CRASH RIDE

T GEPHART

CRASH RIDE
Copyright 2015 T Gephart
Published by T Gephart
Smashwords Edition
ISBN 10: 0992518830
ISBN 13: 978-0-9925188-3-7

Discover other titles by T Gephart at Smashwords or on Facebook, Twitter, Goodreads, or tgephart.com

This eBook is licensed for your personal enjoyment only. This eBook may not be re-sold or given away to other people. If you would like to share this book with another person, please purchase an additional copy for each recipient. If you're reading this book and did not purchase it or it was not purchased for your use only, then please return and purchase your own copy. Thank you for respecting the hard work of this author.

This book is a work of fiction. The names, characters, places and scenarios are products of the writer's imagination or have been used fictitiously and are not to be construed as real. Any resemblance to persons, living or dead, actual events, locales or organizations is entirely coincidental.

Edited by Nichole Strauss from Perfectly Publishable
Front Cover by Gianni Renda
Cover Image by Angelique Ehlers
Back Cover by Hang Le
Formatted by Max Henry of Max Effect

To Gep,

forever unscripted.

Trent Harris
thanks
Bumby
Joel Ogden

1

Megan

MY HEAD WAS FUZZY. I'D DEFINITELY DRUNK TOO MUCH. CHRISTmas parties were the work of the Devil. Under the guise of holiday cheer, you were suckered into swallowing punch that had a higher alcohol content than the city of Tijuana. It burned going down, but unsurprisingly the more you drank; the more appealing it tasted. I was going to be pissed if I threw up all over my new Gucci boots.

Some guy I barely knew invaded my personal space and almost spilled his drink on me. "Oh ... hey, Megan, how's your dad? I sent him a study I'm trying to get published." I wasn't drunk enough to see his thinly veiled attempt at conversation was a chance to use me to get to my father.

"Wouldn't know." I took another sip of the demon elixir from my cup. "He and my mom are in Vale at the moment."

"Too bad." Random guy shrugged before trudging off to go find someone else to talk to.

This was typical of my work situation. My dad, Dr. Mitchell Winters, was one of the head cardiothoracic surgeons at New York Presbyterian and even guest lectured at Cornell; he was highly respected and very influential in the medical field. My mom, Dr. Mary Winters, was a pediatrician and my older brother, Dr. Thomas Winters, was an ER attending physician. Yeah, you guessed it; there was a definite trend in my family.

Don't get me wrong, I loved my job. Being a clinical psychologist at Mount Sinai was an amazing opportunity, but I knew that my dad had been instrumental in me securing my position. People either wanted to be my best friend or give me a wide berth because of my last name; I was like the *Harry Potter* of the hospital world. Unlike Harry, I didn't have magical powers and I could sure use some magic tonight.

Use some of that magic on Troy Harris. The mohawked, hazel-eyed drummer from the band Power Station that did things to my girlie parts.

Troy Harris. Ah, he who cannot be named. Well, I can name him; I just can't *do* anything with him. Why am I even thinking about him? I'm supposed to be getting loaded and possibly hooking up with that cute guy from radiology. See—*that* guy—he was a guy I could actually have. That is where my energy *should* be focused, not on a rock star that only saw me as a friend.

Troy Harris. Damn it, the more I tried to stop, the more I thought of him. He was permanently burned into my brain. I had shamelessly thrown myself at him the night we met. My judgment had been clouded by one too many Long Island iced teas and years of pent up lusting. I'd had that longing from way back, but I never imaged our paths would cross. Not in real life at least. I had gone to the concerts, but I wasn't the type of girl who got invited backstage. Not that it bothered me, it was what it was.

I had always been a fan. Power Station was an amazing live band and their music was more than just good, it was something else. It was real. They had purpose. They gave hope. They evoked emotions. It was one of the best therapies I knew and *therapy* was my line of work, so I should know.

CRASH RIDE

Meeting Troy had felt like a dream. No, really. Like an actual altered state of lucidity. Ash, my best friend, and I had been celebrating. Not that I fully remember the occasion and all of which seems inconsequential now. My sobriety had taken the Staten Island Ferry, sailing away from me without a second thought. That is when, in a noise-filled nightclub, that my stumbling introduction to Troy was made.

Ash had previously, albeit briefly, met Dan and it was this link which had been our *in*.

Troy Harris was nothing like Dan Evans; while the latter had celebrated his status as of one Manhattan's biggest manwhores, his BFF did not share his reputation. Rumors swirled of his bedroom talents, but for the most part no one talked.

Those girls were like a vault. Either he paid them off or he was *that* good. No shady ex's had come out of the woodwork selling their nighttime confessionals, and no hidden camera money shots had shown up online. Not going to lie, the lack of intel on Troy's *goods* had disappointed me slightly—purely from a research point of view of course.

Instead he was touted as the comical, smoldering, nice guy who didn't take himself too seriously. This mixed with his genetic windfall of good looks made him ridiculously attractive. Let's face it, I was going to need someone who wasn't intimidated by my particular brand of enthusiasm. Sounded to me like Troy Harris might just fit the bill.

His jokester reputation for making waves with his fellow band mates was also proven to be true when he caught us trying to sneak into the VIP section where they had been holed-up.

With Ash having been very vocal about her dislike for Dan, Troy was ready to be our best friend.

I liked this. A lot. So much so that after our drunken introductions were made, I wrapped myself around him like a vine. After all, chances of seeing him again were probably low and he was ripe to be climbed. I was too intoxicated to care about the implications and not coherent enough to care what he thought. I wasn't going to possibly miss the only chance I had to lay my hands on him, and I very much liked what my

3

hands discovered. Troy Harris was most definitely not photoshopped.

Unfortunately my clingy, juvenile routine wasn't my only misdemeanor. No. I was *allegedly* defeated by a pair of Louboutins and an uneven sidewalk. I say allegedly because I actually have no recollec-tion, though regardless of the finer details, I ended up with a bad ankle sprain and Troy Harris taking me home. Sadly, he didn't nurse me back to health

Ugh, my cup was empty. The paint stripper I had been drinking had sadly been drained of its last drop. Unlike Troy Harris, the empty cup was an easy fix, so I strolled over to the makeshift bar and helped myself to another drink.

Mmmmm ... much better. The warm alcohol spread through my body like a wildfire and prompted me to giggle. The subject of what I found so hilarious eluded me but whatever it was, was funny. I was funny. Hey, you know what else would be funny?

Without properly thinking it through, I reached into my purse and pulled out my phone. Saved within in its memory banks was a number I had acquired for a previous and unrelated exercise and wisely, not deleted. Who cared if holding on to it made me seem creepy? I dialed before I'd had a chance to reconsider. I felt brave. Like a gladiator, but with better shoes.

"Hey, Megs." He answered almost instantly; my hand gripped the phone tighter upon hearing his voice. I fumbled as I tried to play it cool.

"Oh hey, Troy Harris, it's Megs." I cringed realizing he had already said my name.

"I know." His low laugh rumbled through the phone.

"I saved your number. From before. I'm not a stalker." I doubt he was convinced, the words coming from my mouth sounded slurred and chaotic. It had not been a good sell.

"It's okay, I don't mind you calling me." I heard the smile in his voice.

"God, you're sexy." It leapt out of my mouth before I had a chance to stop. "I can't believe I actually called you. Can you just sit on the phone with me a while and breathe."

CRASH RIDE

"Er, Megs? Are you okay?"

"Yeah, I'm good. *Really good.* I love it when you say my name. Say it again," I slurred into the phone.

Did I sound as lame as I thought? I tried to regulate my breathing so I didn't sound like a complete creeper. Speaking to him short-circuited my brain. It was like being star-struck, only amplified. Nervous didn't even cover half of it.

"Megs, are you drunk? Where are you?"

"At work, Troy Harris. Mount Sinai. You need any medical attention?" I giggled.

Who knew I was a comedian. How he was able to resist me was a mystery. "Shhhhh don't tell anyone, but I'm Harry Potter, the movie version. I haven't read the books."

"Jesus. Megs, stop drinking. You sound really loaded, so unless you tell me that you have a ride home tonight, I'm coming to get you."

I brought my cup to my lips and took another swallow. "You're going to let me ride you tonight? Santa must have got my Christmas list early." The thought alone was deserving of another drink.

"Wow. Can you do me favor and stay out of trouble? I'll be there soon."

"Boooooo. Stay out of trouble? How is that any fun?"

"I'm getting into my car. Please, just sit down or something. I'll call you when I get there."

"Fine, Troy Harris, because you said please."

"Bye, Megs."

I ended the call and tossed the phone into my purse, unable to suppress the huge smile on my face or stop my excited victory dance. Lucky for me the blaring music meant that my rhythmless hyperactive shuffle was not out of place.

He—Troy Harris—was coming for me. For *me*. The thought looped in my head. It was something that I never thought would happen and fully expected my interactions with him being tied to a third party. Yet, Dan or Ash were nowhere in sight, and Troy Harris was on his way to

5

see *me*. How quickly my luck had turned. I was king of the world, or at the very least Manhattan. I resisted the urge to outstretch my arms to celebrate my newfound sovereignty. That would be overkill, as would be a tiara.

Rather than wait until Troy called me again— like a regular person would—I decided to go wait for him downstairs. Smart. In case I missed him or something, there was no way I would risk that. Besides, I had spent enough time with my drunken coworkers to be polite; no one would even notice I was gone.

And just like, I slipped out of the room. Probably *not* with the stealth and coordination as the word slipped implied, but I didn't fall on my ass or twist an ankle. I was out the door and down the wide and empty corridor as fast as my designer boots would carry me.

The cold air hit me like a punch in the stomach as I opened the main outside door. Every breath I inhaled felt like tiny daggers in my lungs. Why, was I so damn cold? Oh, crap. I had been so excited to leave I'd forgotten my coat inside.

Oh well, hopefully he would get here before hypothermia set in, so I'd just suck it up and wait. I didn't need something as silly as warmth. Pfft. Didn't I say I was a gladiator? I would be brave.

Okay, so five minutes outside with snow flurries swirling around me and I'd decided I wasn't that brave and it was freakin' cold. I ran back inside the building and into the room where my coat had been slung over a chair. I was in and out like a ninja, grabbing what I needed without making eye contact with anyone. I followed my previous path back down the corridors and out the main doors again.

Not sure in which direction he would be arriving, I walked out from the main entrance way and onto the street, keeping a look out for his souped-up '74 VW Baha Beatle. Not that I'd stalked him or anything, it was like common knowledge. Any self-respecting Power Station fan would know what set of wheels they drove; unfortunately my research didn't extend to the license plate.

The noisy activity of the emergency department was on the opposite

CRASH RIDE

side of the building so the howling wind was the only sound that broke the silence. Two large headlights pierced through the darkness, the huge black pick-up truck they were attached to rolled slowly up the road toward me. Shit. I was alone. This was not good.

It was probably just a dude who was lost, or at least that's what I told myself.

I decide to walk in the opposite direction, away from the truck. Sure, that's the smart thing to do, walk *away* from the main entrance. I was paranoid, alcohol delusions messing with my head. The truck had nothing to do with me. My heart thumped hard as I looked down the road. Troy would show up any minute, I just needed to not freak out.

The pick-up stopped, its engine idled before it performed a K turn and started to drive toward me. Shit. I was *not* paranoid. I was being followed. If this was fate's way of giving me a big fuck you by dangling Troy Harris in front of me only to have me mugged or killed moments before I got to enjoy him, then fate was a fucking asshole. I wouldn't die, not tonight.

The truck got closer, flashing its lights and I did the only thing I could think of—I ran. My arms pumped as the cold wind lashed at my face, my footing unsteady in my heeled boots. My feet screamed in agony as they pounded against the pavement. I promised my feet if we survived the night I would buy more sensible footwear. Just not Birkenstocks, I mean, comfort can still look good, right?

I heard the noise of the engine close in behind me, the beast of a vehicle picking up speed. Okay, okay I prayed to whatever deity who would have me—I'll buy Birkenstocks, just let me not die. It was too late; tires screeched as the truck mounted the curb and cut me off. I was a goner. I didn't even get to kiss him. Life was so unfair.

"Megs, what the fuck are you doing and why are you running?" Troy jumped out of the still idling truck and grabbed me around the waist.

He pinned me against the warm hood as I stared at him in confusion. "Huh? You drive a VW Baha." The most intelligent thing I was able to utter.

"I have other cars; I blew the transmission in my VW last week. I haven't had a chance to replace it." He moved his face closer to mine. "How do you know what kind of car I drive?"

"Google. It's a sickness. Don't hate me." The uncontrolled words spilled from my lips. His eyes were like truth serum. I couldn't lie when I looked directly into them. Which is what I was doing. He had such amazing eyes.

"You Googled my car?" He laughed, a big throaty laugh. "What *else* did you Google?"

Look away, don't look into his eyes, it's a trap. It's a TRAP. "Shoe size, favorite food, taste in women." I swallowed as my subconscious self cowered in horror. Now I actually *wanted* to die.

"Size thirteen, Mexican, as for women—varied. I don't have a type. Anything else you want to know?" His face was inches from mine; I could feel his breath tickle my neck. The sensation intoxicated me further, awaking every cell of my body as his frame pressed against mine.

I closed my eyes, saving myself before I asked him, *why won't you kiss me* and shook my head.

"Okay, let's get you off the street before you hurt yourself or someone else." His fingers wrapped around my arms and peeled me off the hood. "I flashed my lights at you, to let you know it was me."

"Gangs do that. I'm sure I've read it somewhere," I explained as I righted myself on my feet. "They flash their lights at you so you think they're friendly and then they kill you. I am pretty sure it's for initiation."

"Do you realize how crazy that sounds? Why would they warn you if they are going to kill you?"

"I don't know, Troy Harris; do you see me flashing gang signs? They're gangsters. I wouldn't argue with them."

Troy chuckled as he moved to the passenger side door and opened it. "You are so funny when you're drunk."

I stared at the space between the doorframe of the car and the floor. It

CRASH RIDE

was so high up. Was I supposed to take a running jump? "Do you have a ladder?"

"Here." Troy smiled and tapped the black steps along the outside of the car. "One foot here and the other here. I'll stand behind you, just in case."

It wasn't pretty, but I managed to haul myself into the beast without incident despite contorting my body into a weird angle to get into the cab. Why I made things harder than they had to be, I'll never know.

Once I was safely inside and buckled in, Troy moved to the driver's side and hopped in. He was able to do so in one swift, graceful movement —something I had been unable to do—and I couldn't stop myself from staring.

He cocked his head to the side. "You good?" He fastened his seatbelt.

I nodded slowly as he dismounted the curb and pulled back onto the road.

Suspended reality was the best way I could describe it. The surprise and the shock of the situation I found myself in stunned me momentarily. Had I ever been alone with him before? I'd imagined it so many times but now that I was sitting beside him, I had no idea where to even start.

It was quiet. His stereo was off and the only noise to break the silence was the hum of the engine.

"Hey, so I never thanked you for your help." It was the first thing that came to mind. "With Dan and Ash. I know you were skeptical about stepping in, but they needed us. So thanks."

Troy didn't take his eyes off the road as he answered me. "I'll admit getting involved in Dan's business was not high on my agenda, but you made a solid case. Doesn't mean I want to play interference on a regular rotation though."

"I think they are going to be fine now." Ash and Dan would no doubt have their ups and downs like any couple, but I had faith they were in it for the long haul. "You can probably go back to playing drums and being sexy." Did I actually say that last bit out loud? I wasn't even looking at his eyes this time. I had no excuse.

Troy glanced at me and laughed. "I think I'll just stick to the drum part of your proposal, being sexy sounds like too much work, but thanks."

Little did he know, he didn't even have to try. Oh no. In fact, the only thing the man had to do was show up and sexiness took care of itself. It was in him. The way he walked. His I-don't-give-a-fuck attitude. The haphazard fashion sense—no other man over thirty could wear a *Hershey's Chocolate* tee and rock it. It all cumulated into a simmering vibe. Like one big melting pot of *yum*, I involuntarily licked my lips.

"Soooooooo," I fumbled, twisting my hair nervously around my finger. My mind and my mouth were at odds as to which statement would come barreling out next. "We should go out and celebrate. Both of us returning to our respective fields of expertise." It was worth a shot. Not like I had a lot to lose. My dignity had checked-out a while ago.

The truck stopped in traffic as we approached a red light. My eyes kind of stared off into the distance in a state of semi-disbelief. Was I really in this car or was it just a dream? Having him close felt like a fantasy. I wonder if I just reached out and... The loud blaring of a cab's horn punctuated that it wasn't a dream.

"Megs, do you really think that is a good idea?"

"What idea?" I tried to untangle the lock of hair that was cutting off the circulation of my finger as I mentally retraced the steps in the conversation. Oh. Right. I had asked him out. This was the part where he gave me the gentle brush off. It's not like I hadn't alluded to my interest for weeks. We had been playing this little flirty game since I met him and while I'm not the hang-from-the-chandeliers kind of girl, I'm certainly not a wallflower either.

"Us, going out." He took a breath, the playful vibe of the conversation evaporated, taking along with it any chance of the two of us dating. "Megs, you are an amazing girl. You're funny and beautiful, and when you aren't repeating my name five hundred times, I dig spending time with you. But Dan and Ash. They just got back together. I know you and Ash are tight, and I think it goes without saying that Dan and I are... well he's my brother. I just don't want to complicate things, you know what I'm saying?"

I pushed back my errant hair and bit my lip; forcing myself to look at him and smile sweetly. "Troy Harris, it was just a night out. It didn't have to be complicated." I didn't bother trying to hide my disappointment. It wasn't a maybe, it was a definitive no.

"Megs. What happens if we go out and I do something stupid like not call you or some shit? Then it gets awkward and people have to choose sides. People we both care about. Before you know, it's like we're on a fucking reality show. No matter how many times people say they won't let shit get complicated, it ends up complicated. I like you, I think you're awesome and I don't want to screw it up. I want us to be friends."

Wow. Friend-zoned. He was pretty clear. Perhaps he was looking for a commendation, for his honesty and all, but rejection is still a rejection. Even one that made sense. It still stung. He was right about one thing. If we did go out, and things went bad, either for us or for Dan and Ash, then it would inevitably spill into a big cesspool of suck. Of course, common sense didn't ease the disappointment of the situation and solidified the fact my nighttime illicit fantasies would be staying just that...fantasies. Can't blame a girl for trying.

My teeth toyed with my bottom lip as I closed my eyes. I couldn't believe I was being so brazen. "Can we at least be friends with benefits?" It couldn't hurt to put it out there, even if I assumed the answer was probably going to be a no. Nothing ventured, nothing gained. I was still stunned I was having this conversation and I wasn't sure if I was thankful I had alcohol to blame or I was going to hate myself in the morning. Probably a little of both.

"Wow, Megs," Troy laughed. "I'm going to pretend you didn't say that, 'cause we've already established I think you are awesome and that situation would not be a hard sell. Maybe we could just be *regular* friends."

"Okay, Troy Harris. Let the records show that you *had* the opportunity to sleep with me, and you turned it down." Who the hell says that?

If he hadn't turned me down before, that sure as hell would be the nail in the coffin. Crap. That freaking punch I'd been drinking had a lot to answer for.

"Noted, your Honor." He pulled up to the curb beside my apartment. "Do you think you are ever going to just call me Troy?"

My heart sunk, my excuse for being in the car was over as we stopped in front of my building.

"We'll have to wait and see I guess. I should let you go, thanks for driving me home." I knew I had to get out and go up into my apartment, even if what I actually wanted to do was try and convince him further. I wouldn't be one of those desperate girls who asked him to come upstairs, even though I wanted nothing more than to throw my self-respect out the window and beg. Beg for one night with him. Toe-curling red-hot sex. That's what that body promised and I was going to have to walk away. It sucked. Big time.

He let out a long steady breath, and if I didn't know better I'd assume that maybe it hadn't been so easy to turn me down. "Yeah, you should be safe enough from gangstas and uneven sidewalks from here." His voice softened. "Oh, and Megs ..."

My heart pounded so loudly I was sure he'd hear it. "Yeah, Troy Harris?" I looked into his eyes. Throwing caution to the wind with the powers they held over me.

"Just 'cause we aren't sleeping together doesn't mean you can't call me sometime. You know. If you need something... or if you just wanna hang."

I closed my eyes and smiled. The intonation of his voice was so seductive it hurt, even if the words weren't sexy. "I'd like that. Can you sometimes take your shirt off?" I laughed as I slowly reopened my eyes.

His chuckle reverberated through the cabin. "Ha. I'll see what I can do."

"Bye, Troy Harris." I turned and jumped out of the car, my feet landing heavily on the sidewalk.

"Bye, Megan Winters."

Troy

6 Months Later/Present Day

"So you wanna come up with me, maybe have a drink?" She smiled, not even trying to hide what she had on her mind, and a beer was not it.

"Thanks, but I'm going to pass." The engine idling should have been a big tip off. Not going there. There were many places my dick was not going tonight and inside of her was at the top of the list.

"Oh? I can go down on you right here if you like?" She didn't take the hint, her hand sliding up my thigh. Seriously, what did I need to do to clue this girl in I wasn't going to fuck her?

"Going to have to pass on that, too. Thanks for the offer though, that was sweet." Or desperate, we could go either way. The asshole in me was leaning toward the latter, but I didn't care to find out. No point. Getting her out of my car and gone were my priority right now, not working out the finer points of this chick's seduction technique. If my dick was any less hard I was going to need to pop a Viagra just to take a piss.

"Well... I guess I should go then?" The look of surprise on her face floored me. Seriously? She hadn't joined the dots yet? Clueless. Fucking perfect.

"Yeah, I need to meet Dan. We have a band thing." A lie, but an easier let down than *I have no interest in you, please get out of my fucking car*. Being an asshole was one thing, being unnecessarily cruel was something else. "See ya, Lacey." The I'll-call-you or let's-do-this-again-sometime wasn't tacked onto the end. There was no chance I'd do either of those things.

"Okay... Thanks." She leaned in and kissed me, no doubt in a last ditched effort to change my mind. She was persistent, I'll give her that but still no cigar.

"Yep. Thanks." My hands tapped on the steering wheel as I pulled my mouth away.

If Lacey wasn't up to speed before, she sure as hell was then. Her fingers snatched her purse from the console and stormed out of my ride. The slamming of the car door behind her, muffled the "fuck you" as she left. It was deserved and yet I couldn't make myself care. At least she was gone, even if it meant I would probably lose a friend on Facebook. Once again, care factor, zero.

It was nine-thirty on a Friday night and I was heading home. Living the fucking dream.

My fist tapped against the big wooden door. "Douchebag, Open up."
"Hey, asshole." Dan smirked as he cracked open his front door. "Nice

shirt. Brings out the color of your eyes." He stepped aside so I could walk in.

"I'm glad you approve. I wore it especially for you." Wiseass. I hadn't bothered to change, still wearing the bullshit button down and jeans I'd worn to dinner. "You and Ash got plans? I'm so fucking bored, taking a nap looks like a good time."

Ash moved into Dan's apartment pretty soon after they got back together. Not that there was any doubt of what their zip code was going to be, her place had been a shit hole in a bad part of town. So being that Dan and my real estate shared the top floor of a high rise, it meant I was now kicking it with a new female neighbor.

"Didn't you have a date?" Dan looked over his shoulder as we walked into the living room. He silenced the dipshit on his large screen television before tossing the remote onto his fancy, new distressed wooden coffee table. His pad recently overhauled at the hand of his girl.

"Yep, Lacey. Masturbating with a cheese grater would've been less painful. I called time early and bailed." It wasn't an exaggeration. I was so done with airhead bimbos, I didn't give a fuck how well they sucked dick.

"Sounds like a fun night." Dan laughed as he disappeared into the kitchen, emerging a few moments later with a couple of ice-cold long necks. "Beer?"

"Hell, yes." I snagged a bottle out of his hand. "So, you never answered my question. You wanna do something tonight?" The leather of the couch creaked as I sunk my ass into the chair.

"Ash is going out. With Megs. Just the two of them." He took a swallow of his beer, but his face said it all. He wasn't cool with his girl hitting the town without him in tow. I'm convinced Dan missed all those classes in Pre K when we all were taught to share.

"Interesting." My grin widened. I couldn't help myself. He was too much of an easy target.

"Don't even fucking start, Troy. This whole girls' night out thing is fucking bogus. I just know some motherfucker is going to try and hit on my girl. I'm not cool with this, not at all." Dan planted his ass in the opposite matching leather two-seater. Edgy was the understatement of the century. Poor bastard, looked like he was ready to gut some poor SOB.

"Earth to neanderthal, she's coming home to you. Even if some douche hits on her, you know she's probably going to tell him to go fuck himself or knee him in the nuts. Don't you remember how *charmed* she was when you hit on her?" I hated to admit it, but Dan pussy-whipped was kind of fucking nice. He had given James and Alex so much shit when they'd done the ball and chain thing. It was poetic justice that he was tied up in knots.

My pep talk fell on deaf fucking ears as he continued to sulk like a two-year-old. "You know, we could go out too," I suggested, knowing he was going to be a moody asshole whatever the location was.

"You want to go out?" Dan lowered his beer, carefully placing the bottle on a coaster. Yep, well and truly whipped!

"Sure, why not? We can go shoot some pool, or go see a band?" It had been awhile since we'd been out. The band had been holed-up in James's studio for the last three months while we laid down the new album.

"Dan, can you zip me?" Ashlyn appeared in the doorway, wearing a tight blue dress. "Oh, hey, Troy." Her eyes widened, as she grabbed at the material exposing her back. I couldn't help noticing the amount of skin she was flashing. No wonder Dan looked like he had swallowed glass.

"Hey, Ash, what's shakin'?" I tilted my beer in greeting, unable to suppress my grin. "You look great."

"Shut up, dickwad." Dan got to his feet and yanked at Ashlyn's zipper. His effort to hurry the process made it snag. "Fuck!" He shook his finger, obviously coming off second best against the teeth of the zip. "Babe, seriously, why don't you and Megs hang here? We'll go to Troy's if you want have a girls' night. I'm pretty sure there is a Zac Effron movie on *Showtime*, and there's ice cream and cookie dough in the freezer."

"Aw, Dan, are you jealous?" Ash smiled as Dan finished fucking around with her dress. "You are just going to have survive without me for a night. Megs is working some tough cases and she needs a night out. You understand don't you, baby?" Ash wrapped her arms around Dan's neck and it didn't take a genius to work out where this was heading.

"I don't want some asshole trying to touch what's mine." Dan tipped Ash's chin and he clocked her with a look that claimed her more than his words.

"No one is going to touch anything." Ash moved in closer, her mouth getting cozy with the side of his face. I wondered if I shouldn't leave the room and give them a moment. Not that either of them seemed to give a shit I was still around.

Like the big guy upstairs was listening to my silent prayer, there was a knock at the door that gave me an out. I'd seen enough of Dan getting busy to last me a lifetime and even though I dug Ash, I preferred to leave some shit unseen.

"I'll get it, anything is better than listening to you two clowns." I don't think they even noticed the knock or me leaving. I moved off the couch and made for the door, hoping the lovin' feeling wasn't going to spill into the hallway as I walked out of the room.

My gratitude went to whoever was on the other side as I grabbed at the solid wooden door and yanked it open. And there she was, the five-foot-four blonde bombshell that made my dick twitch every time I saw her.

"Megs." My grin got wider as I looked down at her next-to-nothing outfit. I didn't have to imagine too hard to guess what was underneath her tight black dress, her perky tits straining against the material. Once again, I was throwing my thanks to the man upstairs.

Megan Winters was straight up beautiful. Long, wavy blonde hair that went half way down her back with the sexiest, clearest, blue-green eyes I'd ever seen. Topped off with a knockout fucking smile. Her body was nothing short of perfection, with the right combination of tits and ass that would force even the strongest man onto their knees. Add to that her wicked sense of humor and her ridiculous fucking IQ, and you had a girl that most men would give their left nut to call their own. Not that it would ever go beyond the silent appreciation I had for her, still it was hard not to notice. No matter how many times I saw her, it did nothing to diminish the punch in the gut I got every time I laid eyes on her.

"Hey, Troy Harris." My name rolled out of her mouth with a smile, and damn if it didn't make me stand up a little straighter. Her little quirk of tacking on *Harris* after *Troy* didn't bother me anywhere near as much as I pretended. Her eyebrow lifted as she moved through the doorway, "Dan and Ash making out again?" Like me, it wasn't her first rodeo with those two boneheads.

"I'm sure they've moved on to dry humping by now." I stepped aside so she could stride past me, which also treated me to the most superb view of her ass. Total scumbag move, but I couldn't help myself. I had already decided she was a no-go zone, a decision I was having a hard time reconciling with at the moment.

"Ha, remember the good old days when they could be together in a room and not be all over each other like a rash?" She glanced back at me as she made her way to the lounge room.

"Preaching to the choir, Megs." My eyes glued to the sway of her hips as she moved in front of me. Yeah, not creepy at all. I shook my head as I tried to focus on something other than trying to imagine what kind of underwear she was wearing.

Putting the brakes on the chance to bed Megs was not an easy task. At first, I considered it —more like my dick demanded it— but I wasn't going to be a douchebag. I knew too well what it was like to get caught up in the misery that came with fucking around with a friend of a friend.

High school, junior year, I had dated Quinn Sinclair who happened to be the best friend of Kim Evans. Kim and Dan hadn't only shared the same last name but they also shared DNA. And while I would never have dated Dan's sister, Quinn seemed like fair game.

Shit had been fine and dandy while things were going well, but it all went to hell the minute we broke up. Kim constantly gave me the stink eye anytime I went around and saw Dan, and Dan was catching heat from his sister, and from Quinn. What I had thought was a mutual break-up, Quinn had seen as me breaking her heart. Enter drama, stage right. Needless to say, I avoided the Evans house like the plague for a solid three months and Dan threatened to kick me in the nuts if I even looked at one of his sister's friends again. Granted shit died down eventually, and last I heard Quinn was still in the old neighborhood, happily married to her accountant husband with her two-point-five kids, but that pact I made to Dan, still stood.

"Why don't you two just make a porno already?" Megs laughed as we walked into the lounge room; Dan and Ash still lip-locked like a pair of freshmen.

"Don't encourage him," Ash giggled as she rubbed lipstick off Dan's mouth.

"Megs." Dan tipped his chin as he looked over at us. "You know I'd never share my girl with anyone. And I got all the footage I need locked up here." He tapped his noggin with the hand that wasn't wrapped around his girlfriend.

"Ever the romantic." Ash rolled her eyes. "It's a good thing I love you." She squeezed Dan's chin in another loved-up exchange. Fuck, at this rate we'd never get out the door.

"Right, so if the two of you are done being adorable, maybe we can get out of here. I have had the worst week at work, if I don't get to lose myself in a good time in the next thirty minutes, I'm going to be rocking manically in a corner." Megs smiled but I could tell there was something else underneath it. Something in her tone didn't sit right, made me all kinds of uncomfortable.

"Is everything okay, Megs?" I had to ask. Rationally I chalked up my concern to Megs being a friend. While technically not part of this circus of crazy, her connection to Ash justified me taking notice.

The excuse also meant I didn't have to advertise my other interests. The ones that were less about who she was friends with, and more about the woman standing in front of me. The whys of the situation were still unclear, but it wasn't just about her ability to get me hard. Nope, it went deeper than that, and if there was something going down, then I wanted in on that intel.

She shrugged it off and it didn't take a genius to realize she was holding shit back. "Nothing I can talk about, just a rough case load. I can handle it though, just need a night out."

"You girls want a ride in? Dan and I are thinking of hitting the town as well. That is, if I can convince cry-baby to stop bitching into his beer and get out the door." Extra time with Megs would be a bonus. Hopefully I could get a bead on what was clouding those beautiful eyes. Yeah, it made no sense for me to be protective of her, but it was a lost cause pushing down the urge. I'd learnt not to fight it.

"We were going to get a cab. You guys are going out too?" Ash asked, as she turned to look at Dan who was still weighing my offer. Like it or not, he was riding shotgun. I wasn't going to be sitting here all night with his miserable ass. Lord knows, I'd paid him that courtesy more than just a few times.

"Yeah, guess so." Dan got on the same page, not like I'd given him much choice. "Give me five and I'll change." He pulled off his T-shirt as he walked toward the bedroom.

I grabbed my cell and started dialing. "We'll get TJ to drive us in. He can take you ladies wherever you wanna go, and then we'll come get you when you're done."

"Well if we're all going out, why don't we just go out together?" Megs volunteered, and I'll be damned if her face didn't light up at the suggestion.

Ash played devil's advocate; her concern was an easy read. "Megs, are you sure? I thought you wanted it to be just us." She'd made a point of not being one of those girls who was constantly under thumb. Just as well too, 'cause that's sure as shit not what a *real* man wants. All that yes-sir-shit was great in the bedroom, but outside of that, they needed to be able to think for themselves.

CRASH RIDE

Megs's lips curved into a smile. "Ash, I know you. You're going to be thinking about Dan the whole time anyway and he is probably going to be texting you every five minutes. It's fine. We can go out as a group. That is, if Troy Harris is okay with it?" She turned to me, nailing me with a single look.

Wow, did the temperature of the room just raise a few degrees since she'd walked in? There wasn't a lot she could ask me for and I'd say no. Her suggestion—us hanging out tonight— had zero chance of me not being on board. "Oh, I'm more than okay with it. I'm immediately a fan of anything that means I won't have to deal with Dan being a whiny bitch the whole night."

"So it's settled." Megs flicked her hair from her shoulders, her spectacular tits getting my attention as she breathed in and out with excitement. "I get to pick the venue though. If Dan has his way, we're going to end up at Hooter's."

"Hooter's? What are you guys talking about?" Dan was back, freshly changed into a clean pair of jeans and Misfits T-shirt. "Megs, you know I like you and all, but talking shit about that fine establishment is blasphemy in this house."

"Dan, no one was talking shit about your tits-n-wings haven. Relax." Ash shot him down pretty quickly. That right there was one of the biggest reasons I liked her. She picked up my slack, so to speak, where Dan was concerned. "Megs has decided we should turn girls' night into a foursome."

"Wait. What? Is this some kind of test?" Dan looked confused, the color draining from his face.

I threw back my head and laughed, putting him out of his misery. "Not that kind of a foursome, you moron. Fuck, man, seriously. We're tagging along on Megs's magical mystery tour."

"Well, hells yeah!" Dan grabbed Ash around the waist, looking at her like she was dinner. "That mean I get to be down and dirty on the dance floor with my baby?"

"I'm already regretting this decision." Megs sidled up close to me, rolling her eyes.

"Oh no, Megs. You've already committed. No take-backs." I slung my arm around her shoulder and pulled her into a hug. Hmmm. I liked the way she felt against me. Very fucking nice.

"Well, if everyone's agreed what's say we get out the door and see if we can't get Megs to forget her shitty day," Ash offered, putting a stop to Dan's wandering hands. "Dan, shouldn't you change? I'm not sure they are going to let you into a club wearing a T-shirt."

"Oh Ash, I love you, babe." Dan's mouth curled into a grin. "But green supersedes dress code every time, sweetheart. Besides, name a club and I know most of the dudes at door. I could walk in wearing a chicken suit and they'd still let me in."

Ash gave him a friendly shove. "You are so conceited, you know that?"

"I know, babe. It's part of my charm." His fucking grin getting wider.

The man was an idiot, but he wasn't wrong. Call it unfair or social unjust, but along with the fame we attracted, we got one hell of a free pass. People just gave us shit and treated us differently, even if we didn't want it. Fuck, I couldn't even remember the last time someone told me I couldn't do something. As for establishments, short of taking a piss on the bar, we could pretty much wear, do or say anything we wanted if it meant that it got people through their door.

I moved my arm lower, feeling Megs's soft skin under my calloused fingers and my cock stirred, all kinds of interested in what my hands were doing. Yeah, not going to happen buddy. We needed to eject ASAP or it was going to be really fucking obvious what my thoughts were about. "As much as I'd like to see Dan in a chicken suit tearing around Manhattan, I think we should make tracks. You good?"

"Ready." Dan tucked his arm around his girl's waist, the shit-eating grin on his face a dead giveaway he was ecstatic with the development of the evening. Great.

Megs smiled, her face happier than a kid in a candy store. "Okay, so

CRASH RIDE

I'm feeling sentimental. Let's go back to where it all started. Let's head to *Panic*."

3
Megan

IF ANYTHING WAS GOING TO MAKE ME FORGET MY CRAP-TASTIC day at work, it was Troy Harris. Ah, sigh. He was like the Holy Grail of good times wrapped up in one badass package. Not that I knew, it was all assumptions and measured guesses, but surely a man built like that wouldn't disappoint. And disappointment is one thing I didn't need tonight.

It wasn't like I didn't have an amazing life. My quota of *great* was straining against the maximum. A loving, supportive family, a beautiful apartment, wonderful friends and a fulfilling job, how did I get so lucky? Sure, Prince Charming hadn't shown up yet, but I hadn't had to give up one of my shoes either, so it wasn't all bad.

Not a lot of people understood my career choice, but working with troubled kids was something you could never attach a dollar value to. While angels didn't cluster around me like a renaissance painting—I'm still partially bummed about that— what I did, mattered. There was no greater reward than seeing one of my *kids* weather the storm. Nothing

CRASH RIDE

even came close.

My latest *kid* was Brad Hemsworth. A sixteen-year-old who, despite coming from a middle class, well-adjusted family, was dealing with adolescent depression. He was struggling to find his place, not fitting in with the jocks or smart kids at the school and generally spending most of his time alone. He had tried to commit suicide once before and he was admitted into the ER yesterday after another failed attempt. This time with pills. His reasoning, it was neater than slitting his wrist like he had done the time previously. I tried not to take it personally, but a part of me felt I'd failed him. Tonight, I needed a night to just forget. Selfish, I know, and I hoped that feeling this way wasn't going to guarantee me a place burning in Hell, but I needed distance. Distance from the sadness and distance from the guilt.

Panic was the club Ash and I had fatefully found ourselves in so many months ago when we were trying to cheer up Ash. It wasn't a coincidence that I chose this place, hoping it would rework its magic. Troy Harris, along for the ride, well that was the cherry on top.

True to Dan's word, dress code hadn't been an issue with the bouncers falling over themselves to raise the rope for both he and Troy. Not even a look was thrown in our direction as we breezed right in. They didn't even check ID. I could have been a sixteen-year-old runaway with a purse full of blow and I would have received the same nod and smile. Lucky for them I *was* of age and *not* packing narcotics—they had dodged that bullet.

"You going to get drunk and fall over?" Troy playfully bumped my shoulder as we entered the club, the light sweeping through the room in an erratic wave. The noise wasn't any less obnoxious since our last visit, but strangely, that excited me. My senses exploded with the familiarity of the room; the darkness and the light were at war with each other as a soundtrack of destruction played in the background. Panic was an appropriate name for the place, the thumping of my pulse matched the bass booming from the speakers.

I playfully nudged him back as we waded through the crowd. My hands probably lingered a little longer than was necessary, but it was crowded and dark, so the touching was totally acceptable. That was my story and I was sticking to it. All that was needed was a suitable justification for my hand wandering to his ass and my night would be complete. Just putting it out there and if the universe wanted to reward me, then what could I say? I would be grabbing that opportunity with both hands—pun totally intended.

"If I fall, will you promise you'll nurse me back to health, Troy Harris?" Seeing as sleeping with me was out, a little TLC from those strong capable hands would be worth another tumble.

Dan and Ash were a few feet in front of us, Dan's arms wrapped protectively around Ash's waist. No one would have missed his territorial vibe, and short of actually marking her, he was doing a fine job so that no man would think twice about approaching her. It was kind of adorable.

"I've got an icepack waiting in the car, just in case." His lips teased into a smile.

I liked that. His smile. It was so contagious and it did amazing things to those hazel eyes. It also managed to do other amazing things, *tingly* things to parts of my body. He didn't even have to touch me. Look Mom, no hands —just that smile and those eyes. It was his superpower. I wasn't entirely convinced he was human.

The stress of my day had already started to evaporate. This was definitely one of my smartest decisions. Troy had a kindness in his face that contradicted the roughness of his body. All those hard lines converged into big walls of flesh. He was solid and I wanted nothing more than to rub myself up against his mass.

Wearing a fitted, black button-down he left undone at collar and at the sleeves, he was looking particularly good tonight. He'd teamed it up with a pair of black jeans and black heavy boots, the pop of color coming from his intricate and artful tattoos that poked out from the fabric. His tats were beautiful, covering both arms, most of his chest and back. Not that I'd actually seen all of them up close, but I'd stalked enough pictures to know. Have we discussed my Google habit? Yeah, it wasn't a coincidence that when you typed "TR" into my search bar, *Troy Harris* was the first thing to pop up. If he ever checked out my computer's history, I would be totally screwed. Mental note— clear my cache when I get home.

My want for him, that hadn't diminished despite him telling me it wasn't happening. Masochism was the only explanation for it. Because despite our flirting back and forth, I knew he didn't feel for me what I felt for him. Did I stop? Nope.

The lust I had ran deep; it was an itch I just couldn't quite reach no matter how hard I scratched. No one else seemed to satisfy it either. Not like I hadn't tried and not like I bet he could. And I needed that more than I cared to admit, especially tonight. To help me forget the thoughts that were unrelenting in my mind, and to help me remember the pleasure that my body had long been denied.

A couple rushed past, almost knocking me over. They didn't even notice I'd almost fallen on my ass as they pushed through the crowd. Too busy laughing and wrapped up in their own excitement to worry about the fact they had shoved me. My body swayed as I tried to regain my balance.

Troy instinctively pulled me to his side. "You okay?" His hand moved around my body, forming a protective barrier around me as he tried to right me back onto my feet. His concern for me dissipated my anger at the couple for being rude assholes. I actually might thank them —Troy's hands on me as a result of their handy work, that was a serious positive.

"I'm fine, thanks." My hand brushed up against his arm, hoping he would hold me a little longer. Sadly, I needed to get my thrills when they came and Troy touching me definitely fell into that category. If only I could convince him to touch me a little lower, and possibly while we were both naked. Too much?

"Maybe I should hold on to you, just to be sure. We wouldn't want for you to end up injured so soon. You can't even blame the booze this time around." He lowered his hand so that it circled my waist and I had to remember to breathe. My body pressed against his side as he guided me through the crowd. Instinctively, I reciprocated and wrapped my arm around his waist. After all, I wouldn't want to seem rude or ungrateful; manners were a big part of my upbringing. I sure wasn't going to argue. He could keep his hands on me for as long as he wanted. Not that I would vocalize that encouragement, I still had my pride.

"I can assure you, I'm going to do everything I can not to end up on my ass." I leaned against him, his scent intoxicating me. I had to stop myself from actually pressing my nose against his chest and sniffing him. It would not be something that would have been easily explained even though the pleasure would have been worth the embarrassment. He smelled good too. All that masculine-sexy- whatever it was spliced with cologne. Yum. I actually had to stop myself from licking my lips. I seriously needed to get laid, and preferably by someone who knew what he was doing.

It's not like I had spent the last six months pining after a guy I couldn't have. No, I had brushed myself off and went full steam ahead in trying to find a distraction. Any distraction. Not that I started bedding strange men and having one-night stands, but I was certainly more open to a *casua*l relationship. I was actively dating and I'd always had a healthy sex life, but the last couple of months... well I was a little bored with what the life buffet had offered me. Maybe it's the bad-boy hang up or the allure of the forbidden, but the reasons why Troy and I shouldn't sleep together were making less and less sense. After all, we were adults. Rational ones even. Well, for the most part. Feelings wouldn't even have to come into it. Who says it has to be a relationship? It could just be just sex. Maybe once we'd *had* sex, the whole forbidden fruit issue would be gone, thus remedying the situation. Maybe, it would be like a vaccination, sort of like when they give you the live virus of something to prevent a full-blown outbreak. It would definitely cure the sexual frustration I had going on.

"Um, Megs? Where did you go?" Troy's raised eyebrow hinted at the

CRASH RIDE

fact I'd zoned out again. It seemed to be a real hazard when I was around him. I hadn't even noticed we reached the stairs that lead to the VIP area.

"I was just thinking…" I swallowed. My heartbeat raced as I contemplated what I was about to say. Best not to over thinking it, I didn't want to lose my nerve. I was also stone cold sober, as Troy had helpfully pointed out, so there was no way I could blame my future actions on inebriation. Still, there was a sure fire way to stop the loop of crap rolling around in my head and *that* way was standing in front of me. Sue me if I sounded desperate, I really didn't care about public opinion, what I needed was to lose myself for an hour or two. And the person I wanted to do that with was Troy. Here goes nothing. I was about to test my theory once and for all to prove that honesty is in fact the best policy.

"We should have sex."

"Whoa. Um. Megs. Maybe we should get a drink first. Maybe sit down?" Troy smiled but didn't act shocked. After all, the flirting was nothing new so he probably assumed *this* was just an extension of *that*. Turning it up a notch, if you will. I could tell he didn't think it was a legitimate proposition. I would fix that.

"No seriously. The more I think about it, the more I'm convinced we should do it."

He lowered his face inches from mine. "Megs, didn't we already agree dating would be a bad idea?"

"Who said anything about dating? No, I'm talking about fucking. Just sex. Purely physical," I clarified in case there was any confusion. I figured if I was going to sell this baby, I had to do it justice and leaving wiggle room in the interpretation would not do.

His eyes narrowed, realizing I was serious. "Were you drinking *before* you got to Ash and Dan's?"

Laughing would be inappropriate, and would not help my cause, so I tried not to. It wasn't easy. Sure what I was asking was slightly out of character—scratch that, extremely out of character—but I had suggested it in the past. Granted I'd been drunk, and my lets-have-sex had been off-the-cuff, but a proposal had been made. What did I have to lose? "No.

I'm completely sober. Actually, this is the clearest my mind has been in a long time."

"So we're just supposed to *fuck* and then stay friends?" His eyes were a mix of contradiction and confusion. Strangely, it just made him even more alluring. "I really don't think that works out that way for anyone."

While I admired his integrity on the issue—really, give the man a round of applause—it was his other attributes I was interested in tonight. It wasn't going to turn into some long and romantic love story. I was okay with that. I was surprised I hadn't come to this conclusion sooner. Sex was definitely the answer. "No, not if they go in with other expectations. Of course, we know better. No emotional attachment, just fulfilling a primal need."

His mouth curved into a grin and despite my indecent proposal, he didn't seem pissed. "Megs, think about what you are saying. Once you go there, you can't un-go there. We both know it's not that simple."

"Are you two coming up or what? I thought we were going to party tonight, not have a PTA meeting on the stairs," Dan called from the top of the stairs, his arm around Ash. I guess they had finally noticed our absence, or potentially heard the whistle of the crazy train threatening to take me away.

"Shut up, asshole. We'll be there in a minute." Troy turned and called back to him over the noise. Secretly I was glad he hadn't just shot down the conversation. It would be premature to high-five myself just yet.

Dan rolled his eyes but didn't seem overly concerned as he allowed Ash to pull him away. She gave me a quick wink and a smile just before they disappeared from view. I would have to thank her for that later; her intuition guessing it was a conversation that didn't need an interruption. She didn't need to know the finer details, especially seeing as I had no idea what I was actually doing.

I leaned in closer to Troy, needing to know if I was fighting a losing battle. "Aren't you even the slightest bit turned on by me?"

"Megs, my dick is about to get choked out by my jeans. Trust me, not being turned on is *not* the issue here."

CRASH RIDE

So I wasn't imagining it. He was interested. Or at the very least his *dick* was, and lets face it, that was the only part we really *needed* to be on board. Yep, we can officially declare me out of control. Maybe the stress really was getting to me? Whatever the excuse, I was going with it. I'd come this far, might as well jump off the cliff. I had always been an overachiever.

"I think you are over-thinking this. Here is the way I see it. I have had a really bad week, horrendous even. And what I would really like right now is sex. Just to lose myself in a raging, screaming orgasm. Nothing fancy, as long as we both get off. Now, I know I could find some random guy and take him home, but I would really prefer for it to be you. Who gives me the orgasm, I mean."

Troy cocked an eyebrow as he considered my offer. "And you think we can just have sex and shit won't be awkward later?"

"I know so. Besides, I think it might actually help us." At the very least help me. Possibly even cure me of my crazy obsession all while helping me forget my mental baggage. There really wasn't a drawback as far as I was concerned.

"How do you figure?"

I took a deep breath. This is what I like to call my finishing maneuver. The final wrap up. The end argument. "Well, I've always had a thing for you. I'd go to shows and see you on stage and secretly wonder what it would be like. Knowing you hasn't really stopped me from thinking about it. If we did it, then maybe I could stop looking at you and wondering what it would feel like to come with your cock inside me."

His jaw tightened, as his eyes raked up and down my body. The intensity of his stare made me feel naked.

"Fuck." He hissed out a breath.

"That's what I'm trying to facilitate here—"

"Seriously, douchebags. What's the hold up? You stand on that step any longer and the club is going to start charging you rent." Dan reappeared, his timing horrible. Fortunately he was alone, but he was descending the stairs toward us. Well, this was about to get interesting.

"Give me a minute, Megs." Troy eyed me intently before turning to Dan who was now standing beside us. "Dude, what the fuck is your problem? Can't you see we're talking?"

Dan rubbed his neck as he looked between us. "Yeah I see, what I don't get is what's so important you can't talk up here?"

"I've had a shitty week," I began to explain. Not a lie. My week had been horrible. "Worse than normal, and I just needed to offload some steam. I know Ash will worry if I talk about it up there. Troy was just lending me a friendly ear. Trust me, it's not the kind of conversation you want to hear." There was the understatement of the century, if ever I'd heard one.

"Why? Are you ok?" Dan's face turned serious. "Megs, if you are in some kind of trouble, you need to tell me and we will handle that shit. You're Ash's best friend; I don't give a fuck what's going down, Troy and I will to be front and center on it." His concern was endearing. Granted he could be conceited, but underneath it all, he had such a good heart. Sadly, this was not something I wanted him front and center on, however impassionate the plea.

"Stand down, asshole. I've got it covered." Troy tapped Dan across the chest and shot him a look in warning.

"I'm fine, really." I smiled. I really didn't want to explain to Dan that the real reason we were standing here was that we were deliberating the finer points of Troy's cock giving me pleasure. It sounded so crude when I said it like that, so it definitely shouldn't be repeated.

Troy placed his hand on the small of my back, asserting *he had this under control.* "We're just going to take a walk around the club, okay? Just tell Ash we're dancing or something."

"Fine." Dan's eyes darted between us, somewhat appeased. "Go do what needs doing but if you need reinforcements, I'm your first port of call." He poked Troy in the chest.

Stopping myself from getting my hopes up was not an easy task. The what-did-it-mean dominated what thoughts while the tugging in my lower belly prayed I wasn't getting ready for another brush off. Not after

CRASH RIDE

I'd laid all my cards on the table. Surely, that would be too cruel.

Troy laughed, tapping Dan on the shoulder while his other hand stayed glued to my lower back. "Always. Now stop busting my stones and go hang with your girl before she wises up and realizes she can do better than your sorry ass."

Dan flipped Troy the finger and wisely retreated back to the VIP area, where no doubt he would make out with Ash until we returned. If we returned. Was he actually considering doing this? He easily could have had an out, citing that we would attract too much attention if we slunk off into the darkness. Could it be that this sexual tension I had been feeling was not just one-sided?

He lowered his head and whispered in my ear. "You called me Troy."

"Huh?" That was not where I thought this conversation was heading.

"When you were talking to Dan, you didn't tack on my last name."

"Oh, yeah I guess I didn't." I hadn't really noticed, but I guess now that I thought about it, I had just called him Troy. Though I didn't see how this piece of information was conducive to us getting horizontal.

His lips rested against my ear, his breath tickled my skin. "Hmmmm, so now that has me curious."

His beautiful eyes seared me. My body wondered if he was going to touch me in a way I needed, and my brain needed to know what he had meant. Internally, I was mess. I was both turned on and confused. "Curious about what?"

"About how you are going to scream out my name when I fuck you."

I swallowed, hard. "Are you going to fuck me, Troy Harris?"

"You bet your ass I am. Let's go."

4

Troy

I HONESTLY TRIED TO FIGHT THIS. NO, REALLY, I DID. IT'S NOT LIKE I hadn't fantasized about the five hundred ways I could fuck Megs. Hell, just seeing her and knowing the possibility was off the table had been torture. Of course, I'm not a fucking deviant who can't think with anything but his dick, so I kept that shit locked down and pretended like my cock didn't get hard every time she walked into the room.

See, apart from my pact with Dan, I actually really liked Megs. I mean *genuinely* liked her, and the last thing I wanted to do was make shit weird between the two of us. So, while I *wanted* Megs in the biblical sense of the word, it was the other shit she offered that actually made me sit up and take notice. She was funny and smart and wasn't scared to stand up for herself. She had also been a sweetheart to Dan when Ash had broken up with him. That brand of kindness, the kind that doesn't attach strings, it isn't just rare in our world— it's almost non-existent.

There's always something, some fine print bullshit that came with the preverbal *free lunch*. Megs, she was one of the exceptions. As I said rare, and there was no way I would do anything to disrespect her.

However, she was now offering herself to me on a fucking platter and as pathetic as it sounded, I didn't have the fucking strength to turn her down. Telling me that she wanted to come with my cock inside her flipped a switch in me that I had no hope of controlling. Shit, now it was all I could think about and I couldn't even remember all those reasons for *not* having sex with her.

I should be saying no, be a better man and tell her this would be a mistake but my mouth wouldn't say the words. My dick …well it was already wondering why the fuck it had taken us this long to get to this point. I tilted her chin so I could get a better look at her, see if maybe there was some indecision in those drop-dead gorgeous eyes. Nothing. Not even a hint of freaking hesitation stared back at me.

Her perfect tits heaved up and down as she breathed heavily, and if I had any willpower left in me, that vision alone ensured that it took the expressway out of here. Without talking, I snaked my hand around her waist, her eyes widening as I pulled her close to my body and lead her down the stairs back to the Gen Pop part of the club. She didn't fight me, keeping in step as we sifted through the bodies that lined the space between the blood red walls.

"Where are we going?" she asked, her eyes darting between the crowd and me as we continued along our way.

I could tell from her tone she was uninitiated in what was about to go down.

She may have talked a good game, but the quick-fuck-thing obviously wasn't her usual speed. Megs was different and I liked that she probably hadn't done this before with someone else. It shouldn't have mattered, but it did. Juicing me up even more with the prospect.

She wasn't looking to advertise what we were about to do for status points. Nor was looking to sink her claws in and get a ring from me.

It excited me that she wanted to go there with me, knowing she was about as far from a groupie as I could get.

Fucking me right now, in the club hadn't been her suggestion. I was being an asshole and I knew it and yet, the chance to change her mind was not an option. I'd given her that, and she hadn't seemed keen, so now it was all about doing what both of us seemed to be starving for. And no, I'm not being fucking dramatic. Starving is how I felt.

She was beautiful and sexy and I'd stared at her for months, pushing down the urge to kiss those lips and sink my cock into her. Months, I'd convinced myself not to go there, needing a cold shower after seeing her and a fucking pep talk as to why we weren't going down that road. There was no fucking way we *weren't* doing this.

"You're playing with fire, Megs; and I'm not feeling very gentlemanly right now." I hissed through my clenched jaw, my balls so tight I thought for sure they were going to explode.

"Are you going to fuck me on the dance floor, Troy Harris?" Her eyes lit up in a weird excitement that made me almost consider it as a possibility.

"Not interested in giving anyone else the pleasure tonight, sweetheart, just you."

"Oh." Her beautiful lips formed an O to back up the wide-eyed expression as the penny finally dropped.

We walked past the security and straight out the front door. I spied the Suburban parked up against the curb, TJ leaning up against the hood shooting the breeze with one of the bouncers.

"Hey, Troy, you looking to leave already? Ms. Winters, you ok?" TJ looked at us suspiciously, like we'd suddenly grown extra heads.

"Yeah man, just need the keys." I gave him a look not to argue with me and held out my hand. It wasn't the first time one of us had commandeered the ride for something other than transportation; it just had been awhile.

TJ eyed my hands around Megs's waist and hesitantly pulled out the keys from his pocket. He didn't give me any lip, but he was far from liking the idea. His death stare translated the you-better-know-what-the-

CRASH RIDE

fuck-you're-doing without the need for an audible. It didn't take a brain surgeon to work out what we were up to, but he was smart enough to keep his trap shut, even if he thought that it was a bad idea.

Of course it was a bad idea, it was full-blow idiotic. Megs and I were about to get down and dirty in a fucking car while our two best friends were ignorantly partying no more than five hundred feet away. This wasn't going to be some hit-and-run. She wasn't just a girl who I wanted to fuck, we'd already established that when it came to Megs, it went beyond just the physical. Not that my dick wanted to hear the argument right now. We were both going to have to play nice after the fact, and pretend we hadn't seen each other naked. The fall-out if shit went bad had the potential to be fucking huge and yet none of those reasons seemed good enough to stop me.

I hit the keyless entry on the remote, the door lock popped open as I guided Megs to the passenger side door.

"You ready?" I pulled open the door and waited for her to climb inside the cabin. Part of me waited for her to tell me she'd changed her mind and to take her back inside the club.

She slid her toned legs into the car as her ass sunk into the seat, biting her lip seductively. "Let's go." She yanked the door I had been holding open and shut it. I watched through the glass from my place on the sidewalk as she fastened her seatbelt.

Ok then, no second thoughts. Good to know. I walked around to the driver's side and climbed in. My ass barely hitting the soft leather seat and I cranked the ignition.

I shifted into drive, reaching around for the seat belt as we eased away from the curb into the flow of traffic.

"Are you taking me home?" Megs shot me a sideways glance as the lights of the club faded in the rearview.

"Nope, we aren't making it that far." I hung a right and pulled into a narrow one-way street. I wasn't even sure if it was a legitimate street or if it just an alley used to facilitate deliveries for the businesses that backed onto this narrow strip of asphalt. My care factor on the matter was less than zero, other than thanking God that it existed.

The car jerked as I hit the brakes and shifted into park, stepping on the emergency break as the car continued to idle. My head swiveled to Megs, her eyes wide as she surveyed the alley before she turned and looked at me, her hand slowly moving down her side to unfasten her restraint. *Good idea.* I hit the eject button on mine and let the seat belt slide off as I killed the engine.

"You want to go into the back?" I leaned over the console and brushed her cheek with my thumb. Translation. You sure you want to do this? While my balls had reached Defcon 1, I wasn't going to be a complete asshole. It was bad enough I was about to fuck her in a car on some dead-end street, I wasn't going to do this without giving her one last out if she wanted to take it.

She didn't answer, instead she moved closer and slammed those sweet lips on mine. Well fuck me. No seriously, fuck me. My dick punched out in protest against the fly of my jeans as she opened her mouth and allowed my tongue to slide inside. It was better than I imagined. Her hungry mouth opening wider as her tongue wrestled with mine, my hand having a mind of its own reached up, palming one of her tits. She whimpered as I thumbed over the material of her dress and teased her nipple, the peak rising to the occasion with very little encouragement.

"In the back," I groaned against her mouth. I wanted unrestricted access to that body and the front seat wasn't even close to cutting it.

She pulled back, her hand reached up against mine as I kneaded her tit. "That feels so good." Her eyes watched me closely as I continued to play.

"I can make it better. C'mon Megs, jump into the back." I reluctantly moved my hand away and cracked open the driver's side door. My already rock-hard dick throbbed in my pants, wanting to know what the hold up was.

Megs followed suit, both of us exiting the front seat and moving into the back. The car's back doors slammed in unison as we scrambled onto the bench seat. My hands sliding up her legs at fucking warp speed as they made their way to her ass.

She was just as enthusiastic as she clawed at my shirt as I hauled her onto my lap and attacked her mouth. Her lips opened, allowing my tongue to slide inside, the invasion far from gentle. She moaned into my mouth as she rocked against my hard-on, my hands slid from her ass to her naked thighs as I tried to lift her dress.

Megs continued to writhe in my lap, the friction making my eyes water as I hovered between sweet pleasure and motherfucking torture. I wanted to tear the clothes from my body and torch them purely on the fact they were hindering shit right now.

Her nails clawed down my chest and abs with enough pressure I was sure it was going to leave a mark, and damn if the prospect didn't make me even more excited. We made out like a pair of fucking teenagers under the bleachers, dry humping each other with enough intensity I wasn't sure if I was going to blow my load or get the worst case of chafing known to man. Either way, I wasn't stopping. With her dress pulled up out of the way, my hand once again moved to her ass, my fingers making contact with bare skin. Fuck. I moved a little further along her skin in my quest to discover if she had decided to go commando or not, and came across a thin strap of fabric. G-String. Very fucking nice. I yanked the strip to the side, allowing my finger to slid down the seam of her ass and watched her shudder as I travelled further down. The nails that were previously embedded in my skin were now wrestling with my belt; the leather flicked me as she violently tore it from my jeans. She didn't stop, ripping open my fly while we remained lip-locked and I teased her ass.

My cock sprung free as she pushed down my boxers, my hard-on hitting my stomach. I was so turned on I could barely speak, but there was no way I was ready for this to be over without tasting her first. I lifted her off of me and Megs yelped as I tossed her down onto the seat. The confusion on her face priceless as I smiled and then gently parted her thighs.

"Oh!" The tension in her legs relaxed as my tongue lapped at the edge of her G-string. "But I want to touch your cock," she half-moaned as I pulled across the material and flicked across her hot, wet center.

"You can touch it all you want." The edges of my lips curved before I lowered my mouth back down and sucked gently on her clit. "You want me to stop?" I asked, slowly sliding a finger inside her. "Megs, holy hell, you are so wet." My finger was instantly coated as I slid in another. It was a challenge not to throw this game plan out the window and just move to a bootleg play, the one where my dick got involved. It had been screaming to get into the game since she mentioned the word "cock" and was wondering why the fuck it was still on the bench. Easy there buddy, you'll get your chance to play, but not until I fucking make her come with my mouth.

"Don't stop," she moaned, her hips lifting closer to my mouth as I resumed licking and sucking her clit while I gently finger-fucked her. "Oh God, please don't stop." Her plea unnecessary, 'cause I had no intention of stopping. I continued to work her over with my mouth, her body bucking against me as I tried to ignore the pain in my balls. They too, like my dick, begging to get in on the action.

"Oh fuck," screamed Megs, her voice echoing around the car as I moved my other hand to her ass, gently thumbing over it while my fingers stretched her pussy. One last flick of my tongue was all it took and her legs clamped around my head and she screamed. Her body convulsed as I felt the orgasm rip through her, her pussy pulsing around my fingers while I continued to gently lick her. Each pass of my tongue made her body shake as I teased every last inch of pleasure from her. Not going to lie, watching her pant with my head between her thighs was even better than I'd imagined.

"Oh. My. God." She paused between each word. "That. Was. Amazing." Her chest heaved up and down as she sucked in air, both of us still mostly clothed despite my dick poking proudly out of my boxers.

"I think it's time these came off," I gently slid my fingers out of her and pulled at her G-string taking it with me as I moved my hand down

CRASH RIDE

her legs. I threw them onto the other seat as I spread her legs open and got a better look. Her glistening, wet pussy was fucking beautiful and I had to stop myself from going down on her again, my fingers circling her opening as I shuffled up onto my knees.

"Holy shit!" Her eyes widened as she stared down at my crotch. A slight look of fear flicked through her face as she caught sight of my cock.

"Well, you do know how to make a guy feel special, don't you?" I laughed as held it for her to get a better look; my cock jerked the minute it made contact with my hand.

"Is that metal? In your—?" She couldn't peel her eyes away as she stared at the thick metal ring that circled the tip to just below the head of my cock. It wasn't the first time I'd caught a girl off guard. It's not like I'd broadcasted that shit in *Rolling Stone* Magazine, nope. It was on a purely need-to-know basis. Sure, the rumors were out there, so on more than one occasion, girls had asked to see it backstage. Their eagerness to see my dick had almost convinced Dan to take the plunge. We got right to the piercing shop too, but he chickened out when a dude tapped the chair and told him to pull down his pants.

"It's a piercing. Trust me, I think you'll enjoy it." I shoved my jeans down, reaching into my back pocket and pulling out a condom.

"Did it hurt?" she asked, genuine interest flicking through those beautiful eyes.

"A needle getting driven through the head of your dick sure didn't tickle, but it wasn't that bad." I was beginning to wonder if show-and-tell was as far as we were going to get.

"Can I touch it?"

"Well, I was hoping you would." I grinned, gently stroking the length of my shaft as I brought it closer, sitting on the seat beside her.

So maybe we weren't just going to be playing show-and-tell. Excellent.

Her fingers tiptoed up the length of my shaft before she curled her hand around my length. "That's so fucking sexy, Troy Harris." She grinned as she slowly stroked me.

I eased back into the chair, her fingers around me felt so fucking magical, I had to fight the urge not to blow my load all over her hand. "Megs, you just came on my mouth. I think we're on a first name basis now."

"I want to lick it; I want to feel it in my mouth." She moved closer, not bothering to wait for permission. She bent down and took me into her mouth in one big thrust.

"Jesus, Megs," I hissed as she wrapped her lips around the head of my cock. Her tongue flicked around my shaft before circling around the tip, her teeth gently pulling on the ring. I'm not sure which deserved the greater applause, her initiative on the blowjob or that fact she was sending me into outer space with that sweet mouth of hers. The jury was still out, but what I did know is — the deeper she took me into her mouth, and the more she sucked me, the harder it was for me to maintain any type of control. Fuck, at this rate I was going to *need* her to repeat my full fucking name 'cause I sure as hell was having trouble remembering it.

Caught between wanting to ask her to stop and begging her to keep going, I gently pulled on her hair and freed my cock from her mouth. There was no way I was going to come without making her eyes roll back into her head at least one last time. I grabbed the condom that had fallen out of my hand and onto the seat beside me and tore open the foil. She watched as I pulled out the rubber and rolled it down my hard-on, licking her lips as her eyes followed my hand, smoothing the latex over my piercing and all the way down to the base. Damn, if there wasn't a part of me that regretted pulling out of those beautiful lips.

"Do you know how long I've wanted to do this?" She moved onto my lap and straddled me. "I almost want to pinch myself to make sure it's real." Her face inches from mine.

With my hand firmly around my shaft, I teased her pussy with the head of my cock. "Does this feel real?" The ball from the ring hit her clit and made her whimper.

CRASH RIDE

"Troy," she moaned. "Please don't stop." Her eyes closed as I slowly pushed into her. Not a lot— just barely an inch— trust me, that was a fucking exercise in restraint if ever there was.

"Holy shit!" Her eyes flew open and I felt her pussy clamp around the head of my cock, the only part of me which was actually inside of her.

"You ok?" I asked, steadying her hips to stop myself from pushing any deeper.

"Yes, I'm ok. It just feels... So amazing."

"It will feel a lot better once I'm all the way in, but I'm going to need you to relax. I don't want to hurt you."

Megs dropped her head so that her forehead rested on mine. "I don't care if it hurts, I want it all. Deep. Hard. I. Want. It. All." Her voice so full of fucking want, it was like I'd been smacked in the jaw.

That grand plan I had —to take this slow—yeah that shit just sailed right out the window as I pulled her down onto me and sunk deep into her in one hit. She moaned and I blew out a curse as her tight wet pussy clamped around me like a fist. So fucking tight.

"Fuck, Megs." I slowly breathed out as I started to move, my hands on her hips guiding her as I picked up the tempo. She quickly got on the same page and met each one of my thrusts with one of her own, twisting her pelvis as she lifted up before slamming back down hard. I grabbed the top of her dress and pulled it down, needing to suck on one of her gorgeous tits. The bra she had on underneath was some sheer fucking mesh that I was sure I could rip just by looking at it. I pulled down the front, rolling her nipple between my fingers and guided it to my mouth. We were panting so much, the windows had fogged up.

I slammed into her, harder and faster each time. The gloves were off, and I couldn't have been gentle if I'd tried. The fact we'd both wanted this but had kept our distance had just made it that much more intense. My mouth moved from her tit to her mouth and I slammed my lips on hers. I felt desperate, like I couldn't get deep enough into her, it was fucking euphoric and maddening at the same time. She bit my lip as I pulled her down, my hands once again around her perfect ass. She bucked against me, wild with each thrust and I knew she was close.

"Touch yourself, Megs. I want to see you finger that amazing pussy of yours while I fuck you."

"Oh," she moaned as her hand moved from behind my neck, to slither down her body and between her legs. Some girls got weird when you ask them to do it, but Megs didn't even miss a beat as her fingers twisting over her clit while I continued to pound her. It was fucking beautiful, watching her touch herself with my cock inside her, the tips of her fingers making contact with my dick as I moved in and out. I couldn't look away. It was the hottest thing I'd seen in a long time, more so 'cause she was so into it. The fact that it was Megs elevated it to eleven.

"Troy, I'm going to come." Megs closed her eyes and her fingers moved faster, her body tense as she rode me.

"That's it, Megs. I want to feel how hard you come." I moved my fingers across the crease of her ass, teasing it before slowly sliding in a finger. Megs's eyes flung open as I invaded her ass, her pussy milking my dick as she came hard. The pulses she sent up my shaft giving me no hope to hold off any longer as I exploded into her. "Fuck." I groaned as my load hit the tip of the condom and I wasn't sure it didn't tear the fucking thing in half.

Megs collapsed against me, her head on my shoulder as she sucked in each breath. "Wow, that was incredible." Her muffled voice sent tiny vibrations against my skin.

My finger slowly slid out of her ass, her body shaking as what was left of her orgasm rode its way out. "That was more than incredible." I tried to rein in my own breathing as I wrapped my arms around her. "Megs, you're fucking amazing."

"Aww, Troy Harris, you'll make me blush." She hid her face against my chest as she giggled.

"Really? After what we just did, me talking is what makes you blush?" I couldn't help but laugh. She was definitely not the *good girl* I had her pegged for. Hell no. She was one of these girls who looked all straight laced and turned into a nympho in the bedroom. Shit. Just

CRASH RIDE

thinking about the crazy things she might be up for made my dick twitch, which conveniently was still buried inside of her.

"We should get back." Megs sighed as the reality of the situation hit us both. Sure, this isn't awkward. We now had to go pretend like we *hadn't* just had fucked each other's brains out and be social. Yep. This was going to suck. Hard Core.

"Yeah. You're probably right." I rubbed her back wondering if I should say something. I mean, we hadn't really discussed what was going to happen after. Sure, she had said all it was going to be was sex, but I still felt like an asshole fucking her in the car, in some alley. Shit, we hadn't even gotten totally undressed, screwing like two crazy animals in heat. Not my best moment, that's for sure.

Megs lifted off me, her teeth biting down on her lip as I slid out. "You don't regret it, do you?" I guess she felt the weird vibe as well.

My eyes were firmly locked on hers. "Are you kidding me? Hell no. I'm just trying not be a complete douchebag and ask if that was a onetime deal."

She smiled, obviously pleased I was looking for a repeat. "You would do it again? With me?"

My hand moved up and down her thigh, her skin so soft it almost didn't feel real. "Megs, I'd do it again right now if we had the time. You were incredible. I know I'm probably breaking all kinds of rules right now but yeah, I really want you to come home with me tonight."

She relaxed, sinking into the seat beside me and smiled. "I'd like that. A lot. I guess if it's the same night, technically it's still the same one time. Right?"

"I'm all about the technicalities." Especially ones that meant I was going to be able to do *that* again.

"Good, so we do this tonight and then we both move on." She fished her underwear off the seat and started to smooth out her dress. "No one has to know, nothing has to get weird and we can just go back to the way things were."

So that was the plan. One night. One night to fuck each other's brains out and then we'd go back to friends. I didn't even care how fucking shady it sounded, I wanted it. I wanted her. One night and then maybe we both could get over this twisted infatuation we seemed to have. One thing was for sure, I was going all out and making it count. Tonight she was going to scream out my name so many times she was going to be sick of it and I was going to enjoy every second of it. And while we were both going to be moving on, she would never forget it.

5
Megan

HOLY—EXPLETIVE-EXPLETIVE-MY-BRAIN-IS-SO-FRIED-I-CAN'T- think—Hell, I just had sex with Troy Harris. Yep, the use of his first and last name was still required, if only to try and get my head around it. Did a twister suddenly pick me up and transport me to OZ? The absence of ruby slippers told me no. It was like the ultimate crime and I had gotten away with the robbery of the century. I've been a bad, bad girl, officer go ahead and take my prints.

The whole trip back to the club I couldn't even think straight. My thoughts jumped in a suspended state of what-the-fuck-just-happened. Oh, and I couldn't sit straight either, but that was on account of his HUGE cock.

The size-thirteen shoes should have probably been the tip off; his hands were big too, so it would stand to reason… And yet I was still unprepared for what he was packing.

Damn. Was I going to be walking funny? It would totally be worth it. And while we were on the subject of "ta-dah" moments, that big giant ring in the head of his aforementioned huge cock just about made me choke. Literally, as in I couldn't freaking breath. Me and my friend, *Google* were going to be having some serious words when I got home. How the hell could I have not known about that? And more importantly, how could I have ever orgasmed without it in the past? What would possess a guy to pierce *that* part of his body, I'll never know, but I am saying a silent thank-you to the person who had the balls—no pun intended— to start that trend. If the talented penis wasn't enough to get me on my knees and sing Hallelujah, the *other* things he had in his bag of tricks, sure did.

So, the anal play. Yeah, didn't see that one coming. Sure, guys had asked me to go *down that road* before, but the answer had always been a resounding, oh-hell-no. Wow. Boy, was I wrong. I'm not going to lie and say that at first the invasion didn't make my eyes bug-out like an old school cartoon character, but that uncertainty lasted about a quarter of a second till the freaking mind blowing orgasm rolled in. It was less like a wave and more like a tsunami. If I'd had pockets, I would be checking them for sand.

I'm not sure if that was some kind of signature move, or if he just felt inspired, but the man had some serious talent when it came to pleasuring a woman. Between his hands, his mouth and his cock, I was seriously wondering how the hell a man like that was legal. Maybe the ultimate crime was his. There sure as hell would be no police report filed by me.

"You doin' okay?" Troy stopped the Suburban in front of *Panic*, the short ride back to the club over.

"Uh-huh." My head nodded slightly more enthusiastically than I would have liked.

"You just look a little…" His truth serum eyes seared me. There would be no controlling my mouth.

"Well-fucked?" Was what I'd offered. Not like it was a lie, but I could have been a little smoother. Nothing else seemed to fit, so I was going to stick with that.

His low laugh rumbled through the cabin of the car. "I was going to

CRASH RIDE

say *antsy*. I'm not good with you being so unsettled. Makes me think I didn't take care of what needed to be taken care of, you get me?"

He leaned across the console all cool-and-unaffected as the smell of sex and his cologne assaulted the air around me. It just didn't seem fair. He wasn't allowed to be talented, good looking, able to produce mind-blowing orgasm *and* be cool. Greedy much?

"Oh, it was taken care of. Twice." My head bobbled like an idiot as I tried to play off the goof-ball grin that was plastered across my face. No one was fooled. "We should get back inside." Thank you mouth for finally kicking in. Look at me acting close to normal. He'd never know it was all an act. Move along folks, nothing to see here.

"Yeah, they've probably noticed by now." Troy eyed TJ who had walked around the passenger side door and opened it for me.

"Ms. Winters." TJ spared me the judgmental stare down or the cold shoulder. I nodded my appreciation, as a gigantic hug thanking him would have been overkill.

"Ready?" Troy appeared beside me as TJ helped me from the car to the sidewalk. For that, the big burly security-guard-come-driver deserved another thank you. The length of my dress hem not conducive to climbing in and out of a tank-like vehicle.

Who can get out of a car *that* size *that* quickly? Seriously, was he Batman? "Yep." My mouth popped on the P as I adjusted my dress and added *stealthy* to Troy's list of attributes. The list was extensive.

"Here you go, man." The car keys flew out of Troy's hand and landed in TJ's steady palm before he pocketed them. The extent of the exchange limited to a few grunts and a nod as Troy lead me back to the main entrance of the club. Maybe they had a code? Whatever, it was a mystery that didn't need solving tonight, certainly not by me.

"Just so we're clear on our story." My voice rose to compensate for the loud mayhem we had stepped into. "Crappy week at work. We went to the bar, had a few drinks and then I need to step outside for some air." Sounded plausible. Yeah, let's go with that.

"Sure, but we never did discuss your *crappy* week." Troy's hand

49

pressed into my lower back as he guided me up the stairs. The same stairs we had neglected to climb earlier. He leaned into me, "I'm not buying it's just a tough case load." His hot breath in my ear was making all kinds of parts of me tingle and I had to remind myself not to press myself up against his body and bury my tongue in his mouth.

"I'm fine." The rehearsed response was automatic when it came to work talk. The added shrug wasn't. I couldn't have been any less convincing, and for once it hadn't been my mouth that let me down. Kudos traitorous body, you are now on my shit list.

"You know you can talk to me, right? I'm pretty good at keeping secrets." Troy's lips spread into a grin as he reached the top of the stairs.

Well then. So, my plan to inoculate myself with a good dose of Troy Harris and be cured was a bust. It certainly didn't help that he was being so sweet, and that grin he had going on just made me want him more. Maybe I needed more exposure. Like I literally needed to fuck him out of my system? I certainly owed it to myself to explore the options.

"I'm fine, promise." I made a cross-my-heart motion over my chest and walked to the entrance of the VIP lounge area. The bouncer waving us through the minute he laid eyes on Troy.

"There you are!" Ash rushed to greet us. Her eyes were red and puffy, her mascara *less* enhancing her lashes and *more* giving her smudgy panda eyes. And unless you are *Courtney Love,* that look is not intentional.

This was certainly not the welcome I thought we would be walking into. Dan followed slowly behind her. He looked guiltily responsible; the hands shoved into his front pockets and the dopey look on his face a dead giveaway.

"Ash, are you ok?" I grabbed her hand and shot a death-glare at Dan. "What did you do?" So help me if he'd made her cry by doing or saying something stupid, I was going to end him. I don't think I could go through another one of their break-ups. The last one had almost sent *me* into therapy.

"Relax, Megs. It's not what you think." Dan circled his hands around

Ash's waist and pulled her against his body, she didn't fight him so I'm guessing that's a good thing. Someone needed to start talking.

Ash dried the corners of her eyes with the tips of her fingers. "Dan asked me to marry him."

Huh? All muscle control of my mouth was lost as it fell open in disbelief. My eyelids peeling back to their capacity was also a nice touch. *Wow.* Did *not* see that one coming. Marriage? How long were we gone? Had Marty McFly shown up in his Delorean and we'd somehow time travelled? Maybe Troy's penis had an in-built flux capacitor and zipped us through the time-space continuum. His talented cock knew no end.

"What? Just now?" My shaking head complemented the attractive facial paralysis I had going on as I tried to wrap my brain around what I'd obviously missed.

Troy, who obviously hadn't shared my stunned reaction, moved in front of me. "Congrats, man. Good move on making it legal, it will be harder for her to dump your sorry ass when she finally realizes she can do better." He shook Dan's hand and gave Ash a warm hug.

Dan was unmistakably pleased, the smile barely contained on his face as he patted Troy on the back. "Thanks, man. You know you're going to have to be suited up and stand beside me as my best man, right?"

"Wouldn't miss it for the world, dude. Whatever you need."

My brain kicked into gear and demanded I say something. My best friend just announced she was getting married and I had been standing there speechless while the revelry went on around me. *You're happy for her. This is a good thing. Congratulations.* All acceptable responses, pick one…any one! "Wow. Congratulations, Ash. I'm so happy for you." Thank you, sweet baby Jesus.

Ash beamed, her excitement and happiness palpable as she tugged on my arm. "And Megs, I need you to be my maid of honor. I know it's kind of soon, but I know Dan's the one. There's never going to be another guy for me."

"Of course I will. I would love nothing more than to stand beside you." It was a given that I would be there in whatever way I was needed.

Being partnered with Troy? Time will tell if that was a blessing or a curse. "I'm so glad you're happy, that's all that matters. Who cares how long it's been? When you know, you know. So which one of you two is going to spill the details? Is there a ring?" My mouth spewed every random thought as I grabbed Ash's left hand and noticed a sparkling diamond was absent from her ring finger.

Dan held up his hand as he entered the *ring* debate. "There ain't no way in hell I'm choosing an engagement ring without Ash's input. I know Stone and James took a knee with a box full of carats, but I wanted to be sure that whatever she wears is something that she loves." He punctuated his stance by pulling her in close and kissing her neck.

Ash smiled. "The ring isn't important. I don't even need one."

"Yeah, you do." Dan made it clear where he sat on the *no ring* stance. "No future wife of mine is going to be without an engagement ring and don't even think about the money. So you can either choose a ring you like or you get one the size of a baseball when I go buy one myself."

"I don't think he's bending on this one, Ash; might be easier just to take the hit and get the bauble." Troy winked with a laugh. Ash nodded, agreeing it was probably a losing battle.

While their touching exchange was endearing, I was still no closer to know how or why Dan decided to pop the question in a club. That information was something I needed to know. Not that it was any of my business, but that had never stopped me before. I was an information girl. It was a sickness and I was very unwell. "So... getting back to the proposal. You know I need details."

"Well, to be honest I hadn't really planned it." Dan took the reigns on this one as he explained how he decided they needed to become husband and wife. "But being here reminded me of that night and how it all started."

It was evident in the telling how much he loved her. My heart swooned despite the absence of rose petals and sunsets —and probably no bended knees either—but he was a fly-by-the-seat-of-your-pants kind of guy so I wouldn't expect his proposal to be anything less. I felt my eyes water as I looked at my friend, so happy and in love with a guy who adored and loved her like she deserved. It was fitting that she was finally getting her little slice of happily ever after.

"I'm not sure if that's romantic or kind of creepy." My eyes blinked rapidly, trying to keep my tears at bay.

Ash joined me on my journey to Tearsville, her fingertips trying to salvage what was left of her eye make-up. She needn't have bothered. It was a lost cause. "Oh hush, Megs, it's beautiful and it's perfect."

"Ok babe, you're going to need to stop crying." It had been a long time since I'd heard Dan sound so serious, he stroked Ash's arm with concern. "I know you said you're happy, but the tears are starting to mess with my head. Last time I made you cry, you left me."

"Aww Dan, stop. You're going to make me cry now." His words plunged my own make-up at risk as my eyes started to water. Damn him for being so incredibly sweet.

"Ok, ladies," Troy waved over a waitress and ordered some champagne. "No more crying. What we need to is celebrate."

He was a God. Troy, I meant. His intervention saved me from a full emotional outburst that would have unleashed my unattractive crying face. No one needed to see that. He would *so* be getting a blowjob for that act of kindness; I was a really ugly crier.

We moved over to one of the vacant couches, coupling off as we sat down. It should have felt weird— sitting next to him, acting normal—but it didn't. Instead we laughed and chatted about the impending nuptials as the waitress handed out our champagne.

"To my best friend, who's been more like a brother to me." Troy held up his glass. "I'm so freaking glad you didn't waste time and asked the best woman who ever walked into your life to marry you."

His smile made my heart skip a beat before he continued. "Ash, I know we haven't known each other long but I can tell you are the real deal, and I couldn't be happier to have you as a sister-in-law. Sorry to tell you, but you marry this loser, you get us as well. It's all good though, 'cause it means you can stare at Alex's ass anytime you want now."

We laughed— Ash and I. She *had* stared at Alex's ass so it was funny. Dan didn't share the amusement as he shot Troy a dirty look and flipped him the bird. "I hate you, asshole."

"Back at ya, sunshine." Troy grinned back.

"To Dan and Ash." Troy paused before adding, "Nothing but love for both of you. Congratulations."

"Dan and Ash." The words left my mouth with very little effort. Troy had said it all so I showed my support by taking a drink. It was the least I could do and would keep me from declarations of how amazing Troy was. I was thinking it but the world didn't need to know. Best I pin that thought for later.

The drinks flowed freely, which could have been dangerous. My hands seemed to spend more and more time on Troy Harris; his arm, his knee, his thigh. No one noticed and more to the point, no one stopped me. I would have stopped had he asked, but he didn't so I didn't. Did that sound right? Probably not. Oh look, another glass of champagne.

"So you wanna team up, beat the two of them into submission if either of them fucks this up?" Troy gently bumped my shoulder—*he* was touching *me*— as we watched Dan and Ash move from the couch and onto the dance floor.

"Yes. I think that's part of the job description when you sign up for the wedding party." My voice came out breathier than I would have liked, possibly on account that I wanted to nuzzle against his chest.

Troy's arms stretched out over the top of the couch, his skin making contact with my back. The shiver travelled down my spine, all the way to my toes. "Funny how we worried about them noticing us being gone and they couldn't have cared less."

Yes, no one had noticed. Let's go back to car was what I had wanted to say but instead the watered down version of, "Yeah, I guess we lucked out," was what I actually said.

It was a compromise and it meant I didn't sound like a nympho, so positives all around. Yay! "Did you still want to… get together…later?" My voice was unsteady, either champagne or concern that our night of

CRASH RIDE

debauchery was going to be put on a permanent hold, to blame. Best to be prepared.

Troy's hand slid off the couch and gently caressed my back. "Of course I do, why wouldn't I?" His smile convinced me that he had no plans to sleep alone.

I stifled a moan, allowing more skin to connect with his hand. "I just wanted to be sure you hadn't changed your mind."

"Changed my mind? I'm the best man, you're the maid of honor. I'm pretty sure there is some unwritten law that we have to sleep together." There was a smile but no humor in his voice.

"I'm fairly sure there is no such law." My eyelids may have fluttered; I couldn't be sure as the silliness of my words made me giggle.

"Going to have to disagree with you, Megs, respectfully of course." Troy's hand slowly slid down the couch to rest on my hip. "I'm not going to be held accountable if you doom their marriage 'cause you didn't follow the rules."

"Oh, so that's the reason?" My chin tilted as my body relaxed against his. Cooling it would have been the smart thing to do. Dan and Ash could walk up at any moment, we were in a public place and I was practically in his lap. Did I care? Nope, and I couldn't make myself either. He was intoxicating. My lips moved closer to his ear. "You afraid we're going to curse them if we don't sleep together?"

Troy turned his head, his lips hovered above mine and I was sure he was going to kiss me. "No." He paused, his voice husky and low. "The reason is 'cause I want to own that body of yours tonight. I couldn't give a rat's ass about anything else other than making sure that happens."

55

6

Troy

IT WAS SOMETIME AROUND TWO IN THE MORNING WHEN WE finally wrapped it up and piled into the Suburban. That was about three hours later than I would have liked. Patience and virtue—yeah I didn't get the memo. Instead I concentrated on what it would feel like to have my hands on her ass while she rode my cock; it gave me the incentive to hang back and let the night play out.

Dan and Ash got cozy on the row of seats in front of us while Megs and I took the ones in the back. Two things it had been good for. One, the two lovebirds didn't get an eyeful of my hard-on. And two, my hands were able to stay busy on Megs without any raised eyebrows or suspicion. And busy they were.

That dress she was wearing deserved a standing ovation, 'cause other than looking outstanding on her, it didn't hinder my access. My fingers got on a first name basis with her thong while she rubbed the front of my jeans with her hand. It was a beautiful thing.

The little moans she had going on didn't help either. They weren't loud enough for our audience to hear. Nope, she'd saved that privilege for me alone. Almost made me forget where the fuck I was, reaching for her mouth with my own on more than one occasion. That probably would have required some explanation. My tongue down her throat? Yeah, really no way getting around that unless she needed mouth-to-mouth resuscitation.

Both Ash and Megs had both consumed their fair share of drinks at the club. If the collection of champagne bottles hadn't been a clue, the giggling sure was. Sober? Not likely. And while they weren't loaded, they were fairly lit up.

Of course being the stand-up guy that I am, I kindly offered Megs the use of my guest room so she wouldn't have to go back her place alone. She happily accepted. The brownie points I'd won from Ash were a nice touch, my concern for Megs's well-being, commended even. I know, I'm a regular fucking saint.

The elevator ride up to the Penthouse had been excruciating. Being in such a confined space and not being able to do anything, yeah that was brutal. I had to mentally recite the batting order for the Yankees to try and calm the raging hard-on I had going on.

The minute we'd said our goodbyes and Dan and Ash disappeared through their front door, I grabbed Megs and pushed her up against the wall. I'd waited as long as I cared to and I wanted her mouth, and every other part of her on me.

She gave me zero resistance as my tongue continued to fuck her mouth. That was the preshow as I fumbled with my keys and opened my front door, both of us ready for the main event.

The door slamming behind us was all we needed to take it to the next level, clawing each other like savages. We didn't even make it to the bedroom. Instead we dropped onto the hardwood floor of my entranceway and tore our clothes from our bodies like they were on fire. I'd take her to my bed later, what I needed was to get my mouth on her—

every part of her.

Her neck, her tits, her thighs— my tongue got real familiar with it all, and she was almost begging by the time my mouth hit her pussy. Her back bowed off the floor as I continued to tease her, invading her, making her squirm. She twisted beneath me, changing her position and demanded to suck my cock. I wasn't about to argue as I turned to give her access, her hot lips wrapping around me made me lose my damn mind. I'd had my fair share of blowjobs, but the way she worked that mouth of hers had me convinced I'd been dealing with amateurs all these years. Good to know.

My thumb circled her clit as I pushed a finger inside her, my cock muffling her pleasured moan. The charge coming off our bodies would have been enough to power a small country. Energy crisis solved.

I felt her body tense as her pussy tightened around my fingers, her breathing erratic as she thrashed beneath me with my dick in her mouth. She was close, and so was I. The heat in my body rose as I fought a losing battle to prolong the inevitable. My dick made the decision that it had gone on long enough. "Megs, I'm going to come."

Her body convulsed as she beat me to it, every inch of her shook as I shot my load into her mouth. She continued to suck and swallow as I pulsed into her. Little muffled whimpers escaped from her lips as I drew out the last of her orgasm. My hands and mouth still busy between her legs.

It was awhile before we actually made it to my bedroom. Moving? That shit was obsolete for a good ten minutes while we both came down from the monumental sixty-nine in the entranceway.

Taking her to bed was high on my agenda, but it turns out all the good intentions in the world didn't count for shit. 'Cause after getting cozy on the floor for a while, my hard-on came back, interested as to why we weren't fucking yet. The bastard was out of control. Megs didn't seem to mind.

We'd made it about thirty feet. Which considering the backtrack to my discarded jeans by the doorway; it had been a fair effort. The condom was fished out of the pocket and onto my dick in record time. It was the rug on the living room floor that got pleasure of hosting *that* action. The couch had just been too fucking far.

That was followed up by a blowjob in the kitchen to which I happily reciprocated by going down on her in my study. Being that she was a psychologist, I'd assumed she appreciate the house tour with positive reinforcement. Who said I didn't pay attention in school?

By the time we eventually crawled onto the bed, the alarm clock on my nightstand was hinting the sun would soon be playing peek-a-boo. What hadn't changed with the flicking over of those florescent green digits was my need to take her again. She was like sexual heroin and I was a junkie with an unrelenting addiction.

We were both covered in sweat, panting, as I pounded into her from behind. Megs was on her hands and knees in front of me, my hands locked around her waist.

"That's it, fuck me," she screamed. "Harder, Troy Harris. I'm so close."

My thrusts deepened as I picked up speed. "Hard enough for you?" I pushed every inch of me into her, my finger once again sinking into her ass as she clawed the sheets.

"Oh. My. God," she screamed as her pussy gripped my cock, the pulsing sensation sending me over the edge as I came with her. Her body shook uncontrollably as muscle fatigue set in and she collapsed onto the mattress, pulling me down with her.

"Fuck, Megs." I rolled on to my side, taking her with me so I wouldn't crush her. "I can't believe you are *still* calling me Troy Harris." I laughed in between sucking breaths, pulling my finger from her ass.

"Yeah, that kind of slipped out." She shrugged. "I got caught up in the moment."

Her body shivered as I moved my hand up her side. "You cold?" I kissed her neck wrapping my arms around her. My A/C had kicked in at some point and was blowing cold air through the room.

"A little." She shuffled back against my chest. I liked it. A lot.

My dick slowly slid out of her and I pulled off the condom. The used latex reunited with the foil wrapper in the wastepaper basket beside my bed. More of their friends would probably be joining them later.

The comforter that had been kicked off the bed—courtesy of either her foot or mine— was quickly snagged by my hand and wrapped around us. My plans for not moving changed as my hands rubbed over her body. Goosebumps covered her damp skin. "You want to join me in the shower? Warm up a little?"

She turned to me and smiled. "Is this your attempt to fuck me in the shower?"

I couldn't help but laugh. It hadn't been my game plan but I liked her thinking. "Megs, I think we've got a good ten-fifteen minutes before I'll be operational again. No fucking. Just a shower."

"Sure, I'd like that."

The shower had been as promised— just a shower. We'd stood under the spray of the warm water, my cock stirring the minute my hand started soaping her. Up her body, down her body, other side, repeat. It was mechanical but necessary if I wanted to keep my word. Lathered up and shut up, I even washed and conditioned her hair, which had been a first.

Girls in the shower were usually a precursor to shower sex, so the experience had been a new one for me. Megs sure as hell wasn't making things easy either, the little noises she made while I massaged her head were putting my resolve to the test. Got me wondering if I couldn't make her come purely from washing her hair. It seemed she'd gotten almost as much pleasure when she'd washed my 'hawk, her fingers twisting through my hair while her wet, slippery body pressed against me. It was driving me insane and while the plan had been to get clean, all I could think about was getting dirty.

Done fantasizing about screwing her against the tiled wall of the

CRASH RIDE

shower, I cut the water and put myself out of my misery. The only rub she received was courtesy of a couple of over-sized towels. Her hands, not mine.

When it came to blow-drying her hair, I opted out. Sure, I would have loved to stay and watch a re-enactment of a *Whitesnake* video play out in my bathroom. Tits and hair flying wildly sounded like a good time, but my dick was having serious problems with the *look but don't touch* scenario I had us locked into.

So while she took care of *that,* I ripped the sheets from my mattress and freshened it up with a pair that weren't sporting our DNA. Managed to get in between them as well, leaving the dirty sheets I'd stripped piled in a corner. A run to the laundry wasn't on the cards. Not if it meant I'd risk missing the view. And what a view it was.

Megs stepped out of the bathroom, her hair doing that floaty thing around her shoulders, and the best part —she was naked. She didn't even do that lame-ass hand-wrap manoeuver to cover her tits or her pussy that some girls do. Thank Christ for that. She just strolled out with her head high and a smile on her face, crawling back into bed beside me. Oh, she also shot me a look that clued me in that the *hands off* thing I had going on was no longer working for her. This was not a problem for me and I was more than happy to continue playtime. Her lips tightly wrapped around my cock was a very nice start.

I wasn't sure how many times we'd fucked. It was irrelevant, but I do know I spent more of the night/morning inside of her than out. Not one of those times did the thought *I shouldn't be doing this* cross my mind. The sunlight cracked through the drapes, flooding the room, before we finally admitted defeat. Exhausted, I wrapped my arms around her and we both fell asleep.

61

7

Megan

I'M AN IDIOT. THE PLAN HAD BEEN— I HAVE SEX WITH TROY, I GET him out of my system and I move on. Simple. It's what I had convinced myself would cure this borderline obsession. It was basic psychology, like craving chocolate the minute you go on a diet purely because now you *can't* have it. My initial approach hadn't been affective. My taste of Troy had only stimulated the craving, not diminished it, which is why I decided on another approach. Binging. Getting my fill of Troy Harris so I would be sick of the sight of him. Literally screwing him out of my system. Sounds like a reasonable theory. Turned off by saturation. So binge I did. All. Night. Long.

It didn't take.

What the hell was wrong with me? Not only had I *not* cured my addiction slash infatuation, but I'd also reinforced how much I was attracted to him. It hadn't helped that he had been so freaking awesome, and funny, and sexy. Not to mention his amazing, long, hard co… Damn it! I was supposed to not be thinking about it and now all I can do is

CRASH RIDE

think about *it*. I wonder if I asked nicely if he'd let me take a mold for a dildo? Everyone is so DYI these days. That wouldn't be creepy at all. Yep. I was a self-diagnosed deviant nymphomaniac with addiction disorder. Glad all those years at Georgetown paid off, my parents must be so proud.

Reality check. It was not going to be so easy to just move on. I had even started to look for reasons why we weren't compatible. Surely that's the way to get over this silly crush. My investigation had been fruitful.

Troy Harris was a closet *Star Wars* fanatic. You heard right. Star. Wars. He had one tattoo dedicated to the *Dark Side* as well as one to the *Rebel Alliance* and they reflected each other on opposite parts of his arm. A representation of his inner light and dark. Kind of like a nerdy yin and yang. I should have been weirded out by this sci-fi, cult classic revelation; instead... I found it adorable.

The life-sized R2D2 in his kitchen, that was not cute. In fact, it had scared this shit of me. Who has movie memorabilia in their kitchen? See, there was something I could work with. Robot in the kitchen kicked off my mental tally of "cons."

And another thing, the man had no coffee in his apartment. None. Who doesn't have, at the very least, a rogue tin of *Folger's* hiding behind a prehistoric box of crackers? What if the Zombie apocalypse hit? I can tell you that the people *without* coffee would be the first suckers turned. Have you seen people in the morning before their cup of Joe? The caffeine would be the only thing that would distinguish us from the Walkers. Apparently Troy is not a coffee drinker. Gasp. I didn't know these people existed. Who doesn't drink coffee? I'm still trying to get a handle on that.

So two— flimsy at best— excuses as to why I shouldn't sleep with him again. And when was the last time I had achieved that many orgasms in one night? Never. My argument as to why we shouldn't be *back in the saddle again* was very quickly negated. He had even very sweetly offered to take me to breakfast, apologizing for his lack of coffee. I had to decline of course. Showing up to a coffee shop in last night's dress and heels? No. Just No.

My morning-after coffee was when I did my post mortem. A break down of the night that was, and I had a system. Go home, shower, change and *then* you go get coffee. The side order of a muffin was standard— the heart-to-heart with Ash, was an added bonus.

Yeah, that would NOT be happening. How would I even start that conversation? *So Ash, remember how I've wanted to sleep with Troy in like forever? Remember how we decided it's probably for the best if I don't because let's face it, other than hot sex, nothing good will come of it? Well, funny thing. You're going to love this. I disregarded all that common sense nonsense and threw myself at him... with my vagina. Yep. That's right. While you and Dan were busily planning your happily-ever-after, I was getting some sexual healing in the back of the Suburban.*

Yep. Some things really are best left unsaid.

So after kissing Troy goodbye —I lingered, sue me — I hailed a cab back to my Greenwich Village apartment. I quickly showered, changed into my favorite sundress and took the short walk to my favorite coffee house.

Jilly Beans was always bustling with activity, the recycled wooden tables and chairs crammed in between cotton candy pink walls and the checkerboard linoleum floor. It was in the tiny corner café where I sat with a half-full latte trying to stop myself from going back to Troy's apartment and tying him to the headboard. Or he could tie me. We could take turns. That would be fun.

"Hey!" Ash pulled out a chair and sat down at my table. Fresh-faced with her red hair pulled back into a ponytail, she looked gorgeous without even a hint of makeup, casually dressed in jeans and cotton tee. "Why did you run off? I went over to Troy's this morning and he said you'd already left. I would have thought you would have been trying to steal his bath towels or rub yourself on his bed sheets." Ash laughed, reminding me of previous conversations where I had threatened to do just that.

She had no idea.

"Yeah, I didn't want to over stay my welcome." I picked up my cup and took a swallow of my now lukewarm coffee. "Besides, the man had no coffee in his place. Did you know he doesn't drink coffee? He must be some kind of freak." I contorted my face in mock horror trying to steer the conversation away from me being alone with Troy.

"Definitely a freak if he doesn't drink coffee," she mused sarcastically, rolling her eyes. Unlike me, she didn't need to play the pick-Troys-flaws-so-I-don't-sleep-with-him-again game. It was quite a mouthful.

A lot like Troy.

I needed to stop.

Ash's smile lit up her green eyes. "I guessed this is where you'd be after I checked your apartment and no one answered. So predictable." She was right; this is where I could be found most mornings.

Whether it was a quick stop for a takeaway or a more relaxed sit-and-sip, my day didn't start until I'd stopped at *Jilly Beans*. God knows if for some reason I happened to miss a couple of days in a row, the staff would probably file a missing person's report. They understood my caffeine addiction and happily enabled me. "I like it here, they know my order and the baristas are cute. I'm thinking of asking the dark-haired one out on a date. Good looking and knows how to make good coffee. That's husband material right there. I could potentially beat you to the altar."

I wasn't seriously thinking of dating him, it was a throw away line. Our witty little banter just made my day more interesting. I'd flirted with him for the last few months, but he wasn't my type. My type was rockin' hot drummers who inspired scorching hot drive-by sex. Clearly I had a specific palette. I was in so much trouble.

Ash looked over at the tall, lanky, and shaggy-haired man standing behind the counter. His smile was barely visible beneath a neatly manicured beard. The attention we were suddenly throwing his way caused him to adjust his large, thick-rimmed glasses.

Ash laughed. "I think he noticed us staring."

"Good." My lips twitched into a flirty smile as I gave him a friendly wave. He waved back discreetly before he turned his attention back to the important task of working a milk jug and a steam wand. A man making coffee was sexy.

Maybe I should ask him out. It wouldn't hurt. He seemed to be good with his hands, expertly having made a smiley face in my coffee foam. Perhaps I was looking at this all wrong? Maybe Troy actually wasn't *that* good.

It had been a while since my last sexual encounter. It's not like I had accumulated tumbleweeds in my girlie bits, but in recent times I had been spending a lot more time with my vibrator than with a living, breathing penis. Seeing other people would prove that it had been the break in my man-drought that had made last night so toe curling. It probably didn't even matter that it was Troy. I could have had sex with Jimmy, the creepy emo/goth EMT guy, and today I'd be sitting here fantasizing about white skin and eyeliner. Ugh. I shuddered. I dodged a bullet with that one. I mentally made a note to avoid the ER for a while, at least until I was able to scrub that image from my mind.

Ash disregarded the conversation of my dating future with the wave of her hand. "Well, you're a big girl so you can date who you like but I need you to put off your rendezvous with nameless-coffee-dude for one night. Please come over for dinner tonight. Dan has rehearsal; we can eat ice cream and talk wedding stuff."

"Tonight? I guess I can postpone my date with destiny for one night." I squeezed her hand. It was hard to believe my friend, who had seen marriage more as an amicable merger not twelve months ago, was happily living her own fairytale.

"Thanks, Megs." A slight blush crept up her face. "You're not only my maid of honor, but with my mom and my sisters being back in Boston, I don't really have anyone else to get excited with me. Unfortunately you've drawn the short straw. Besides, who else can I trust to kick my ass if I turn into Bridezilla?"

CRASH RIDE

"Aw, sweetie, I love that you've chosen me to share this with, and you couldn't be a Bridezilla if you tried. Although I think this is a good time to tell you, if you make me look a pink marshmallow, I will kill you." I laughed. Not that there was any real danger of that, Ash hated pink but I figured it was best to put our cards on the table. I was still haunted by the nightmare that had been my senior prom. I really wish I could go back in time and tell my seventeen-year-old self that Barbie was not the fashion icon I'd believed her to be. God help me if those pictures ever got out.

Ash grinned, fully aware of my aversion to large bouffant-ed ball gowns. "Damn, I had the pink tulle tutu already picked out."

"Ha. Ha. Very funny. Just remember karma's a bitch and I'll be the one planning your bachelorette party." I threatened, only half kidding. "Have you told your folks yet?"

"Yeah, this morning. Mom cried and Dad got quiet. I could tell he was emotional. Can you believe Dan asked for my dad's blessing? Apparently while we were home for Christmas he told Dad that he wanted to make me his wife and would ask me when the time was right. I know he can be an ass sometimes, but God I love him." The smile on her face reinforcing how happy she was.

I couldn't help myself. Dan was entirely too easy a target. "That's beautiful, Ash. By the way, you should totally call him an ass like that in your vows. I think everyone would love that."

"Are you kidding me? Troy already suggested I work in douchebag and numbnuts. If I didn't know them better, I'd swear they hated each other."

Just hearing Troy's name sent a shiver down my spine. For five minutes I had successfully not thought about him and yet, as soon as he *was* mentioned, I was back imagining bad, bad things. *Good* bad, bad things. Things we had done and things I would love to attempt.

Not helping. Think of something else. I drained the last of my cold coffee from my cup as I realigned my thoughts with Manolo Blahnik's new season's sandals.

Black, strappy patent leather. They would complement that Marc Jacob dress I loved so much but rarely wore. This was good. Positive reinforcement. Shoes. Shoes would be my savior.

"So what time do you want me tonight?" The smile fixed firmly on my face as thoughts of those strappy Blahniks resting on Troy's shoulders while he fucked me, now dominated my mind.

I was in. So. Much. Trouble.

I had returned to the scene of the crime. Well, close enough to it anyway. Criminals not being able to resist the urge? It was all true. A weird sense of curiosity taunted me. Compelling me to walk out of Dan and Ash's apartment where I sat, surrounded by Bridal publications, and revisit the location of one of the most erotic nights of my life.

I didn't.

That's why murderers always got caught on CSI shows. It wasn't the killing that did them in; it was the poking around after the fact. The compulsion to relive the act. I understood it now. Morons. Both me, and them.

My limbs stretched out in front of me as I made myself comfortable on the floor, rolling onto my stomach. The plush area rug underneath me was soft as I propped myself up onto my elbows, oblivious to my surroundings. I heard the faint sound of murmuring in the distance, probably Dan saying goodbye to Ash before he left to go be a rock star. Best left ignored. Spoiler alert, they were probably making out.

My head lowered into the glossy pages of whatever bride magazine I had been flicking through as I pushed a spoonful of *Chubby Hubby* into my mouth, and tried not to think about fact that Troy was only a few feet away. Just through the doorway and down the hall. The ghost of him haunting me, I could almost *feel* his presence and *smell* the sex.

"Megs," Troy's husky voice startled me, almost making me choke on

CRASH RIDE

the spoon still in my mouth.

There he was. Like a conjured-up dirty dream. Except he wasn't an apparition, instead he'd walked in, crouched beside me and rested his hand on my bare leg, all while I was blissfully unaware in my self-imposed oblivion.

The spoon was hastily removed from my mouth as I yanked it out. If I was going for seductive, I'd failed. "Oh. Hey, Troy Harris." Quickly swallowing as I scrambled to my knees. Sure, *that* wasn't a more compromising position.

He grinned as he wordlessly took the spoon from my hand and dug it into the pint of ice cream that sat on the coffee table. His hand brought the ice cream loaded spoon to his mouth and his lips closed around it. Hot. Oh hell.

He pulled the spoon from his mouth, with the seduction I hadn't managed. The surface licked clean before scooping more ice cream. "You want some?" His smile widened as he held the spoon inches away from my lips and waited for my response.

"Yes." It was almost moaned, the word clearly too difficult for me to speak. My mouth opened wide like a freak-show clown at a carnival, and he lowered the spoon inside. The ice cream spilled across my tongue that played against the cold metal. Delicious.

It had nothing to do with the ice cream. Just so we're clear.

He slowly pulled the spoon from between my lips, my resistance making him grin.

He raised an eyebrow, "More?" Whatever he was offering, I most definitely wanted *more* of it. Every. Last. Drop.

"Dude, you ready to go?" Dan called from off in the distance, shattering my iced confectionary erotica. I could have wept at the loss.

Troy eyed me intently and then licked the spoon—the one that had just been in my mouth, God that was so fucking hot— and placed it beside the pint on the coffee table.

And like he hadn't just mind-fucked me, he slowly rose to his feet, his lips curled into a sexy smile and he strode to the doorway. "See you later,

Megs." He waved as my eyes stayed glued to his sexy ass as he walked away.

He didn't even look back. Just left me there. Frustrated. And it had nothing to do with my so-called man drought, and everything to do with him. I wanted him. I. Was. In. So. Much. Trouble. I seemed to be saying that a lot lately.

"Alrighty. Boys are gone!" Ash cheerily bound into the room carrying her own pint of goodness. Ice cream would never be the same again. "So, I'm ready to make fun of all these crazy wedding dresses while feeding my face." She giggled as she slunk down onto the floor beside me. "Hey, what's wrong? You look weird."

Weird? Or sexually frustrated? It was a fine line. In either case it was not a conversation I wanted to be having. "I'm fine." I lied as I picked up the same bridal magazine I had been flipping through when Troy had waltzed it. Not that my brain connected with the pictures that were in front of me. It was all a blur.

Ash joined me, picking up her copy of *bride-something* monthly and I forced my head to nod in all the right places as she pointed out dresses. My mind was M.I.A.

Right. So what were my chances of being able to stay away from Troy Harris? Slim to none at best. Not great odds. So, maybe one more time? Yes, just one more time and then I'll stop. Promise. At least that's what I told myself.

Denial. It wasn't just a river in Egypt.

8

Troy

RECIPE OF DISASTER. THAT'S WHAT LAST NIGHT HAD BEEN. JUST because shit hadn't gone pear shaped didn't mean given half a chance it wouldn't. Did I want to go there again? Abso-fucking-lutely.

My head was not in the game, pretty sure it was on the smokin' hot blonde who'd walked out my door this morning. My dick got instantly hard just thinking about her, which given the amount of times I blew my load in the last twenty-fours was ridiculous. How she was still walking this morning was also a mystery. I hadn't been gentle.

"Hey, asshole, you channeling your inner Don Johnson?" Dan's face scanned the length of my new ride as we entered the undercover garage. "Fuck... Miami Vice just threw up all over this car."

"Don Johnson drove a Ferrari not a Lamborghini, douchebag." My morning had been busy. Impulse shopping wasn't usually my thing. I'd survived my thirty-two years without a set of Ginsu knives or an Ab-

Cruncher. Then again, I'd never needed the distraction.

"Magnum P.I.?"

"Ferrari."

"So you just woke up and decided to buy a car?" His mitt hit the handle and raised the scissor door on the passenger side. The action repeated by me on the driver's side.

"I wanted to go fast." More like needed the rush. The junkie high from Dr. Winters wouldn't be happening anytime soon. It was a substitution. My hands fisted the steering wheel as I slid into the seat.

"This thing is a fucking dinosaur. Did they run out of new Lamborghinis?" His ass sunk into black leather seat.

"The Countach is a classic, show some motherfucking respect." New cars weren't my style and I had a thing for the classics. This one came in the form of a wedge-shaped aircraft-grade aluminum sports car with a V12 that sounded like Armageddon. My latest throw-back was going to be leaving one hell of a carbon footprint, best start planting trees or some shit to try and even the score. My boot kicked the gas pedal, the rev of the engine reverberated off the garage walls. Fuck that. The environment had no hope.

"Mike Lowry. Bad Boys 2." Dan snapped his fingers, shit-eating grin on his face.

"Still a Ferrari."

"Fuck it. Just drive this fucking thing and don't kill us." Dan buckled his seatbelt and thankfully shut his mouth. Not that I was worried about him flapping his gums, the roar of the engine would drown anything out.

The session tonight had been my saving grace. A last minute addition to the album, and we were skating pretty close to the wire on production time. It was either record it now or forever hold our peace. James wanted a song included and had floated the suggestion. Everyone gave the nod, so Casa Bowden is where we would be kicking it for the evening. Fucking brilliant because hitting the skins is exactly what I needed. Help me work out some of this shit I had looping around in my head. Not going there.

Megs being at Dan's was unexpected. My plans had been simple, pick up the douchebag, get in the car and leave— things hadn't worked out that way. Ash casually mentioned that Megs was in the living room and I suddenly got very interested in saying hi.

It would've been rude to not at least stick my head in, considering she'd spent the night in my guest room the night before. All about appearances, right? What was the harm?

Seeing Megs splayed out on the living room floor was like a punch in the balls. Yep, I was a goner. Let's blame it on impulse, or the fact all the blood from my brain had drained into my cock, but all I could think about were those sweet fucking lips and owning that mouth. That shit we had spoken about, being friends and *not* fucking, yeah that went right out the window. So maybe licking her spoon was playing dirty, but I didn't give a fuck. What I did care about was making my intentions clear, and I wasn't subtle about it.

Megs and I, that shit was not over.

We pulled in along Jason's Mustang and ejected from the Lambo. The drive had been pleasurable even if the occasional conversation interjected wasn't.

"I swear, dude. The vibrations in that car when you drive—you could jerk off with no hands." A sample of what I had to endure.

We walked in, said our hellos and got down to business. Getting the track laid down was the priority, getting Megs off my mind, an added bonus.

"Hey man, you wanna go over that last bit again? It sounds kind of tired." Alex stopped mid strum, the new song not sounding right.

"It's missing something." James ran his hands through his hair. "The verse is okay but the chorus fucking blows."

"I don't think it's the lyrics, dude," Jase added to the mix. "I think it's the timing. It's too slow."

"You know my feelings on this," Dan piped in. "Every song should be faster."

"We're not playing death metal you tool." Alex threw a guitar pick at

Dan.

"Don't be jealous, asshole, it's not my fault I can play faster than you."

Alex rolled his eyes. "Does your future wife know she's marrying a child?"

Dan's claim was laughable at best, just yanking Alex's chain like he always did. Usually the back and forth amused the hell out of me. Tonight, not so much.

Before Dan had a chance to respond, I picked up my sticks and started playing the chorus again. This time faster on the snare and giving the double kick a little more love. Beside the obvious benefit of drowning out any further bitching, it released some of the tension I'd been feeling.

What came out was aggressive but catchy as fuck. Jase was right; it was a timing issue. Sped up, it sounded amazing.

"That's wicked, dude." James grabbed the mic off the stand, his excitement almost as big as his grin. "Play it again, exactly like that. Alex…"

"On it." Alex turned up his amp and sped up the tempo. His fingers owned the fret board as he moved through the complicated progression. The smug watch-me-shred-like-a-demon look he shot Dan wasn't missed by anyone either. Jase snorted a laugh, punching Dan in the arm before they both joined in and rounded out the sound. It was magic.

James was more excited than a kid on Christmas morning as we hit record. The track was cut and polished a few hours later. And while my poor DW kit took the mother of all poundings, at least I wasn't thinking about the pint-size blonde who'd been dominating my thoughts and making my cock stir.

It was late by the time we made it back to the apartment, and Megs would for sure be tucked up in her bed at home. That piece of information both pissed me off 'cause it meant not seeing her, and made thankful as fuck my torture session for one day was over. It was a fifty-fifty split.

CRASH RIDE

The minute I walked through my front door, I pulled off my boots, tossing my keys on my kitchen counter before I stripped off my T-shirt and socks. It was easier to dump my gear in the laundry on the way through, so I peeled off my jeans and boxers as well and walked to my bedroom, naked.

The place was dark but the layout had been permanently locked away in my brain so I didn't bother hitting the lights. Instead I navigated through the hall, allowing my eyes to readjust. This was a journey I'd made a million times — sometimes drunk, sometimes sober, and sometimes with a girl around my waist. Yeah, only one girl I was interested in at the moment and we were not going there. My dick showed interest even though there was no prospect of that happening. Not like I blame him.

By the time I'd reached my bedroom, I was seriously contemplating skipping the shower and collapsing into bed. Not like I couldn't get one in the morning. Who the fuck cared that I smelled like last week's gym socks? The sooner my eyes closed, the sooner I would stop this fucked up fantasy I had. The fantasy where I call Megs and tell her to get her sexy little ass over here, and let her ride me until the sun comes up. If my cock wasn't complete awake before, he was sure as hell taking notice now. My hand was tempted to reach down and at least give myself some relief.

"Holy fuck!" My voice bounced off my black bedroom walls, yelling a little louder than I'd meant to, My eyes shut and then reopened just to confirm it wasn't some fucked up optical illusion that I was looking at as a naked and shocked Megs shot up in my bed, pulling the sheets up around her.

"Is this some crazy fucking dream?" My hand raked through my mohawk. Hadn't it been like two minutes ago I'd wished for this very thing? If I'd somehow managed to score three wishes or some shit, they could keep the other two. Megs, in my bed, more than enough for me.

"Shit, Megs. I didn't mean to scare you." I moved closer to the bed. Not sure if her look of surprise was over the fact I'd yelled or the fact I was standing there naked with a hard-on.

"Hey, Troy Harris." Her eyes dipped down to my cock. "I was waiting for you to get home." She gave me an appreciative smile when she saw that part of me was already good to go.

There were a million important questions I should've asked. Starting with "how did you get in?" You know how many I asked? Zero. I didn't give a fuck if she picked my locks or teleported into my bedroom. What I did care about was the fact we were both naked, alone and still not getting busy. "Come here." I ripped the sheets off my bed and exposed her beautiful body. She was so fucking perfect.

She gasped but I didn't buy into that shy bullshit as she moved off the bed and strode over to me. She opened her mouth to talk, not sure whether it was to explain or something else, but I claimed her mouth before she had the chance. All that crap we spoke about last night, about the one-time deal? I was no longer on board. From the looks of things, neither was she. Good, 'cause while that bullshit made all kinds of sense, as far as I was concerned, it was still fucking bullshit.

Her arms wrapped around my neck as our kiss deepened. Never in a million years had I thought *this* was what I'd be coming home to. Hell, had I known, I might've blown off the whole recording session. I palmed her ass and lifted her onto me. She was all about it and wrapped her legs around my waist, little whimpers escaping her mouth as I kissed her. My mouth was too busy to ask, so I made an executive decision and carried her to my bathroom. Last night's shower might have been relatively tame but that was not going to get a repeat performance tonight.

"Troy," she moaned as pushed her against the cold tiled wall. Her hands travelled down the length of my chest.

"You want me to stop?" My mouth moved down her neck, kissing her naked skin. It was going to take a hell of a lot of restraint to stop right now, so I prayed she wasn't going to tell me to put the brakes on.

"Don't stop. I want this. I want you." Her tits heaved up and down as she sucked in a breath.

I pulled her body back against me and into the shower stall. Our lips and hands busy with each other as I turned the faucet and let the cold water hit our skin. It was like a million needles poked us simultaneously but even that wasn't enough to stop us, my skin on fire with fucking need. Megs unwrapped her legs and slithered down my body, giving me a free hand to adjust the water temperature.

She sunk to her knees in front of me, her hands pushing me against the shower wall as her tongue trailed down my abs to my cock. She smiled as she licked the ring, her tongue swirling around the head of my dick. My hands fisted her hair as she took me into her mouth, her blue-green eyes looking up at me as she sucked me hard. It was more than I could stand.

I pulled my dick from her mouth and joined her on the floor of the shower. She protested until my tongue flicked her nipple and then she arched her back and let me do whatever I wanted. What I wanted was to put my mouth on every part of her. My teeth gently teased her pink peak while I snaked my hand down between her legs. She lowered herself down onto her ass and gave me better access. Fucking amazing. Her legs spread and my fingers teased her clit. She was wet and not from the water that was raining down on us from the showerhead.

She reached out and grabbed my shaft, her tight hand moving up and down my length while my fingers rubbed circles around the opening of her pussy. I plunged two fingers inside her; Megs's grip around me — both her pussy around my fingers and her hand on my cock— tightened.

I wanted to be deep inside her but with the closest condom in the nightstand, my hand and tongue were going to have to be the only parts that got that pleasure. The other part, the one that was about to blow its load into her hand, would sink into her the minute we were out of the shower and suited up in latex.

We didn't talk; moans seemed all we were capable of as our hands got each other off. I was torn between wanting to watch her get worked up with my fingers moving in and out of her sweet pussy, or watching her jerk me off, both had its benefits. Her back arched toward my hand and I knew that she was close, I was trying to hold off, wanting it to last just a little longer. It felt so fucking good. In the end, biology took over and my mouth slammed down on hers as we both came hard on the floor of the shower stall.

"Hey," I whispered against her shoulder as I wrapped my arms around her.

"Hey," she giggled back, slowly opening her eyes. God she was beautiful.

"You going to spend the night with me so I can do that properly?" My fingers traced little circles on her back.

"It felt pretty good the first time."

"You know it can be better."

"I can probably stay."

"Good. Let's get cleaned up so I can get you into my bed."

"Aren't you curious how I got into your apartment?"

"Well, it crossed my mind for about a second until I saw you were naked and then I no longer gave a fuck. You could've busted my locks and I'd still have a smile on my face."

I'm sure there was a story, and in truth part of me was curious but currently it wasn't *that* part of me that was running the show, so whatever the explanation was, it could wait.

"I didn't bust your locks."

"You have a life of crime you've been keeping under wraps? Vandalizing and boosting cars when you were a teenager?"

"Would that turn you on, Troy Harris?"

Her smile would've knocked me on my ass if I weren't already on it. "Megs, you just have to show up and I get turned on. Anything else is just gravy."

While the first time had been frenzied, the second time I would be taking it slow. I wanted to feel every inch of myself inside her and get familiar with every part of her body. There was no way I would be wasting the opportunity, even if I knew when the morning cracked through my drapes, it would probably be the last time.

9

Megan

OKAY, SO *THAT* HAD TO BE THE LAST TIME.

I would go cold turkey and there would be no more slipups. Yeah, because *that's* what happened. We accidently found ourselves naked and his penis *slipped* into my vagina—again.

So what if he was incredibly hot and made me orgasm like it was an Olympic sport. I refused to accept there was more to it than that. That just being around him didn't make my heart squeeze a little. Or that his smile didn't make my shitty day infinitely better. No, it was purely sexual. It had to be, and there were other attractive guys, ones who had talent. Men who didn't have a connection to any of my friends or their partners. I just needed to find them.

So how did it come to pass that I ended up in Troy's apartment, naked? Well, watching Troy Harris lick that spoon bordered on obscene. He might as well have just licked me between my legs. The same effect was achieved. Who could have resisted that? Certainly not this girl. I needed to sleep with him again. More so to prove to myself that it wasn't as fantastic as I remembered it, so I could move on. Like a reality check of sorts.

The first time—all right, the first six times— we had sex, I was caught up in the fantasy. It was Troy Harris for God's sake. I'd fingered myself to his image so many times I should have been embarrassed. It had to be the hype that had made it so outstanding. No man was *that* good. Of course the theory needed testing. It meant overlooking the fact that my theory testing hadn't worked out for me so well in the past, but it was a hardship I figured I had to endure. What? Everyone makes mistakes. Moving on.

The plan had been to wait with Ash until Dan and Troy got home, and then knock on his door.

I hadn't really thought beyond that brilliant idea. *Winging it* was going to feature heavily. But the hours ticked over, and Ash yawned a few too many times so I said my goodbye.

Hope had almost been lost.

When I got Ash's front door I *remembered* that I had left my bracelet in Troy's apartment. Which was a lie. It was sitting at the bottom of my purse with a broken clasp.

I was going right to hell; sadly at this point, I didn't care.

Ash very kindly offered to let me into Troy's apartment with the spare key he kept at their place—something I'd hoped for. Cue me exiting Troy's bathroom with the bracelet triumphantly dangling between my fingers. We left, with me pulling the door shut behind me, and said our goodbyes in the hallway.

Two things didn't happen. One, I *didn't* pull Troy's door all the way shut.

I gently eased the door just enough into the jamb to catch but not enough for the lock to engage. The second thing was I *didn't* leave.

Instead, I pretended to walk away and then promptly returned to Troy's door. My relaxed strut probably making me look like a catwalk reject from fashion week, but at least I wasn't sprinting.

God, I hoped no one actually watched the surveillance footage.

CRASH RIDE

Once I was at Troy's front door, all that was required was a gentle push and *boom*, I was in.

My rap sheet now included wild sex with a rock star *and* breaking and entering. There goes the neighborhood.

So I was inside; now, what the hell I was supposed to do? Pacing nervously only held my attention so far before I gave up to the magnetic pull of his bed.

I was discreet at first, kicking off my shoes and crawling slowly over his covers to his pillows. Their intoxicating scent overwhelmed me as I nuzzled them.

Insanity—the only explanation as to why I was on my hands and knees, ass in the air with my face in his pillow. Thank you sweet baby Jesus no one walked in sparing me the *what-the-fuck* moment.

Somewhere in between taking off my clothes and rubbing myself all over his sheets — yeah I did it, don't judge me—I fell asleep.

Maybe it was the tension, or perhaps pure exhaustion, but instead of a light doze, I fell into something close to resembling a coma. It wasn't until I heard a very loud "Holy Shit" that I was awakened from my peaceful slumber.

No need to guess what happened next. My oh-it-can't-be-that-good-I-must-have-imagined-the-toe-curling-orgasms was blown right out of the water. How could it keep getting better? How could he know exactly what to do and when to make my eyes roll back into my head? How was I ever going to willingly give this up? Whatever trouble I thought I had been in before had doubled in magnitude now.

So my fate had been sealed. I would be damned to mediocre sex with other men because that had been my last hurrah with Troy. He made me come so hard, I actually cried. Mourning the orgasms that would no longer echo through my body and overwhelmed by every nerve ending in my body feeling like it was on fire.

It had never been like that, not like *that*.

And it hadn't been just the sex. The seemingly bleak caseload I was juggling, and the mountain of guilt I was battling had me on a hair trigger and I was primed for an explosion. It should have been awkward—crying after sex in front of Troy Harris— but strangely, it wasn't. He made me feel safe and he was cool enough to not get all weird after. No questions were asked, he just held me in his arms.

Which is why it could never happen again. I couldn't lose him. Never feeling him again inside me was a horrendous thought, but what would be so much worse was if we ended up hating each other. I *really* liked him and it wasn't just sexual, and there was no way I would jeopardize that.

Cold turkey, I repeated my mantra. It was the only way.

Avoiding Troy wasn't going to work. Apart from the fact he was deeply involved with my best friend's soon-to-be husband, he was also going to be the best man to my maid of honor. What was I going to do? Pretend he had cooties? I *could* be around him, *not* strip naked and drop to my knees. It just took practice.

I buried myself in work. Even though I missed his beautiful enigmatic smile, the time away made me stronger, more prepared to deal with the attraction I was denying. It could totally be done. Totally.

"My parents are assholes. This whole therapy shit blows and I don't need you. I hate them for making me come here. Am I supposed to sit and cry like a fucking loser?"

All thought of Troy vaporized as I looked over at the skinny, fair headed boy who sat in the chair opposite me. Brad Hemsworth had been discharged yesterday into the care of his parents. His release had hinged on regular therapy sessions with me, as well as very close monitoring by his folks. It was either that or he would be admitted to a facility. He flat out refused to stay in the hospital.

He was angry but hopefully not beyond reason. "Brad, I know you don't want to be here and no one is going to make you talk about

CRASH RIDE

anything you don't want. Why don't we just get to know each other a little better? This is your time and we can talk about whatever it is you want to talk about."

He got out of his chair and started to pace around the room. "How about we talk about *you* convincing my folks I'm not going to slit my wrists or take a bunch of pills. I made a mistake. I'm not taking your mind-altering drugs either. I swear it's a way for them to control me. I'm not about to be dumbed down on Ritalin."

My eyes followed his agitated, twitchy movements as he paced, while I remained in my chair. I stayed calm, neutral. "Brad, first of all, I'm a psychologist not a psychiatrist so I can't prescribe you anything. We just talk here, no drugs involved at all. And secondly, Ritalin is used for treatment of attention deficit disorders; it wouldn't be effective treating depression."

He balled his fist at his sides; his face flushed with anger. "I'm not depressed. God, you are just as bad as my fucking parents. I wasn't going to actually kill myself. It was a fucking mistake. Like I told the shrink in the hospital, it was a moment of weakness, I'm fine now."

"Brad, depression can take on many forms. Let's not worry about the label right now, let's talk about making you feel a little less angry."

It was a balancing act, knowing how much to push and when to back off, and he was putting me through my paces. I worried about him. He was severely in denial but I needed to win his trust, to get through to him. Today, however, that breakthrough wouldn't be happening.

I spent the rest of his appointed hour trying to coax him to a safe place, one where he felt comfortable talking to me, a place with less anger. But at the end of the sixty minutes, I wasn't entirely sure that any of it had broken through.

"So, we done yet?" Brad impatiently kicked the chair leg with his Converse-covered foot. He yanked at his *30 second to Mars* T-shirt that looked as if it had seen better days. The worn-out jeans he was wearing were frayed at the hem. "Can I go?" he asked again, flicking his long blond bangs so they covered his tormented brown eyes.

"We're done for this week, you can go," I responded, lifting myself out of my seat, smoothing out my tailored skirt as I stood. "I'll see you next week."

"Yeah, whatever." Brad sunk his hands into his pockets and walked out of my office.

His exit gave me permission to sink back into my chair and let my head drop into my hands, mentally and emotionally exhausted. The blue painted walls of my office were not as bright as they used to be, my large wooden desk was filled with notes and files that would take at least another hour or two to put in order. Some days were harder than others, and today had been a difficult day.

My cell buzzed silently on my desk and I welcomed the distraction, reaching across and answering it without bothering to check who was on the other end.

"Megs," Ashlyn's excited voice broke through my mental fog, "tell me you have no plans tonight."

"Ash, it's a Wednesday. What plans would I have?"

"I wasn't sure if you'd set up your hot date with coffee boy yet." Ash laughed, I had almost forgotten about him and my faux dating interest.

"I'm playing hard to get," I joked. "What's up?"

"Hannah, James's wife, is having a little engagement dinner for us at their house. Nothing fancy, just the band really and their significant others, but you have to come."

Great. That would be a perfect punctuation mark to an already crappy day. An evening spent avoiding Troy and pretending like hanging out with Power Station was no big deal. No one was that convincing. I mentally waved my fist in the air and mouthed, "Fuck you" to the universe.

"Ash, I don't really know her that well. Besides, you said it yourself. It's a band thing."

"Hello? I'm sorry but where is my friend Megs?" Ash sarcastically slurred into the phone.

"Very funny. I just think maybe that you should probably go without

CRASH RIDE

me. Besides, my laundry hamper needs some serious attention." I cringed at my bogus excuse. Why hadn't my brain manufactured something better? A case report that needed to be written or a patient review that needed to be read, anything other than laundry. I might as well have said I was washing my hair.

"Did you fall and hit your head?" She almost shouted through the phone. "This is *Power Station*. I'd have thought you'd be so excited that you would be humping my leg, not making lame excuses not to go."

She wasn't wrong; a few months ago that very reaction might have been accurate. "Ash, I'm not going to start using you to get to the band, that wouldn't be cool. It's fine, go have a good time."

"Okay, stop that. I know we joke about your love for the band, but I have never felt used nor do I think you would ever do that." She took a breath before continuing. "Is there something else going on? I know I have been a bit wedding obsessed lately; I'm sorry if there is stuff that I've missed."

I weighed her words for a minute, glad she had missed the change between Troy and I, the subtle glances between us. No one else needed to be tied up in that mess. Seems you can't play the it's-only-sex game with someone who is so intimately woven into your life. Troy had tried to convince me of that very idea early on. I hadn't wanted to hear it. Well, it was really fucking obvious now.

Humor was my go-to in my bag of tricks, that and sarcasm. I employed them both in equal measures. My dad, in the past, accused me of using them as diversionary tactics; he wasn't wrong. "Well, I didn't want to say anything, but your perpetual happiness is kind of annoying. You think you can kick it down a notch?"

Ashlyn laughed, thankfully not pressing the issue any further. "I promise to be less happy if you come. I might even manage a frown."

"Now who is sounding like they hit their head?"

"Well, Dr. Winters, I didn't want to have to pull out the big guns but you've left me no choice. I need you to be there. I love Dan, but being in his world still feels kind of awkward. Pretending that those guys weren't a big deal was a hell of a lot easier when I didn't have to see them up close. I'm a realist and it's tough being in love with someone that comes with all of *that*. I know it's my hang up and whatever weirdness I feel is worth it, but I need you in my corner. I also need for you to know just because I'm with him it doesn't mean I'm no longer with you. I'm not going to join the rock-star-wives-club the minute I marry Dan and forget who I am."

"I knew there had to be a club. It's probably for the best you aren't joining though; organized groups were never your thing."

"So are you going to quit being a dumbass, and help me even out the ratio of people featured on *MTV* verses people not featured on *MTV*?"

The magic words "*I need you*" was all Ashlyn had to say. All jokes aside, there wasn't a lot I wouldn't do for her, even if it meant making myself uncomfortable. She was like the sister I'd never had, balancing out my crazy as I pushed her out of her comfort zone.

"Sweetie, if it's that important to you, of course I will come. Although, I will say it's rather hurtful you think I'm not going to be on *MTV*. I can play the *hell* out of the recorder and that shit is poised to be the next big thing."

"You know you're leaving yourself wide open here for jokes about oral skills."

"Wow, Ash, I think you've spent too much time with Dan and he has burrowed inside your brain. If you start calling me a douchebag, I'm telling you right now, I'm going to stage an intervention."

"Deal." Ash's tone did little to hide how delighted she was. "We can come and pick you up around seven."

While I was prepared to sit across from Troy Harris and not sleep with and/or pretend I hadn't slept with him, I also needed the means for a quick escape. Sure, in a perfect world things wouldn't get weird but if they did, at least I could say my goodbyes and privately berate myself for my stupidity.

"Actually, it might be easier if I borrowed my mom's car. It's just sitting in the garage since Dad whisked my mom to Providence for some romantic mid-week getaway. I cringe at the thought of them having sex, so I have convinced myself all they will be doing is antiquing and exploring lighthouses." *Thank you parents for having a healthy relationship, which has taken you out of state.*

Not that it would have been a problem to use either of their vehicles; it was just easier without the third degree. My father still couldn't wrap his head around the fact that I didn't own one myself. I lived in Manhattan. Enough said.

"Blissful ignorance, huh?" Ash laughed. Having been around my parents, she knew they were more likely to be holed in a charming Bed and Breakfast enjoying adult time, rather than scaling a narrow, winding staircase of a decrepit lighthouse. "Okay, I'll text you the address."

"Awesome." It was so *not* awesome. "I'll see you there."

We ended the call and I closed my eyes. The soft leather of my office chair cushioned my head as I leaned back against it. It was time to get over myself and do what I said I was capable of doing. Remain calm, unaffected and enjoy my evening regardless of Troy being there or not. It was ridiculous. I was ridiculous. I was not going to let a moment—okay, several moments— of weakness ruin my night. I would pull up my big girl panties, put my money where my mouth was, practice what I preached, and any other cheesy analogies I could use to tell myself that I would be okay.

The breath I had unconsciously been holding slowly spilled from my lips and I felt my body slowly relax. It would be okay; I repeated it in my head. It had to be, because the only thing worse than seeing Troy Harris and it being weird would be to never see him again. That would crush me more than I cared to admit.

'10 Troy

MEGS HADN'T CALLED, SENT A MESSAGE OR SHOWN UP NAKED ON my doorstep in days. All of that —especially the last part—really fucking sucked. Yeah, we both knew we had to cool it and get back to *friend zone,* but it agitated me.

Why? Who the fuck knew. What I did know was the past few days while we were on radio silence, I was pissed off, worked up and so fucking edgy I was wondering if I should just sit down with whatever Oprah's latest book club recommendation was and feed my face with Ho-Ho's.

The more I tried, the less I was able to get her off my mind. Thinking about what a cool chick she was and wondering what she was doing. Yeah, all the bullshit what-ifs weren't helping; instead it was giving me an even bigger head fuck.

We'd had sex. Big deal. True, it had been monumental sex, but we agreed that's all it was. It's not like I was never going to have that again. Well obviously not with *her*, but my dick hadn't fallen off and I hadn't suddenly turned into a fugly mutant.

I could get laid any time I wanted. As much as I wanted. With anyone that I wanted. I was living the fucking dream, and I needed to remind myself of how good my life was. There were men who would kill to be in my place. I couldn't even begin to describe how awesome things were.

Right, just keep telling yourself that buddy and you might actually believe that shit.

Megs. Yep, and we were back to that. Should I have called her? I'm not the kind of asshole who fucks a girl and then doesn't call. That had been Dan's M.O., pre-Ashlyn days of course. We were in some lame ass limbo of being friends but not talking to each other. It made zero sense to me.

Fuck. This call-or-don't-call bullshit was giving me a headache. I pinched the bridge of my nose and closed my eyes, wishing I had a magic eight ball or something.

"Yeah." My phone had been blowing up all morning and I'd finally decided to give it reprieve.

"Hey, man." It was James, not Megs, and fuck if I was disappointed. Wanting to hear from her more than I cared to admit. "Hannah has decided we need to have a dinner to celebrate Dan finally putting a ring on it. My place, tonight."

"Funny, I didn't hear that as a question."

"Probably because it wasn't."

"Dude, I still remember the last time your wife was pregnant. That Jekyll and Hide thing fucking scares the crap out of me."

"Good, we'll expect you then. Seven o'clock and Hannah said don't be late."

Not even going to pretend to know how a chick can turn from happy to murderous on a dime, but one thing was for sure—you do not mess with it, ever. No, seriously. That's some prehistoric survival shit. It was easier to agree than have my balls ripped off.

"Yep, I'll be there at seven." Guess my evening was set.

My new Lambo slid in beside Stone's Escalade and Jase's Mustang. Sure, it got like five miles to the gallon and probably elevated me to douchebag status, but driving it got my mind off all things blonde and beautiful. I'd take the win when I could.

Dan's Benz was parked on the other side of the driveway along side a flash, high-end red Lexus sedan. Huh? Who the hell drove a Lexus? Fuck it. The owner of the corporate coffin didn't rate high on my give-a-shit meter. Snagging the large white box that had been sitting on my passenger seat, I climbed out of my car and strolled to the front door.

"You're late." Hannah stood in the open doorway. The hands on her hips clueing me in she was less than pleased.

"Sorry, Han, traffic was a bitch until I got out of Manhattan." My head dipped and I gave her a kiss on the cheek. "I brought dessert. Dan's favorite." I grinned, tapping the box in my hand.

The peace offering seemed to thaw the chill Hannah was throwing at me. "Aw, Troy. That is so sweet. Come in, everyone is waiting." See what I mean? Mood swings.

I followed her through the hallway and into the back end of the house. From the back, you'd never know she was in the family way, the only clue the small basketball-sized belly you got an eyeful of when she turned around. The baby was due just before we went out on the road, which was cool.

Noah, James and Hannah's first, had been on the road with us in the past, and I was almost certain Grace, Alex and Lexi's little girl, was tour bound as well. Long gone were the days of wild parties and drinking till dawn. It was a different kind of backstage party these days, one that involved juice boxes and *Nick Jr.*

Thinking of the tour gave me something to smile about, even if it was going to be dominated by kids. The sooner we got on the road, the sooner I could stop acting like a moody asshole. Put some distance between the Megs situation and me. Who knows, maybe find someone out there that would happily be my distraction. It certainly was worth a try.

"Sweetheart, I'm just trying to get Noah off to bed." James met us in the hallway; trying to wrangle Noah, who wasn't convinced it should be bedtime. "Oh, hey man. You made it." James tipped his chin hello given his hands were tied up with a defiant two-year-old.

"No. No Bed." Noah pushed against the arms of his dad, his face red from the effort. Poor little guy was giving it a shot but was no match for James's strength.

"Hey, buddy." I tickled the back of Noah's neck. "You giving your old man a hard time? That's Uncle Troy's job. You wouldn't want me to lose my job would you?" Hoping it didn't turn on the waterworks, I gave the kid my best puppy dog eyes.

Noah looked over me, giving it some serious thought. "Nu-uh Uncle Troy."

"Okay, so why don't you let your dad get you off to bed." I planted a kiss on his forehead and rubbed his back. "And I promise I'll make sure your dad gets a hard enough time for the both of us."

"Okay, Uncle Troy, night-night." Noah waved his little hand then curled his arm around his old man's neck. James mouthed me a silent thank-you as he carried Noah to his bedroom.

Hannah's hand went to her belly and gave it a little Buddha action. "You boys are so sweet with him. He's been impossible lately. He refuses to do anything I say, and everything is *no*." Thinking I dodged the waterworks bullet might have been premature as Hannah's eyes started to water.

"He's just pushing your buttons. I would've thought that after all the practice you had with us, this would be a walk in the park." I put my arm around her and gave her a hug. "Han, you are an amazing mom."

"Thanks." Her fingertips mopped the tears that were pooling in the corner of her eyes and gave me a smile. "Hormones are a bitch."

"Preach, sister." I shot her a grin. "Just the other day I was telling Dan about this fucking water retention I had going on. You should see the size of my feet."

She sucked in laugh. "You are an ass, but I still adore you."

"Back at ya, Han. Now let's go celebrate my best friend being off the market." We walked in to dining room, my box of goodness still in my hand.

"Hey, Troy Harris." Megs walked slowly toward me with a big ass smile on her face. "Fancy meeting you here."

Fuck.

So there goes my quiet evening not thinking about the sexy blonde who can get my dick hard just by walking into the room. It felt like I'd been sucker punched as she moved toward me in slow motion. She looked fucking amazing too; the short green dress she was wearing was showing most of her tanned legs. Her long hair hung loose. She was stunning.

"Hey, Megs." I quickly recovered, thanking my mouth for getting with the program. "Yeah, big surprise. It's good to see you." Not a lie. It was really, really good to see her.

"Do you need a hand with that?" she asked, her eyes dipping down to the box that I had completely forgotten I was carrying.

Yeah, your hand around my cock would be nice, thank you very much.

"Nah, I got it. You look… good." Good didn't even come close to covering it. Mouthwatering was more accurate.

"Why thank you, Troy Harris." She gave it a little *Scarlett O'Hara*, her voice taking a stroll below the Mason-Dixon line. "You look mighty fine yourself."

What's mighty is this hard-on I'm packing, let's talk about that.

Shit. I was a fucking pervert. Thank God she couldn't read minds.

"Whatcha got there?" Dan moseyed over, all kinds of interested in the box. The dude had perfect timing, pulling my ass from the fire. "Fuck, yeah! This is why you are my best man." The dozen frosted cupcakes inside the reason he was grinning like an idiot.

CRASH RIDE

"I don't get it?" Alex shook his head, walking over to join the party. "What's so special about cupcakes?"

"Hi, Troy." Ashlyn waved, rolling her eyes before playfully nudging Dan's shoulder. "Alex, don't even get him started."

"Heathens, the lot of you." Dan waved them off dismissively taking the box into the kitchen.

The exchange in front of me did little to change my view. The one that had my eyes glued to the knockout blonde in front of me. Megs stayed and watched it played out; her interest in it seemed on par with mine. Non-existent.

"Here." Jase handed me a long neck, ignoring Dan and the staring competition I obviously had going on with Megs.

"Thanks." Nod. Swallow. Just what I needed to put these flames out.

"Megs, want a beer?" He offered her the other.

Don't take it. Not sure I'd be good with sitting on the sidelines watching you swallow.

Her eyes dropped to the frosty bottle before they came back to me. "Thanks, but I'm fine."

Yes, you are.

Pin. Drop.

Neither of us able to tear our eyes from each other but our mouths staying clamped shut.

Well, that wasn't awkward. Not one little bit.

"Okay then. Good times, guys." Jase slapped me on the shoulder. The asshole decided to bail. "Going over to chat to Alex, can't get a word in edgewise over here." He walked. Didn't even look back.

"I might go see if I can help Hannah or Ashlyn." Megs followed Jason's lead and hightailed it to the other side of the room.

Awesome. This was going well.

"Hey, Troy." Lexi gave me her usual warm smile, her eyes a little more tired than I was used to seeing.

"Lexi." I welcomed the distraction and noticed we were one Power Station rug rat short. "You leave the little lady home alone? Hope you gave her enough vodka and cigarettes to get her through."

"Ha, very funny. Grace is having a sleep over with Alex's mom." She gave me a smug smile that meant trouble. "So... you and Megs."

"Don't start." My sideways glance was also a warning. "There's nothing there. We're just friends."

"Oh, really?" She clearly wasn't letting it go. "Huh, because I could have sworn that when you walked in and saw her your eyes almost bulged out of your head. Followed by your tongue hitting the floor. That's the way I always react when I see my *friends*." The sarcasm on the word friend wasn't missed.

While shit might have slid past Dan and Ash, Lexi didn't miss a thing. The clearing of my throat didn't help either. "I thought the matchmaker bullshit was Hannah's deal; don't tell me having a baby has made you soft." I deflected hoping she would let it go, the situation not needing the heat or the attention it was getting.

"Not soft, just more invested in what's important."

Megs was on the other side of the room, laughing with Hannah and Ashlyn. No less beautiful than the last time I'd looked. "Yeah, well regardless of any of it. It ain't happening. That's a whole lot of fucking complication no one needs."

"I'm not really the person you should be talking to about avoiding a complicated relationship." She glanced to where Stone was deep in conversation with James and Jason. "I think Alex and I covered about every aspect. Long distance, crazy exes, miscommunication, misunderstandings and more baggage than the Parisian flagship store of *Louis Vuitton*." She laughed. "But when the right person comes along, complications... they just make it more worthwhile."

"Thanks, Lex." I wrapped my arms around her and pulled her in for a hug. "Hey, if this gig with us doesn't work out, you know can always go write cards for Hallmark."

"Whatever, Troy." She smiled, her arms wrapping around me. "You guys would fall apart without me."

"True." It's not like I could disagree.

Hannah waved her oven-mitted hand and called everyone to attention. "Okay everyone, grab a seat. It's time to eat."

The rowdy group that we were moved to the table. Asses found their seats with no real thought given to the seating plan. Conversations not interrupted during the process.

Rather than pussy out, I pulled out a chair and gave her a nod. "Megs."

It could have gone either way, but I was glad when she took me up on my offer and sat down. Keeping my hand from running down her bare arm while she took her seat had been fucking difficult. Although the bigger challenge was not looking down the front of her dress, which was doing a wonderful job and showcasing her perky... not fucking helping.

Megs shuffled back in toward the table, rewarding me with a big smile. "Thanks, such a gentleman."

"For pulling out your chair?" I took my seat beside her; surprised she'd had been so easy to impress. I know the whole pulling-out-the-chair thing was a bit cliché, but when the mood took me, I could play nice.

"Nope." Her eyebrow rose as she leaned in to whisper. "For not looking down my dress."

Uh-hum, had it suddenly gotten warmer in here? "Oh, I looked; I'm just good at not being caught," I lied, and apparently I was a comedian because my response had made her laugh. Like a real laugh— not some half-assed chuckle. It was a nice sound too and I really liked the way it made me feel. I was going to need to hear more of it.

A bunch of separate conversations zigzagged over the mountain of food that sat in front of us. Alex and James were talking shop. Hannah, Ash and Lexi were talking babies, and Dan and Jason were in a fierce car debate about whether American muscle was more superior to European design. No one paid us any attention.

"Have you been good?" I leaned over and picked up a plate of some kind of chicken and offered it to Megs.

She smiled and helped herself to some food before answering. "Yeah,

I've been buried in work but I've been okay. How about you?"

This felt good. We were having a normal conversation, and look we weren't fucking each other senseless up against a wall. Who knew?

"I've been doing band stuff. Same old, same old." I grabbed a spoonful of potato salad and slapped it onto my plate. "I'm glad you came tonight."

Megs scrunched her nose up at the potato salad, opting for the garden salad instead. "I'm glad too. I'll be honest, I didn't want to."

I froze. She didn't want to? Not sure I wanted to know the answer, but I had to ask anyway. "Why? Because of me?"

"Yeah," She shrugged. "We said we wouldn't let it get awkward and it got awkward. I wanted to call you; I just thought it would be easier if I didn't."

Yeah, not happy with that. Last thing I wanted was for her not to wanna be around me. How was that a good thing? Nope, that was not okay. The only way the stupid hell of not being with her would make any sense was if I could still be sure she was okay. Wow. When did that happen?

"We both probably could have handled it a little better; I mean, I didn't call you either. But, Megs, you want to call me, call me. We said we'd stay friends and we can't do that if we are avoiding each other."

"You're so wise, Troy Harris."

"Well playing drums only takes up so many hours in the day, everyone needs a hobby."

She laughed again, this time the light hit her eyes and made them sparkle. If I hadn't already been sitting down, I would have needed to. She was so freaking beautiful and when she laughed she did things to me I just didn't understand.

So this was our deal now, laughing and talking but no fucking. Yep. This was going to blow.

11
Megan

THAT FIRST POST-SEX ENCOUNTER HADN'T BEEN SO BAD. AFTER THE initial, hey-let's-pretend-I-don't-know-what-you-look-like-naked, we were actually in a good place. Not to say that I didn't wish things could be different and that we could see each other naked again—with everything else that comes with that— but friendship is where we seemed poised to stay. So I kept telling myself.

Because I couldn't leave well enough alone— really, I'm a hazard to myself— I suggested we should *probably date other people*. The conversation went something like this: "So, Troy Harris, seeing as you aren't dating me, and there's no hope of that happening, you should let some other lucky lady have the privilege. It will help me move on and this is, after all, all about me."

Okay so maybe the conversation didn't go exactly like that, but it was mentioned we should see other people—by me, the idiot — and Troy, who seemed to have no problem with it, readily agreed. I'm not even sure how it was interjected into the conversation. Clearly I suck when it comes to making my mouth not say stupid stuff, so it really wasn't surprising.

At least we'd finished the evening on a positive note, promising to stop avoiding each other and work our way to a decent friendship. More than sleeping with him again, it's what I desperately wanted. Just to be able to call and see him again without it being weird would be a start. Okay so not weird was a tall order, maybe less weird than it had been was what I should be aiming for.

Troy and I became somewhat of phone-buddies—yeah I know it sounds like some obscure anime themed App— but we often called each other and had lame-ass conversations. Ridiculous even, but I looked forward to them. Completely nonsexual and everything. At first it was a challenge trying to not picture him naked but we eased into a friendship that was actually kind of nice.

The person to make the first call had been me, when on Monday I dialed his number.

"Megs." Troy answered the phone almost immediately.

"So, I was thinking." I didn't even bother with formalities like hello.

Troy laughed. "Sounds good to me, I usually like it when you get thinking." I didn't need to ask where his mind had wandered.

"Awesome, so can I sign you up to be on the next season of *The Bachelor*?" Genuinely curious as to what he would say.

"No, you can't." He shot me down, not even entertaining the idea.

"You are no fun, Troy Harris." I pouted, despite him not being able to see it. I'm sure he heard it though. I had a very pouty voice.

Troy laughed. "Goodbye, Megs."

The next volley came from Troy on Tuesday.

"Hey, Troy Harris." I smiled as I placed the phone to my ear. Did I mention how much I really liked seeing his name on my caller ID?

"Hey, Megs, I heard one of the Jonas brother's is single. I have no idea which one it is, but they all pretty much look alike. You want me to set you up?"

"Please. Like I'd date a Jonas brother." I exaggerated my displeasure.

CRASH RIDE

He chuckled. "Right, you like your men a little more rock and roll, got it. Ummm let me check TMZ and see who's available. I'll call you back."

My follow up had happened on Wednesday and the conversation had turned from dating to something else entirely.

"Hey, Troy Harris." His name left my lips as soon as he'd pick up the receiver.

"Hey, Megs, I hope this is important. The Vampire Dairies reruns are on and that Nina whatever-her-name is hot."

"Oh, I love Vampire Diaries. Damon Salvatore is so misunderstood. This is important. Does your cock ring set off metal detectors at airports? I mean, do you need like pull your pants down and let them wand you?"

"Er, no. Why?"

"Oh, I was bored and thought we could take a drive out to La Guardia and mess with some TSA people. Back to square one I guess. Bye."

By Thursday I was not only expecting his call but also anxiously waiting for it. My pulse racing a little every time my phone went off.

"Megs." I heard the smile in his voice. "I hope you found another satisfactory way to amuse yourself yesterday."

"Oh I sure did. I bought a huge dildo online instead, and I'm going to pack it in my carry on for my next trip." It took everything I had to suppress my laugh.

"That's awesome; remind me never to fly with you. Anyway, I got a new Tat today and while I was there I picked up a gift certificate for you. Figured we could get a *return to* label inked on your ass, you know in case you fall down again."

"Aw, you shouldn't have. You are so sweet."

"My pleasure, Megs. There was also a discount on *Ace* bandages at *Walgreens*. I know I shouldn't spoil you, but I couldn't help myself."

"Goodbye, Troy Harris."

"Bye, Megs."

Friday had me buzzing with anticipation over his call.

"Hey, Megs."

I loved hearing him say my name. "Hey, Troy Harris."

"I used your address to do some internet shopping. I know I should have asked first, but we're so cool with each other, I figured you'd say yes. I really hate it when people see my name and address and then before you know it…boom a stalker."

"Sure, no problem at all. What did you buy?"

"Chinese throwing stars and a sword. Hopefully it doesn't get flagged by the FBI; you don't have an existing record do you?"

I couldn't even respond I was laughing so hard. Those calls had been the highlight of my day. It wasn't just phone calls; there were voice messages as well. At the end of my workday, there would always be a missed call and message from Troy. I'd put my headphones on and would listen on my cab ride home from work. It almost became a sort of therapy for me, a way to unwind.

The mix of feelings that I was experiencing for him was new and exciting. They confused me slightly, not being able to package them up neatly, but I knew my days were better with him in them; even it was just phone calls.

It was official— apart from being sexy and so incredibly funny— Troy Harris was also very sweet and sincere. It was so unexpected. One more thing to add to the list of his perfections; I'd stalled greatly on his imperfections after those original two. Hated coffee and the R2D2 in the kitchen (in case anyone needed a refresher) and even now, those two didn't seem so bad. The no coffee thing could actually be a positive. I would never have to compete with him for the last cup.

Saturday's call had been a little bit different. Rather than wait until later in the day, I instead gave him a five a.m. wake up call and played Britney Spear's "Oops!...I Did It Again" at ear-splitting decibels through the phone. Even though I had also been affected by the sleep deprivation, it had been worth it to hear the expletives that spewed from Troy's mouth while he tried to work out what was going on. It had taken me at least ten minutes before I had been able to catch my breath. Tears streamed down my cheeks, I had been laughing so hard.

CRASH RIDE

After Troy warned me that we were now at war, the conversation took a more serious turn.

"So, are you dating anyone?" The words leapt out of my mouth before I had a chance to stop them.

"Not really, Jase and I hung out with a couple of girls on Wednesday but nothing really serious."

"Oh, okay," I managed to say without choking. My voice almost sounded normal, indifferent. There, something to be proud of.

The thought of him with someone else made my blood run cold. Did I want to know any of this? I should have stopped, but of course I didn't. I had to dig a little bit deeper, maybe torment myself a little more. It would have been too much to ask to just end the call on a happy note.

"Why didn't you tell me?" It wasn't any of my business and I had no right to ask.

I heard a small sign. "It wasn't important. It wasn't some hot date or anything. What about you? You dating?"

What about me? I hadn't even looked at a guy since I'd slept with Troy, not seriously anyway. I mean, I'd appreciated the guy in his underwear on the billboard in Time's Square, but it would have been rude if I hadn't. The poor guy was in his underwear, demanding attention.

"Me? Sure, there's this guy I've kind of been interested in. Who knows, we might even go out tonight."

"Really? Well that's good."

What did that mean? He wanted me to date? Why couldn't *he* be jealous? Not that I was jealous. Nooo, of course I wasn't. I was just curious. "What are you doing tonight?"

"Not sure yet. I'll probably go out."

It was his non-committal reply and lack of jealousy that was responsible for my next move. Rational Megs would have never suggested what I was about to suggest. A time machine would have been good. So I could've either gone back and kicked myself for being so stupid or clamp my hand across my mouth so the words didn't come out.

"Well, you know what would be fun," I said. The world moved in slow motion as I finished the last part. "We should go on a double date."

It was like a car crash. The minute it left my mouth, I regretted it and prayed that Troy would shoot down the idea. Who even suggests something like that? You didn't have to look too far to get your answer. This was by far my dumbest idea.

"Sure." His words had sealed my fate.

Panic set in as the reality hit me. I needed a date, like now. That guy I had kind of been interested in—Fictional. Non-existent. It was something to say so I didn't sound like a pathetic loser who had been sitting at home waiting for someone who wasn't interested in her. Yeah, all right. I'll admit. Me being cool with Troy and I not dating wasn't entirely the truth. I was fine with it as long as he wasn't dating someone else. Now I was not only going to have to be *okay* with it but watch it, all night long. Damn it.

So was there dial-a-date service? I sure as hell could use that right now. Trust me, at this point hiring an escort was not off the table. I had no shame and I would rather turn up with Juan Pablo on my dime, than show up alone.

It also didn't help that I was working against the clock. Assuming I could find someone who would be bearable, what would be the chances they were available on a Saturday night?

I could do this. It was one night. It would be fine. Troy and I were fine, now. I could even look at him and not need to stick panty liners under my armpits to stem the ridiculous amount of perspiration he seemed to induce. See? Totally, fucking, fine.

Was it too late to fake an illness? Something contagious but not so grotesque he would never want to see me again. I paced nervously around my living room. Fuck. I was in deep shit. Think. I willed myself to come up with some master plan but nothing happened, other than giving myself a headache and the possibility of an angina attack from the stress.

The walls were closing in on me as the first two hours ticked over with not even a possible name of a willing victim I could ask. I pulled on my runners and left my apartment for the solace of *Jilly Beans,* my lack of caffeine adding to my distress.

It was there while I ordered my extra large, extra hot latte with an extra coffee shot from hot coffee guy that inspiration struck me. Or was it desperation? Which ever it was, I was thankful. And if I didn't think it would have earned me some seriously judgmental stares, I would have gotten on my knees and praised God.

"Hi." I handed over a twenty-dollar bill and gave my best flirty smile.

"Hi," hot coffee guy responded. His cute smile teased beneath his neatly manicured beard.

"I've been watching you for a while..." What the fuck was I saying? I've been watching you for a while? I sounded like a freaking stalker. Had I suddenly lost the ability to flirt?

"I meant, I've been coming here for a while and I've noticed you." Not much better but we were going to work with it. "And..." I continued hoping that at some point the seductress in me would kick in. "I was wondering if you had any plans for this evening?" Not my best work and probably too direct, but I was on the clock.

"Are you asking me out?" Hot coffee guy leaned against the counter, amused.

Look buddy, this isn't a sideshow. It's a yes or a no. "Well, sure. I mean, if you want to. I understand if you have plans. It's short notice."

"Do you even know my name?" He raised his eyebrow as his grin widened.

"Um..." I looked down at his apron hoping to find a name badge but was disappointed when my search came up empty.

"I'm sure I'll find out, if you go out with me tonight." Lame. Why didn't I just hang a sign around my neck that read desperado? I swear I had better moves than that.

Thankfully hot coffee dude had a good sense of humor and didn't laugh his ass off at my feeble attempt. After he whipped up my order, he took a break and sat with me while I enjoyed my coffee. His name was actually Callum and he was incredibly sweet. The thirty-three-year-old New Jersey native took the trip across state lines with dreams of opening his own retro-style coffee house. I didn't want to crush his spirit by pointing out his business venture was probably better suited to New Jersey than New York, so instead I smiled and promised to be one of their first customers when he opened. That wasn't a hard promise to make, regardless of my feelings for Callum, my love for the liquid God of caffeinated goodness would stand the test of time.

So with my coffee all consumed and Callum's break over, we exchanged numbers with a promise from me that I would text details sometime that day for our hot date that evening.

It was with this new found relief that I floated back to my apartment. I had a date, he was cute *and* he wasn't on an hourly rate. So many positives, I could barely contain my excitement. I texted Troy and told him that *Project Double Date* was a go and because I had been cocky, told him to name the time and pick the place. Clearly I hadn't learnt from my earlier overconfident idiocy.

Callum—like most residents of NYC —didn't own a car, so we decided it would make more sense to meet at *Jilly Beans* and split a cab to our destination. Troy had picked a club—standard— in midtown and silently I was glad it was somewhere noisy that lacked intimacy.

We stepped out of the shiny yellow cab sometime around nine. It was a Saturday night and the streets were filled with excited locals and tourists ready to party away the weekend in the city that never slept. Smoke bellowed from a grate in the ground; the heat of the day not willing to give anyone a reprieve.

I'd worn a short black backless dress that teased at my upper thigh—no bra. I knew it was sexy but if I had any doubts, they had been put to rest by Callum's eyes almost bugging out of this head. My strappy

Manolo's —the ones I had purchased while trying to manage my Troy obsession— were the perfect compliment. Callum had dressed nice too, black skinny jeans, black pointy-toed shoes and a blue and red checkered button down shirt, rolled at his biceps. I still hadn't decided whom I was trying to impress.

There was a short line, but Troy had informed me that my name with a plus one would be left on the list to ensure I would be allowed entry quickly and with no trouble. Sure enough, after the mention of my name, the rope was lowered and we were ushered inside. No cover charge was demanded, nor were our IDs checked, such was the power of celebrity.

The inside of the club was like a hundred others in the city. It was as if all the designers had all compared notes or they'd been styled by the same person. A marriage of industrial and modern, the walls had been painted to look like exposed cinder blocks. Lights swirled randomly from the exposed metal truss that hung from the celling. The bar, metallic and mirrored. Even the music sounded the same. Wash, rinse, and repeat.

"How did we get in so fast? Are you famous or something?" Callum naïvely asked.

It had been mentioned, in passing that we *might* be catching up with a friend or two of mine. Sure, the boundaries of honesty had been stretched, but telling him it was a double date right off the bat would have sent him running a mile.

"Oh, those friends I told you we may run into? They come here a lot, they said they'd leave my name at the door." My web of deceit became more intricate.

"That's cool, Megsy." Callum smiled and slung his arm around my waist. I wasn't crazy about the *Megsy* thing but didn't set him straight. His overfamiliarity felt weird, like an ill-fitting belt that ruined a good outfit.

"Megs." We'd barely travelled five feet when Troy's smiling face greeted us, his arm around the shoulder of some blonde skinny whore.

Okay, maybe she wasn't a whore and I was being catty, but the smug look she wore on her face was enough of a reason to hate her. And did he have to pick a blonde? He couldn't have diversified and picked a brunette or something?

"Troy." I forced the smile on my face and tried not to hiss out his name through gritted teeth. I hated seeing him with someone else. "Fancy meeting you here."

"Yeah, big coincidence." Thankfully he continued my rouse though his smirk very plainly showed he was enjoying making me squirm.

"Callum, this is my friend, Troy." I childishly sidled up closer to my date as I made the introductions. "Troy, Callum."

"Hey, man. Good to meet you." Troy shook Callum's hand amicably. It annoyed me how easy it seemed for him.

"Wow, are you Troy Harris? The drummer for Power Station?" Callum's smile widened.

"He sure is." Skinny whore weighed in, tightening her grip on Troy. Oh look, she speaks. I had been worried she wouldn't be able to move her exaggerated collagen-inflated lips.

"Yeah. Guilty as charged, and this is Amber. " Troy nodded and gave his cheerleader a squeeze. Amber, she even had a stripper name. Perfect.

"Hi," Amber squeaked. "And you are..." She deliberately left her voice trailing as she looked me over.

I am the woman who made the guy whose arm you're clinging to come so many times he could barely walk two weeks ago. "Megs." I compromised. "A friend of Troy's," I added, not entirely content with my amended introduction.

Amber, obviously bored with me, turned her attention back to Troy. "Are you going to take us to the VIP section?" she whined, sounding like a toddler pleading for candy.

Troy shrugged. He didn't seem as excited as he had been when we walked in. "If that's where everyone wants to go."

"Sounds good to me. Megsy? You cool with that?" Callum's hand moved down the exposed skin on my back, dangerously close to my ass.

Troy's eyes followed Callum's wandering hand and his jaw tightened. "Megsy?" His eyebrow raised at my new found nickname. "Any

CRASH RIDE

objections?"

"None here." I smiled brightly and pretended like the hand on my ass or the nickname wasn't bothering me.

Amber clasped her hands together excitedly. "Great, follow me."

We tried to squeeze through the crowd but had to stop every ten steps when someone recognized Troy. Every time he was polite, spending a few moments with each fan before moving forward. Amber seemed to enjoy the extra attention and always made sure she was tightly on Troy's arm at every photo opportunity.

The VIP area carried the same theme as the rest of the club, metallic, industrial. What was different were the plush bright blue chairs that spliced through the harshness of the place. It was either some nuevo style technique I wasn't cool enough to understand or the designer had been colorblind. The glass-topped coffee tables that were randomly scattered through the room were also a mystery.

When I had suggested this double date thing, it had seemed like a bad idea. The reality was so much worse. Amber poured herself all over Troy; her hands, legs, mouth, tongue on him at all times.

It was enough to make me sick.

My hands were balled so tightly that my fingernails had cut into my palms. I smiled politely while Callum spoke passionately about different Columbian coffee beans and his aspirations to open a coffee house. Amber commandeered the conversation when she could, chatting excitedly about who had been ostracized from the catwalk in Milan— The fact the coffee table legs were wider than her thighs should have been a tip-off that she was a model. I hated her even more.

We sat and drank, the smile fixed to my face while I lived out my private hell. Troy seemed relaxed, his arms draped around the back of one of the plush blue chairs —they might look like an eyesore but at least they were comfy— with Amber perched in his lap.

Despite having a fairly decent buzz from the copious amount of alcohol I had consumed, I was still far from having a good time. Mentally I made the decision to keep a handle on my inebriation. Drunk

Megs was not as diplomatic as sober Megs, and also lacked the filter between her mind and her mouth. The last thing I needed was a slurred and emotional purge of my feelings or alternatively, to grab Amber by the hair and tell her to *back the hell off*. I'll admit that the last part made me smile.

As the warmth of the alcohol spread through my body and made more me relaxed, my body discovered it had other needs—ones that required a bathroom. I had already filled my quota of listening politely and was skating to the end of my self-control. So rather than sprout the drunken, emotional confessional I had been avoiding, I decided I needed to get away from there.

"I'm going to the bathroom," I announced loudly as I stood up, my body swaying unsteadily on my feet. Not sure why I felt compelled to broadcast my bodily need, but I didn't wait for a response or an acknowledgement. Instead I opted to turn my back on the farce that was my night, both literally and figuratively and stalk to the nearest bathroom. The trip somewhat reminiscent of the first time I'd met Troy.

The private restrooms of the VIP area were extremely luxurious. The white tiled walls and chrome accents made it feel like I'd stepped into a private utopia. Luckily for me, I was the only occupant, which allowed me the ability to explore. My high heels echoed off the white marble floor as I inspected the space that featured a large, white leather chaise and an old-school bureau filled with designer lotions, soaps and colognes.

It was in the bathroom that I could finally breathe. The noise of the club and the memory of my horrendous evening could be shut behind the large metal door. It was heaven. I wondered how long I could stay here. Or if I slunk off without saying goodbye, if anyone would notice? I had been okay with not dating Troy, or at least I thought I was. What we had now was great, he made me laugh and I loved spending time with him either on the phone or seeing him briefly when I went to visit Ash. But I wasn't prepared to see him dating someone else. To see another woman touching him, going home with him. It was selfish and unreasonable and

I knew that, but I would give anything for that the girl he took home tonight to be me. News flash. It wasn't going to be. Great. I was emotional, confused, far from sober and hiding in a bathroom. I had reached a new level of hell.

'12

Troy

AMBER—MY DATE—WAS AS DUMB AS TWO PLANKS. ACTUALLY, that would be insulting to the wood—she was probably dumber than that, and the only interest she had in me was my ability to get her into the restricted VIP area and continue to pay for the overpriced pink cocktails she was sucking down. In all honesty, that situation was perfect with me, so I didn't feel like a complete and utter asshole in having zero interest in her.

Her number was randomly selected from the collection of crumpled napkins, matchboxes and scraps of paper I had accumulated over the last couple of weeks. Not that I called any of them before—I wasn't interested in dating— but Megs's bright idea had required me to play the number lottery.

When Megs had suggested this double date thing, I thought she was kidding. No shit, I fucking laughed. Firstly, because we weren't in junior fucking high— who the hell went on double dates, and secondly, 'cause the last thing I wanted was to see her with some other dude. Fuck that. NO.

We'd played it cool for the past few weeks, doing the friend thing. It seemed like every day I got a little bit deeper, and even though we saw each other and spoke all the time, it was never enough. Our phone conversations were hilarious and the highlight of my day. I even pretended like shit was all fucking fine even though I was less than happy that I couldn't touch her. Yeah, and it wasn't just about not being able to fuck her either. I missed the weight of her against me. Her smile. Her laugh—made my world go around.

Tonight had been its own special brand of hell. She strolled in looking like sex on legs, and I had to spend the night hiding the hard on I'd been rocking since she walked in. God, she was beautiful.

While there was no denying Amber was pretty, the girl had yet to take a breath since the minute we'd sat down. No seriously, I was surprised she hadn't passed the fuck out. She had been running her mouth about a bunch of bullshit I had no interest in. The hipster douche from the wannabe *Starbucks* that Megs had walked in with was fucking riveted. Awesome, maybe those two should get together seeing as neither of them had even noticed when Megs left to use the bathroom.

My quota with sitting around and pretending like I gave a shit was full. So rather than listen to the mundane world of those two morons, I excused myself to go take a piss. Besides, Megs had looked a weeble-wobble when she'd stood up and I could smell the disaster.

The idea of her going home with Callum fucking pissed me off. He had the nice guy routine down, but I knew nothing about this kid other than he had a Jersey accent and he had a hard-on for coffee. The thought of her sleeping with him— that put me on a whole different level of rage.

The bathroom was tucked away in the back right hand corner, and was found with very little effort. I debated whether or not I go in, or earn myself creeper status by standing outside and waiting for her to come out. The decision was made for me when after a two-minute internal debate she came barreling, bull-in-a-china-shop, through the doorway and slammed right into me. I caught her.

"Hey, Troy Harris, do you need to use the little boy's room?" Those big beautiful eyes clocked me as her tits pressed against my arm.

I bit back my grin. "Come on, Megs. You know there is nothing little about me."

"True, Miss Stripper USA is in for a treat tonight," she slurred sarcastically. She sounded drunk and maybe a little jealous.

"She's a model not a stripper," I corrected. Not that I wanted to talk about any girl other the one in front of me.

"Model, stripper—the girl needs a sandwich." Megs waved her hands animatedly in front of my face. "You might want to spring for a burger or something. It would be kind of awkward if she passed out while you were having sex."

"Thanks for the tip." My grin got bigger. "Would you like me to get your date a burger while I'm at it? My forearms are bigger than the dude's legs. Incidentally, you might want to check your wardrobe when you get home. I don't think the pants he is wearing are his own."

"They are called *skinny* jeans." Megs rolled her eyes. "They're supposed to look like *that*."

"Skinny jeans? When did real men start wearing girl's pants?" Horrified! It would be a cold day in hell before I'd be rocking a pair of pants like that. How the man hadn't spoken three octaves higher had me dumbfounded.

"Oh, you are just jealous they don't make them in your size." Megs poked me in the chest, big ass grin on her face.

"You're right, I'd be lucky to get a fucking toe in a pair. How do those pants not strangle his sack? Oh, I know *you* probably have bigger balls than he does." I laughed as I pulled her closer, her body up against mine.

"It's not the size of his balls I'm interested in." She smirked as she breathed into my face. "It's whether or not he can make me come."

Right, now she had my attention. I lowered my head and whispered in her ear. "Well it's a good thing you bought that huge dildo early in the week, 'cause it looks like you're going to need it tonight."

"Wow, thanks for the great idea." She turned her face, those beautiful lips almost touching mine. "I can get myself off with the dildo while I blow him."

Detonation. Something inside of me snapped. Like a fucking avalanche of sexual tension unleashed all at once and there was no stopping it.

My mouth slammed down on hers, my hands grabbing her ass and hauled her onto me. She got with the program, wrapping her legs around my waist and I walked us back into the bathroom she had just walked out of. My tongue got to know every inch of her mouth as I pinned her against the cold tiled wall. My hands busy palming her ass.

She moaned my name as I used the bulge in my pants to rub up against her hungry pussy, her head thrashing from side to side as I worked the length of it up and down between her legs.

I reached out an arm and slammed the bathroom door shut. My hand fumbled for the lock, twisting until I heard the telltale click of the metal sliding into place. If I weren't so fucking turned on right now, I would have thanked the club management for their progressive stance on public fornication by installing a lock. But the only thing rocking my thoughts was touching every part of the woman whose tongue was currently in my mouth.

"Megs." I pulled my mouth away; my hand brushing the hair out of her eyes. "We're in a whole world of trouble right now."

"Oh God, stop talking and touch me. That feels so good." Megs's hands clawed at my back and pulled me closer toward her.

"You going home with him tonight? You and Callum, is this a thing?" This shit wouldn't go down if she was with him. No fucking way. She moaned against me trying to get the friction she needed. "Megs, I need to know."

"No, he's just a guy. Coffee shop. Needed a date." Her mouth on me making her words come out jumbled. "Amber?"

"You're not her type, sweetheart, and neither am I."

Green light. Her eyes widened as my hands moved to her inner thigh and pulled aside her panties. She was soaking wet, the tips of my fingers coated as I circled her opening.

"Yeah, is that what you want? You want me to make you feel good?" The pads of my two fingers stroked her while I thumbed her clit.

"Yes." She circled her hips in rhythm with my hand. "It's been two weeks and I need to come so fucking bad."

Fuck, I wanted her. I wanted her to yell my name so loudly that even with the fucking music blaring in the club they'd hear her. I wanted to make her pant and pulse and come so hard she wouldn't be able to walk straight in the morning. She had me by the balls and I didn't give a fuck, my sole mission was to give her what she was begging me for.

"Megs, you have a dirty little mouth when you're horny." My hands palmed her tits, pinching her nipples through the material of her dress. "You want me to make you come with my hand?" My thumb got cozy with the opening of her pussy.

"No, Troy." She leveled me with a stare and looked me dead in the eye. "I want your cock. Fuck me."

I'd lost the ability to think.

I ripped the tiny black thong from her body and tossed what was left of it on the floor. It had no business covering what I wanted. Her legs unfurled from around my waist, sliding them down so she could stand. Not that she was going to be able to do that for long if I had my way. Her hands went straight for my belt. Fuck. We were going to do this.

Fingers wrestled with my buckle and my zipper, as my thumb rubbed circles around her clit. I was so hard, it fucking hurt. My objective, get suited up and inside of her. Like five minutes ago.

She pushed down my jeans and boxers below my hips. My dick springing free was her reward. Her hands palmed my shaft, giving me a stroke or two while I plunged two fingers inside of her.

"Yes." She writhed against the wall as I continued to play, her head flailing from side to side as I slid my fingers in and out.

It killed me to stop touching her, my cock punched out in protest to let me know he wasn't happy either. From the minute I'd seen her walk in, this is exactly what I wanted to be doing. Sadly the condom wasn't going to magically fly out of my pocket and land on my dick all by itself. And not having sex with her was *not* an option.

"No, don't stop." She grabbed my wrist as I moved my hand. Trust me, I didn't want to either.

"I need to get a condom on, Megs. Give me a second."

"Hurry, Troy. I need you in me."

I yanked the condom from my back pocket, ripping open the packet with my teeth. The packaging was tossed to the floor as I fought with Megs's hands, needing her to let go of my cock long enough to slide the latex down my shaft.

As soon as I was suited up, her hands went straight back to my dick, gripping me so tight it bordered on pain. "Fuck," I hissed, as she continued to jerk me off. It felt freaking amazing but there was no way this was going to end in a hand job.

My mouth was once again on hers as I pried her fingers from around my cock and captured her hands. She protested, bucking against me as I raised them above her head. My lips moved to her neck as I sucked against her skin. Knowing it would probably leave a mark made me even harder.

I grabbed her wrists with my hand and held them steady against the wall. "I need to be in you." My other hand rubbed the head of my cock against the opening of her pussy. She arched her back to get closer and making me feel like king of the fucking world, she was just as desperate for this as I was.

She wrestled her hands out of my hold and gripped my ass, pulling me toward her. I met her half way and slid into her in one, swift stroke.

"Megs." It was halfway between a moan and a prayer. She felt so tight and wet that I had to stop for a minute and just let myself feel it. My lips panted against her neck. This girl was going to be the death of me.

Not one to sit around and wait, Megs starting moving. Restricted by my body caging her up against the wall, she swiveled her hips from side to side, which created some crazy-good twisting sensation. It was like be jerked off—by her fucking pussy. My mind almost exploded.

I grabbed her legs and locked them around my hips, needing to get in deeper. She gasped as I gave her everything I had. I pulled out slow before sliding back in fast, my finger marks indented on her ass. She fought against me each time, not wanting me to pull out.

"Holy Shit." Megs scrunched her eyes tight as I plunged into her, her pussy clamping around my dick.

Yep, playtime was over. I slammed into her deeper and faster, her hips meeting my every thrust. It was out-of-control crazy and unrestrained, pumping into her while I kissed her hard. God, nothing should feel this good and be legal. I wanted every part of her.

"Don't stop. I'm so close," she mumbled against my lips.

"You going to come for me, Megs? I want to feel it."

"Troy."

One word. That was all she said.

It was more a muffled scream than a word, but it was clear she had said my name— and then I felt *it*. Her body tightened before it finally let go, and she shook in my arms as I rode out the rest of her orgasm. I'd been holding back, wanting to see her face when she'd finally come, not allowing myself to finish. That look alone tipped me over the edge. It was like chasing down a runaway train as I continued to pump, my load shooting deep as I panted against her throat.

We didn't move. Her legs still pinned around me with her face buried against my shoulder, both of us breathing hard. She didn't say a word, which made me edgy. Had me wondering if she was going to give me the we-shouldn't-have-done this speech. But I couldn't make myself regret it, being with her.

She tilted her head toward me and whispered. "Fuck."

Yep, that was pretty much an accurate description of it.

I released her legs and she slowly lowered them to the floor. Her body was still unsteady as she tried to smooth out her messed up hair. Her make-up? I was wearing more of her lipstick than she was, but she still looked like a knockout. Keeping away from her had been impossible, and what's worse was now I didn't want to. Not just to get my rocks off, this girl was different. Things were different.

"I told you we were in a world of trouble."

'13

Megan

WHAT THE HELL HAD I DONE? WHO HAS SEX IN A BATHROOM WITH one guy while on a date with someone else? I was some kind of freak. What's worse is that if given the same chance, I would do it all over again. All that rhetoric about having wisdom in hindsight is bullshit. I take your hindsight and raise you one mind-blowing orgasm with the guy I'm obsessed with. Obsession, that's what it was.

That's how the whole mess started. He was the unattainable guy who looked like a sex God. He was famous. It would be fun. One time wouldn't hurt anyone. Ok, so maybe just a few more times, but I could stop at any time I wanted. What does that sound like to you? Yep, I was going to need a twelve-step program and a sponsor.

Troy and I had fucked each other senseless while the two people each of us walked in with sat maybe twenty feet away in blissful oblivion, awaiting our return. Sure, technically neither of us was dating either of them but still, that was a very slippery slope. I mean, who does that? It's like I couldn't control myself— not at all.

Was it a mistake? That was a massive trick question. My brain was telling me yes, but something that felt that good could never be a mistake. Herein lies the biggest problem. Not the fact I had crazy, bathroom sex with Troy while I was supposed to be on a date with someone else i.e. the issue that I *should* see as the problem, but that we couldn't seem to be able to be alone together and not end up naked.

How is that healthy? It's certainly not a relationship. We weren't dating, we were just fucking and while at the start of this little arrangement that had been fine, it didn't sit well with me anymore. No, I didn't think I was a whore or a pervert. Highly sexed with compulsion issues? Okay, so no one was perfect.

"Hey, we should get back." I straightened my dress and picked up my shredded panties. They weren't going to be much use to me so I tossed them in the trash and made the conscious effort to remember I was now sans underwear. Suddenly I had a new found affinity toward *Britney Spears*.

Troy pulled off his condom and tossed it the trashcan, ironically where it would lay with my discarded G-string, a tribute to our *good time*. "Are you okay?" He looked at me, concerned— probably wondering if I was going to start crying hysterically or insist he declare his intentions for me.

It was his lucky day, because not only did he just *blow his load*, he wasn't going to be getting any emotional drama from me. Nope, not doing it. Not after I had told him shit wouldn't get complicated, and I was capable of sex without emotion. There was no denying things had changed. Or at least they had for me. This wasn't just about him being sexy and us having a good time, this was about the way he made me feel. Emotions—that dirty word—were most definitely involved.

"Megs, do you want to talk about what just happened?" Troy grabbed some paper towel and handed it to me before taking care of himself.

The clean up —the stark realism of the situation. It's not like we could walk out back into the club with goo everywhere. I prayed no one would be murdered in the bathroom in the near future and it got swabbed for DNA.

"We had sex. We seem to do that a lot when were alone," I responded drily as I turned on the faucet and washed my hands. Act normal I told myself and for God's sake keep it together.

"Yeah, so..." Troy cocked his eyebrow looking for me to continue.

"So... we should probably try harder not to?" It was the best I could offer. What else could we do? Short of locking up my vagina, there wasn't a lot it seemed. One of us was the weakest link and I couldn't be sure it wasn't me.

"Yeah, probably." He nodded as he took his turn at the sink. It was all so civilized.

"Good, we agree. That was the last time." The paper towel I was using went sailing into the trash. I got the distinctive feeling of déjà vu. We've been here before and I had been just as convincing, hopefully this time, it would stick.

"Okay." Troy dried his hand. The zipping of his pants and adjusting of his T-shirt happened soon after. "So we're good then?" He looked skeptical, liked he expected more. Maybe he honestly did believe I was going to cry.

"Yep, we're perfectly fine." I was amazed at how easy the lie passed through my lips.

We did our best to tidy ourselves up so we didn't look like we just had sex, but there was only so much I could do with a compact and a lipstick. I already had a massive hickey developing on my neck, the thrill of explaining that to friends and co-workers was something I hoped to avoid.

Troy walked out first and then I followed after the obligatory five minutes. It was ridiculous really, the cloak and dagger routine. No one in the club gave us so much as a secondary glance and the only people who may have shown some concern were our *dates*, but even they didn't seem to wise up.

When I had gotten back to our little awesome foursome, Callum and Amber were laughing hysterically about some joke they had shared. The two of them discovered they both had *so much in common*, how nice for them. Troy looked bored as they generously got me up to speed on everything in the conversation I had missed. They needn't have bothered, it was plainly obvious Troy and I had been replaced.

Sitting across from Troy after just having had him inside of me was weird. There was no getting around that. Oh I gave it my best shot, playing it off like I had sex in club bathrooms all the time, and this was no big deal, but the truth remained—it was a big deal. He gave me a few concerned looks from time to time, but each time I met his eye I gave him my best it's-all-good smile and calculated when would be a good time to make my exit.

Another drink later and I had reached a respectable arbitrary length of time for me to leave. I did the whole I-have-work-in-the-morning excuse and said my goodbyes. Troy offered to call TJ for me but I declined. I'd already received one ride courtesy of Troy Harris that evening. I didn't need another.

Callum walked me outside so I could hail a cab. His hug goodbye warm but noticeably less familiar than when we'd walked it and just like that— I'd been friend-zoned.

"Hey, Megsy, thanks so much for asking me out tonight. I had a ball. Your friends are awesome."

I smiled as I returned the hug. "Yeah, well I really only know Troy. Amber, not so much."

"She's pretty great." His sheepish grin alluding to the fact he thought she was more than just *great*.

It should've been awkward, his interest in another woman while he was speaking to me, but it wasn't. Let's be honest, I was in no position to judge. He hadn't been the one to sneak off for a quickie in the bathroom.

"Yep. So I guess I'll see you at *Jilly Beans*." There was no need to see each other socially again. It was clear he was interested in Amber and the connection between us was non-existent.

"Extra large, extra hot, extra shot." He rattled off my usual order.

"That's me. Just want a little extra of everything." I laughed but it was so *not* funny. Extra trouble is what I would be getting whether I'd ordered it or not.

No more sex with Troy Harris.
Ever.
It can't happen.
Not again.

It was like my daily mantra reminding me that the *casual fling* hadn't worked. Hold on to your seats folks, I had feelings for Troy Harris. Not just the ones that make your girlie bits tingle, I'm talking about the ones that make your heart ache.

I had stopped seeing him just as someone to be lusted over and craved for him to be my *one*, and I wanted to be his.

When that actually happened, eluded me and honestly it didn't matter—what mattered was we weren't good for each other.

The intensity we had would eventually burn out, and then what? You can't sustain a relationship on sex alone; you would eventually have to be regular people and do normal stuff. We lacked that capacity.

He had made it clear from the start; he wasn't interested in dating me. Stupidly I had convinced myself that it didn't matter. Like this girl could suddenly be ok with having feelings for a guy that weren't reciprocated. Not likely.

We were friends, and I had to push it and open my big mouth. *Sleep with him; get him out of your system, have your fun and you will be strong enough to walk away.* That is what I had told myself. Yeah that was all a big fat lie.

So do I tell him —*hey remember when I said I could handle this and wouldn't ask for more? Yeah, I take that all back, I'm asking for more.* Or do I pretend nothing has changed, try and move on and really—and I mean *really* this time— try to date someone who is going to fulfill all my needs, and be available in the boyfriend sense of the word. I wouldn't beg, not for a guy to want me, so that left only the latter option.

Troy had called the next day and I had pretended it was business as usual. I avoided talking about *us* and asked him where the tattoo voucher he'd bought me was. We fell into our usual rhythm of daily, nonsensical fodder with the plan that I slowly wean myself. Eventually I wouldn't have to fake the we're-just-friends thing, it would just be. And what a glorious day that would be.

The wedding was a good distraction. Ashlyn and Dan had finally set a date. A few months from now, in November. The bridal party was limited to two —Troy and me. Yeah, it took me a few minutes breathing into a paper bag to calm down.

Forget. That's what I needed to do.

14

Megan

IN MY BID TO FORGET, I TRIED TO AVOID SOCIAL SITUATIONS WITH Ash and limited our contact to a few phone calls and coffee catch-ups. I blamed work— it was a believable excuse.

I hated keeping my distance but couldn't risk running Troy, so I stayed away.

So what does a person do when they are trying to forget? They go and get a permanent reminder etched into their skin. Just like that.

Oh look, a tattoo parlor.

Tattoos had always fascinated me, but I had always chickened out. First, because I knew my parents would freak out and later because I couldn't choose something I could live with for the Rest. Of. My. Life. That tramp stamp isn't going to just wash off when you decide it's no longer cool. The pressure was too great.

It was a whim and I assumed that my feet would *hit* the door before the needle *hit* my skin, but then I met Josh—the tattoo artist. He made me so comfortable, I actually wanted to do it. We talked about what I

CRASH RIDE

wanted and placement and before you knew it I was laying on his table in my panties, getting a stunningly, beautiful gray-scale feather etched above each hipbone. They were soft and feminine and just for me. My own little private rebellion.

The tattoos had hurt. A lot. I couldn't even imagine the pain ink-work like Troy's would have caused. I just closed my eyes and absorbed it. It was real, tangible and in a crazy way actually made me feel better.

Josh the tattooist was hot. His tall muscular frame was covered with intricate artwork. His black hair that was shaved short and tight against his skull made his stunning blue eyes stand out. He made me laugh, which helped considering the world of hurt I was in, and was a consummate professional while inking me. He didn't look at my rack once. Well, not that I saw anyway.

After it was done, he suggested maybe we could go out—if I was interested. No pressure.

I said yes.

Not that I wanted to, but figured it was best to get back on the horse and at least pretend I was interested in other men. Besides, he'd already seen me in my panties.

Our first date had been relatively low key— a new fusion restaurant in Chinatown. The usual first date conversation followed, favorite foods, movies and uh-hem... music. He was a Power Station fan too— sure, that wasn't weird at all.

I steered the conversation away from all things Troy Harris to talk about my work at the hospital. He didn't out and run the minute I'd told him I was a psychologist, *or* ask me to read his future. Oh it happens and *psychic*, I am not. But I'd known in the first date he was never going to be my forever.

The second date was a little more fun. We watched the goofy classic, *The Rocky Horror Picture Show* at *Landmark Sunshine Cinemas* on the Lower East Side. Josh joined me in the aisle for a loud, off-key rendition of "Time-Warp" —neither of us would be quitting our day jobs.

It was on the second date when he'd kissed me.

After the movie we'd stopped in at my old work place *Garro's* for a drink. Our waitress had just sauntered off with instructions to load us up with cheese fries and soda when Josh leaned across the table and kissed me.

While unexpected, it wasn't all together horrible. More of a savor-my-lips than tongue-down-my-throat kind of kiss and when it was over, I smiled and said thank you. Thank you! Like the man had just handed me a napkin or a bottle of ketchup.

After that second date, I told Troy about Josh.

It was the right thing to do. Sure we'd never dated and were no longer sleeping together, but I still felt I needed to tell him. If I was honest with myself, I told him hoping to illicit some reaction. Maybe a *hey, don't date him* or *I really miss sleeping with you* —the second response probably more likely than the first— but I just thought he might, I don't know, have an opinion.

He didn't. Well, at least none he shared with me. He instead let me talk about my dates and didn't even make a wise-ass remark about the guy kissing me. Part of me was disappointed. Whatever Troy and I had shared romantically, it was now the past.

With the third date came a certain amount of anticipation. He'd already kissed me and while it had been very PG-13, he would probably want to up that rating. Possibly get some hands on action.

Usually not a problem for me— a good make out session with some dry humping was good for the soul. Like chicken soup for your libido. But, my soul and my libido were playing a solid game of hide-and-go-seek when it came to tattoo guy Josh. I was attracted to him; I just wasn't attracted to him *enough*.

So the third date was the deal-breaker. Either some magic started to happen or we said our friendly goodbyes and saved ourselves the trouble. To test the chemistry, I decided to go all out— sexy outfit, sexy shoes, a venue that would be conducive to *the mood* and alcohol. Lots of alcohol. Might as well give poor Josh a fighting chance.

Josh arrived at my apartment around seven. He looked great, dressed

CRASH RIDE

head to toe in black —black baggy jeans, black button down shirt and black heavy boots; his tattooed arm sleeves and neck on display. He smiled with appreciation at the plunging neckline of my new red dress. Discreetly readjusting his man-bits as we got into his Jeep Wrangler. Objective of the dress—met.

For this monumental make-or-break date, I'd pick a little basement bar in Soho. Not the typical eye-rolling ultra trendy club that usually graced the sidewalk of that locale, no, it was a bar. Like a speakeasy but without the jazz band or moonshine.

Donavan's was a hidden gem. With no markings or signage—word of mouth was the only way you found this dirty little secret. It promised a plethora of liquor, dartboards, pool tables, and good music at the hand of the hottest DJs in town.

"You sure this is the right place?" Josh followed me down the narrow, rickety stairwell.

"Relax, where's your sense of adventure?" I tapped on the dilapidated door.

"Do we need a secret handshake?" Josh grabbed my hand and gave it a squeeze.

"'Sup." The security guard was huge. His large menacing body filling the doorway he'd opened.

"Hey, umm is there a code word or something?" Neither my cheesy grin nor my attempt at humor impressed the giant in front of me. My bad.

"IDs?" Amazing how that small demand translated into *show me your IDs and stop wasting my time*. Powerful and scary. It kind of excited me. The night was definitely not going to suck.

"You really know how to pick a place." Josh slung his arm around me, his pleased smile teased at the corners of his mouth.

On the inside, the place was huge. It expended into a large but slightly uneven rectangle. And like a Steampunk wet dream, it featured celling to floor matte black walls with gold gilded cornices.

"Rumor has it, anything goes in this place. Don't ask, don't tell." I pulled his arm playfully.

"Is that why there's a dude smoking a joint in the corner?"

"Could be medicinal. So judgey."

"Want a beer to go with the contact high?" Josh wrapped his arms around me and nuzzled my neck. Okay so the touchy-feely stuff was going to happen sooner than later. In that case I was definitely going to need that drink.

"Um, can I have a Long Island Iced Tea instead?" Beer wasn't going to cut it.

"Sure, baby. You can have whatever you want." Josh brushed the hair away from my face. Calling me *baby* was a new development.

We made it to the bar through the maze of people and ordered our drinks. Josh handed over some cash as the disinterested bartender prepared my Long Island and twisted the cap off Josh's Coors Light. He didn't look up at us once. Perhaps this was the anti-*Cheers* of the bar world— "where everybody knows your name" didn't apply. They didn't only *not* know it, but they didn't care to either.

"Have I told how great that dress looks on you?" Josh's smile hinted he was more interested in what was under the dress, as he leaned up against the bar.

"Thanks." Smile. "It's new." Smile. Why was this drink taking so long to make? Next time, order shots.

"Megan."

He refused to call me Megs, preferring to use the name that graced my birth certificate. It all stemmed from a previously owned pet cat named Megs that had died when he was eight. I wasn't sure if I should be horrified that someone had named their cat *Megs* or if I should book this guy in for therapy. You were eight, dude—she is in a better place, move on.

"Are you nervous?" His hand grazed across my cheek.

"No." My exaggerated laugh didn't fool anyone. "Yes."

"It's the whole third-date-third-base expectation. I'm not sure I am ready to sleep with you." What the fuck was I saying? My mouth spewed words my brain was convinced I should not be saying.

CRASH RIDE

"Baby, you are far from a foregone conclusion." He smiled; it was a nice smile. Just not as nice as Troy's. "Have I done anything to make you think that?"

Thank you, sweet baby Jesus, my drink was finally ready. I snatched the highball the minute it hit the bar, sipping the icy alcoholic goodness through a straw. Smile. "No, of course not." Smile. Hiding emotions was something I clearly sucked at.

"Megan, we're not going to do anything you're not comfortable with. No expectations here, okay?" He grabbed his beer from the bar and took a sip.

"I don't usually suck this much at dating." It was more of an apology than an explanation. My *game* was very much missing in action.

"Why don't we go shoot some pool or something?" His head jerked to the direction of the back left hand corner where we were told we'd find a couple of tables. "Get the ball action out of the way so you can relax." The smile lit up his blue eyes.

I laughed. And not the fake kind. "I'd like that." God he was sweet. That alone deserved a kiss.

He looped his arm around my waist and led us to the back end of the club. The pool tables were situated in little secluded alcoves, almost like little hidey-holes. Kudos management — it was a cute way to give the players privacy and probably facilitated more than just a blowjob or two. Things were looking up; I was thinking about blowjobs and not having a full-on panic attack. Awesome.

As we rounded the corner and stepped into the pool cave the brighter light of the gaming area distorted my vision momentarily.

"Megs?" Troy's eyes widened as he stood from taking his shot at the table. Every curve of his chest was displayed through the tight fabric of his white *Nirvana* T-shirt.

Wow. He looked *good*. Wearing faded blue jeans and black boots; he was his usual mix of unpretentious sexiness. Why tonight did it seem so much more... sexier.

"Megs, aren't you going to introduce us to your friend?" I was guessing from his tone I had been staring and unresponsive. It had been a while since he had affected me like that. Usually, I had time to prepare myself to act normal. Psyche myself up to see him and play my usual game of pretend. This was something else, I had been blindsided. I had also been drinking, so we can put some blame on that. I ignored the fact the couple of sips I had taken wouldn't qualify as drinking.

"Yes, of course." My brain kicked into gear as I peeled my eyes away from Troy's chest. Jason, who I hadn't noticed up until now, gave me a friendly wave.

"Troy and Jason, this is Josh. He's a friend. Josh, this is Jason and Troy." I stopped short not knowing how to explain my affiliation. *Here are two members of Power Station, my best friend's fiancé's band and before I forget to mention it, I slept with one of them*, didn't seem like a good idea.

"Hey, dude." Jason stepped forward and shook Josh's hand, Josh returned the handshake with a mix of shock and genuine awe on his face. I was wondering how long it would be before he broke out the you-didn't-tell-me-you-knew-Power-Station speech. Jase gave me a huge hug and a cheeky smile before adding, "Megs, you look like you're going to start some trouble in that dress tonight."

"She sure is." Troy eyes steamrolled over the length of my body and I had to remember to breathe. "Josh, nice to meet you." He took his turn to do some handshaking.

"Wow, Megan. You know Power Station? How could this have never come up?" Strangely even though this conversation was directed at me, Josh was too busy shaking Troy's hand and smiling at the guys to actually look at me. "Jason, Troy. I'm a big fan."

I rolled my eyes. I couldn't help it. While Josh had been a *fan*, he wasn't a *big fan*. He didn't have every album like I did and certainly hadn't been to the number of shows I had been. But no, put a couple of the band members in front of him and suddenly he becomes star-struck and is instantly their biggest fan.

"It didn't seem like a big deal." I lied, not sure what would be an acceptable excuse seeing as we had actually spoken about the band. The time when we compared musical tastes on our first date and their name had come up probably would have been an excellent time to throw in there, oh yeah, I know them. "I didn't want to name-drop like I was bragging," I added, figuring it would redeem me slightly.

"Oh, Megs, you're such a sweetheart not wanting to exploit us like that." Troy leaned in and gave me a hug, his hands pressed against me making me feel like I was on fire. "This isn't your usual hang out, *Megan*." I didn't miss the emphasis on my name.

To say it was horrible to see Troy was a lie. I had wanted to see him, but I couldn't trust myself. Being close to him when I didn't have my emotions in check would be dangerous, with reasonable thought thrown out the window. I would want him— to touch, to taste, to savor. It wasn't just the instant arousal the minute I'd walked in the room; it was my thumping heartbeat I couldn't rein in. My inability to be near him without telling him how much I wanted him to hold me.

"No, not my usual hang out." I suppressed the urge to press my lips against his neck. "I thought I would try something different." I didn't just mean the club. Josh was also neatly pigeonholed in the *something different*. Or maybe it was just the same but different. Having a stand-in bad boy for the one I couldn't have. The one I desperately wanted.

"Wow, so how do you all know each other?" Josh seemed oblivious to the fact I wanted nothing more than to throw Troy across the pool table and kiss him.

I usually had my shit more together than this; we had been talking and seeing each other for weeks without incident and now I was willing to throw away our perfect unblemished record. What the hell was I doing? I was here with another guy. One who had asked a question that I still hadn't answered.

"My best friend, Ashlyn— the one I told you about who used to work with me at the bar," I explained turning back my attention to Josh, you know the guy I was considering kissing or perhaps maybe sleeping with tonight. "Well, Ash is engaged to Dan, so I kind of got acquainted with the band through her."

It felt dirty after I'd said it, like my friendship with Jason and Troy was an incidental after effect of Ash and Dan's relationship, which wasn't true. I don't know why I didn't say, we'd met in a club one day and all become friends. Maybe I was worried that my real feelings for Troy would be revealed unless I kept it light and uncomplicated. I hated myself for saying it all the same.

"Really?" Jason laughed. I was petrified by what he was going to say next. "I don't think Ash can take all the credit for it. Megs made a pretty memorable first impression." Busted! I prayed the walk down memory lane would end there.

"Yeah, that was a great night," Troy added, his voice tight but his face unreadable. "You might want to keep an eye on her, buddy; she has a tendency to fall down if she has too much to drink." Okay, that was a cheap shot. He hadn't reacted this way on our disastrous double date *or* after our numerous sexual encounters. The tension in the air crackled between us.

"Um, did I miss something?" Josh looked awkwardly between us. It was obvious that *something had been missed*. Even Josh in his post-Power-Station-appreciation glow could spot it a mile away.

Troy answered before I had a chance to open my mouth. "Miss something?" He let out a huge laugh. "We're just messing around. I'm not used to seeing Megs so serious, that's all."

While Josh seemed satisfied with Troy's explanation, I didn't miss the edge in Troy's voice. My heart was beating so fast I was positive that any minute it was going to leap out of my chest and land on the pool table. Was Troy trying to prove a point? And did he have to do it so publically or so sarcastically? It seemed I hadn't been the only person who caught the things-are-getting-strange vibe with Jason studying both Troy and I carefully before stepping in.

"Hey, Josh, why don't you let me buy you a beer while these two rack up the balls for the next game." Jase tapped Josh on the shoulder. "They have this awesome microbrew that is off-menu, I'll get us hooked up."

CRASH RIDE

If it wouldn't have attracted too much attention I would have thrown myself at Jason and kissed him, his plan to give me and Troy *a moment*, an answer to my silent prayer that this eyeballing contest we seemed to be playing would come to an end.

Josh looked genuinely pleased that Jason had extended a private invitation. If he'd suspected it was anything more, he wasn't letting on. "Sure, as long as Megan doesn't mind. You want another drink, baby?"

"No, I'm fine." I gave him a polite smile and lifted my mostly full Long Island. "Thanks for asking. Go ahead with Jason. I don't mind." Pushing him out the door and telling him not to hurry right back would probably raise alarm bells, so I went with nonchalant.

"Awesome, thanks, baby." Josh gave me a squeeze before walking off with Jason, his voice trailing off in the distance. "So you guys are releasing a new album soon huh?"

"Your new boyfriend I assume." It wasn't a question; Troy tipped his chin toward the direction that Josh and Jase had left. He didn't smile as he folded his arms in front of his chest.

"He isn't my boyfriend, just a guy I'm seeing," I snapped, wondering why he was acting so cagey. "I don't know why you are being weird about it. I told you I was dating someone."

I didn't trust myself to be near him, knowing how twisted he made my emotions.

Troy didn't have the same concerns about getting closer to me it seemed as he took a step in my direction. His hand tilted my chin to look him in his beautiful eyes. "You might want to clarify that with him. How many more times can he call you baby?" I could feel his breath on my skin as he spoke. "And I'm not the one being weird, *Megan*."

It was much harder to be strong when I had to look at him, to deny that I wasn't making a huge mistake by being with someone else. "What do you want me to say? You want me to tell him we slept together? I didn't think that would help our cause of keeping *that* in the past."

"Jesus, Megs, there is a lot of room between not knowing me and fucking me." His hand grazed across his chin. "You didn't think to pick somewhere in the middle?" His forehead crinkled in confusion.

"I panicked. I wasn't expecting to see you here. I wasn't prepared to answer questions about us. I just thought it would be easier…"

"Questions about us? Aren't we supposed to be friends, I don't understand why that's so complicated. You had no problem telling *me* about *him*." I saw the hurt flicker through his hazel eyes. "You introduce me as your friend, not just some fucking dude you happen to know because of Ash."

"I don't know what to say. You were never just some dude. I'm sorry that I said it and more than that, I'm sorry that I implied that you weren't my friend."

Sorry didn't even begin to cut it. I felt horrible, there had been no need to lie about how I'd known Troy and yet, I had. It was the guilt. As ridiculous as it sounded, I felt like I was cheating. Cheating on Troy and cheating on myself by being with someone else. It took seeing them together in the room to put that in perspective. Troy wasn't some guy I could just forget by dating someone else. He wasn't someone I could just replace. I had been stupid to assume that I could, and even more stupid for falling in love with him. Yeah, I had avoided the word, danced around infatuation and lust, but what I felt was beyond those.

"Fuck, Megs, when you give those puppy dog eyes, it's really hard for me to be pissed at you." Troy rolled his eyes and he gave me a smile I didn't think I deserved. He moved in closer and rubbed my arm with the tips of his fingers.

I shook my head softly and whispered. "Don't be pissed at me, I'm already pissed at myself."

"Yeah?" Troy raised an eyebrow. "And why are you pissed at yourself?"

A slow breath escaped my lips as I closed whatever distance there was between us. "There isn't enough time to list all the reasons right now, Troy."

It was instinct. I couldn't be this so close to him and not touch him. It felt natural, like where I belonged. It wasn't about sex or lust, it was a

CRASH RIDE

comfort I couldn't describe and it's what I needed. My head fell against his chest as my arms strained to wrap around him.

"Megs, what are you doing?" Troy chuckled against my hair.

My eyes closed as I absorbed him, savoring the moment. If I could have stopped us both from talking I would have. "I just need you to hold me right now. I know they are going to be back really soon, just hold me for a minute."

"Megs, if there is something wrong you would tell me, right?" Troy gently ran his hand through my hair; there was a concern in his voice that hadn't been there before. "This guy isn't being an asshole is he?"

I signed as I answered honestly. "No, the only asshole here is me."

He held me close to his body for a while and I let his warmness envelop me. It was selfish and I had no right to the comfort it afforded me, but I wanted it anyway. He wasn't mine, he had never been mine and there would never be a time he would be. I'd tried to forget him, get over him and even talk myself into the fact that what we'd had was purely a sexual connection. What I had completely ignored was the truth, that I'd fallen for him—God it was so much more than that—and I wanted to have a relationship with him. Any other guy that came into my life was never going to measure up. It hadn't been fair to anyone, least of all not to Josh.

I reluctantly peeled myself away from Troy's chest, giving him my best smile to reassure him I was okay. The last thing Josh deserved was to come back and see me in the arms of another guy, especially when he'd held such high hopes for tonight. It was bad enough my heart already belonged to someone else; I wasn't going to lie about it as well. Maybe Josh didn't want a relationship, maybe he was looking for a good time; in any case, I wasn't the girl for either of those things. The only fair thing would be to tell him.

Troy studied me curiously as I moved to the opposite end of the pool table and racked up the balls in the triangle. I had no intention of playing but it gave me something to do, something to take my mind off the mess that I had apparently got myself into.

Troy edged closer to me, his hand resting next to me on the pool table. "Megs, don't go home with him," he pleaded, my heart fracturing with the sound. His beautiful eyes were focused and serious. It hurt to look at them.

"Hey, baby. This beer is the *shit*. You want a taste?" Josh waltzed in, a half consumed bottle of beer in his hand and just like that, whatever moment Troy and I had had was over. Josh's eyes flicked over the racked-up balls on the felt and grinned. "Awesome, you set up. Who's breaking?"

Never had a more appropriate question been asked. *Who's breaking?* I was, and I didn't want to. My feet miraculously took a few steps in front of the other and ended up by Josh's side. "Would it be okay if we didn't play. I'm a little tired."

"Come on, Megs." Jason looked disappointed as he grabbed a pool cue from the wall. "Stay and play a game."

Josh put his arms around me and I tried not to flinch. "You sure you don't want to play for a bit?" He was disappointed. His chance to rub shoulders with the rich-and-famous sabotaged by a moody date.

"You can stay if you want, you don't have to leave." Honestly at this point it didn't matter. I was going home alone, so regardless if I walked out the door by myself or not, our date was coming to a very quick finale.

"Sorry boys, looks like Megan wants to call it a night." Josh looked hopeful as he waved to the guys. "Maybe some other time?"

Troy leaned against his pool cue and gave us a tight smile. "Sure, anytime." I was almost positive that offer was not genuine.

"Bye, Jase, Troy. I'll see you soon." I gave them both a half-hearted wave and let Josh put his arm around my waist.

He quickly swallowed what was left of his beer and placed the empty bottle on a nearby table. "See you, Troy, Jason. Thanks for the beer."

Jase nodded and gave us a warm smile. "No problem, enjoy your night."

I forced my way back though the maze of bodies, just needing to get out of the club. It felt like I couldn't breathe, a condition made worse by Josh's hands around my waist. I was almost dizzy by the time we made it to the front door.

"Hey baby, what's the hurry?" He eyed me curiously as the bouncer who had let us in earlier opened the door to let us back out.

I didn't answer, instead I climbed the stairs that lead to the sidewalk, all my concentration on putting one foot in front of the other so I didn't fall on my face. A trip to the emergency room was not on the agenda for tonight.

Relief flooded me once I'd finally made it to the top, the street still brimming with night traffic. "Megan, slow down." Josh grabbed my wrist as I tried to hail a cab. "You want to tell me what that was about?" He spun me around and forced me to look at him. He didn't seem mad, which was a plus, but he wasn't going to let me get into a cab without some kind of explanation.

Words eluded me. What did I even say? He was a fun guy, sure, we weren't a perfect match, but he'd been so incredibly nice to me. He had been a distraction and that hadn't been fair. So rather than continue the lie, I went with the truth and hoped it would stop me from feeling like a total jerk.

"Look, you're a nice guy but we can't see each other any more. I thought I was ready to date someone but I'm not. I don't want to give you the it's-not-you-it's-me line but it really is *me*. I just can't do this."

He slowly let go of my wrist. "Is this because you're running away from *him*?" His head jerked to the direction of the rickety stairwell.

"Huh?" My mouth dropped open. How did he know? Did one of my subconscious thoughts actually come out of my mouth or had he seen us together? Did I deny or confirm it? Now would have been a good time for some random act of God. In the end, my silence had been enough.

"Megan, you and me, we're in a similar line of work. You'd be surprised how much you learn about a person when they are lying in your chair, waiting for you to tattoo them. Some get chatty, some stay quiet like you did; either way, you can read all you need to read from their body." There was a kindness in his eyes when he spoke, it made me hate myself even more. "There are usually three different types of people who come and get ink."

He held up his fingers and started to list them. "One. The living canvas. For these people their skin is blank pages that they use to tell their story. There is no separation between the art and them. It's a part of them as much as an ear or a toe. It's an addiction as well as an expression. Two. The weekend warrior. They go under the needle to earn cool points or to follow trend. These are the people who usually get some lame tribal band around their arm or a tramp stamp. They get tats that are highly visible and often cheesy. I don't judge, but I assume that five to ten years down the track they will be spending time with a laser. Three. The tortured soul. They use the art as therapy, to memorialize something or a loved one. They mark their skins with tributes and dedications or a connection to something or someone. It's just for them; displayed or not displayed it wouldn't mean any more or less.

"I knew when you came into my studio that you weren't a weekend warrior and you had virgin skin so it just left the last option. That's why I asked you to sit down and let me draw something. I could tell you needed it."

"They are beautiful." My hands involuntary brushed across my hips where my tattoos were safely hidden.

"Like the girl who's wearing them." He smiled. "I didn't know it was a guy, but I sensed your head was elsewhere. You're *really* pretty though and I just thought I'd take a chance. Hoping whatever demon was chasing you would hopefully quiet down and we could get to know each other a little better. You seemed like you would be a lot of fun. The not wanting to kiss me should have tipped me off that you weren't interested, but you know..." He gave me an adorable smile. "I figured I'd keep trying."

"I'm sorry." I swallowed. "I feel so fucking terrible right now."

Apparently the pedestrians on the street didn't care for my heart felt apology, nor did they seem invested in our chat; their heated stares glared as they jostled past us as we stood in the middle of the sidewalk. Josh gently took my hand and guided me away from the foot traffic and onto a nearby stoop.

"Why? 'Cause you went out with me?" He rubbed the base of his chin, his eyes confused like he could comprehend why I'd felt bad.

Because I used you, because there was never going to be anyone else other than him. The words I eventually said were softer but no less true. "Because I let you believe there was more than there was."

"You didn't do anything like that." He laughed. "I had a ball, didn't you have fun? Cheese fries and drag queens, I don't think I've ever had a date like that."

"Yeah, it was nice." I agreed, for the most part it had been pleasant. It certainly wasn't terrible and as horrible as it sounded, he had been a lovely distraction.

"Megan, I really like seeing that beautiful smile and it's been cool hanging out with you over the last week or so. But a man can't really compete with a memory, especially one that is still very much in your life." He gave me slight shrug of the shoulders.

Did I explain further or did I let it go? I'd never met a guy who'd seemed so relaxed about the fact his date wasn't actually interested in him. It confused me a little but most of all, I was glad. Josh had been right about one thing, we *were* in a similar line of work. He knew exactly what to say and exactly how to say it. There was going to be no dramatic showdown on the street and I was glad that I had walked into his shop that day. He'd given me so much more than the beautiful feathers that now graced my skin.

"Do I owe you any extra money for the counseling? I feel like those tattoos were hugely under priced," I asked cautiously, thankful that out of all the tattoo shops in all of New York, I walked into his.

Another shrug, another smile. "Nah, you were a nice canvas to work on. I got to look at your beautiful skin for hours instead of a big sweaty biker. You also smell a lot nicer than they usually do."

And just like that it was over. It had been almost anticlimactic. We both knew we probably wouldn't be seeing each again, not unless I decided to get another tattoo, and there was an easy sense of calm around the end of it. If I didn't think it would send the wrong signal, I would have given him a big hug but instead I opted for a shoulder bump and a smile. "Thanks, Josh, I showered that morning and everything. I'm so glad I didn't stink."

He playfully bumped me back and smiled. "I know the date's pretty much a bust, but will you let me drive you home?"

"Yeah, I would like that."

15
Troy

I CAN'T BELIEVE SHE JUST LEFT WITH THE ASSHOLE. SHE HAD ASKED me to hold her, and then she turned around and left with *him*. One thing was fucking clear— she still wanted me as much as I still wanted her. I felt it and I saw it in her eyes when I'd wrapped my arms around her. It was not fucking one-sided and all she had to do was *not* go home with him.

I didn't say a fucking word when she told me she had started dating some dude. The chair I threw at the wall, well that couldn't be helped. She was so cagey about how they'd met. He wasn't even her type as far as I could tell but if she was happy, then I'd keep a lid on it. I'd even kept my trap shut when she mentioned he'd kissed her. Yep. That had been a fun night. I'd gotten into my Lambo and redlined the shit out of it before I calmed down enough to finally go home. There was no reason why she shouldn't be kissing some other guy, not unless you counted the fact that I didn't want her to. Nope, those lips I only wanted on me.

Seeing his hands on her, calling her *baby*, was more than I could fucking stand. But the kicker was her playing it off like she barely knew me. The fucking icing on the cake.

I'd been ready to tell her to forget it; I wasn't really interested in being some chump who sat on the sidelines. But those eyes, when she said she was sorry, there was no way those words would come out of my mouth. She didn't just look fucking sorry, she looked sad. Tore me up. I didn't care if it was me or the situation— I wanted it to stop. The hug; it was the beginning of the end.

My hands on her were something I'd avoided. Why torture myself? But the minute that I had her, there was no way I could pretend she didn't matter, that I didn't want her. That I didn't think about her, each and every fucking night.

So what did she do? She turned around and left with some other guy who, as far as I was concerned, hadn't proved he deserved her.

"Dude, that vein in your neck bulges any more than it is now, you're going to spring a leak." Jase's stare nailed me from across the table.

"I just think she can do better than him. C'mon, Jase, even you can admit she doesn't belong with him." The pool cue in my hand was probably getting a little more pressure than it would have liked.

Jase shrugged. "He seemed okay." He pulled the cue out from my death grip before it snapped. Smart move.

"Okay? Are you serious, brother? He called her *Megan* the whole fucking time. Everyone knows she prefers Megs." None of this shit was even close to being okay.

Jase took a swig of his beer, his smirk poking out from behind the bottle. "So it's her date's tendency to use her *real* name that has you in a mood. Good to know." His shit-eating grin got wider. Smug bastard.

Too juiced up to stand still, I paced around the room. "And what the fuck is up with calling her *baby*? He's known her for like five fucking minutes. Maybe he should've just pulled his dick out and taken a piss on her, it would have been less obvious."

Jase eyeballed me hard, planting his ass on the beat-up couch beside the table. "So you going to tell me how long you've been sleeping with her or we going to insult the poor dude some more?"

"Fuck."

I thought it as well as said it. No point denying it now, I'd been acting like a moody asshole since Megs had walked in. It was only a matter of time before he wised up and put two and two together. Must've been why he asked Josh to go have a friendly beer with him at the bar, not his hard-on for the off-menu microbrew. He'd clued up that we needed to talk, and like the stand-up guy that he was, he made it happen. I parked my ass on the chair next to him and slowly let out a breath.

"I'd suspected as much." Jase casually took another mouthful of beer. "Dan might have his head up his ass, but I've noticed your little secret squirrel meetings with Megs, and your lack of female company."

"We thought we'd kept it under wraps." I pinched the bridge of my nose and hoped no one else had caught the vibe.

"Trust me, dude, I'm almost positive no one has noticed. James and Alex are so focused on the album and we've already established Dan's main concern is making Ash his Mrs."

"Why didn't you say something?"

"I figured if you hadn't mentioned it, you probably didn't want to talk about it. I wasn't going to push the issue."

That was the big difference between Jason and Dan. If I'd been sitting here with Dan, he would have run his mouth for the next few hours demanding to know the how's and what's of the situation. Jase on the other hand, had no interest in the details. He just sat back and relaxed, and if you wanted to spill your guts then he'd happily listen. No pressure, either way. It was the main reason why I'd called him and asked to shoot some pool with me tonight. I didn't want the fucking twenty questions that usually came with a night out with Dan.

"Megs had said she had a date tonight, I had no idea she was coming here. He'd already kissed her, third date and everything. Do the math. I wasn't going to sit at home like a fucking little bitch."

"So I'm your rebound. Nice." Jase tipped his chin with a grin.

"Well getting loaded and other women were off the table so... No one gives a fuck who we are here. I just wanted to shoot some pool, maybe have a beer without someone trying to crawl into my lap."

That had been the plan at least. Then she'd walked through the doorway; looking so hot I'd had to nail my feet to floor so I didn't walk straight over to her and attack her mouth. The fact she was with a dude meant jack shit to me. As far as I was concerned, the asshole was touching what didn't belong to him.

My head fell back against the couch, wondering if while I was sitting with my dick in my hand, the tattoo king of NYC was rounding second base. "This is so fucked up, man." And wasn't that the understatement of the fucking century.

"So, I'm guessing this was more than just a sex thing." Jase proved how smart he was by reading between the lines.

I shut my eyes and let out a breath. "Yep."

"You love her?"

Jase's simple question was like taking a bat swing upside my head. Did I love her? I didn't want to be without her, and if that's what love was then yeah, I was there.

Well, fuck me. I wasn't just being a jealous asshole, nope. It went much deeper than that, but there was no way the first time I would be saying it would be to Jase. It would be to Megs, or not at all.

"What I do know for sure is, that I like her a hell of a lot and I don't want her with someone else."

Jase drained the rest of his beer and cracked his knuckles. "Sounds like we have problem."

"Yep."

"You want to go get a burger or something, talk some of this shit out?"

"Should we paint each other's toenails as well?"

"Well I sure as hell ain't going to try and braid that shit you call hair."

"Let's get out of here, I need some distance."

"Right behind you."

While we'd decided against painting each other's nails, we did end up back at my place. Somewhere in between throwing a few hands of poker and tossing back a few beers, I'd given Jase the rundown on the Megs dilemma. It didn't solve shit but it kept me from punching holes in the drywall. I didn't even want to think about how Megs had spent her night. Nope, not going there. I was pushing that shit to the side of my brain that had a big do-not-disturb sign hanging off it.

We must have crashed at some point because when I woke up in the morning there was a half spilled bottle of beer on the floor and a passed out Jason Irwin snoring on the rug.

"Dude." I reached down and gave him a shove. "How much did we drink last night?"

Jase peeled open an eye. "Fuck, man. Your floor sucks." He scrubbed his face with his hand. "I have the mother of all headaches. I need about ten Excedrin and five gallons of coffee."

"On it." I fished my phone out of my pocket and sent Dan a text to bring some coffee around. The day wasn't going to be pretty for either of us. The empties of the floor gave me a hint we'd drank more than a case between us.

My stomach rolled as I made it my feet. "Grab the door when he gets here. I'll get the Excedrin so this sucks a little less." Not that I was convinced they were going to make a shit of difference, nothing in my medicine cabinet was even going to make a dent.

I needed out of here. The place, the situation and the mind frame. At least that's what I kept telling myself as I snagged the bottle of pills from the bathroom cabinet and went back to the living room.

"Fuck, you both look like shit. Rough night?" Dan tossed me the what-the-fuck the minute I walked back in.

Awesome. My morning hadn't sucked enough.

"Don't start asswipe. I have zero mood for your shit."

"Wow. You seriously need to get laid." Dan handed me his usual response as he parked his ass on my two-seater.

Yeah, *that* was the fucking solution. Not likely. "Thanks but I don't think any amount of pussy is going to cure the migraine." I tossed the bottle of Excedrin to Jase.

"Shit going down I need to know about?" Dan eyeballed me as I collapsed into the chair beside him. He didn't need to say he had my back— the look was enough.

"Nope, just need to sober myself up so I can drive." That's about as much as I was willing to share. My head fell back and I squeezed my eyes shut, willing my liver to kick in and get the show on the road.

"You taking off?" Dan asked.

"Yeah, a couple of days. Maybe Atlantic City?" My eyes rolled back into focus as I lifted my lids. Who knew where I'd end up. The location was irrelevant. The distance was what mattered.

"You want some company? I've got no where to be." Jase swallowed his pills followed by his Java chaser.

"Fuck it, we should all go. We'll be like the Wolf pack. Let me square things away with Ash." Dan didn't bother to check if I wanted the tag along. I guessed this was his version of trying to make me feel better.

"No offence, but I don't need my hand held."

"Stop being a buzzkill. We'll even find someone to suck your dick while we're there. Trust me, it will improve your *zero mood* bullshit. Bring your suit too, I want to play the tables and I'm going to need a spotter," Dan added, not giving a fuck that he hadn't been invited.

"Fuck me, this isn't about your scheme for counting cards is it?" Jase lowered his cup.

Dan folded his arms across his chest not willing to admit his plan was bogus. "Hate all you want, but that shit is full proof."

"Hey Rain Man." I didn't even bother addressing how much we weren't going to be getting my dick sucked. "You get caught doing that, a big scary asshole takes you into a little back room and messes you up so badly you're going to spend the rest of your days shitting into a bag."

"Seriously, Troy." Dan rolled his eyes. "I'm going to need to hook you up with Megs with some therapy. That is just messed up."

Silence.

"Okay. Someone want to tell me why we're eyeballing each other and don't give me some bullshit excuse about being hung over." Dan shot us a both the start-talking look.

"We saw Megs last night." This was going to be fun. Of all the things I didn't want to talk about, *Megs* and *last night* were at the top of the list. "I was less than polite to her and her date."

"Megs was on a date last night? Huh, must have been the last one. Anyway, you need to jump on the horn and make that shit right." Dan poked me in the chest. "No need to be a pussy about it, just tell her you're sorry and move on. She'll forgive you. That girl is a sweetheart."

Ain't no way things would be smoothed over by a phone call but the dude wasn't to know that. How would that call even go? Hey, I know you were with some other dude last night but I wised up to the fact I'm in love with you and need you to be my girl. Too little, too late on that one. And what the fuck was the rest of the stuff he was talking about?

"Wait a minute. What do you mean by *last* one?"

Dan waved it off, already bored with conversation. "I mean she called Ash last night, she isn't seeing the tattoo guy anymore. Something about it not working out. I didn't pay too much attention."

"Dan, I need you to focus." I grabbed him by the shirt and leveled him with a stare. My heart thumping like the fucker was keeping time to Metallica. "Are you sure that's what she said?"

"Lay off asshole, fuck." He pushed off my hands and straightened his shirt. "Yes, that's what she said. What's the big deal?"

The big deal was that last I saw of Megs she was upset and needed to be held. I didn't know the why's or the what's, but shit wasn't right. I'd asked her not to go home with the asshole she'd walked with, but she left anyway. His fucking hands on her as they walked out. She didn't fight him so I assumed any further attention was going to come courtesy of the guy who kept calling her *baby*. They didn't look like they were heading for splitsville.

"When we saw them, they didn't look like they were about to break up." I was still trying to wrap my head around it.

"Well maybe after you saw them they got into a fight or maybe the kid found Jesus and was no longer interested in pussy? Whatever the reason, they ain't together anymore." Dan clapped his hands together and rubbed in anticipation. "Now let's talk AC."

There was no way I was getting in a car and going anywhere right now unless it was to Megs's apartment. I didn't give a fuck if I had to bang her damn door down, she was going to talk to me and tell me why she'd been so sad, and then I would tell her that this bullshit about keeping away from each other was just that—bullshit.

"Yeah, that trip ain't happening." I needed to see her. "Dan, you're right. I need to go make this right."

"Oh fuck, man. I was looking forward to taking down the house." Dan whined like it was an actual possibility. Poor fucker didn't stand a chance at a legit casino.

"Please go home before you hurt yourself. I have genuine fear for you, brother." It was bewildering to me how he had managed to skate through life without doing jail time.

"With pleasure." Dan smirked before flipping us off. "Unlike you two morons, I have an amazing woman to go home to."

Dan headed to my door and I followed him out. The clock was ticking and I was still pissed I was standing in my apartment and not on my way to her.

Dan stopped in my doorway. "Troy, smooth over whatever needs smoothing. I don't want to have to punch you in the sack 'cause Megs won't talk to you at the wedding."

That wouldn't be happening. Her and me, we were going to work this shit out, and she was not going to be dating or kissing any other douchebags. Nope. I was done sitting back and pretending that what we were doing made sense. Whatever the chances were, I'd be taking them, and short of her telling me she felt nothing, I wouldn't be walking away, any time soon.

Maybe I was a cocky son of bitch, but I had zero hesitation in looking at Dan and telling him, "I've got this."

'16

Megan

WHAT TIME WAS IT? MY EYES SLOWLY OPENED TO SUNLIGHT burning my retinas. Like a dumbass, I'd forgotten to close my drapes last night before I'd collapsed into bed. It was too early and I had no reason to be awake. Ugh. I needed coffee.

Josh had driven me home, given me sweet kiss on the cheek and then said goodbye. He even waited until I was safely inside my apartment before leaving. He wasn't even weird about. I hoped this didn't mean the next guy I dated was an asshole, not that I would be dating anyone anytime soon.

Rather than going to bed like a *normal* person and trying to forget my horrible night, I instead voted to stay up watching cheesy RomCom reruns. With a box of Kleenex and obviously no common sense, I watched as time after time the hero found his way to his heroine and they walked off into the sunset together. It was enough to make me want to hurl my snotty, scrunched up tissues at the screen. But instead of doing that—which would have been totally reasonable— I just sat there and

CRASH RIDE

watched another. The definition of insanity is repeating the same action and expecting a different result. I was clearly insane.

Damn it. I tried to squeeze my eyelids shut and hoped to ignore the happy beams of light that danced on my comforter. Assholes, I didn't want to be awake, and I sure as hell didn't want to be happy. Yet, ironically, my eyes were wide open and I didn't feel so bad. Maybe it was a new day's perspective or maybe my fatigued brain was giving me a reprieve, whatever the reason, I was grabbing onto it.

Ugh, my legs kicked off the covers —it was too hot. Wordless pictures played on the television, the same screen that had tormented me. While I had been smart enough to mute the stupid thing, I hadn't turned it off. The remote nestled within the mess of crumpled tissues —the graveyard of fallen tears on my bedside table. Tragic.

The buzzer from my front door demanded attention; the relenting sound meant my fantasy of staying in bed was not going to happen— my second disappointment for the day.

I assumed it was Ash. She had wanted to come over last night after I called her. No amount of telling her it was unnecessary would appease her. I was just glad she waited until the morning, letting me have my pity party undisturbed. Hopefully she had a really big coffee and maybe a muffin.

Reluctantly, I swung my legs off the mattress. My feet hit the floor heavily as my hands scrubbed my face. I tried to not imagine what I looked like. Nightmare came to mind. Or possibly, one of those scary zombie walking dead dolls. Ash was going to have to overlook my bad hair day and my puffy eyes.

Slowly I trudged to the door, the buzzer continuing to sound. Geez, Ash, give me a minute. My finger hit the release on the lower external entry and I cracked open my front door, waiting for her inevitable arrival. I really hope she brought that coffee, I needed the caffeine hit like no other.

The sounds of footsteps echoed up the staircase, my door flew open to reveal… Troy Harris? Huh? My head couldn't reconcile what I seeing.

"Troy? What are you doing here?"

He didn't answer.

Instead, he kissed me. *Really* kissed me. Like those stupid, sappy movies I'd watched, he wrapped his arms around me and he lifted me off the floor. His mouth was on mine like he needed me to breathe.

I didn't care I hadn't brushed my teeth or that I looked like shit, none of it got any airtime. I wanted the kiss to last forever, for him to hold me with the desperation that he was…forever.

"You've been crying." He peeled his lips from mine and lifted my chin to look at me. "Did that asshole hurt you?"

"He wasn't an asshole, and no, he didn't hurt me." Josh had been far from being an asshole. He should have hated me for using him as my rebound guy but instead had been sweet and kind. I shook my head and repeated. "He didn't hurt me."

"Did I hurt you?" Troy's finger trailed against the edge of my jaw.

"I hurt myself." I shrugged. "You did nothing wrong." He hadn't. He had just followed my fucked up diagram on how to screw up a friendship, relationship, whatever it was. I still have no idea what we actually were.

"That's bullshit. I did plenty wrong." He lowered his lips and kissed me on the mouth again. I guessed that was the end of the conversation and as long as he kept kissing me, I didn't care.

Troy's hands threaded through my hair, his fingers tangled in the messy waves as the kiss intensified. He moved his hands down my neck and then across my shoulders like he was trying to remember me by touch. It was erotic and sensual and sweet baby Jesus— it was really turning me on.

While my mind was currently being dictated by the throbbing need between my legs, it had occurred to me in a small window of clarity that we were standing in the entranceway of my apartment with my front door *wide* open.

That would *not* do. I pulled him closer and kicked the door closed, the wooden doorframe shaking under the force of it being slammed shut.

CRASH RIDE

Troy responded by pushing me back into my living room, my feet doing their best not to trip over my rug.

We should probably have moved to the bedroom—that would have been the smart thing to do— but we had already established that when it came to sex, Troy and I weren't very smart. So rather than fight it, I gave in as we tumbled onto my large sofa.

Our bodies were pressed together as we clawed at each other, our mouths too preoccupied with kissing to be worried about something as silly as words. I didn't want to speak. Not at that moment anyway.

I'm not sure how it happened but I pulled off his T-shirt. One minute I was grabbing at the soft cotton fabric, bunching it in my hands and the next minute it was off his chest and on the floor. It seemed like a better place for it.

He seemed to have the same idea, with my thin cotton tank top magically being pulled over my head and disappearing over the back of the couch. His hands moved to my naked breasts, he grunted in appreciation over my lack of a bra. It also meant less to take off, which was another plus.

Troy laid back across the cushions of the sofa and pulled me with him. His hands alternated between rolling my nipples between his fingers to palming my breasts.

I wiggled on top of him as my hands moved down his chest, my fingertips feeling each curve and ripple of his defined torso. The bulge in his pants got harder as I straddled him and rocked against it.

His hands left my body and I whimpered a protest but was quickly pacified when I saw they were getting busying unzipping his fly and pulling down his jeans. Ok, then. He toed off his shoes and reached down to yank off his socks, my body rocking against his erection while he tried to undress himself underneath me.

He had only managed to maneuver his jeans half way down his thighs when he'd lost his patience, lifting me off his hard cock and moving me to the other cushion of the couch. The jeans that had been giving him so much trouble were kicked off violently as I watched beside him. His boxers, they were the next to go—a casualty in our desperation to get naked.

"Get them off," he growled as he tugged at my sleep shorts. My clothing, the next victim, his attention focused on getting me as naked as he was.

His body was so toned and defined; the way his muscles flexed when he moved made him look lethal. The tattoos that covered his chest and arms enhanced an already spectacular view.

"Megs?" He stopped the desperate tugging of my shorts as my feather tattoos came into view. His finger gently traced the delicate outline. "When did you get these?"

The confusion in his eyes was an easy read. Skin that had previously been bare had two small but delicate feathers marking it. "A couple of days after we last…"

"Why?"

"Because I thought we'd never have this again." The emotion was thick in my throat as I tried not to cry. "I needed the memory. When I was with you it felt like feathers in the wind. Crazy, flying out of control—exhilarating. But when it stopped— when we stopped, they floated away. It was the only way I could get them back."

"Fuck." He cradled me, running his hand over my skin. "They're beautiful. You're beautiful and I've never seen anything more perfect."

"Troy Harris." My lips gently kissed his chest.

"Yeah?" His hands played with my hair.

"I don't want to talk anymore about things that make me sad. I'm still wearing pants and you're naked. You want to do something about that or—" I didn't get the chance to finish.

Hands, fingers, lips and a tangle of limbs, he pressed his body back to mine. My sleep shorts and panties quickly left my body and joined the pile of discarded clothing. I wasn't sure if it had been by my hand or his, but I was thankful we were now skin on skin.

The head of his cock teased at my opening as I wiggled beneath him, it felt amazing as I arched my back using friction to rub against me. The mental piercing hit me in just the right spot.

"Easy," he warned as he reached down in between my legs and thumbed circles around my clit. "I'm not suited up yet."

"I can't wait." I bucked against him, wanting to be filled with him. It felt like I had been waiting for an eternity. "I want you in me."

His jaw tensed as he lifted off me, his eyes raking up and down my body as he fished for jeans on the floor. I couldn't look away, the shine of the metal in his cock catching the sunlight each time he moved.

Success, he held up the small foil packet with his fingers that he'd dug out of his jeans pocket and all I could think of was that shinny ring that I wanted so desperately inside of me. I couldn't wait. Moving across to him I placed my lips around the head of his cock, my mouth closed around him and I flicked my tongue along the length. "Megs," he hissed out as his hand went around my head, his body thrusting with each and every suck I gave him.

My teeth pulled gently against the ring and I saw his eyes roll back from pleasure, the throbbing between my legs almost unbearable.

His fingers wrapped around his cock and pulled it from my lips, his grip travelling along his length as I watched him rip open the condom wrapper with his teeth and the slide it out with his fingers. It was mesmerizing as he quickly went to work, the piercing carefully encased in the latex before it rolled down the rest of his cock.

And then, in one thrust he was in me. Yep, just that quickly. One minute I'm sitting down watching him stroke himself, and then the next minute, I'm on my back. It was hard and fast and my body tightened around him. Had it always been this good?

"Troy," I moaned, my head flying back in ecstasy as my body welcomed the invasion. "I need you." And I meant it. I needed him in every sense of the word and I didn't want this to ever stop.

"You've got me." His hands found my hips as he moved in and out of me with long, deliberate thrusts. "You've got me," he repeated, getting deeper with each time.

It wasn't going to take long, the anticipation had worked me up into a state that was making me feel crazy. I wanted this, wanted him, so badly that I hadn't even explored what this meant. Had we returned back to the let's-have-sex-but-not-date or was this something else? At that moment, I didn't care.

Our bodies crashed into each other, his thrust countered by mine. The movements of the frenzied pace getting me so close that I teetered on the edge of bliss.

"Touch yourself. I want to see you play with yourself with my cock in you." He groaned as he bit down on his lip.

I reached down to the slickness between my legs, twisting my fingers over my clit as I exploded around him. Tingles travelled up and down my arms and legs as the wave of my orgasm rode out. One more thrust was all it took, his cock pulsing inside of me as he came hard.

He collapsed against me, panting as his heavy body almost crushed me beneath him. I loved it, the heat and his weight on me. It felt real, tangible. Raw. It's what I needed.

Troy's arms covered me, wrapping around my body as he shifted to the side. His large frame wedged between the back of the couch and my body. Our legs intertwined at the knees.

It was at around that point that my post-coital buzz started to dissipate, and my common sense kicked in. I had slept with Troy again. After I had promised myself I wouldn't do this anymore.

Did I have any self-control? Like, at all?

Troy's lips tenderly kissed my neck and in a moment of braveness — or possibly fear— I asked what I had never had the courage to ask before. "So… where does that leave us?"

It was probably too ambiguous a question but I needed to know what it was we were doing. I would leave the scary *are we dating now?* chat for at least a few minutes, following up with *so does this mean you're my boyfriend?* And my pièce di résistance would be *oh and we have to be exclusive.* That would be a fun conversation that would surely send him running out my door. Still, what choice did I have? I couldn't do the sex and no commitment thing. Even if Troy Harris was the provider of that sex, it just wasn't enough for my fragile heart to handle. Troy's fingers lightly circled my skin, sending chills up my spine. "It leaves us right here. Together."

"*Together*, together or just together and not together?" There was a lot of gray area that needed to be clarified and now was probably a good time to do that. You know, before we did something stupid like have sex again without discussing it. Sure, like that could happen *again?* Every single time I was around him alone, I swear I ended up naked. If we were going to continue to get naked, we would have to be in some kind of, I don't know, commitment.

"It's going to be complicated. You said so yourself." I expected him to start running any time now. Complicated was usually like mood cyanide. Things going well —here, add some *complicated* to it—boom good feeling gone.

"Turns out, I was wrong. It's actually really simple." Troy's fingers tiptoed down my arm and across my stomach. His voice had no hesitation. "I want to be with you, you want to be with me. No one else needs to come into that equation."

I took a breath and really had to concentrate not to hold it. "Troy, I know I said we can just have sex and be casual." I slowly exhaled. "But I don't think I can do that. Not anymore. I need more."

Yeah me! There you have it. I finally said it. Who claimed I couldn't admit when I was wrong, and I was clearly *very* wrong about my earlier judgment.

"Look at me." Troy stopped toying with my naked body—which I had to admit was slightly distracting in the most delicious sort of way— and positioned himself so he could face me. "You think you are the only one who's wanted this for the last few months? This isn't just about sex."

"I still don't know what that means?" I whispered quietly as I looked into his eyes. Tell me, I wanted to beg. Tell me exactly what this means. Tell me that you are only mine.

"It means that we do the couple thing. Exclusively. No more talk about dating other people. That was a dumb idea."

The world's problems that existed an hour ago still existed. Sickness, hunger, war etc. they were still very real, present. But in my little world—the bubble I was in— there was only a Zen-like bliss I couldn't have even imagined.

Can a heart actually fill with happiness? Because if it could, mine was about to burst. I would stop short of chasing rainbows and unicorns but to me, this was the best-case scenario multiplied by a hundred. It was my half-time shot at the free throw, and I had nothing but net.

"You know," I giggled, loving the lighter conversations we were familiar with. "I don't want to ruin the moment because I like where this conversation is heading—but this is sort of your fault." I bit my lip and looked up at him under my lashes. Yeah, it was a total cheesy move and I didn't care.

"Oh yeah? How do you figure?" He raised his eyebrow and grinned. "It kind of feels like a two person mess to me."

"Well... if you had just dated me in the beginning." I shrugged innocently.

"What? And missed out on that stellar seduction in between." He chuckled "Not a chance."

"Do we need to tell people?" Ok, that was probably a bit sudden and didn't need to be said at that point, but my mind and mouth had this impulsive thing going on since it had been unleashed a little while back.

"We don't *need* to do anything." Troy gave me a pointed look. "It's up to us, we're making the rules."

So maybe it could wait— the telling everyone we were together part. Would our friends even care? It could definitely be left for a day or two. Or not. I pushed the thought to the side to dwell on later.

Sadly the next thought that floated into my cerebral cortex was not pleasant. The trivial *do-we-tell-them* problem that concerned me five seconds ago seemed wonderful in comparison and I desperately wanted to go back that.

The silence ate away at me as it tumbled in my head. Did I want to know? Would it make a difference? I opened my mouth before I was able to answer either of those questions definitively.

"Were there other girls? Like, after me?"

"You really want to have that conversation, now?"

I nodded silently, it would kill me but it would be worse not knowing. Like a Band-Aid, I just had to rip it off.

Troy sighed and I prepared for the worst. "No, I didn't have sex with anyone else. I was hung up on *someone* and had no interest in fucking around. I'm not a scumbag, Megs. I am more than capable of keeping my dick in my pants."

I had no right to expect him to *save himself* for *me*, but I'd secretly hoped for it. The relief to hear that he had, flooded me in a rush. My words bubbled out erratically.

"I didn't either. Sleep with anyone I mean. Obviously I couldn't keep a dick in my pants because I didn't have one to keep there. And with vaginas it's more about whether or not the pants are on them or not...they are so much more tidier."

"You are so weird."

"Why thank you, Troy Harris."

His grin widened and lit up his eyes. "I missed hearing that."

"I thought you hated it?" I coughed out a laugh.

"Not even close. It was like foreplay." He smirked.

"Troy Harris." I whispered as low and seductive as I could manage.

"You know I'm going to have to fuck you again, right? No complaints from you if you can't walk."

I brought my mouth up to his neck and parted my lips, my tongue trailing up to his jaw. If he was trying to scare me off with his threat, it didn't work. There would be no complaints for me and I would say his name, every single syllable of it every opportunity I got. My hand moved leisurely down his chest as I tilted my head to look at him.

"Well then, take me, Troy Harris."

17

Troy

"SO THE TATTOOS." WE HAD EVENTUALLY MADE IT TO THE BED. Her body laid on mine. "Josh?" The mystery of how she met him, solved.

"Yeah, he did a great job." She didn't lift her head. Didn't need to. I liked feeling the vibrations on my skin as she moved her mouth.

"Not sure I liked the idea of his face being that close to your pussy, but as much as I want to hate the guy, he obviously has skills." The detail on the feathers so fine, it was obvious one kickass artist was handling the needle.

"You're cute when you're jealous."

"Can we think of something more manly than cute?" In truth, I didn't fucking care what she called me as long as we were done with the let's-be-friends shit.

People rarely surprised me and yet with Megs, the surprises didn't end. I loved the way she felt against me. Her hair fanned out across my chest and her little quirk for hooking an ankle around my calf when we curled up after sex. It was adorable even though my leg would go numb after a while. There wasn't one thing I didn't like about her. Not a fucking thing I would change and while I'd I had my hesitations for doing this from the start, none of it made sense to me now.

"This feels like a dream, being here with you. I'm almost expecting to wake up and find out I'm hugging a pillow. It wouldn't be the first time." She giggled, not sold on the smooth-sailing-from-here-on-out.

"Just so you know." I lifted her head so she could look at me. There wasn't going to be any misunderstandings on this. "There isn't going to be a break up between the two of us. We're not going to fuck this up. I'm not being a cocky son of a bitch—both of us are capable of doing stuff that is monumentally stupid—but we're going to always work it out. There isn't an alternative. We'd tried being apart. It sucked. So we aren't going to do that anymore."

The more time I spent with her, the more I knew it. Nope. Together is where we belonged. Whatever it took, and however fucking difficult it would be. Complicated? Hit me with your best shot, I'm ready.

"Troy, I don't want to fuck up Ash's big day." Megs scooched up the bed, the smile she had before no longer there. "If we are doing this then we have to keep it quiet until after the wedding. I don't want her worried about us fighting or something happening. It's only a little while longer. Besides, think of how much fun we'll have sneaking around." The smile was back but a little uncertain.

"That sounds like a recipe for trouble, Megs." She pouted before I had a chance to finish. "But as long as we're finally seeing eye to eye on the being together part, I'm not going to argue." Saying no to her wasn't in my vocabulary. Besides, if it made Megs happy then it was an easy ask.

Leaving Megs's apartment that afternoon wasn't easy and not for the reasons you'd think. Sure, I would have loved to have stuck around and worshipped her body— we had lost time we needed to make up— but more than that, I just hated not being with her. Funny how just knowing she was tucked up beside me was enough to put me at ease. Still, she had some patient reports she needed to write and I figured she'd get them done sooner without me trying to pull her into bed.

I wasn't bound to the ball and chain that was the nine-to-five, but she worked some hella long hours at the hospital and I wasn't going to be an inconsiderate asshole. So I kissed her goodbye in a way she wouldn't forget in a hurry, and I booked it back to my place before I could change my mind. Chances were I'd probably be finding myself back there anyway.

We started our old game of phone tag, with me hitting the call button the minute I got back to mine.

"Hello, Troy Harris," she purred as she answered. Made me want to get back into the car and drive right back.

"Megs." I did my best to keep it together and not suggest she talk dirty to me while I jack off. Jesus. I was turning into Dan. "I have to say I'm a little disappointed in you."

"Oh, really?" The intonation of her voice clued me in she was digging the role-play. "And why is that? The blowjob I gave you in a shower not deep throat enough?"

The memory alone forced me to swallow, *hard*. That had been one hell of a blowjob. "No, the blowjob was fantastic. It's your tattoos that's upset me."

"I thought you said you liked my tattoos, you liar," she answered defiantly.

"They're beautiful." No way I could lie about that. "But I had already spent money on that gift certificate for you. What's the chances of getting my name tattooed on your ass?" I cursed the fact I wasn't able to see her face.

"Oooo can we get matchy ones?" She didn't miss a beat. "With an arrow going through a heart?"

"I'll get your name but I'm not getting an arrowed heart. That shit is so fucking cliché it hurts." No way would I get a fucking heart. Power Station wasn't a fucking hair band.

"Fine, barb-wire it is." She sighed. "Make a booking."

"Bye, Megs." I hated saying those words to her, but I knew I had to let her go.

"Bye, Troy Harris." She was so fucking precious, I hated that she was going to be spending the night alone. Megs wasn't the only one I was worried about. That first night alone I didn't sleep worth a shit. I tossed and turned until I just gave up and turned on the television. Ironically "The Vampire Diaries" was on and my curiosity got the better of me. Two vampire brothers fight over a human girl who happens to have a vampire doppelgänger. Or maybe the human is the doppelgänger? How can these vampires go out in the sunlight? Is it like "Twilight"? No one is sparkling. Someone needed to draw me a fucking diagram 'cause I didn't understand any of that shit.

The early morning phone call waking me meant that at some point I had eventually fallen asleep. I reached for the phone and answered it without even bothering to open my eyes.

"Yeah." I didn't waste my time with hello. Anyone who was calling me this early would have to deal with me not being Mr. Happy.

"Aw, did I wake you Troy?" Megs giggled into the phone. My mood took a really quick upswing at the sound of her voice.

"Yeah, not everyone has to be up at the ass crack of dawn. You could do me a favor and sound a little bit sympathetic." She could wake me anytime and I'd never fucking care.

"Poor, Troy Harris." She didn't even try and hide how pleased she was. "This should cheer you up though. I watched part of Star Wars last night."

"Wow, Megs, that's kind of hot. Was it "A New Hope"?" Not gonna lie, the thought of her watching Star Wars turned me on.

"I didn't really hold any hope for it, I'm not really into Sci-Fi but it wasn't all bad."

"Fuck, you're adorable." Her confusion was so cute, I laughed so hard I could barely breathe. "The name of it, was it the episode four, "A

New Hope"? The first one of the original trilogy."

"Okay so you've already lost me. How can it be episode four, if it's the first one? That makes no sense." She took a breath before continuing. "Anyway, I'm not sure which one this was, but *Luke Skywalker* finds out that his dad is *Darth Vader*. Their reunion wasn't pretty, his kid didn't even give him a chance."

"Oh my God, we need to have some serious words, sweetheart. I think I might actually cry. That was "Return of the Jedi"; you can't watch them out of order."

"See this is why I shouldn't watch these things. Although that light saber thing, tell me that wasn't some nerdy way of comparing penises."

"Okay, hanging up now. You've crushed my soul and desecrated the force enough for one day."

"So be it, Jedi." Megs laughed, her off-the-cuff quote from the movie proved she paid more attention than she led me to believe. If I had any doubts before, they'd just incinerated. This girl was it for me.

"Bye, Megs."

"Bye, Troy Harris."

One night alone was enough; I wasn't willing to do it again. We could go to bed early so she could sleep but it would be with me by her side. Besides, I was scared if she watched any more episodes of *Star Wars* by herself, I wouldn't be able to undo the damage.

Given that we weren't advertising being together just yet, it meant I was spending my nights at Megs's apartment. The chances of being caught less likely when we didn't have to worry about Dan and Ash living across the hall. I couldn't give a shit where I slept as long as it was in the same bed as Megs.

So that's how the week went. Megs would go to work and I would head back to my apartment. Shower, change and then fill my day with shit I needed to get done so I could spend the nights making sure Megs came so hard her voice would echo off the walls.

It wasn't all sex, though it seemed to take up most of our time. We'd talk for hours. Sometimes it would be just about the stuff we'd filled our hours with, it didn't matter that it wasn't important. I just wanted to know about her day or how many times she'd laughed. It was hearing her recount of the hours I wasn't there that made the time away from her bearable.

Jase knew where I was spending my nights. There was no point hiding it, he hadn't missed my feelings for her before we started dating so I came clean and told him we were doing the couple thing. He wasn't surprised and was glad we'd sorted out whatever it was that needed sorting out. It was good thing too, he'd pulled my ass out of the fire a couple of times when Dan wanted to hang out by making up some shit about us going to get laid at clubs. Jase was a fucking team player.

"Hey asshole, are you just getting home now?" Dan had opened his door as I'd stepped into the hall from the elevator.

"Yep, I was busy last night." Not a lie, my night had been spent getting very busy.

"A skirt?" He strolled over to me obviously wanting to continue the conversation.

"Yep." I nodded, pulling my keys from pocket. I wasn't in the mood for show and tell, especially not with Dan.

He grabbed my arm, pulling my hand away from the lock of my front door. Perhaps my one word answer wasn't satisfactory enough. "You've been doing that a lot lately. You haven't been home all week."

It was so freaking weird being on this side on the fence. Dan, playing the role of concerned friend, me, the man-whore. "I'm sorry, Mom." I barked out a laugh. We must have stepped into some parallel universe, "I didn't realize I missed curfew."

"Very funny." He rolled his eyes, the irony of the situation not lost on him. "Is this one girl in particular or you playing the field? Looks like you're going for some kind of record."

Dan giving me the third degree was almost touching. He'd changed and I had to say, I liked this version of him a hell of a lot better. It sucked that I couldn't tell him shit, and that all his worry wasn't necessary but Megs and I agreed to wait and I'd eat my own hand before I'd break a promise to that girl.

"Just 'cause you're reformed now don't pretend like you weren't out every fucking night for years getting tail." Deflection. Easier than telling him stuff that wasn't true and at least I wouldn't feel like a total asshole.

"Fuck, Troy. I don't care if you are fucking two girls at once if that's what you want to do." Dan let go of my arm and ran his hands through his hair. "I'm just saying it's not like you. Look, I'm not going to pretend I didn't screw more than my fair share of women, but I know now that it's 'cause I had no idea what I was missing. Trust me, all the pussy in the world doesn't hold a candle to what I have with Ashlyn."

The heart-to-heart hadn't been necessary; the reality of *that* had already hit me. His delivery was flawed but the man spoke the truth. There was no other girl that would compare to Megs.

"That's fucking beautiful, man. Alex and James should really let you write some lyrics on the next album." My hand cupped the back of his neck and I laughed. "Oh, by the way, don't ever compare the love you have for your woman to *all the pussy in the world*. Not if you want to keep your balls." For most guys it was a give-me, but I'd hate to see a domestic dispute arriving 'cause the man could sometimes be an idiot.

Dan backhanded me across the chest. "I meant it in a positive way."

"Yeah, it will still piss her off. Trust me on this one."

"Point taken." Dan shrugged it off, hopefully having learnt his lesson. "So you doing anything today?"

I didn't have plans, well none than that went beyond the first hour or so. "Just getting a shower and then maybe watching the tube, why? What did you need?"

"I'm bored." Dan shrugged. With the album recorded and no tour dates set, the days were kind of slow for both of us. "You wanna go buy dirt bikes and ride through Central Park?" he suggested.

"You feel like getting arrested today? How about *no* on the dirt bike riding through Central Park." I shot down his idea, not wanting to spend my afternoon in lock-up.

"This is why you don't have a girlfriend, dude. You are so fucking negative."

"Yeah, that's exactly why, asshole. If you're really that bored why don't we drive to Jersey and go ask Jon Bon Jovi is he's still livin' on a prayer."

"Shit, that's brilliant. Hurry the fuck up and get ready. I'm driving."

It was just after eight when I climbed the stars that lead to Megs's loft. Having been with Dan all day and most of the evening meant I had barely spoken to her and I wasn't sure if I was going to ask her how her day was or kiss her.

Buzzing me up minutes before, she was standing in the doorway waiting for me. She looked fucking beautiful. Her face had been scrubbed of make up and she'd changed out of work clothes and into her sleep shorts and tank top. No bra. It didn't get much better than that.

The debate I'd been having— about whether to kiss her or talk— was over. I crossed that last step and took her mouth right there. She let out a little whimper as I circled my arms around her and lifted her off the ground. I couldn't get close enough to her— holding her, kissing her— I'd never get tired of that.

"Well, hello to you too." She smiled wrapping her arms around my neck.

"I missed you today. I'm just trying to catch up." I lowered her to the floor as my hands got reacquainted with the rest of her body.

"We going to move this inside or you want to give my neighbors a show?" She looked over my shoulder signaling to the other doors in her hallway.

I grinned looking down at what she was wearing. The tank top she had on, showcasing the curve of her tits. "I think you already gave them a show." My hand reached up and gently squeezed one of her nipples.

She jerked on my arm, pulling me inside. The door got a kick from her foot and closed behind us. "Be thankful I'm wearing clothes. I could have answered the door naked."

"You would have received no complaints from me." We moved through the hallway and into her living room as my mouth went back to work, this time making its way down her neck. I pulled down her tank top as I continued my journey, her beautiful tits popping out the top.

"Troy." She closed her eyes as my tongue circled her nipple.

"Shsssh, I'm trying to have conversation with your breasts." Any other conversation would have to wait.

"I want to give you something first." She pulled her body away from my mouth, and had she not added the next part I would have been extremely pissed off. "Something... sexy."

"Well now you have me interested." I smirked as I moved my mouth away from her body. I'd finish that later.

She gave me a gentle shove in the direction of the couch. "Sit," she demanded, placing both her hands on her hips.

No idea where this was going, but it was kind of hot. My grin got wider as I sunk into the chair behind me. "Is this where you slap a collar on me and pull a whip out of your ass? We both know I'd make a terrible submissive."

"I don't want you as a submissive." She joined me on the chair and curled up in my lap. "I want you naked."

Her arm reached across to the coffee table and picked up a file that had been sitting there. Her eyes were full of excitement as she handed it to me.

"If that was your goal, you would've got me naked quicker my way of doing things." I kissed her neck before looking at the folder she was pushing against my chest. "What's with the paperwork? I thought you said it was something sexy."

She smiled, opening the folder and insisting. "Read it."

"Urrrr... Female. Caucasian." I started to read off the notes. "If this is to confirm you're a female, it's okay, I worked that out myself. But thanks, I appreciate the reassurance." I glanced up from the pages of

CRASH RIDE

words I wasn't interested in.

"It's my blood work, silly. I had a sample taken on Monday and I got my results today. Screenings for STDs and other stuff. See? I'm all good." She pointed to the part on the page that revealed not only her blood type but also a list of potential nasties, all which read negative.

"This is your health screening? Why are you showing me this?" I placed the folder beside me, it's purpose having been served.

"Because I wanted to feel your cock in me without the condom." She smiled sweetly liked she'd just asked me to take her to the mall.

How she was able to say those things with a straight face bewildered me. I loved that she was unfiltered and that she could say the word cock without getting all embarrassed. There was something so fucking hot about a woman who knew what she wanted and wasn't afraid to ask for it.

"Jesus, Megs. You keep talking like that and you're going to get your wish sooner than later." My already hard dick concurred on my assessment. Both of us down for the skin on skin action.

"So does that mean you want that too?" She looked up at me, a patch of vulnerability shining through all that bravado. It just made me want her more.

Did I want to have sex with her, bare? Hell-fucking-yes, I did. We hadn't had the are-you-on-the-pill talk, and I didn't want to assume she was. But the prospect of slipping inside of her with nothing between us got me so hard my balls ached. "Of course I want to. That's not even a real question. But you could have just told me. You didn't have to show me all this." I tossed the folder back onto the coffee table.

"I wanted to make it official." She smiled as she nuzzled against my chest. "I'm on the pill as well so you can come inside me and everything."

FUCK. Well then. I guess we've now had *that* talk.

"Wow. I'm going to need a minute to stop visualizing if we want *that* to actually happen. I'm dangerously close to coming in my pants right now." I wasn't even kidding. One sweep of a hand on my dick, and it was all over.

My reaction obviously satisfied her, the grin evidence of that. "See, I told you it was sexy."

I liked that look on her face, her being happy and knowing I had something to do with it.

"We're screened every six months for insurance purposes." It was my turn to do the I'm-all-good talk. "My last one was two months ago and I always have used condoms. I'm good. I can pull the paperwork if you want to see." Seeing as she had produced paperwork, it was only fair I offered to do the same. I didn't carry personal medical records around with me but they wouldn't have been hard to get.

"No, I don't need to see." She shook her head and smiled. "We can get to the sex part now, you kissing my nipple at the door made me so freaking wet."

"Do you practice these things before you say them to me? I swear every word out of your mouth is hotter than the last." I brushed the hair off her shoulder wondering how the hell I got so lucky.

"It's a natural talent, now come here and kiss me again." She brought her lips inches away from mine. "I need things that only you can give me."

I tiled her chin so that I could look at her, her lips parted, waiting for me to take her mouth. I loved her. I'd never been more sure of anything in my life.

"I'll give you everything you need, and things you didn't even know you did."

18

Megan

I WAS IN LOVE WITH HIM. I HAD FLIPPANTLY USED THOSE WORDS TO describe my feelings for Troy Harris in the past, having seen him on stage but *those* feelings, they hadn't even come close to what I felt now. Even having known him for months still hadn't prepared me and, while we hadn't said the words out loud, he had my heart. Completely. Every part. I wanted Troy. I needed Troy.

"Troy Harris." I managed to moan in between kisses. "Why are you still wearing clothes?"

There was a sexy laugh against my neck. "I can fix that." He pulled away from me for a second to remove his T-shirt, his beautiful sculptured chest on display. Every time I saw it, it was just as impressive. His arms came back around me. "Now let me see how much wetter I can get you."

A loud buzz from the speaker beside my door broke through my lust-filled fog. Whoever it was didn't stand a chance. Not. A. Chance.

"I'm not answering it. It's probably someone who's got the wrong apartment." My hands moved to his belt and started to fumble with the buckle. It felt like I was going to explode.

"Megs, if we're going to do this, you need to be naked too." Troy pulled at the edge of my tank top. He was such a smart man, and one hundred percent right. Naked was an awesome plan.

My fingers moved from trying to undo Troy's pants to lifting off my top, I tossed it onto the couch without a second though. The warmth of his body on mine was mind blowing.

My cell started ringing loudly from beside me, the illuminated screen doing its best to attract my attention. What? What was so important that needed me to be taken away from this moment? Was the world trying to conspire against this happening? Screw it. It could go to voice mail.

"Fuck, this cannot be happening." Troy laughed as once again my buzzer started being obnoxious. I hated that thing. Where was a baseball bat when you needed one?

My phone once again lit up, the buzzer and my cell at war with each other as to who would get my attention. It was clear that getting Troy's naked cock into me would need to wait. I kid you not, I almost cried.

"Yeah?" I palmed the phone and pressed it against my ear. The cell won out because I could still straddle Troy and neither of us had to put our clothes on.

"Megs," Kyla huffed into the phone. "I know you're home. Let me up."

Kyla Heatherington was one of my closest friends and she lived about a block away with her bestie, Brianne. Ashlyn and I had been working at *Garro's* sports bar for about three months when the two of them waltzed in and poured a pitcher of beer over Brianne's cheating boyfriend's head. Turned out it had been the same guy who had been hitting on me since I'd started, so we bonded over a mutual distaste for him. One margarita-filled evening later and the four of us became instant friends. Some things were just meant to be.

Nooooooooooo. I bit down on my lip to stop myself from screaming it. That would be rude, right? As much as I loved her, now was not the time for a social call. My eyes closed as my fist tightened around the phone, I needed to keep my voice light.

"Kyyyylaaaa." Ok, too light, you sound high. Try backing off a bit. "You're here?" Now you sounded stupid. Of course she was here, she just said that. "What are you doing here?" Better, but was still going to get questions. Maybe I should have stuck with sounding high.

"Are you high? You sound funny." Kyla's voice snapped back. See, told you. A career in espionage was something I could safely rule out.

"Umm. I was just…" My brain searched its recesses for something plausible. I had nothing. "Give me a minute and I'll let you up." I ended the call and tossed my phone onto the couch beside us.

My eyes glanced longingly at Troy's naked chest— it wasn't going to happen. Not until I could get rid of her. "Fuck. I have company." My teeth clenched so tightly I'm surprised any words got out.

"Okay, I'll put my shirt back on." Troy calmly reached for his T-shirt hanging of the arm of the couch.

"No." My head shook as my voice rose. "No, you can't be here." My wide eyes went with the rest of the crazed expression I had going on.

"Megs, she knows we're friends." Troy pushed the tee over his head. "Just tell her I stopped by." He shrugged calmly.

"Stopped by?" My voice rose yet again as I tried to rein in my panic. "Are you kidding? She will smell the sex on you." My discarded tank top was retrieved and shoved back over my head.

"Ah, Megs we haven't had sex yet." Troy smirked as he kissed me.

"That is so unhelpful right now, I'm going to ignore it. You need to hide." I jumped to my feet and yanked on his arm. Yes, that was solution. Where could I hide him? The closet wasn't even a contender.

"What the fuck?" He laughed it off; my incessant pulling of his forearm did nothing to move him. "I am not going to hide." He stood up defiantly and made for my front door.

"Yes you are." He had to. Kyla had a big mouth and a tendency to gossip. If she knew—everyone knew. And I wasn't ready for everyone to know. This was so not good. I raced him to my door, flinging my arms across it like a barrier. Ha! Like that would stop him if he wanted to get past.

"She can't see you. Please go to my room." My plea sounded desperate. I wasn't even trying to hide how freaked out I was.

"Megs." He rolled his eyes, saying my name like I was being ridiculous. Maybe I was being ridiculous. We could argue later, right now I needed him to hide.

"Please," I begged, my arms still stretched out either side of me, barricading the door.

"Fine." He relented, and my body relaxed a little. "But know this, the minute she is out the door, your ass is mine and I'm not going to be gentle about it." He didn't sound like he was kidding.

"Sure, sure." I nodded so furiously I hoped it didn't result in a brain injury, and pointed toward my bedroom door. "My room. I'll be quick and take the file with you, I can't have her seeing it."

Troy muttered something under his breath and huffed a few times but thankfully turned and walked toward my room. He picked up the file from the coffee table, more muttering, and closed my bedroom door. Thank you God, I mouthed silently as I released the external lock and opened my front door.

"Oh hey, Kyla." I leaned my body lazily against the jamb as I tried to sound casual. Kyla took the final few steps before she reached the landing. "What brings you here?"

"Why aren't you answering your door? What took you so long? You're already in your pajamas? It's not even nine o'clock." The barrage of questions had started and she hadn't even entered the apartment. This was not going to be easy.

"I'm tired. I had the music on. I didn't hear the door." The answers rolled out of sequence from my mouth, and with very little conviction. The wave of my hand ushering her inside as I shut the door behind us.

"What the fuck happened to your hair?" She looked around my apartment like it would yield an explanation. I silently prayed Troy would not pick this moment to come out, thinking the jig was up. "And why is your face so red?" Her raised brow hinting she wasn't going to be easily fooled.

"I was exercising." The lame excuse leapt from my mouth before I had a chance to think of something better.

"In your pajamas? I thought you said you were tired." Another raised eyebrow, with the folded arms thrown in for good measure. This wasn't going well for me.

"Yeah I was, from the exercising." I bounced in place to demonstrate like an idiot. You know, in case she didn't know what exercising was.

"Okay, this is weird even for you, but whatever." She waved and started wandering around my apartment. Being that throwing my head between my knees would attract attention, I tried not to have a panic attack.

"Ash called, said you'd had a few rough days at work so I came by to drag your ass out. Get dressed, we're going out." She picked up the latest edition of *Cosmo* that was sitting on my coffee table and started to randomly flip.

"No, I can't." I almost shouted as she went to sit down on my couch. The same couch Troy had been on moments before.

"Why not? Have a shower if you need, I can wait." She ignored me, sinking into the seat as she thumbed the glossy pages.

"No, I have an early start tomorrow," I stuttered. "I can't go out tonight."

"Tomorrow's Saturday. You don't work tomorrow. What's so important you need to be up?" Once again it earned me a raised eyebrow, the magazine was also tossed aside in disinterest.

"I have plans." Once again my mouth opened without proper thought.

"Doing what?" She folded her arms across her chest, giving me her full interest.

"Tae Bo." There was no hope. My ship was sinking fast when *that* was the best I could come up with. It was only a matter of time before it all unraveled.

"Tae Bo? Is that still even a thing? Didn't it go to fitness heaven sometime after the 90's? Megs, seriously, I'll ask you one more time. Are you high?"

"No! Of course not." The giggle and the indignation intertwined wildly in my tone. Did I mention how much I sucked at this?

"I'm not judging you, who hasn't had a *special* brownie or two. Just saying if you were, it would be nice to share." Kayla shrugged like it was no big deal.

"Well you're out of luck because I've got nothing."

"Okay, so stop being lame. Go get changed. We won't be back late."

"I really can't."

"Why the hell not?"

"Because there is a man in my bedroom I'd really like to have sex with."

The truth startled us both into silence. Well then. This wasn't going to be an easy fix.

Kyla opened and shut her mouth a few times, words obviously eluding her. Her eyes flicked to my closed bedroom door. "You have some man holed up in your room?"

"Yes. It's new. I'm not ready to share him yet." It was the most honest thing that had come out of my mouth since she'd walked in.

"Are we going to get to meet him?" She didn't even try to lower her voice, probably hoping to flush out my hidden guest.

"Eventually, just not now. Can you keep this to yourself for a little while?" Not sure why I even bothered to ask, she was going to be on the phone to Brianne and Ashlyn before she'd even left my building.

"Fine, but you know I'm not good with secrets." She huffed impatiently before lowering her voice. "When the hell did you hook up with this one? Weren't you dating Josh like not even a week ago?"

"Yeah, I was. It's…" There was no other word I could think of that was better suited, "…complicated."

"Honey, you know I love you, right?" She planted her hands on her hips and I prepared for the I'm-worried-about-you speech. "But your life is complicated enough with your work, maybe you need to find some guy who isn't going to add to that. Find a nice guy, someone you can…I don't know, settle down with. Oh, there's this nice guy I work with. He'd be perfect for you."

"Kyla, thanks but this guy *is* a nice guy and I don't need anyone setting me up."

"Fine, just don't let him break your heart." She gave me a hug before raising her voice intentionally. "And make sure he treats you right because we have friends that can take care of it if he doesn't."

I cringed knowing Troy would have probably heard. "Thanks for that. I'll call you." My arms returned the hug before I pushed her toward the door. "And don't worry about me, I'll be fine."

She wasn't happy about it but she left, the door slamming punctuating her exit. I assumed I'd have about a ten to fifteen minute grace period before she caved and told someone. If anyone was going to make those ten minutes count, it would be me.

"Troy Harris, it's time for you to make good on that promise." I almost ran to the bedroom and flung the door open. My hopes of a happy reunion were crushed as I was greeted by Troy's pale face.

"Megs, you need to sit down." He tapped the bed beside him and not in sexy kind of way, in the we-need-to-talk kind of way.

"Look, I know you probably heard Kyla be all protective but she is just looking out for me. She doesn't know it's you and trust me, she doesn't have friends who can take care of *it* if things don't work out, she was being dramatic." The words bubbled furiously as I made my way to the bed; I wouldn't let Kayla's good intentions ruin what was supposed to be an amazing night.

"Besides, I know you aren't going to hurt me and you already said this was for the long haul and I believe you, truly I do." My mouth refused to be still, the look on his face putting the fear of God into me. Please don't think this is all too much work, please don't regret being with me. "And as soon as the wedding is over, we'll go public and it will all be fine and this will be just—"

"Megs, shut up." He placed his hands over my mouth as I sat down on the bed beside him. Probably for the best, it didn't show any signs of letting up. "I need you to tell you something and I need you to listen to me."

My head nodded being my mouth was still covered, not that I think words would have been able to come out right now, I was so afraid of him ending us, I couldn't talk.

Troy took a deep breath but kept his hand over my mouth. "I love you. I know we have only been together officially for a week but those feelings have been coming at me for a while. Nod if you are on the same page with me." I nodded wondering if it was declarations of love we were sharing, why I couldn't be free to declare mine.

My heartbeat starting thumping wildly as I waited for the "but" that was inevitably coming, the look in his eyes too intense, too serious to be simply wanting to tell me he loved me. Perhaps my self-assurances that he wouldn't break my heart had been premature.

"So there is something else you need to know."

I braced myself, wondering if he was going to go the this-isn't-going-to-work-out or love-doesn't-conquer-all route, either would hurt just as badly.

"We're pregnant."

"What?" My mouth mumbled against his palm as my brain screamed what the fuck. How the fuck can I be pregnant? I'm on the pill for fuck's sake. We've been using condoms. We haven't had unprotected sexy time yet. I don't feel any different. When was my last period? Oh my God, I'm going to pass out. The garbled noises continued from underneath his hand.

"Megs, I'm going to take my hand away. Don't freak out on me." He slowly unpeeled his hand from around my mouth.

"What! What? How can I be pregnant?" My head shook in disbelief, I was no virgin so divine intervention was out. Not that I thought I was a suitable mother for the second coming but... "How?"

"I have no idea, but this file." He picked up my blood work and opened it to the second page. "Says that you are."

And there it was a *pregnant* followed by the letters hCG and a bunch of numbers I didn't understand.

"I—I..." I had no idea what to say, my brain went into free fall.

"No, no I." Troy took my chin in his hands. "*We*, do you understand me? Us— together. This is our baby."

"I got pathology to take the blood but submitted the samples to the lab anonymously." Words had started to come out but the voice didn't sound like mine. "I said it was a patient of mine, a minor. They didn't ask questions. My brother works in the ER and my dad... I didn't want my name on the sample and people asking questions." It seemed so harmless. It wasn't the first time I requested an anonymous sample. It happens a lot when a minor is scared they might have an STD or knocked up (trust me the irony was not lost on me) and didn't want their parents to know. Patient, doctor privilege meant it could happen. We used a coding system instead.

"You didn't read it all the way through I take it?" Troy pulled the file from my hands, the papers scrunched at the edges underneath my death grip.

"I wasn't looking for that. It's on the second page. It wasn't even a possibility, I just wanted to prove I didn't have gonorrhea."

"Well, good news — you don't have gonorrhea." He smiled like it was no big deal.

"This isn't funny." His calm or his smile didn't reassure me this *wasn't* a big deal. "How can I be pregnant when we have used condoms and I've been on the pill? That's like zero chance. Do you have like super sperm or something?"

"Megs, we need to get you to a doctor. I don't know what these numbers mean and we don't know how long junior's been cooking in there. You're also going to need stuff, vitamins and shit." He put his arms around me, pulling my body closer to his. "We are going to work this out, you're not in this alone."

"Do you want to keep the baby? This is a big decision, Troy, like a *life long* decision. We can't just decide we're done— we'll be parents."

My fingers wrapped around his forearms tightly like I could some how extract the definitive reassurance I needed. This wasn't playtime, this was real life.

"What part of we're not breaking up did you not understand? You think even without the baby, I could just be done with you?" He took my face in his hands. "I said I loved you and I meant it. Marriage, kids, that was always in our future. Someone just hit the fast forward button."

"You are too calm, why aren't you freaking out? I'm freaking the fuck out. You know how crazy I can be, I'm going to be someone's mom. That's insanity of the highest level." Holy shit, there is a baby inside of me. Puking right now would not be out of the question.

"You're not going to be someone's mom, you're going to be our baby's mom. And I'm calm 'cause life throws you a curve ball every once in a while, big deal. It's not like we're sixteen with no futures ahead of us. Money isn't an issue, we're both healthy and we love each other. So maybe the timing sucks a little, we've got to roll with it."

He was so sure, not even the slightest hesitation. Part of me was mad that I was the only one about to hyperventilate, granted he had a few more minutes to adjust to the news before I did, and *he* wasn't the one who was going to be blowing up to the size of Shamu.

"I love you." I realized Troy had been the only one who'd said it, my wordless nod not really qualifying. "I want to have this baby— *our* baby." It sounded so weird saying it but he was right, this wasn't mine or his— it was ours.

To think my plans for the evening were a night of unrestrained sex, without a condom and then boom, I'm knocked up.

"Good, let's get some sleep and see if we can't get you an appointment tomorrow. I need to hold you." He turned and pulled off his boots. The socks came next and then the shirt.

Woah. Sleep hadn't been the plan, who was going to be able to sleep?

"Wait, sleep? But we were supposed to have sex. The whole getting pregnant is a non issue so there's no concerns there." Look at that, a silver lining. Let's concentrate on that and stop with the no sex talk.

CRASH RIDE

"As much as I want to, and trust me— I really want to— we need to wait until a doctor checks you out." He stood and unbuttoned his jeans. They dropped to the floor, as did my hope for action tonight.

"People who are pregnant have sex all the time." Valid argument, thank you brain for stepping in. Was good of you to finally show up.

"Yeah, but they knew they were pregnant and were taking care of it. We can wait. As soon as we're given the all clear, I promise I'll make it worth the wait." Troy moved back on to the bed and pulled the covers aside and waited for me to crawl in.

"But I'm going to get fat and moody and then you won't want me." It was childish but I pouted, shoving myself into bed like an errant child. The moodiness had already started; we were in for a treat in the next nine months or so.

"You're not going to get fat, you're going to be carrying our baby and it doesn't get sexier than that. Trust me, it's going to be you who turns me down, not the other way around." Troy crawled in and rolled me onto my side. We laid face to face, his arms around me, and his hard-on pressing against my leg. The danger of hyperventilation was back.

"I was wrong, you're the one who's crazy." Or maybe we were both crazy. This poor kid didn't stand a chance.

"We'll see. Now shhhh, I need to love on my woman." His hands moved up and down my back as he kissed my neck.

"Troy, I want our baby to have your last name."

He stopped kissing me. "I was kinda hoping you both would."

"Do you mean?" Tonight was not the night for misunderstandings.

His eyes said it loud and clear even before he opened his mouth. "Yeah."

"Just so we're clear, you're talking about getting married, right?" Again, clarification was needed.

"That's exactly what I'm talking about, but we're not doing anymore talking tonight. Go to sleep, Megs, I promise you this will all be okay."

He kissed me and with that kiss I believed him. Believed that it would all be okay.

'19

Troy

THE ONLY THING MORE RIDICULOUS THAN HIDING IN MEGS'S BED-
room, had been sitting around with nothing to do but listen to her stumble over herself like an amateur. I loved my girl but she couldn't lie for shit. So it was either crack open the file and find out what blood type she was, or walk out there and put her out of her misery. I never found out what blood type she was. The word pregnant had put the brakes on my future reading.

Wow. A dad. Mind blown. There you go, my life was about to change.

"Megs, I think you should probably lay down. The pacing is making me edgy, and I can totally see your ass from the split in your gown. Don't think the doc is going to appreciate my hard-on if you catch my drift." Nervous? Megs was about as close to a breakdown as I'd ever seen her.

CRASH RIDE

"I can't sit down. Sitting down does nothing." She continued wearing a hole into the floor, her gown flapping open with each stride. We'd been here for a couple of hours, running tests and trying to find out answers, she'd been done with the sit still routine after thirty minutes. "What's taking so long? I'm losing my mind." The statement wasn't necessary, I'd kind of guessed that on my own.

"You need to calm down. All the stress isn't helping either of you." Now she was making me nervous. The look on her face was not one I wanted to be seeing. I tried to coax her back to the bed and lay down. Yeah, that wasn't going to happen.

"On top of everything else I've done? Troy, I've been drinking. I've taken birth control pills. I've been in smoked-filled rooms. I think the stress is the least of the baby's problems. God, I'm a horrible mother and he or she isn't even born yet." She threw her hands up in the air as her feet kept moving. Nothing I said stuck, her head hell bent on thinking up worst-case scenarios.

"For fuck's sake, you didn't know." It was an effort not to drag her to the bed and make her lie down. The guilt she was putting on herself was enough for me to want to toss the chair I was sitting on through a wall. "It's not like you went out and did crack. It will be fine, let's just wait and see what the doctor says before we go off the deep end."

The sooner they gave us the all clear and we got out of here, the better. Seeing Megs like that did something to me I didn't like. Like chest-thumping-macho-caveman shit that demanded I made it right.

"Good morning, Miss Winters." The doctor strolled in the room with no fucking urgency and placed her files down on the desk. Wonder how long I can be polite before I tell her to hurry the fuck up and reassure my girl.

"Yes. That's me, but you can't tell anyone I've been here." Megs's feet had stopped moving but now her hands were getting the attention. Her fingers twitched as they locked and unlocked with each other. If a baby hadn't been involved, I'd have suggested a double dose of Xanax.

"Miss Winters, I assure you, your confidentiality is safe." Dr. sorry-missed-her-name-the-first-time-and-didn't-care-enough-to-ask-again sat down. Once again, no fucking urgency. "You know that I couldn't talk about anything that goes on here without your written consent."

"She's freaking out, Doc. Safe to assume anything you think she knows might need to be reiterated." Figured I needed to light that fire under her ass and maybe get some intel on what we were dealing with.

"You're the father I assume?" Wow, the woman was a genius, was her first clue me putting my hand around my girl and trying to get her to calm down?

"Yep, Troy Harris. I'm the father."

"Megan, can I call you Megan?" She waited for a go ahead before she continued. "You need to relax and let us get all the facts before you start getting too excited okay? The unnecessary stress isn't healthy for you or the baby."

And where had I heard those words before? Oh, I know. They'd come out of my mouth not five minutes earlier.

"I just… I don't understand. How could it have happened? I didn't know. I didn't suspect. Were the tests wrong, there can be false positives right?" Megs pushed her hands through her hair, still hanging on to the thread of denial.

It had been a fucking ordeal to convince her to call in a favor and get an appointment on a Saturday, but waiting till Monday wasn't an option. The private clinic was happy to accommodate us for the right amount of green. It was a no brainer.

"Megan, I looked over your initial blood results and compared that with the blood samples we took this morning." The doc looked at the paper work almost as if to prove her point. "Your hCG levels are consistent with you being five weeks pregnant."

Any hope I had of calming Megs went out the window. "Five weeks? I've been pregnant for five weeks. I haven't been sick. I had a period. I've been on birth control."

"Let's start with addressing the birth control issue. Have you taken it uninterrupted? Been on any other medication? Been sick? Any one of those factors would reduce the efficiency of that method of contraception." The doc eased back into her chair as we played the how-did-it-happen game.

"I take it...." Megs swallowed before continuing, "...when I remember. I mean, I mostly remember. Sure there was some missed day here or there but only a few."

"Megan, missing one pill is enough to start your cycle. Ovulation can happen at anytime. As far as condoms, yes they are reliable but accidents happen. Heat can damage the latex or it can break, and there can be leakage. Penetrative contact with no ejaculation can also result in pregnancy."

Well that took care of my hard-on. Talk of penetrative contact with no ejaculation. Don't even get me started on the condom leakage. Still not that it fucking made a difference, what mattered was it was official. There was a baby. Ours.

"Looks like we were that one in a million chance, Megs, lucky us." I hoped the squeeze I gave her was enough to offset the dry heave that looked like was about to happen.

"What about the fact I kept taking the pill? What about my period?" Megs refused to sit down; instead we played the twenty questions while we stood up.

"Obviously it's not ideal that you continued to take them but these things can happen and in most cases have no long term effects. As far as your period, some women menstruate right through to deliver. It might have also been an implant bleed. We'll know more as you progress."

"Are you sure I haven't screwed up my baby? Tell me he or she is okay!" Megs demanded, her voice tight.

"Doc, put us out of our misery here. I'm not good with seeing her like this." That was the watered down version of what was pumping through my head, but this didn't seem like the kind of place that I could slam my fist on her desk and demand answers. It wasn't the rent-a-cops that worried me; it was that they'd refuse to help us.

"Megan, what you are experiencing is normal. Even a woman who is fully prepared and who has been actively trying to conceive will have moments of fear. But your results look great and no sign of any complications. We're going to do an internal ultrasound to get a better look, is that okay?" She moved from behind her desk and pointed us to the bed I'd been trying to get Megs on since the start of this conversation.

"Okay." Megs shuffled up onto the bed, her eyes no less scared than when this visit started. "Will you hold my hand?"

"Never going to stop, Megs, never going to stop." One of the easiest promises I'd ever had to make.

She laid back and squeezed my hand so tightly I was sure she was going to crack a bone or two. Did I give a fuck? Not even one. My girl and my baby would be worth a broken hand.

A tiny blip showed up on the screen, small and blurry but there was definitely something there. The little dude or dudette who hadn't cared that his or her parents were behaving like a bunch of loony tunes. Seems to me like junior was already smarter than the both of us, knowing what we should have fucking known from the start.

"That's our baby, Troy." Megs started to cry and I had to swallow hard a few times myself.

"Yeah, sure is." Damn if my eyes didn't get wetter the longer I looked.

There were more questions and answers but for the most part, there was a bunch of wait-and-see shit that needed to happen. We grabbed a script for some vitamins that Megs needed and left with a grainy picture of what looked like a whole lot of nothing but meant everything to us.

"Can we go get a milkshake? I really want a coffee but it's on the bad list. " We'd barely made it out the door as Megs reread over her lists of dos and don'ts.

"She said you can have it moderation." The way Megs sucked down her coffee, the avoid was going to be a hard ask. "Maybe down grade to a small or switch to decaf."

"Decaf? I'm going to assume it's the shock of impending parenthood that has made you say such horrible things to me. Yuck, no way. It's the real deal or nothing, and a small one is just going to make me want more. I have poor impulse control."

"Yes, I've noticed."

We rounded the corner to where my Lambo was parked. The car didn't seem like such a good idea now and would probably be gathering dust after a few months. Guess I would be Escalading like James and Alex. There were worse cars I could be driving.

"Oh and you are so much better. I don't recall a lot of times you said no." She folded her arms in front of her chest which happened to give me a superb view of her tits. The distraction causing my car key to almost hit the paint as I tried to open her door.

"Probably because I loved your lack of impulse control, made my job a hell of a lot easier." I braced my arms on the roof of the car, her body in the middle as I leaned in for a kiss.

"You." She mumbled against my mouth, not having the chance to finish her sentence.

My body cursed me as I pulled away and popped open the door, watching her slither into the seat. That erection that had sailed away earlier was back and it meant business. I jogged to the driver's side of the car and jumped in and tried to concentrate on the more important things we needed to deal with, other than getting me inside her.

"So you want to go tell your folks? I think that should probably happen soon." We eased into the flow of traffic, the road doing its best impression of a Manhattan parking lot.

"I think we should wait a little bit longer. There's no reason why we have to tell anyone." Her hands got busy doing that wringing action again. My brain flew into overdrive.

"Megs, come on. You're pregnant. You don't honestly think we were going to keep pretending like we weren't together did you?" I'd assumed the baby would have put the final nail in the sneaking around BS we had going on. Surely, that was done and dusted.

"Well, yeah. I did."

"No. No more."

"Troy, but…"

"No, Megs, this is bullshit." My hand slamming on the steering wheel made her jump and my regret was immediate. She was scared enough as it was without adding my frustration to the mix.

"People are going to say shit I don't need to hear right now. Some are going to say I'll be too emotional to do my job, some might even say I trapped you. Why does anyone have to know?"

"Who gives a fuck what they say. I know different and that should be the only opinion that matters." That thought had never been given any airtime.

"No, I love you, but it isn't the only opinion that matters. Do you know how hard I've worked to establish myself? It's hard enough being Mitchell Winters's daughter, everyone thinking that you only got where you did because of your last name. Add in pregnancy and it will kill any professional respect I've earned. They will think I'll be checking out soon, off to go shack-up with my *rock star* boyfriend and have little *rock star* babies."

"That's bullshit, they can't judge you 'cause you're having a baby or because you are dating me." The car inched forward before having to stop again, the break in the flow giving me the opportunity to look at her.

"It's bullshit, but it's what will happen." Her eyes convinced of what she was saying. "Trust me. We will tell people when the time is right. Now is not that time."

"Fine but you're killing me, you know that right?" Me letting go would only be carried so far. But the minute she looked like she was in the family way, I would be making it clear that I was the man responsible for that.

"Looks like we both have something that will be worth waiting for." She smiled; no doubt pleased she'd gotten her way.

"So you going to shack up with your rock star boyfriend and have rock star babies?" My grin got wider than the one she was wearing, the idea of us being a family rocking my fucking world.

"Considering I'm already knocked up, I'd say your chances are pretty good." She nodded, looking a lot less stressed than when we'd left the clinic. I liked that. Seeing her happy and knowing that while she wasn't totally cool with everything, she was slowly coming around.

"Let's go get you that milkshake and then you're heading to bed." That shake better be quick too, we'd have to get it to go. I needed to get her home.

"Bed? I'm not tired. It's the middle of the day and I'm pregnant, not sick." Her tone let me know that she had no intention on doing what she was told. Not that I expected anything less.

"You won't be sleeping, trust me." Not if I had anything to with it.

"Do you mean sex?" She sat up in her seat, it seemed like she was no longer interested in fighting me. It was a good thing too.

"Oh yeah. Doctor gave us the green light which means I need to make good on my promise."

"Screw the milkshake, take me home."

"Done."

20
Megan

"TROY." MY HEAD ROLLED BACK ONTO THE PILLOW AS MY HANDS gripped his strong, muscular arms. God he had sexy arms, just look at that definition. Rope like almost. He must go to the gym…like a lot.

"Yeah." Troy lifted his mouth from my nipple; the way he licked me made everything feel so good.

"No, don't stop." My hands gently pushed his head back into position, I hadn't meant for him to stop. He had a very, very important job to do.

Troy laughed against my breast, his mouth closing over the tight peak. It was insane to feel this happy.

"Yeah… Like that." My eyes closed as my chest rose to meet his lips. God he had a talented mouth, almost as good as his hands—almost.

"Megs." Troy rumbled against my skin, moving the talented lip-action to my neck. He body slid higher and wow his erection pressed against me in the most delicious way.

There was urgency and yet a sweetness in the way he kissed me, almost like it hadn't been there before. He was careful and controlled, like bringing a pot slowly up to boil. It was driving me crazy yet I could find the words to make him stop.

We had arrived back at the apartment and predictably it was an epic free-for-all of hands, fingers, and lips. Clothes were hastily removed— not like we needed them anyway— and we kissed and touched our way to my bed.

What had been unpredictable was that once our bodies had hit the mattress, the gears were heavily down graded and everything slowed the hell down. Like really slow.

I had fought it, needing the instant gratification, but Troy had simply ignored my rather vocal protests and continued on his merry way of obscene oral pleasure. No, not licking in between my legs— which is where I'd wanted him—but everywhere else. Teasing me, drawing every last inch of sanity out of me— assuming there was any left.

Hours—okay maybe not hours, but it felt like it—he owned my body, barely allowing me to touch him. My skin felt like it had been licked by a million fireflies with my core ready to explode.

"Troy, please," I shamelessly begged, "this is borderline torture, don't be so cruel."

He chuckled against my neck, "Why don't you tell me what you want then?" Oh he knew what I wanted, he just wasn't done playing with me yet.

"You. In. Me." I mumbled as his lips moved to my mouth.

"Here?" His hand swept tight little circles around my opening, teasing me more. You could have asked me my name at that point and I wouldn't have been able to tell you.

"Yes." It was a moan or maybe a groan, possibly a hybrid that sounded more like dying than sexy but I didn't care. I didn't care about anything other than having him stop the fire that was consuming me.

He shifted his body again, and then he was there. The sweet relief didn't come; instead he kept with his theme, moving inch by inch into me before slowly dragging himself out. Each time he filled me, my body tightened around him, fighting his retreat.

"Look at me, Megs," he whispered slowly as he continued the agonizing assault. "I love you."

"I love you too." The words automatically spilling from my lips, which was just as well because I couldn't have conjured up a conscious thought to have saved my life.

It was then, as we stared into each other's eyes, that I saw what he was doing. Our relationship had started off as *fucking*—intense and out of control. It had been fun and had fulfilled every physical need I had, but this... this was something else. A connection that went beyond what our bodies wanted. Went beyond the orgasm. It went beyond a good time. This, this is what I had waited my whole life to find.

In his eyes I saw the love, I saw his commitment and I hoped he saw the same in mine. There was no mistake on what *this* was, there was no misunderstanding on what it could be. It was home. Mine. His. Ours.

"Troy." My arms wrapped around him tightly as my body finally got what it had craved, my nerves tingling as pleasure ripped through me. I clung to him unable to speak anything else. His release came soon after, murmuring my name and I-love-you's as he filled me, gently raining kisses down on my face as he held me.

I hoped we would still have times where we'd fuck—because no one fucked like Troy Harris— but making love to him was so much better. Lucky for me, I hadn't had to choose. He was mine, all of him.

"Wake-up, sleepy head, your phone is being an asshole." Troy kissed my neck as his hands looked for another part of me to keep him amused. My breasts ended up the lucky recipients. Well good morning to you too, Troy Harris. "I've ignored it the first five times but whoever it is, isn't giving up."

"Ugh..." I hadn't remembered falling asleep, but I obviously had

CRASH RIDE

seeing as now I was trying to open my eyes. "It might be the hospital, I should probably get it."

The mattress moved as he lifted himself off and then compressed again under his weight as he returned. "Here. It's Ash." He placed my phone in my hand as he resumed holding me against his warm body. It would be so easy to drift back to sleep.

"Megs, you need to actually answer it. Holding it isn't going to help you any." Troy chuckled against my ear.

"Hello." My voice sounded groggy, thick from sleep. "Hello." I tried again, slightly less scary sounding the second time around.

"Megan Katharine Winters." Uh-oh. Three names, it couldn't be good if she was using all three names. "You are seeing someone and you didn't bother to tell me?"

Kyla had lasted exactly two days. Better than her usual record, but still I'd secretly hoped for more. "Ash, it's...."

"Complicated. Yes I've already got the down low from Kyla. What's so complicated about it? Why can't we meet him? What does he do? It's not that coffee guy again is it? How long have you been seeing him?" The questions tumbled out of her mouth without even a breath or an opportunity to answer. "Is he good to you? Tell me, he's good to you. Have you told your folks?"

"Ash, slow down." If I wasn't awake before, I surely was now. And here comes the Spanish Inquisition. "He is very good to me and I didn't tell anyone because I wasn't ready yet."

"Well, are you ready now?" She didn't give me the opportunity to answer. There was a definite theme for this phone call. One where Ash talked and I listened. "You are bringing him over for dinner. Tonight. I promise Dan will be on his best behavior and so will Troy and Jase. Kyla and Brianne, I have no control over."

"Wait, what? Troy's coming?" My eyes shot to Troy who could clearly hear the phone conversation beside me. He just shrugged innocently. I didn't buy it, not for a second. Oh shit, I had shown way too much interest in the Troy part of with that sentence. "I mean Troy *and*

193

Jase are coming." I tried to recover. Cringe. It was a bad cover-up if ever I heard one.

"Nice try." Ash didn't miss my slip. Damn it. "Does your new guy know you have a secret obsession? And yes, they will *both* be coming."

"I'm not obsessed and tonight is kind of short notice. He probably has plans." The nervous giggle that came from my throat didn't make me sound any more convincing than I had been.

"So use that magic vagina of yours to get him to change them. Just tell him it's important because your *friends* need to make sure he's not an axe murderer."

"Oh, 'cause that's going to make the invitation so much more appealing. Look, I'll try. My magic vagina can only do so much. No promises."

What could I say? Flat out refusing would have invited too many questions. At least the promise to try would buy me a few hours to work something out.

"Make it happen and no calling me later today with some mysterious stomach bug or headache." Ash nixed the other option I had been considering. Foiled! "So unless you are in an emergency room, you are going to come to dinner. And FYI, I have your brother's number. I'm sure he'd be interested to hear some guy is bedding his sister but refusing to be seen in public with her. Can't think he would be too pleased."

I sat up in bed in a panic. "You wouldn't. I thought we were friends?"

"We are, and you would do the exact same thing if I were dating some guy who no one knew about." She wasn't wrong, not to mention I had involved myself very much so in her relationship not so long ago. Karma wasn't just a bitch; she was giggling her ass off too. "See you tonight. Seven o'clock."

Resignation. I had no other choice. "Fine. I'll see you then." I ended the call and tossed the phone onto the bed.

Fuck. Fuck. Fuck.

"Dinner plans?" Troy asked innocently, like he hadn't heard ninety-five percent of the conversation.

CRASH RIDE

"Yes, ones you apparently already agreed too?" My finger jabbed him in the chest. Not like it would even make a mark on that solid wall of muscle, but it made me feel better so I did it anyway.

"Hey, don't look at me. I didn't know I was going there for dinner. Dan text me this morning and asked me if I could go over later this evening because he needed help with something. He didn't say anything about dinner." Troy put his hands up in defense.

"Fuck." My head fell into my hands. There wasn't going to be a quick fix.

"We can do that, but I don't think it's going to solve your problem." He smirked before kissing my shoulder—which incidentally was so not helpful. "Tell me, beautiful, how you are going to talk your way out of this one?

My mind ticked wildly with possibilities. "Maybe I can ask Callum…"

"No." He shot the idea down before I even finished the sentence. "I don't give a fuck if it's pretend or otherwise, no other guy gets to date you. That shit was hard enough to take before—now that you're mine and have my baby inside you—I'd probably rip the guy's head off."

The vibe he was throwing off was one dictated by pure testosterone. Let's forget to mention that I had dated Josh while I was unknowingly pregnant. There were some things best left unsaid.

"Fine, then I'll go alone." There was no getting out of it. "I'll say *he* had to work or something." Plausible. Short notice. I was liking my idea already.

"Do you know how bad of a liar you are?" Troy's voice softened as he kissed my neck. "I mean, like horrendously bad. I love you, sweetheart, but if I'm ever going to hide a body, you are the last person I'm going to call."

"I'll have you know I would totally rock body disposal. So that would be *your* loss." With my arms folded defiantly across my chest I tried to look insulted.

"We'll see." The smirk was back, the laugh added in for good measure. "Should make for an interesting evening."

"You know, you could enjoy this a little less. It wouldn't kill you." I gave him my best death glare. His smile told me, it had been less than convincing.

"Where's the fun in that?" He laughed, rubbing my arms affectionately. He was going to need to stop that if I wanted to continue to be mad. "I'm assuming you won't be travelling with me to Dan's or with your *boyfriend*."

"You assumed correctly." Showing up with Troy would look suspicious. No, I would catch a cab. That would give me more time to create a backstory. "I might make him a fireman. And he got called away, he's a hero you know."

"So many pole jokes, and so little time."

"Please don't make fun of my fictional boyfriend, it's not classy." I rolled my eyes.

"Fine, I'll leave your fictional boyfriend alone, but your *real* boyfriend is sending a car to come pick you up." He held up his hand anticipating my rebuttal. I was more than capable of getting around by myself. "Don't get all feisty on me. Dan has probably already organized TJ anyway."

"Okay. I won't fight you." At least the ride would be one thing I wouldn't have to worry about.

"Good. Now come here and let me give you a proper good morning." My body was yanked back onto the mattress; an involuntary yelp accompanied me on the way down.

While my concerns for the evening weren't solved, not yet at least, I lost myself in Troy's kiss. It was easy to do and it was definitely the best way to wake up. Whatever stress the phone call had caused was washed away, and as luck would have it, it *was* a good morning. A very, very good morning.

21
Troy

"Beer?" Jase handed me a longneck while I milled around in Dan's living room. I was edgy as fuck. "Just a pointer, you checking the time every five minutes is probably not the best way to play it cool." He took a swallow of the beer in his hand.

"It's seven thirty, she was supposed to be here half an hour ago. Where the fuck is she?" My mind got caught up on possibilities I didn't like as I took a swig from the bottle. I was already over this bullshit game and the night hadn't even started.

"Maybe she got held up with her *boyfriend*." Jase grinned and took another swallow.

"Very funny, asshole. Do you know how much this bullshit is pissing me off?" Jase was one of the few people I could talk to about Megs. At least while I was pacing like a caged dog he could help run interference.

"What's pissing you off?" Dan joined us, leaving his wife-to-be to fuss in the kitchen. "What are you two ladies gossiping about?"

"Oh nothing important." I wondered how much he'd heard. "Just that I'm going to have to get into a monkey suit for your big day. It's like wearing a straight jacket." The excuse of the suit gave me a save. Not like I could tell him the fucking truth.

"Damn right you are suiting up. You aren't going to bitch about it either." His eyeballing told me he meant business. Not that there was any doubt. "Wonder where Megs is? You wanna give the loser a hard time?"

"Probably not one of your better ideas. Maybe give the girl a break, huh?" Jase thankfully took the reins on that one; saving me from telling Dan I'd punch him in the sack if he made her cry. Yep. It was going to be a long ass night.

"Fine." Dan pouted, pissed his source of entertainment had been taken for the night.

I pulled my phone out from my pocket. No texts, no missed calls and thirty-three minutes later than when Megs said she was going to be here. Another minute and I'd be getting TJ on the horn— someone had some explaining to do.

Since finding out I was going to be a dad, it was insane how fucking protective and territorial I'd become. It was straight up caveman shit, I didn't understand it but I knew well enough to know there was no fighting it either. And no shit, if I could wrap Megs in cotton wool for the next eight months, I'd do it.

The door buzzer sounded and it looked like I was finally going to be put out of my misery. Thank fucking Christ.

The relief, however, was short lived 'cause when the door swung open it wasn't Megs. The two chicks whose names I didn't quite remember were busy squealing over Ash's newly acquired engagement ring in the entranceway with no sign of my girl.

I'd waited long enough. "Need to make a call, guys. Give me a sec." Neither Dan nor Jase asked questions as I turned my back and put some distance between us so I could get busy giving JT the where-the-fuck-are-you.

CRASH RIDE

"Oh, hi Troy." One of the pair, who'd just walked in, popped up in front of me—her smile was more than just a little friendly. My phone that had barely made it out of my pocket was still in my hand as she gave me a wave to go with the smile. I hadn't even had a chance to dial.

"Hey…" I search my mind for her name. It had to be in there somewhere; both Ashlyn and Megs had introduced us a couple of times. I'd never been interested enough to take notice.

"Brianne." She let me off the hook, adding another little smile at the end. Well at least I hadn't pissed her off, not that she was high on my list of priorities but being out and out rude to a friend of Ash and Megs wouldn't win me any favors either.

"Right. Brianne. How are you doing?" My phone got shoved back into my pocket as I mentally calculated how long I would have to talk to her. One minute? Five? Surely Megs would show in that time. If she didn't— polite or not— I'd be giving Brianne a friendly shove and making that call.

"I'm good. Really good." More smiles and I had to wonder if the girl hadn't taken some happy pills before she'd shown up.

Ash flicked her eyes over to us and gave me a nod. Not sure if she was glad 'cause I wasn't being an asshole to her friend or Brianne talking to me meant one less chick pawing at the rock on her hand. So guess I was stuck a little while longer. Jase and Dan were no help either; the two of them not even giving us a second look as they stood where I'd left them deep in conversation.

"Great." I forced my mouth into a smile. Great? Not even close.

Brianne continued to talk, but a bunch of words was all I heard. My limit for waiting had just been reached when another loud buzz came from the door. And if that door opened and Megs wasn't behind it, there would be some serious hell to pay.

"Hey, everyone. Sorry I'm late." Megs burst through the doorway, her face more pale than when I'd left. My need to be polite put on a back burner as I moved closer to where the action was.

"So where is he?" Ashlyn asked, her head poking out the doorway looking to see if someone else was with her. Not fucking likely.

"Ash, I'm sorry. It was late notice and he had to work." Well what do you know, she sounded genuinely sincere, she must've been working on the act in the car ride over. Maybe that's why she'd been late.

Megs shot me a look but didn't hold it for long, instead giving Ash her attention as the questioning continued.

"It's Sunday, what does he do?" Ash wasn't letting it go that easy, not that I'd expected anything less.

"He's a fireman." Megs smiled like she'd just been given a puppy. I wasn't sure if I should be proud she was really trying to pull it off or pissed that she was pretending she was with someone else.

"He let you slide down his pole?" The expected Dan response didn't take too long to show up. I had tried to warn her about pole jokes— she hadn't listened.

"Dan, really." Ash planted her hands on her hips and gave her head a shake but no one seemed surprised. Megs relaxed a little seeing the heat was off her, at least short term.

"Sorry babe, it kind of needed to be said." Dan shrugged, the shit-eating grin showing how *not* sorry he was.

"So, your fireman." Ash turned back to Megs, the twenty questions far from done. "Does he have a name?"

The more I watched, the more juiced up I was getting. Fuck it. She was clearly not herself, I could tell just by looking at her, and I wasn't sure if it was the fucking stress of sprouting bullshit or if she was genuinely not well.

"So Troy, are you done with the new album? You will be touring soon I'm assuming?" Brianne shoved herself in front of me again, stopping me from hearing Megs's answer.

"Huh?" The words she had said not fully registering in my head because I'd been worried about my girl.

"Touring? The band will be going on the road, right?" she repeated, her body so close to me I had to take a step back.

"Rory's so busy and sort of shy. Maybe some other time...." Bits of

Megs's conversation floated over to me as Brianne waited for a response. Hinting that her interest in the Megs show was done and dusted.

"Yeah, next year sometime," I answered, not bothering to look at her, my eyes focused on Megs who was looking paler by the second.

"Would love to see a show. You guys are fantastic live," Brianne continued. Stepping in front of me when I tried to get closer to where Megs was standing. This dance was getting old.

"I'm sure we can manage to float you some tickets. No big deal." I threw it out there hoping that the promise of free tickets would get her off my ass. I had been done with this conversation five minutes ago.

"Rory sounds like a douche if you ask me. What kind of guy can't get his shit together for his girl." Dan weighed in, adding to my already short fuse.

"Really? You would give me tickets?" Brianne smiled and side stepped in front of me again.

"Yeah, like I said, it's no big deal." I moved again finally getting past her.

"Oh, thank you, Troy, you're the best." She threw her arms around me stopping me from moving forward, her hands getting familiar with my chest.

"Heyyyyyyy. Wow. Easy there." I got to work quickly trying to peel her arms off my body, but she was persistent, tightening her grip as I tried to move her fingers.

My eyes shot to Megs, who because of my edging to get closer, now had a front row seat to Brianne's little show. The seething eyes and the tight mouth enough of a hint she wasn't happy.

"You smell nice, is that some special cologne you're wearing?" She moved her head closer, sniffing my neck as I tried to maneuver out.

"Brianne, hey." I was done being nice. "How about you let go. I don't want to hurt you." I was completely ready to rip her hands off me if she didn't fucking remove them herself.

"I like it, you smell manly." She completely ignored me, like I hadn't just asked her to get her fucking mitts off me.

"Get your hands off him!" Megs seethed as she stormed over to us, yanking on Brianne's arm.

"Megs? Oh hey, sweetie, I was just chatting to Troy." She patted my chest like I was her fucking pet as I freed myself from her.

"Yeah, I saw how you were chatting to him. Any closer and you would be giving him a lap dance." She planted her hands on her hips, her voice full of venom.

"Ah-ha. I fucking knew it!" Kyla pointed at us both, her eyes and grin just as big as each other. "I knew it. I told you we would smoke them out."

Kyla and Brianne high fived each other and the pieces came together. The whole fucking thing had been a set up and we'd both been played.

"Knew what? What?" Dan looked around, confused not knowing what the hell was going on.

"Oh lord, here we go." Jase laughed, knowing the shit storm had just been unleashed.

"Megs and Troy are together." Brianne smiled, proud her little performance had outed us. If I hadn't been so distracted with concern with Megs, I would have seen this shit a mile away.

"Megs and Troy are together? Does the fireman know?" Dan looked between Megs and me, trying to play catch up.

"There's no fireman, you moron. Try and keep up." Jase smacked him on the shoulder.

"Fuck it." I did what I should have done from the start. I grabbed Megs's hand and gave it a squeeze. "Yes, we're together. We were trying to keep it on the DL and not make a big deal about it but now it's out there, we're seeing each other. We're a couple. Whatever you wanna call it, I'm done with this hiding shit."

"Waaiiiiiitttt a minute." Dan held up his hands, giving me the eyeball. "What about all those broads you've been screwing?"

"There weren't any other broads. It was just Megs." I slung my arm around her and tucked her in close. It's what I had wanted to do from the minute she'd walked in. It felt good and I made a fucking promise that

CRASH RIDE

from now on, I wouldn't be holding back.

"Fuck, it's like Lexi and Alex all over again. Seriously, I'm fucking offended. Why the hell wasn't I in on this memo?" He threw up his hands in disgust.

"Dan, not now," I warned.

"People are fucking, left, right and center and I'm none the wiser." He continued to run his mouth at the risk of a beat down from me. His attention turned to Ash who didn't look all that surprised. "Did you know?"

"Not until Kyla came to me with her theory. Although I'm really not surprised." She tucked her arms around Dan and gave us a smile.

"So you played us? You weren't really flirting with Troy?" Megs looked at her friends, apparently needing confirmation on what I already knew.

"Come on, Megs, girl code. I would never go after a guy you've been lusting over for years. But Kyla and I decided that you would probably need the incentive to come clean." Brianne gave her a smile, her delight fucking obvious.

"I hate you both."

"No you don't. Look how awesome it is. All in the open." Kayla smirked, giving Brianne a hug. The pair of them, pleased.

"Whatever." Megs waved them off and turned her attention back to me.

"Well now everyone knows about us, can you give me a minute so I can kiss my girl?" Not that I needed the permission, my mouth on Megs was happening and the fact I'd waited this long was a fucking miracle.

"Oh, so sweet." Brianne clapped her hands together, giving us her endorsement.

"I mean, literally everyone is fucking and not telling me." Dan was still stuck on the same old tune.

"Shut up, dickwad. You are spoiling my mood." I flipped him off as I slowly edged Megs back into the living room.

I didn't give her much time, my hands around her jaw tilting her head toward mine so I could taste her. She parted her lips and let me inside, her hands pulling me closer as I sealed my mouth with hers. It was like being in heaven. I would never get sick of it.

Megs pulled her mouth away from mine; her smile telling me it had been just as good for her. "You don't have to look so pleased with yourself and don't you dare say I told you so."

"Wouldn't dream of it but the pleased look is staying. I am very, very pleased." Not a lie, I was ecstatic about the turn of events. Happy that people knew that we were together and what did you know? Nothing bad had happened.

"Let's not mention the baby just yet, okay?" Megs pulled against my shirt, her eyes flooded with please-don't-fight-me. "I think we've reached our quota for crazy reveals for one night."

"Deal." I could live with that. We had all kinds of time to announce junior. "Why were you late? You feeling okay?"

"I think my easy run might be coming to an end." Megs gave me a tight smile and my inner caveman got very interested in the conversation. "I was feeling weird and puked a bit, but I'm fine now."

"Should we go back and see the doctor?" I cursed myself for not being there to take care of her when she was sick. That shit would be changing, very fucking soon.

"No, from all the reading material they gave us, it sounds normal." She gave a shrug and wrapped her arms back around me.

"Alright you two, come sit down." Ash smiled from the doorway. "We are actually eating dinner tonight."

"Ash, I'm sorry I didn't tell you. I just ..." Megs wriggled out of my hold and started to explain before Ash cut her off.

"Megs, I'm happy for you. Really I am. It doesn't matter, I'm just glad you got your guy." She didn't seem pissed which was a plus. While I knew eventually everyone would get over it —even Dan— the last thing I wanted was Megs upset.

"Thank God, I'm so relieved. I thought for sure you would be mad and worried our relationship would screw up your wedding plans." Megs

CRASH RIDE

grabbed Ash's hand and gave it a squeeze.

"Megs, you're crazy." Ash smiled, giving Megs's arm a little shake.

"How much trouble can you get into in a couple of months?"

"True." Megs laughed. "I mean I can only get knocked up once, right?" She slapped her hand across her mouth as soon as she realized what she'd said. So much for not telling anyone about the baby.

"What?!" Ash looked at Megs before looking at me, obviously putting two and two together.

"Yeah, that's the other bit of news we were keeping on the quiet." There was no hiding my big ass grin. "It's early days, but we're going to be parents."

"Oh my God." Ash's eyes got wide as she got caught up to speed.

"Ash, please don't tell anyone. I can't believe I let that slip. It's so early, we just found out ourselves."

"I swear I won't tell a soul, but no more fucking secrets, okay?" Ash pulled Megs in for a hug, both of them pretty emotional.

"I promise." Megs hugged back, no doubt part of her glad she wasn't hiding more shit from her friend.

"Alrighty, you think I can have my girl back? Have some lost time I want to make up for." And make sure she's okay. The sickness thing still worried me a little.

"Sure, sure." Ash released Megs and I pulled her back to my side. "Five minutes you two."

"Thanks." I tipped my chin as Ash scooted out of the room.

"Now," my hands went to her jaw again, clocking her eyes with mine, "let me do that one more time so I can make sure you are okay."

22

Megan

"Ugh, I feel sick." My stomach rolled as I ran to the bathroom. My morning ritual about to be performed for the second time as I heaved whatever contents my stomach had left into the toilet. "God, this is so fucking gross." I heaved again, hoping to God it would be the last.

"Megs, what can I do?" Troy asked helplessly from the door, the one I'd tried in vain to close before doubling over and puking my guts out. It was bad enough I had to witness it; I didn't want an audience.

It had been two weeks since we'd found out a little life was growing inside me and within that two weeks, my body had already started to change. The biggest change seemed to be the relationship I was now in with the bathroom. I'd contemplated changing my status on Facebook; we were inseparable these days.

"Please don't watch." I waved him off, mortified. "I'm almost done." My hands braced either side of the cold tiled wall as my body hovered in limbo, waiting for the next wave of nausea to rip through me.

"You think I haven't seen anyone get sick before? Megs, I spent most of my teenage years watching underage kids puke their parents' liquor cabinet out onto their lawn."

Obviously the view hadn't been good enough from the door, because despite my protest he came and sat on the tub beside me. I grabbed the washcloth from the sink and wiped my face.

"Awesome, thanks for the visual. It doesn't change that I don't want you to see me. God, could this be any less sexy? I wouldn't be surprised if you never slept with me again." Oh God, please don't let me cry. Cry for the ghosts of orgasms past. I'd had a good run, I shouldn't be so greedy.

"Going to take a little bit more than vomit to turn me off, sweetheart. Do I need to have sex with you right now just to prove a point?"

I grabbed my toothbrush from the holder and squeezed on some toothpaste. It was probably going to make me gag but at least my mouth would be minty fresh. Got to take the victory when you can. "I'd probably throw up on you and ruin your *New York Dolls* T-shirt." I pointed to his vintage Tee before shoving the toothbrush in my mouth.

"Fine, we'll do it in the shower, easy fix." He stood up and pulled off his T-shirt, his face deadly serious. "Let's go, get naked."

"You're insane." I mumbled spitting the toothpaste into the sink. Wow, it didn't get any less sexier than this. How was he still standing there?

"Nope, just know that no matter what happens my feelings aren't going to change." He walked over to the sink while I rinsed.

Things would change. He would go on tour and meet women who weren't moody or emotional and whose boobs didn't sag to their knees. Not that mine did yet, but I was prepared— I've read *Cosmo*. When did I become so fucking insecure?

"They'll change after the baby, when you'll be able to park your car in my vagina."

Troy's face animated as he barked out a laugh. "Seriously, do you rehearse this shit?" And yet again more laughter at my expense. This was so not funny. "You are killing me."

"Stop laughing at me, this is not funny." The damp washcloth I had been using went flying toward his face. My throw wasn't great —I had never been good at sports—and he ducked, the washcloth hitting the wall in a rather defeated splat.

"Look at me, Megs," Troy closing the gap between us and I gave silent thanks I had brushed my teeth. "I am not going anywhere. I love you. We've got this, okay?" He wrapped his arms around me, capturing me in a Troy prison of sorts. It felt nice there. Safe.

"I love you, too," I mumbled against his chest, breathing him in.

"Well then, we're more than half way there, yeah?" His hand played with my hair as he held me close. He showed no signs of letting go, which was awesome seeing as I didn't want him to.

"I hate that you're the one making sense when I'm acting crazy. Worst thing is I know it's crazy talk, but I can't make myself stop. You know I graduated cum laude from Georgetown? I should be the one making sense."

His chuckle vibrated through his chest. "So, even smart people get to fly off the handle. If it makes you feel better, most my twenties were spent *acting crazy*. I've done my time."

"God, you're sexy, Troy Harris." I peeled my head from his chest to admire the view. It was a view that I would never get tired of.

"Must be the company I'm keeping." He flashed a cheeky grin. "I would also like to point out that shower sex is still very much on the table."

"We have to be at my mom and dad's in an hour." Of all the craziness I'd been sprouting this morning, now was when I decided to be responsible? I was so appalled.

"So? I have a Lambo, Megs. I'll drive the thing sideways to get us there in time."

He was making a solid argument and I almost caved, except thoughts of having to sit through a meeting with my parents after just having had sex was probably a little too skeevy, even for me.

"Just kiss me now."

It was a compromise and probably one that would see us being late anyway. Me and impulse control left a lot to be desired.

"Always."

Nerves. They didn't help the nausea I'd been dealing with, nor did the eggs benedict my mother had placed in front of me. Mental note. It's easier to introduce your boyfriend to your parents *before* you get knocked up.

"Troy, would like some more juice?" My mother hovered with a pitcher full of orange juice. Her bright smile thawing some of my nerves. Oh hell, my parents were going to freak the fuck out.

"Thank you, Mrs. Winters, I'd love some." Troy held my hand under the table as I counted backward from ten and tried to regulate my breathing.

"So, you're a rock star." My dad took a sip from his coffee cup, his brow raised in the I'm-not-making-this-easy-for-you position I hadn't seen in awhile. It was his talent—along with being a brilliant heart surgeon—the ability to make me feel like I was sixteen and got caught sneaking out.

"With all due respect, Mr. Winters, anyone who calls themselves a rock star is an ass...." He caught himself before adding *hole* and corrected himself. "...is conceited. I'm a musician and I'm lucky enough to be successful in a pretty difficult industry." Troy obviously wasn't feeling the same fear I was. Good. Only one of us was allowed to freak out at a time and currently I was definitely freaking the hell out.

"Yes, very difficult industry but no career paths are safe these days are they, Mitchell?" My mom sat back down in her seat and gave me a wink. Her support was something I could always count on, and besides I blamed her for some of my quirky antics. Sitting right there in her chiffon blouse and playing with her strand of pearls was an original member of the *KISS* army, I kid you not.

"Of course, I was merely trying to establish what it is you do." My dad took another slow sip from his cup. "You play in the same band with that Dan fellow, Ashlyn's rather taken with?" I didn't correct him that Ash was *marrying* him, slightly more than *rather taken*.

Troy's calm veneer didn't shatter, answering my dad respectfully with a calmness I clearly didn't possess. "Yes, sir. Dan Evans is my best friend; we are both in the same band."

"Do you do drugs?" My dad lowered his cup nonchalantly like he'd just asked if Troy flossed after brushing.

"Dad." I barked out, horrified he'd subscribe to such a clichéd stereotype.

Troy looked my father dead in the eye and answered. "No. No drugs."

"So, how did the two of you meet?" My mom tried to lighten the mood, not like it could get any tenser, mention of drug use will do that to a conversation.

"I had the pleasure of meeting your daughter last year. Just took me a while to wise up and ask her out." Troy smiled and thankfully went with the censored version. I didn't need for my parents to know about my extra circular sextivities.

"Are you alright sweetie, you haven't touched your brunch?" My mom touched my arm, the plate in front of me, untouched.

"I'm just not very hungry, Mom." I gave her my best smile, the lopsided half-grin didn't do much to help my cause.

My dad eyed me up and down, no doubt gathering intel from my lack of appetite. I swear the man had x-ray vision or something. He could always *tell* when something was wrong.

"So, are you getting married or are you pregnant?"

"Dad!"

"Mitchell!"

My mom and I both snap simultaneously. He must definitely have x-ray vision.

"Look, I know I'm an old man but I'm not completely ignorant." He wiped his mouth with his napkin. "You both look like you've been told you need a triple bypass. So which is it? Oh, and I will remind you son, while I am doctor, I still maintain my second amendment rights."

"Mitchell, stop." My mother waved my father off before reaching across and touching Troy's arm. "He doesn't have a gun."

"I didn't say I had a gun, I said I maintain my rights— which means I could get one," my father clarified.

"I'm pregnant." It was time to come clean, after all that's why we were here, right? "We love each other, and we're having the baby."

"Mr. and Mrs. Winters, while this pregnancy wasn't planned, I love your daughter very much and we're going to be a family." Troy took over, not willing to let me face the music by myself. "We're getting married as soon as she agrees. Hell, I'd marry her tomorrow, if she'd let me."

"Is this what you want, darling? I need you to know that your mother and I will respect and support you, whatever decision you make but I don't want you to get married out of obligation. That will never work out. Baby or no baby, this has to be something you need to be sure of."

My dad reached out his hand and touched my arm.

"Dad, of course I want this. I love him." My eyes watered as I nodded my head and Troy squeezed my hand even tighter.

"Sir, me not marrying Megs is not really an option." Troy moved his arm around me.

"Our Megan is an exceptionally bright girl, and usually a good judge of character so the fact that you are sitting here in our home means she obviously thinks very highly of you. But I held that baby girl when she came into this world. I loved her first, and I'm always going to love her, so when I give her away, I'm going to make damn well certain that the man is worthy of her."

"I don't think there is a man alive who is worthy of her, but I can tell you now that I would give my last breath to make her happy."

"Right answer." My dad nodded.

"Dad?" Was this some test Troy was supposed to pass?

"When the two of you eventually have children you will understand. No one will ever be good enough for them; all you can ask for is that they find someone who will give it their all to make them happy."

I was already an emotional mess—hearing how much he loved me—just about sent me over the edge. I should probably buy shares in *Kleenex* for the rest of this pregnancy.

"Does this mean we have your blessing?" I knew it was old fashioned and I would be with Troy without it, but I desperately wanted for my parents to be okay with this.

"Beautiful girl, you will always have our blessing." My father smiled. "Troy, if you mess this up, I know ways to kill you and make it look like natural causes."

"Mitchell!"

"Dad!"

"I'm not going to mess this up." Troy grinned, no doubt or hesitation in his voice.

"Good, now tell me when we can expect this grandbaby."

23
Troy

"SO YOU GOING TO MAKE ME BEG, IS THAT HOW YOU WANNA PLAY this game?" I kissed her neck in the spot I'd knew would make her squeal. Our bodies lying on top of the makeshift pallet bed I'd made out of blankets and pillows on my living room floor. The bullshit movie we'd been trying to watch no longer holding our interest.

"Troy Harris, stop that! You're playing dirty." She threw her head back laughing, but made no attempt to move—not that my arms locked around her would have let her.

"Last time I checked, that's how you liked it." I nipped at her shoulder, loving the noise that was coming from her mouth.

"I do, I do." She laughed as she tried to wiggle out of my hold.

"See, it's not that hard to say. Now, just let me get you in front of a preacher and you just need to repeat that again." I moved my arms from their strong hold and maneuvered her onto her back, my legs caging her in as I hovered above her.

"Who knew you were such a traditionalist." She raised her hands to my face. "God, could you be any more adorable?"

"Can we quit calling me adorable? I thought we agreed on calling me bad-ass, fierce will also work." My hands worked their way up her sides, tickling her.

"Whatever— you are just a big teddy bear, Troy Harris." She threw her head back in a laugh; the smile she was wearing rocking my world.

"You're lucky I'm secure in my manhood." My fingers traced the lines of her body, part of me not believing that she was actually mine. "I thought the idea of a shrink was to make people *less* crazy not give them a complex."

"I'm off duty, so messing with your mind is allowed." Her grin got bigger. Jesus, there was nothing I wouldn't do for this girl.

"Is that why you are refusing to set a date? My mind not pretzeled enough for your liking?" My head dipped down, my mouth deciding it had something better to do than talk.

"I want to marry you, I do —but it's so soon." Her thumbs moved over my lips and her eyes clocked mine. "Like sooooo soon. We have just started telling people we're dating, we get married— everyone is going to know it was a shotgun wedding. Besides, Dan and Ash haven't even had their wedding yet."

"Fuck what people think, and the only shotgun will be the one I'll be lugging if we end up having a daughter. No one is forcing my hand, but I want a ring on yours."

Marrying Megs was not something I needing to think about. Not sure when I'd wised up, but her carrying our baby wasn't the reason. Sure it might have sped up the process, but there was zero doubt that it was what I wanted. Her and me forever, I was more than okay with that game plan.

"But I'll be fat in the wedding photos." Megs screwed up her face in disgust. "Is that what you want to look back and see? Me being poured into a wedding dress like the Stay Puft marshmallow man?"

"You will look fucking perfect, like you do everyday."

"See, you don't need me to mess with your head, you're already delusional." She rolled her eyes not understanding that for me, her body changing was a turn on, not a fucking turn off.

"I sure as hell was in the past. Looking at you and pretending that I didn't want to be with you, yeah —it doesn't get more delusional than that." Ain't that the truth.

"Aw. You're being adorable again." Her smile was back, this time even bigger than before.

"I'm motherfucking fierce I told you." My mouth attacked hers, trying to prove my point.

"Fiercely adorable," she mumbled against my mouth.

"Killing me. You are killing me." My lips moved to her neck, kissing their way down.

"Tell me you love me." Her hands locked into my hair, pulling my head back to look at her.

"I love you, marry me," I said with zero hesitation.

"I love you too. Not yet." Her eyes got glassy as she nodded her head.

"Then I'm going to ask you every day until you say yes."

And so started our game, everyday a new proposal.

Monday I went with funny and got a huge ass teddy bear delivered to her office. No shit, the thing was easily six-foot and had a sign around his neck that said his name was Fierce. In his huge paw I'd taped a card that said *Marry Troy*. Sure I wanted to be the one doing the asking, but I wasn't scared to call in some help if it meant we got to take the walk down the aisle sooner.

She'd jumped on the horn and giggled for ten minutes straight.

"Troy, I love Fierce. You are so sweet."

"Just don't love him more than me; I didn't pay all that money for the bastard to steal my woman," I warned, glad I'd been able to make her laugh.

"I don't know— it's a coin toss right now as to which one of you holds a bigger piece of my heart." She teased as if she was trying to bait me.

"Did he give you my message or was he too busy putting the moves on?" I'd hoped that she hadn't missed the message he had in his hand.

"He did and I'll think about it." It was a step up from the *not yet* I'd gotten yesterday, so as far as I was concerned it was a win.

"Awesome. I'll get the ball rolling for tomorrow's surprise then."

"I can hardly wait. Hey, Troy. Is it okay if I take Fierce to the children's wing to play? I think the kids would really love him."

"Yeah, I think that would be the best place for him seeing as I've obviously got things covered at home. Besides, it will mean I won't have to worry about him hitting on you when I'm not looking." This earned me more giggles.

For Tuesday I went with romantic.

I woke up at the crack of dawn and placed a trail of rose petals from her bed all the way to the kitchen. Then I got busy making heart-shaped pancakes, trying to not set off the smoke alarm while I cooked them. Avoiding third degree burns was also a challenge—accidently grabbing the fucking heart shaped cookie cutter I was using with my bare hand while it was still in the skillet, wasn't my smartest move.

"Rose petals. Awww, did Fierce sneak in last night or was it my other teddy bear?" She yawned as she took a seat at the kitchen counter.

"Oh no, that fucker isn't getting credit for my moves." I swooped around, kissing her neck before placing the plate of pancakes in front of her. *Marry me* written in maple syrup across the top.

"Is this your way of getting me to eat my words?" Her finger slid along the edge of the plate collecting some *Aunt Jemima* before popping it into her mouth.

I moved around to the other side of the counter to where her feet were dangling from the barstool, sinking down to one knee and pulled a candy ring out from my pocket. If she wanted me on my knees, she'd have it. Whatever it took to make her say that three letter word, and I would keep asking until she said yes. There was no one else for me.

"This is just a stand in till we find the right one." I slid the ring onto her left hand. "But I've already found the right woman. Marry me, Megs.

I love you."

"Troy." She teared up as she cupped my face. "I love you too, but maybe we should wait until the baby's born. Do it properly? The baby will still have your last name even if we're not married, I promise you."

This wasn't about our baby having my last name; this was about having the woman I loved as my wife. "When we do it, either before or after the baby is born, it will be properly. I'll keep asking you. One of these days you are going to say yes." And I wasn't giving up.

Wednesday I hid Post-It notes in all of her stuff. So throughout the day she found little yellow squares that said *Marry Me*. I had been busy and stuck them in shoes, her laptop bag, bathroom cabinet, underwear drawer, in her purse and even managed to hide a few in her office. This hadn't been as hard to coordinate as I'd thought. I had been picking her up from work all week and every time, without fail she would need to use the bathroom before we left. So I'd used the time Tuesday evening while she was answering her call of nature to stuff a few in her drawers and push some under her keyboard.

"Troy Harris." The call had come around noon.

"Megs, what a nice surprise." I grinned into the phone like an idiot even though she couldn't see me.

"Did you buy shares in *3M* and not tell me? It's like Post-It notes threw up all over the place."

She was exaggerating, but I hadn't been shy about how many I'd hid. 'Cause I couldn't be sure she'd see them all, I played the numbers game and boosted the amount I'd left.

"I figured killing a few trees was less conspicuous than a billboard in *Times Square,* but give me a week and I'm sure I can get it together."

"Oh just make sure you don't replace Mr. tighty-whities in his Calvins, I really like looking at him."

"You look at him all you want as long as you come home to me." Some dude with his junk on display didn't threaten me, as long as he stayed on a billboard.

"Bye, Troy Harris."

I would never get sick of hearing her call me that, sure as hell meant more to me than calling me baby.

"Bye, Megs."

And so went the rest of the week. Thursday I dialed it down and went with simple. A big bunch of flowers with a card that said *TH Loves MW* was delivered to her office. There wasn't a *will you marry me* on there but it was kind of implied. She called and told me that they were beautiful, and then warned me her receptionist might try and snap me up herself— like that could ever happen. Friday, I surprised her and took her out to lunch. I got a local deli to get together a picnic basket for us and we walked to Central Park where we ate on the grass.

We had made the trek to Yonkers on the weekend and we'd told my folks we were together. My mom cried with excitement, firstly that I'd brought a girl home—something I hadn't done in a really long time, and secondly that we were going to be parents. The whole out-of-wedlock thing hadn't bothered my parents so much, they knew I was going to do the right thing by Megs and my son or daughter, so they did even ask if we were going to get hitched. Besides, my sister had gotten knocked up when she was eighteen—so me being a dad in my thirties —was a walk in the fucking park.

Not surprisingly they loved her and I did tell Megs that she was stuck with me now; my mother would probably disown my ass if I let her slip through my fingers. I'd even managed to ask her to marry me two more times on the weekend.

Everyday we moved a little bit closer, with my calculation being that by end of next week we would be in the courthouse —either getting a marriage license or her filing a restraining order.

It was worth taking the risk.

24

Megan

YOU KNOW WHAT ELSE COMES WITH HAVING YOUR HEAD DOWN A toilet and peeing every five minutes? Fatigue. Like a black cloud, it rolls in and sucks your energy right when you need it most, i.e. having your shit together at work.

"I hate my parents. I wish they'd never had me." Brad fidgeted in his chair; progress with him was going at a snail's pace.

"Why don't we talk about why you have these feelings. Has something happened recently? Have they mistreated you in any way?" It was the same story every session. He was filled with so much hate.

"They are trying to ruin my life. I didn't fucking ask to be born. It's all their fault my life sucks. They don't give a fuck about me." The venom spewed out of him, his feet tapping nervously on the floor.

At some stage something had to get through to him; a tiny *in* was all I needed.

"Brad, I can see you have a lot of hurt and anger, but your parents love you very much. I know things are hard for you to see right now but they are doing everything they can to help you. They care very much; they want you to be happy and well. I care Brad, I need for you to know that."

"I'm not crazy, I know you and everyone else thinks it, but I'm not." He flicked his ruffled bangs out of his eyes and looked at me, his eyes pleading with me to take away some of his pain.

"No one thinks you're crazy, you just need help. Please let me help you." My thoughts flicked to my own child and the things I would do to save them, save them from this pit of despair. "Please Brad, we can do this together."

"I don't know where to start." It was the first crack—the tiny, tiny step to moving forward but it was all I needed.

"We start slow, by being honest." I wanted to weep with relief. "We are going to write some scenarios down, triggers." My hand flew to my desk drawer and pulled out a blank piece of paper. "Things that make you feel not so great." I handed him a pencil. "It can be anything."

Brad leaned forward in his chair and tentatively started his list. "Anything? Like if I hate butterflies and they make me mad, I can write that?"

"Yep, you can write anything." I reassured him as I leaned back in my chair.

Uh-oh. That didn't feel good. The sudden movement back made me feel weird. Now was not the time for morning/afternoon sickness. I shouldn't have skipped lunch—you would think it would be easier on an empty stomach but it just made it worse.

"Dr. Winters? You okay?" Brad looked up from his list as I felt a heat come over me. Yep, this wasn't good. I was probably going to puke.

"Just a little upset stomach." The heat slowly travelled up my body as beads of sweat started to glisten on my forehead. "I just need a glass of water."

The water was a crapshoot—it was either going to settle the urge or accelerate the process, either way, I couldn't leave. I slowly rose out my chair, feeling clammy all over as I slowly walked away from my desk.

My hand started to shake as I poured myself a glass of water from the water cooler in my office. Just keep it together a little while longer, I told myself as my unsteady hand brought the paper cup to my mouth.

"Just keep writing, Brad." My breathing started to hitch as a different kind of feeling washed over me. "I—I'm okay." My voice wavered as I took another swallow of water.

Something was wrong, it wasn't just nausea—the heat, the shaking—it felt like the flu. I felt weak, like I could potentially pass out.

Abdominal pain gripped me—like period pain but worse— as I literally lost my breath. No. Another cramp took hold as I fell to my knees in pain. No.

"Dr. Winters!" Brad leapt out of his seat and joined me on the floor, his face filled with fear. "What's wrong? I'm sorry I was so mad."

"No." I whispered as yet again I felt the contraction of my abdominal wall. This couldn't be happening. My panties becoming wet as I felt the tell tale drip from in between my legs. "No." It was barely audible, my voice gripped by pain and fear as I clutched my stomach.

"Dr. Winters, please tell me what to do? Please?" Brad begged on the floor beside me, I had almost forgotten he was there.

"You need to grab my phone, Brad. It's on the desk. Then I'm going to need you to run outside to Mrs. Bennett in reception and wait with her, okay? Can you do that?" I harnessed whatever calmness I had in me, making sure I didn't raise my voice. He was just a kid, seeing me on the floor was bad enough—freaking out, that would scar him for life.

Brad ran to my desk and retrieved my cell, planting himself back on the floor with me. His shaky hand handed the phone to me as he stayed beside me on his knees.

"You need to go wait outside, Brad. Mrs. Bennett will look after you until your parents come to get you." I forced the smile as pain shot up my back.

"Something bad is happening to you, isn't it?" His eyes were so wide with fear.

"Please wait outside, Brad; I promise I am going to be okay." I wasn't sure if I believed it but I needed it to be the truth.

My fingers started dialing the ER department as I watched him reluctantly move to his feet. His scared eyes looked back at me from the doorway before he finally disappeared through it.

"Hi ER, Ronda speaking." The call was answered on the second ring.

"Hey Ronda, it's Dr. Winters from Psych room 3, I need a wheel chair and some assistance. I think I'm miscarrying my baby." I breathed through the pain as my hand squeezed the phone.

"Dr. Winters, I'll get someone up to you A.S.A.P. — just hang tight."

It's not like I had a lot of options other than *hanging*, there wasn't anything I could do but sit there.

"Okay, Okay." I nodded even though she couldn't see me, my eyes welling as I ended the call.

"Jesus, Mary and Joseph." Carrie Bennett ran through the door, sinking to her knees beside me. "It's going to be alright sweetie, just hang in there."

It wasn't going to be all right. No doctor or nurse would convince me of that.

"Please go out and stay with Brad, he's scared. Please go sit with him." My breathing was labored as I stared down at the floor. I couldn't raise my head.

"He's with Lani, sweetie. He's fine. I promise you." Her voice softened as she told me he was safely waiting with the other receptionist.

"Then please go wait with them. I just want to be alone." I couldn't do this and be strong for an audience. I was about to fall apart.

"Dr. Winters…" She started to protest.

"Please, Carrie." I interrupted forcing my head up to look at her, "Please."

Carrie slowly rose to her feet, her eyes flicking between me and the door. "I'm just going to be outside."

I nodded as I maneuvered the phone back into my palm so that I could make another call. My fingers were barely able to hit the number keys the pain was so intense.

"Megs," Troy answered; in his voice I heard a smile. "You going to try and sneak out early? I think we should definitely eat in tonight."

"Troy." My throat was thick with emotion as I tried to speak. I just needed to hold it together for a few more minutes, just a few more. "I'm losing the baby. I'm sorry."

It was all I could say, unable to explain or talk anymore as I pulled my cell from my ear, Troy's desperate voice echoing my name over and over before I hit end. He deserved more but I just couldn't give it.

"Megs!" My brother ran into the room with another attending physician, the stretcher behind them rattling into the room. "Stay calm, Megs, we're going to take care of you."

Our schedules rarely synced and I wasn't sure if it was a blessing or a curse that the stars had aligned today.

My head shook as he and the other doctor placed their hands on my elbows as they tried to ease me up.

"It's too late, I know it's too late." My body shook as they helped me to my feet. Blood trickled down my leg as I stood.

"Tom, she's lost a lot of blood. We need to get her lying down." The other doctor moved the stretcher closer to me as he held onto my arm.

"It's too late." They were the only words that seemed to come out of my mouth.

"Lay down, Megs." Tom nodded to the stretcher. "We need to move you."

My legs were on automatic, my body being controlled by the men whose hands were around my arms. I don't remember lying down, or my back hitting the gurney. The words of my brother and the other doctor were jumbled above me as my eyes flashed open to the passing fluorescent lights in the ceiling. The gentle rocking meant we were moving but I didn't care where we were going. ER or the parking lot, the end result would be the same.

"Megs, as much as I want to be in that room with you, I can't treat you. Blake is going to take it from here. I promise you, I'll be outside the whole time. Can I call Mom and Dad?"

I think I nodded, but I couldn't be sure; the thought that he would tell them was somewhat of a relief. The words were just too painful to say over.

"Megs." Tom's hand stayed locked on mine till they wheeled me into the exam room, "Have you called Troy?"

"Yes." It was barely a whisper but he nodded so I'd know that he'd heard.

And then he let go. Pushed out and swallowed by the noise as the curtain was drawn behind him.

25
Troy

"MEGS! MEGS!" I SCREAMED INTO THE PHONE, MY VOICE GETTING nothing but air. "Megs!" It was no use. The line was dead, the call — over.

"What the fuck, dude?" Dan killed the sound on the *Xbox*, the game of *Call of Duty* we'd been playing, well and truly over.

"I need to get to the hospital, I can't talk right now." I tossed my controller onto his couch. So much shit going through my head that I couldn't even focus on where the fuck I'd left my keys.

"Is Megs in trouble?" Dan got to his feet, throwing his controller to join mine while I patted my pockets like a fucking moron.

"Troy! Let me come with you. I'll drive." Dan held up my car keys. The bastards had been sitting on the coffee table right in front of my face the whole freaking time.

"No, I have to do this alone." I snatched the keys from his palm and sprinted to the door. I had no fucking idea what I was walking into, but I couldn't do this with back up.

"Brother, do whatever you need to do but for fuck's sake call me later. Whatever it is." He called after me as I yanked open his front door, his eyes full of I've-got-your-back.

"I've got to go." Were the only words I bothered to give him as the door slammed behind me.

My heart pounded as I jumped into the elevator and hit the button for the basement, the fucker not moving anywhere near fast enough.

"Come on!" My fist slammed against the mirrored wall, willing the metal box to speed the hell up. Every second, it dragged its feet until the steel doors opened at the underground parking garage.

My feet pounded, making my way to my car, cursing the fucking thing for not having keyless entry.

"Fuck." I fisted the keys to unlock the door.

My hand wrenched at the door, sinking my ass into the driver's seat before the thing was fully open and shoving the key into the ignition.

The engine roared as I pumped the gas, pulling the door shut as I tried to make some fucking sense of what was going on.

Megs had sounded so calm, so fucking calm it scared the fuck out of me.

My boot hit the accelerator, fishtailing onto the street as I tried to put on my seatbelt with one hand. Getting a ticket, yeah— didn't give a fuck—too juiced up to focus on anything other than getting where I was going.

Cars jammed on their brakes in front of me, the Lambo hitting a wall of fucking traffic as we pulled onto the main road. "Goddamit." My fist punched the horn as I tried to weave between the lanes to move this shit along faster.

Nightmare. It was a motherfucking nightmare as the minutes ticked by and I was still no closer to where I needed to be. Drivers beeped their horns and flipped me off as I cut them off, driving like an asshole with a death wish.

CRASH RIDE

I punched it on Madison Avenue, making the turn onto 99th and skidding into the parking garage.

"Hey, buddy, slow down." The asshole attendant called from his glass box like I give a shit what he thought.

Muscle memory steered the car into an empty spot, hauled my ass out of the seat and got my feet moving to the E.R. Thank fuck for the auto switch that kicked in because my brain had checked out the minute Megs had killed the call.

"I'm looking for Dr. Megan Winters." My palms slammed on the info desk making the chick behind it shoot up like a Pop Tart.

"Sir, I'm going to need you to calm down." Ms. Not-fucking-helpful rose to her feet and gave me the once over.

"I'll calm the fuck down when you tell me where she is." There was zero chance of me being calm until I found where Megs was and got to see her. The way I saw it, the lady should be grateful I wasn't tearing the place apart.

"Sir. Please, I don't want to have to call security; please refrain from using profanity."

Seriously. She's going give me shit over the word *fuck*? Why the fuck were we talking about what words I was using and not about where the hell my girl was? My fists balled tight to stop myself from ripping the fucking headset she was wearing off her fucking head.

"Lady, I'm not trying to start anything, but my girl and my baby are in there somewhere and I'm not in the mood to be pleasant. So, sorry if your feelings got hurt but I need you to quit eyeballing me and get on that fancy computer and tell me where she is." My fists primed by my sides ready to punch the computer if she didn't start giving me answers.

Her hands went to the two-way that was sitting on the desk near the phone, bringing it to her mouth without breaking eye contact.

"Security, we have a code gray…"

No! I could not get hauled out of there. Not without seeing Megs first.

"Don't call security, please." I prayed she would give me a chance to explain, forcing myself to lower my voice. "I just need to get to her."

"This is security, please advise the location of the code gray." The voice spewed out of the box in her hand.

My eyes flicked to the two-way, then to her. If there was a fucking God, this was when I needed him to get into the game. Every muscle in my body was wound tight as I relied on this stranger to help me. "Please. I'm begging you."

"Disregard the last transmission. False alarm." Her eyes stayed locked on me as she lowered the hand-held. She looked like she wasn't a hundred percent on board with listening to me, but whatever the chance was, I'd take it.

"Thank you. I'm sorry." I held up my hands in a peace offering and to prove I wasn't going to bitch-slap her desk anymore. "Dr. Megan Winters." I said her name slow. "Where is she?"

"Give me a moment." She sat her ass back down as she hammered the keys on her keyboard.

"She was brought in, but only immediate family can go back through. Are you related to Dr. Winters?" Her face told me she already knew the answer, her fingers easing off the keys and inching toward the two-way.

"I'm her boyfriend."

It sounded so fucking insignificant and didn't come anywhere near close enough to describing what she was to me. "She's pregnant and she is losing our baby. I know you have protocol, but I can't let her go through that alone. I need to be there with her."

"Sir...." The sorry-I-can't-help-you, about to be thrown on the end.

"Look, I swear to you, if she doesn't want me there I will leave. There isn't going to be a fight from me and you won't need some asshole rent-a-cop to haul me out, but I can't wait out here. I need to see her."

"Please wait." She sighed and picked up the phone. It was promising but until I was in the same room with Megs, I was still going to be edgy as fuck.

"Hey, are you Troy Harris?" Some blond-headed kid edged toward me.

Not sure if he was a fan or whatever, but there was no way in fuck I was going to do a meet-and-greet. "Listen kid, seriously haven't got time for this shit right now. I'm not interested in being your big news of the day so please just leave me the hell alone."

"O-Okay." The kid shuffled back into his seat like I'd just punched him in the face.

"Troy?" A dude in scrubs came up beside me, his hand landing on my arm.

"Yes. Are you her doctor? I need to get back there." I wasn't sure if this was the new person that I needed to be convincing. I didn't care whom I had to talk to as long as they let me through.

"I'm her brother, Tom." He tipped his head toward the double doors he'd walked out of. "Take a walk with me."

We were supposed to have a sit down sometime during the week. Her brother worked crazy long ass days, making it hard to nail him down; so while I'd known about him, we hadn't done the hi-how-are-yous yet. Not that it mattered now.

"I have to know, man; I need to know she is okay." My nerves were jangling so much I could barely get the words out straight.

"Megs is resting, they have her on an IV for fluids and some pain meds." He directed us through a corridor.

"That's not what I asked." I stopped walking. I needed to know the truth, not hear shit being sugar coated.

"I'm going to be honest with you, she's not doing great."

It wasn't easy to hear it but at least he'd finally come clean.

"The baby?"

He almost didn't need to say it; the look he was giving me told me there was no chance.

"I'm sorry. At eight weeks there is nothing we can do."

It was like a wave washed over me and dumped me on my ass. Or maybe it was a truck that had come and collected me in its grill. My chest hurt so much I was surprised I could still breathe, the lump in my throat also not helping the cause. I blinked fast, my eyes not doing real well with keeping their shit together. Guess they'd been following my lead.

"Can I see her? She can't do this by herself. I need to be there." It wasn't about me anymore, whatever I was feeling, it had to have been doubly worse for her.

"You can go back for a second but if she wants you out, you're going to have to leave."

He was talking as her brother, not a doctor and I had to respect that even if it was unnecessary. There was zero chance of me walking away from Megs, but I wasn't going to let my stupid need to see her make shit worse. I would sit in the waiting room until she was ready but I wouldn't leave. Not ever.

"I swear to you." I looked him in the eye and held out my hand.

He shook my hand and gave me a tight smile. "Hell of a way to meet, huh?"

We started ambling down the hallway again, people in curtained-off areas wailing either side of us.

"Yeah— no offense—but this wasn't how I saw this shit going down." I shoved my hands in my pocket as he rounded the corner.

"She's in there." He stopped short, his chin tipping to the curtain on the right. "Just don't… don't expect too much of her. She might not want to talk about it, you have to let her take the lead on this one."

I took a big swallow, once again fighting the lump in my throat. "Dude, she's had the lead from the start. I'm just the lucky bastard who's trying to keep up."

He gave me a nod and then wandered off, giving me the space to do this on my own. No doubt he wouldn't be far and ready to haul my ass away if Megs asked him to.

My hand hesitated as I pulled the curtain across, the zipping noise on the rail making Megs turn toward me. Her eyes were so red from crying, I didn't ever think they'd be right again. "Hey." I pulled the thing closed behind me and took a step inside, my heart fucking breaking with every stride.

"Hey," she responded, her voice shaky as she unwrapped her arms from around her chest.

There was so much about this situation that I hated. My chest felt like it was tearing in two but the pain that I saw in her, that was the fucking worst. I didn't even know where to start to make this right.

I pulled up a chair and planted it beside the bed. "I'm just going to sit down beside you and hold your hand, if that's okay with you?" My hand stretched out and linked with hers.

"Troy..."

There was so much hurt in that one fucking word that I literally hated my own name.

"Megs, we've got nothing but time, sweetheart. The only thing I need right now is to be here, we don't have to talk."

"I'm so sorry." She sucked in a breath as her eyes started to leak.

"Sorry?" My fingers stroked the back of her hand. I wanted to hold her but I didn't dare push it. "What have you got to be sorry for?"

"It was my fault." She whispered, the torment ripping through her like a freaking knife.

"Megs, no." This was not going to land on her. No fucking way. "It was no one's fault. Shit happens, it just wasn't our time yet."

"When you told me—that day when you read the report— I wanted it to be a mistake. I didn't want the baby. What kind of person does that?" Her eyes flooded.

"You were in shock, it was a surprise," I reasoned. Neither of us had been expecting that the sheet of paper was going to tell us we were about to be parents. Fuck, I'd had to re-read the stupid thing before it sunk in.

"The first five weeks of our baby's, life I put our baby at risk by not knowing and then when I finally did find out, I wished him gone." She ripped her hand out of mine and covered her face. "I'm the reason why. All my complaining about morning sickness and getting fat, I had wanted it to be over and now it is."

"Megs, this isn't on you. Do you hear me, this isn't on you." My feet pushed out of the chair and I sat on the bed, my hand rubbing circles on her back as I tried to comfort her. The pain I'd had before, nothing on what I had now. It killed me that she owned it, like she was in some way responsible.

"I'd changed my mind, Troy. I really did. I wanted our baby and I was sorry, but it wasn't enough." She pulled her hands away from her face and looked at me. Her tear stained cheeks and bloodshot eyes nailing me in place. "God, I'd do anything right now to feel sick again. I would have my head in a toilet all day long if I could just have the baby back. I don't care how fat I get. I don't care how our lives are going to change. I just want..."

"Come here." My arms wrapped around her as she shuffled up the bed, her head buried in my chest as my T-shirt got wet from her tears.

"I wanted our baby. I really did."

"I did too." My eyes once again fought the tears but I needed to keep it together. "I love you, Megs. I love you so much."

"I love you too." She whimpered against my neck as I stroked her hair.

"Marry me." I'm not sure why I said it and I knew that putting it out there wasn't what she needed right now, but the thought of her not being my wife was tearing me apart. For me—what we had—was as real as it got, and going through life without her wasn't an option. Not now, not ever.

"But there's no baby now, we don't have to get married." Her big blue-green eyes were wide as she shook her head.

"Wanting you to be my wife had nothing to do with the baby, and everything to do with not being able to live my life without you." I tipped her chin, needing her to really look at me. "That hasn't changed."

"We were worried that our relationship would be complicated, but every step of the way has been crazy, Troy. We don't have the best track record for easy."

Complicated, crazy —none of it mattered to me. "Where's the fun in a smooth ride? I'd take crashing and burning with you than easy with someone else."

"I just can't right now." Her lip wobbled as I wiped her tears.

"I know, and I'll wait, but I'm not walking away."

Forever, I'd wait forever.

The curtain pushed open again, Tom filling the space with his hands still gripped tight around the fabric.

"Hey, Megs, sorry to interrupt. Mom and Dad are here."

Megs nodded at me him before she looked up at me. "Can you wait outside? While I talk to my parents."

"Megs, you don't have to do this by yourself. We can talk to them together." It wasn't just me manning up, I didn't want to bail—not yet.

"I know, but I would rather do it by myself." She laid her hand on my chest and gave me a weak hug.

No matter how much I wanted to stay in that room, I couldn't find it in me to say no to her. "Whatever you want, sweetheart. I'm just going to be outside."

Walking back through the corridor, the space filled with activity. Bodies crashing into each other, doctors and nurses talking over each other but it felt like a piece of my heart had been ripped out. It didn't matter that I hadn't met our baby yet; I still felt the loss all the same.

I pushed through the door that led out into the main waiting room of the E.R., some of the same people were there waiting for their turn. The blond-headed kid I'd blown off was still there too, his ball cap pulled down to cover his eyes.

Seeing him got me thinking of what an asshole I'd been. He wasn't to know my world had been fucking falling apart. He was probably looking for an autograph or a photo or five minutes of my time. I'd have punched the SOB who spoke to my son the way I'd spoken to him.

"Hey, kid, I'm sorry about before. It was just a really bad time for me."

My apology was bullshit but it was the best I could do, nothing would make up for being a total cock. My head hadn't been right but I never should have pulled that shit. The kid was maybe sixteen? He had no idea that he had just picked the wrong time to talk to me.

"Oh, it's okay. No it's fine. I'm sorry." He pushed his cap back, his

Cons kicks tapping nervously on the floor.

"No, it wasn't fine. No matter what I was going through, I shouldn't have bit your head off like that. I was a complete asshole and I'm really sorry." I took the seat beside him.

"I overheard you." He took a swallow and nodded. "You and Dr. Winters lost your baby?"

Hearing it didn't make it easier the second time. I didn't know what to say, saying the words out loud weren't an option.

"I'm not going to tell anyone, I swear," the kid quickly added. "I didn't even know she was dating you, honest." He stopped, clocking me with an eyeball, his voice shaking so much I couldn't help but know he was scared. "I was with her. It's 'cause of me."

"What are you talking about?"

None of it made sense. This kid being with Megs or thinking he was the reason why in seven months I wasn't going to be holding my son or daughter.

"She's my shrink. I've been such a fucking shit." He pulled the cap off his head and rolled the bill nervously his hands. "I'm just mad a lot, you know? I'd come and talk and I didn't mean to but I always ended up giving her a hard time. I'd cuss her out even though she was nothing but nice to me. We were in a session, and it just happened. I didn't know what to do, I didn't know."

Fuck. No one deserved to see that, let alone a kid. On top of that, he was thinking that his problems were the reason Megs had lost our baby. It was a mess I honestly didn't know how to fix but I needed to try. Megs would have known what the say, I owed it to her to at least try.

"There's nothing you could have done, nothing any of us could have done. It didn't happen 'cause of what you guys talked about, sometimes bad shit just happens."

He concentrated hard on his cap in his hands, not lifting his eyes from their mark. "Bad shit happens a lot in my life. It follows me around, like a curse."

He was way too young to be battling those kinds of demons, way too young to be carrying that load. Were all the kids Megs saw like this? How was she able to do it and not have it mess with her head? In that moment, I fell in love with her all over again.

"What's your name kid?"

"Brad. Brad Hemsworth." He flicked his eyes sideways to me.

"Brad, I'm not a doctor but I can tell you that there is no way you had anything to do with what went down." I had a feeling that talking to him was probably breaking all kinds of rules— but it was one small thing that I could do, hopefully it would make a microscopic difference. "I'm sorry shit isn't going right for you, but Dr. Winters—she really cares. She's changed my life, if you give her a chance she can change yours too."

Brad nodded like he understood but I had no idea if any of it stuck. A fair-headed lady with a panic stricken face bolted toward us from the opposite end of the room.

"Brad! Honey, we've been searching the whole building for you." Her hand gripping her handbag so tight her knuckles had turned white.

"I just wanted to make sure Dr. Winters was okay." Brad shoved his cap back on his head, his eyes nailing themselves to the floor.

"I know, sweetie, but you shouldn't have run off. I was scared half to death." She looked it too; her fingers twisted her wedding ring nervously as she stood in front of us.

Brad lifted his head and gave the lady a good look at his face. "Mom, I'm sorry."

"That's —That's alright." The lady looked shocked, like maybe she hadn't heard it in a while. Her eyes doing the mist over as she looked at her boy. "We should go home now."

Brad stood up, shoving his hands in his pockets as he shifted on his feet. "Hey, I know I'm not supposed to contact Dr. Winters outside of my appointments, but can you tell her— tell her I won't be a shit anymore."

"How about I tell her you said hey, and that you'll be looking forward to the next session." My version was the only version Megs would be getting.

"Yeah, that will do." Brad gave me a nod as he looked to his mom.

"Take care, Brad." I shoved out my hand, the kid clapping it with his own.

"See ya, Troy."

The mom looked on nervously, not wanting to rock the boat as we said our goodbyes and I watched them leave.

My ass sunk back into the seat and I started my game of hurry-up and wait. If I had to sit there until tomorrow, then that's what I'd do. Eventually she would have to come around and let me in—the alternative was just too hard to take.

26
Megan

Dr. Blake wheeled me back into the room where my parents had been waiting. I was still a little groggy from the anesthetic, but the added meds they had pumped into my IV had taken the pain away. The pain in my body, that was, the pain in my heart was still there.

"Megan, as long as you have someone to stay with you over the next twenty-four hours, there's no reason why you can't go home." Notes were scribbled onto my chart, ones that probably said the "clean up" was all over and I was no longer pregnant. It was over so quickly—done, finished.

My dad was doing a horrible job at being discreet, trying to read over poor Dr. Blake's shoulder. "Of course, she can come home with us. Either myself or her mother will be with her the whole time."

It didn't matter that I was a grown woman; my father would always want to take over. He didn't do out-of-control, he wanted everything nice and neat —organized. Something I wasn't right now, and didn't aspire to be.

"Dad, don't take this the wrong way but I want to go to *my* home. It will be easier for me to get back to normal in my own surroundings. Whisking me off and putting me into my childhood bedroom isn't the answer." Neither was pretending what happened, didn't just happen but I didn't bother vocalizing the last part.

"Darling, you've just suffered a trauma and you need time to heal. I think it's best you are around medical professionals who are able to care for you." My mother moved the hair out of my face, her eyes filled with worry.

"I don't need medical professionals, I'm not sick —I lost my baby. I know everyone is tiptoeing around the words but that is what happened. Calling it a trauma doesn't make it easier, so please don't fight me on this. I think that I am more equipped than anyone to make the decision on what's best for me."

"Well, I'll let you guys sort it out, shall I? As long as you promise me you won't be alone, I'll sign your release papers." Dr. Blake looked over at us from his chart, no doubt wanting to avoid the drama of our family politics. Can't say I blamed him—at that moment— I wanted out too.

"I won't be." I promised Dr. Blake who gave me a nod and walked off. Hopefully to fill out the paperwork so I could go home.

Tom pulled the curtain across filling the space that the doctor had just vacated. What do you know? It was Grand Central station in my little cubicle.

"Megs, Troy is still outside and he looks terrible. Can I put the guy out of his misery and let him back in?"

Troy. I had shoved him out of my room when my parents had arrived and then a nurse had come and wheeled me to the O.R.

He'd been here the whole time? I probably shouldn't have been surprised, he'd said he wouldn't leave but it had been so long. I assumed he would have gone home.

I'd lost our baby and then told him to leave. He must hate me. If I was him, I sure would.

"He's been waiting the whole time?" It was stating the fucking obvious but it came out of my mouth anyway. To be honest, I had little control over what I was saying or feeling. My heart almost bursting that he was still here, for me, despite me sending him away. No man had ever loved me like that.

"Yeah, in the waiting room. He hasn't left." The corners of Tom's mouth slightly curled at the edges. The smile he gave to soften the blow when regular smiling wasn't appropriate. I wondered if they taught that in medical school? I sure as hell hadn't mastered it.

"Please let him in." I nodded to Tom and then turned to my parents. "Dad, Mom. You can go, I've got it from here."

"Megan, are you sure, sweetie?" The protest already started to bubble in my mother. "We can stay, or give you a ride home?"

"I can take her home." Troy moved into the crowded space, his face tired and drawn. He looked destroyed. I had done that. That look was there because of me.

"Hi, Troy." My mother rubbed his arm gently.

"Hi, Mrs. Winters. Mr. Winters." He answered robotically but didn't move any closer.

"Well, alright but if you need us for anything, just call. Day or night, just pick up the phone." My dad admitted defeat and gave my mother the we-should-go look. I silently thanked God they weren't going to fight me on this.

"Thanks." Please don't cry, please don't cry. "I love you both." I didn't even attempt a smile—I wasn't delusional enough to think I'd be able to pull it off.

"We love you too." My mother blew me a kiss with my dad ushering her out of the cubical.

"I need to get back to patients, Sis. If you need anything, just buzz." Tom also excused himself, giving Troy a nod on the way out.

"Troy…" What to even say? I was coming up a blank.

"Megs, please. I know you are hurting right now but please don't shut me out. I lost our baby too." He moved quietly to the chair beside my bed and sat down. There was an unmistakable sadness in his face.

"Do you hate me? I assumed you left. It's been hours."

"Why would I hate you? I told you I wasn't leaving and I'm not. My place is here, with you."

"Because…" I couldn't finish. How many tears could one person cry? Surely I'd exceeded my limit, not that my leaky eyes had received the memo.

"Megs, I love you." He was out of his chair and up on the bed before I'd had a chance to wipe away the tears, cupping my face in his hands. "I really, really do, and nothing is going to change that. What happened is no one's fault. I'm mad as hell that it happened, but not at you, never at you."

"Will you stay with me tonight? Will you hold me?" I didn't care how desperate I sounded. I was desperate, desperate for this ache in my chest to stop.

His mouth gently brushed against mine. "Always."

The time alone back at the apartment had been horrible, we both cried and held each other, but most of all we talked— really talked. Nothing was off the table and in some ways, it was almost liberating.

"You know, we never talked about kids before and then I was pregnant." My hands were tucked under my pillow as I faced him.

"I want kids, Megs, not like a basketball team, but I want a family. What about you?" His pose mirrored mine; his face just inches away.

"I want two." It was late and I was tired, but I didn't want to stop talking.

Troy smiled and gave me a nod. "Two's a good number, makes riding roller-coasters easier."

"You can't decide the number of kids you have based on that." The smile teased at my mouth.

"Sure you can." He threw some further conviction behind his voice before he continued. "You try going to Disney World with an uneven number, someone is missing out."

"I can't even argue with that logic." How could I argue? It was adorable, even if it was somewhat crazy.

"Because you know I'm right." He grinned; probably pleased I hadn't been able to come up with a counter argument.

"Moving on, Troy Harris." I waved him off casually. It felt good to be talking about normal things again, both of us even managing a smile. The guilt wasn't lurking too far away as I tried to shove it to the back of my mind and asked another question. "Did you have pets growing up?"

"You mean your detailed Google search didn't give you that information?" His grin got wider as he raised an eyebrow.

"Shut up." I gently shoved his chest. "You make me sound like a stalker." Besides, I hadn't Googled him in a *really* long time.

"Nah, stalking is more like watching me through my bedroom window, so unless you did that…" He left his sentence trailing, waiting for my response.

I winced, giving him a guilty smile. "Well."

"Megs?"

"I'm joking." I laughed, amused by the slight concern that was on his face. "I've never watched you from your bedroom. Although I totally would have done it but— you know— you live on the top floor of your building, and hiring the abseiling equipment would have raised too many questions."

"Okay, it's my turn." He shuffled closer, his hand resting on my hip. "Did you always want to be a psychologist?"

"When I was younger I wanted to be one of the ladies on the highwire at the circus. They looked so glamorous in those sparkling costumes." I sighed remembering my childhood fantasy.

"Let me guess, you had issues with your balance?"

I fell over one time and the man assumes I'm a klutz. "No, smartass. I found out you had to live in a trailer." I grimaced. "Ughhhh."

Troy barked out a laugh and it was too hard not to join him. It felt wrong to be happy but also kind of right. We hadn't forgotten what happened, but we were finding a way to be okay with it.

"I have a question." It had been something I had been curious but hadn't ever asked.

"Well go on, it's not like you to hold back." He smirked, clearly loving our session of truth or dare.

"So that first night you met me, it was pretty clear what I thought of you, but what did you think of me?" My heart pounded as I waited for him to respond.

"I was kind of pissed you were so drunk." He answered honestly with a little shrug.

Well, that had been unexpected. I was thinking he was going to go with I thought you were annoying or maybe—in my fantasies—I thought you were so incredibly sexy. But pissed because I was drunk? There had to be more to it than that.

"Because I was all over you and fell over?"

"No, because it meant that if I tried to kiss you, I would feel like a complete scumbag." His voice was low and so very sexy as his smile curled at his lips.

"You wanted to kiss me?" Had I heard him right? That night when I'd wrapped myself around him like a boa constrictor, he had wanted to kiss me?

"I wanted to do more than just kiss you." He moved his mouth closer to mine. I guess to give me a visual interpretation seeing as I seemed to be having trouble with his words.

"Woah!" My hands pushed against his chest in surprise. "Define more."

He cocked an eyebrow. "Megs, seriously?"

Oh hell yes, seriously. He wasn't getting out of it that easily. "No, no. You have to answer. I confessed about my secret aspirations of being a trapeze artist; you need to come clean, bubby."

"Fine." He took a breath before he continued. "I wanted to take you home and have sex with you. That dress you were wearing wasn't doing a very good job at keeping that hot body of yours under wraps, and watching your beautiful red lips calling me Troy Harris made me instantly hard. The car ride home was brutal; your legs were in my lap and I could totally see your panties. In my head I'd fucked you three times before I'd gotten you settled in your apartment." His are-you-happy-now face waited for my response.

"It's probably warped and twisted, but knowing you wanted me back then really excites me." And made me feel like less of a pervert for having been so obsessed with him. It was reassuring to know it hadn't been one sided.

"Well, I did. The first time you called me, I had a hard-on for hours. And the time I picked you up from your Christmas party after you drunk-dialed me, yeah that was another fun night," he mused sarcastically.

"Oh I remember that, I wanted you to kiss me so badly." And hadn't I almost begged for him to sleep with me? Ugh. Not my finest moment. Thank God, the memories are fuzzy. There is bliss in ignorance.

"Trust me, one of the hardest things I ever had to do was say goodbye to you that night, and you sure weren't making it easy for me."

Yeah, obviously my suspicions had been correct.

"Good." I smiled; it pleased me to know he had been just as sexually frustrated that night as I had. "I'm glad you suffered."

"Well I'm glad my *suffering* stopped." He nipped at my shoulder before kissing my neck.

He had been so gentle— affectionate without trying to turn it sexual. It's like he could read exactly what I needed.

"It feels like a lifetime ago." Or more, so much had changed during those months.

"It kind of was." Troy shrugged. He was right, it was. We were different. *Things* were different.

"So where do we go from here?" We couldn't go back to the way things were. That never would have worked.

"Where ever you want to go, as long as it's together. I can't lose you; I think we've both lost enough." He held me tightly; there was no doubt in my mind that he would never let me go.

"Troy Harris." I whispered against his skin, kissing his chest before bringing my face up to meet his."

"Yes." He gave that smile that meant he would humor whatever lame-ass idea I'd come up with.

"Will you marry me?"

Every reason I had that had been holding me back was no longer relevant. In that moment—just being with him— I'd fallen in love with him all over again.

He dipped his head and kissed me—hard.

"Yes."

27
Troy

"HEY, BEAUTIFUL, IT'S TIME TO WAKE UP."

Watching Megs sleep had been the first time I'd been able to catch a breath since leaving the hospital. Her tired lids peeled opened as I kissed her neck before slamming them back shut.

"Come on, Megs. Let me off the hook here. I feel like an asshole trying to wake you, but it's time." The small shake I gave her earning me a groan.

"So tired." She yawned trying to bury her head in the crook of my armpit.

"I wouldn't be hiding there, if I was you." I warned her, the last time I'd spent any time under a shower at least twenty-four hours ago. Sure I'd hit it with some *Old Spice* but it still wouldn't have been pretty, that's for sure.

"Just five more minutes." She waved me off as she tried to chase down some more Zs.

"Five more minutes and we're going to be on the runway." The plane banked, making its finale approach into JFK. "You want me to carry you off the plane, I have no problem with that— but the attention we were trying to avoid— yeah that will probably be history."

"Troy Harris, I love it when you get all logical on me." Her beautiful eyes stayed hidden behind her lids but she treated me to a smile.

"And here I was thinking you married me for my last name. I know how fond you are of saying it, Megs Harris."

"That sounds so freaking weird." She laughed as she sat up in her seat. "I still can't believe we did it."

"Well it's kind of fitting with our history— impulsive and unconventional. Besides you'd finally agreed. I sure as shit wasn't giving you the opportunity to change your mind."

We had both laid it out on the line when had gotten back from the hospital. Stuff we'd never talked about suddenly got airtime and it went a long way to heal us both.

Megs asking *me* to marry *her* was the icing on the cake. I had been fully prepared to wait and I'd even decided that I'd lay off on the proposals, but her saying those words to me was like being punched right in the mouth.

Being that fast forward had been kind of our speed, we jumped on a late flight to Vegas and made it to *Van Cleef & Arpels* just before they shut their doors. A couple of rings and a seedy Vegas chapel later, we walking down the aisle to the tune of "Don't Stop Believin'" by *Journey*. Yep, the cheese factor was high but it was either that or Shania Twain. So *Journey* it was.

There was no dress, no flowers and no friends. Just the two of us and a preacher who was older than kerosene, but it was legal and we were married, and that was all that mattered.

It occurred to me getting on a plane so soon after Megs had lost the baby wasn't the smartest decision, but she insisted that the risks were minimal. And her wanting it as much as I did was enough to convince me not to wait. I'd waited long enough and if one good thing could come out of the nightmare we'd been through, then I'd take it.

"For the record, I wouldn't have changed my mind but last night was perfect." Megs stared down at her wedding rings, the diamonds doing the twinkling thing they did when they hit the sun, and I didn't doubt for a second that we'd made the right choice. Staying in Vegas wasn't an option. We had no intention of hiding out, or avoiding the shit storm our quickie wedding was going to attract, so we high-tailed it back, ready to face the music.

"Technically it was this morning. Our marriage license says two forty-five a.m. so guess it's still our wedding day." The plane shook as the landing gear was lowered, the runway in sight.

"Well seeing as it's my wedding day, that means I get to choose what we do and my vote is breakfast." Megs squeezed my arm as the plane dropped altitude, my stomach lunging from the dip and the lack of food.

"Megs, it's almost noon. I think breakfast is a bust." While breakfast was out, food was definitely on the agenda. I could murder a burger and fries I was so hungry.

"But I want pancakes and bacon and the biggest coffee we can find. Oh my God, coffee. I missed it so much. I'm going to get two." Her eyes got wide with the promise of caffeinated goodness.

"Then if my wife wants breakfast, we'll get her breakfast." She would get whatever she wanted, whenever she wanted and I would spend my last breath making sure of that fact.

She grinned as the tires on the plane hit the tarmac, the plane knocking us around on the touch down.

"We should probably tell our folks as well." We were back in NYC and the fact we eloped was hanging over us like a big neon sign. No regrets, but we sure as hell had a lot of explaining to do. "No doubt the chewing out we're going to get is going to be massive. Let's hope your dad didn't make good on his threat of getting a gun."

"I'll handle my dad." She undid her seat belt as the plane rolled to the gate. "Do you think our friends will be pissed?"

"They'll get over it." I unhooked my belt too, ready to get off the plane. "If you want to do the wedding thing, we can make that happen. Alex and Lexi did a redo a few months after."

"You know it's funny, I always pictured my wedding a certain way. You know, wearing a *Vera Wang* gown, the fancy shoes and possibly the Plaza, but I just don't want that now."

Not that I knew what a Vera Whatever was, but she had rocked the jeans and T-shirt she'd worn, and I'd never seen her look more beautiful.

"It's up to you, I'm good with the way we did it."

"Mr. Harris, Ms. Winters you can disembark the plane now." The airline chick smiled as she directed us to the jet bridge.

"Thanks." I nodded and grabbed Megs's hand. "Let's get out of here."

Knowing Vegas was going to be a drive-by, we hadn't packed shit. Not even carry on. We were there long enough to say "I do" and for me to add a tiny bit of ink to my collection. We had almost spent more time in the air than we had in the desert, which had suited me just fine. I was glad to be back and pleased we weren't going to be wasting our time at baggage claim.

JFK was freaking pumping, people running to gates and the loud speaker demanding attention. I was glad I'd sent TJ a message and organized a pick up. Getting a cab would have probably been a nightmare. We moved from arrivals to the curbside area, my fingers getting busy letting the big guy know we were waiting.

"Troy, Ms. Winters." TJ rolled up in the Escalade, the two of us piling into the back.

"I just sent you a message." His phone pinged from the front seat. "You have ESP or somethin', dude?"

"Watched the flight schedule and was doing laps. It's easier than having you sitting out there unattended." He kept the engine idling as we climbed into the back seats.

"Thank you, TJ." Megs smiled as she snuggled into her seat.

"No problem, Ms. Winters." He gave her a chin tip in the rearview.

"Yeah, about that." Fuck it—might as well start telling people and TJ was as close as family got without being blood or the band. "She kinda has the same last name as me now but keep it on the down low until we break it to everyone else."

"I figured you probably went and got legal. Not too many reasons for you to be inbound from Vegas when you were in New York yesterday. Congratulations." TJ grinned, giving us a good look at his grill as we pulled away from the curb.

"Thanks, man. It was spur of the moment. Maybe take us to Megs's first. We should probably make a few calls." And maybe get a shower as well, I also still had the promise of breakfast I needed to make good on.

"Yep, can do." TJ nodded as he changed lanes and put us on the road, Greenwich bound.

Megs pulled out her cell and powered it up, the phone having been stuck on airplane mode for the last six or so hours.

"Holy shit!" Meg's hand vibrated with the cell blowing up with a bunch of missed calls and unanswered texts. "My parents are freaking out. They've been calling for hours."

"You want me to talk to them?" I held out my hand ready to take the heat. Fuck, they could unleash whatever they wanted on me, nothing was removing the shit-eating grin I was wearing.

"No, I've got it." Her voice wavered a little like she wasn't all that convinced that she *had it*. Her fingers punching the keypad as she dialed the number.

"Just remember, anyone starts giving you a hard time, you hand that phone to me. I won't have anyone making you feel bad about what we did." Not to mention that the happy-happy-joy-joy was still arm wrestling with the grief of losing our baby. Sure we were smiles and rainbows but that didn't mean the minute we walked back into the apartment that the reality of the situation wouldn't rear its ugly mug.

"You are too sweet, Troy Harris." She bit her lip as she raised her cell to her ear as we navigated through the shit storm that was Manhattan traffic.

"Hey, Mom. No please don't cry. I'm fine." The smile Megs had been wearing slipped from her face. "I'm sorry you were worried. I just…"

She took a breath, not seeming to get a word in edgeways. "Mom, I'm fine. I was on a plane, I had to have my phone off." Megs got defensive as she continued. "Well the doctor didn't say I couldn't fly, I wasn't flying the plane myself."

I was just about to grab the phone off her when she finally broke the news. "Because Troy and I went to Vegas and got married." I stared at Megs waiting for a reaction and hoping her parents weren't going to give her a hard time. My primal need to protect her from anything bad was making me twitchy.

"Mom?" Megs waited. "Oh, hey Dad. Yeah, that's right we eloped. No, no one pressured me. I wanted to. Because I was tired of waiting to be happy and this made me happy." From the one-sided conversation I was hearing, I was getting the gist they weren't pleased. Megs stood her ground though, not going the I'm-sorry-don't-be-mad route. "I don't care about a big celebration; it's what I wanted and it's done."

She pulled the phone from her ear obviously done with defending our actions and brought it closer to her mouth. "Dad, I'm hanging up now. I love you both but I need you to be happy for us." And with that she ended the call.

"Did that go as well as it sounded?" I didn't need to hear the other side of the phone call to know they weren't going to be welcoming us to Sunday lunch anytime soon. I was probably on the top of their shit list as well. Still them being pissed off didn't change that we were rocking matching rings, and that us being married was as permanent as the tattoo I'd gotten an hour after.

"Yeah they are freaking out, they think I'm suffering post traumatic stress disorder and somehow jumped into making a decision. They already knew I wanted this, sure it was sudden but it's not like we hadn't talked about it." Megs switched the phone to silent and threw it into her purse. No doubt her folks would try and call her back, maybe to try and talk some sense into her.

"It's a valid concern, Megs, they are just worried. Let's give them a few days and then maybe go see them." Not saying that they were right, but they were only worried 'cause they loved her. If my kid ran off and married some dude, I'd probably have words to say about it myself.

I reached across and held her hand, my thumb rubbing over the back of her knuckles. Megs gave me a weak smile as I stroked her skin. "What about your parents? Are they going to freak out?"

"Ha! My mom will get down on her knees and thank God I finally came to my senses and married you; she won't care too much about missing the ceremony. She kind of got used to the idea that I wasn't going to settle down, so this is like her Christmas and birthday all coming at once."

And wasn't that the truth. My mom had given up on the pipe dream of me being shacked up. She wasn't an idiot, and knew I had female company but she ignored the press for the most part. And other than a lecture telling me to be respectful and me not being too big for an ass whooping if she heard about me being a scumbag, we had the whole don't-ask-don't-tell thing going for us.

"Troy Harris, the perpetual bachelor?" Megs laughed, obviously my dating history amusing the shit out here.

"Well, considering before I brought you home, the number of girlfriends my folks had met, stood at three—all of which were while I was in high school—she hadn't counted on sitting in a church watching me put a ring on it."

"See, why can't my parents be that cool?" She leaned her head back against the headrest, her eyes getting sleepy with the rock of the Escalade.

"Probably 'cause you haven't been on tour since you were seventeen."

We rode the rest of the way without any further commentary, TJ turned on some jams and Megs dozed off and on till we got to her apartment.

"You good? Need me to hang around?" TJ pulled over to the curb not far from the entrance of her building.

"All good, brother. My car's chillin' in the underground garage. You can go do your *Driving Miss Daisy* thing with someone else." I popped open the door and my feet hit the sidewalk.

"Thanks, TJ." Megs rubbed her eyes, obviously the Zs she'd snagged in between traffic lights not enough for her liking. She ambled out of the car and joined me on the curb.

"Yep. My pleasure." TJ gave us a two finger wave as we shut the door. The tail lights of the Escalade easing back into the gridlock we'd escaped from.

"Come on, Mrs. Harris." I tucked her in close to me. "Shower, change and then I'm going to caffeinate you." My lips landed on the top of her head as we walked through the doorway of the apartment building.

"Mmm. You are such a smooth talker." She nuzzled closer into me as he strolled to the elevator. I liked having the weight of her body tight against mine, and being able to see the rise and fall of each of her breaths. It made me feel like a better man, like a piece of my puzzle was in place. Losing the baby had been bad enough, but if I had lost Megs—not sure I could have come back from that.

The elevator pinged once we got to her floor, the metal doors sliding open to reveal a deserted hallway. Just as well—neither of us was in the mood to socialize.

Megs fished her keys from her purse and twisted them in the lock, the door springing open from the effort.

"Hey!" Megs squealed as I hauled her up into my arms. "What are you doing?" Her feet gave a half-hearted kick in protest.

"Threshold." The one worded explanation enough for her feet to give up. I grinned as I carried her through her doorway.

She slithered down out of my arms, her feet hitting the floor in front of me. The last twenty-four hours had been a rollercoaster of emotions for both of us, and being in the apartment brought back some of the ghosts of yesterday with it.

"Troy…" Megs's eyes got serious, the blue-green pools losing the shine they'd had no five minutes ago. "I can't have sex yet. I'm still…" She didn't need to fill in the blanks. The stash of *Kotex* in her purse gave me all the info I needed.

"Look at me." I tipped her chin so her eyes were on me. "There will be plenty of time for that. When you're ready, you let me know."

"I want to, but…" My finger on her mouth stopped her talking. She wasn't going to be wearing more guilt than she already had. Hell no. End of discussion.

"Megs, I waited for months to have you for the first time, and months for you to be my girl. Going without sex for a few weeks isn't even on my radar as an issue. We've got nothing but time, sweetheart, and neither of us is going anywhere."

"Stop, you'll make me cry." Her chin did the wobble as her eyes blinked real quick.

"No crying." My arms wrapped around hers. "Not over that. Now, let's get cleaned up and go get breakfast for lunch before my stomach cannibalizes itself." No shit—the threat was real, my last meal having been hours ago.

"And coffee." She reminded me, her lost smile creeping back.

"Whatever you want."

"You know, Troy Harris. That's a dangerous promise to make a girl. I could start demanding all kinds of crazy shit." She wiggled her eyebrows, her threat making me laugh.

"Bring it. It's either a done deal or I'll spend my last breath trying." I gave her a quick kiss and unwrapped my arms, the vibrating from her bag getting my attention.

"Trying to amuse yourself with the TSA again?" I raised my eyebrow. "I thought you bought a giant dildo not a vibrator." My grin got wider.

"It's my phone." She elbowed me in the ribs as she pulled out her cell. "Shit, there's a missed call from work." Her eyes floated down to the number displayed on the screen. "It must be urgent if they are trying to get a hold of me. I have a couple of patients that are high risk."

Work— shit. I'd completely mind dumped the run-in I'd had with the kid in the waiting room. I had meant to tell her, but I was waiting for the right time and then it just kind of slipped. I'd promised him I would give her his message, so I needed to make good on that.

"Yeah, I forgot to tell you. I met one of them, one of your kids. Brad Hemsworth. He was waiting outside of the ER."

Megs looked up from her phone, her face getting pale. "Oh my God, was he alright?"

"Megs, he was just worried about you. Said he was with you when it went down." Part of me still was torn up that I hadn't been there. Not that I was delusional and thought I could have changed the outcome. I got that there was nothing anyone could've done— but that didn't put to rest the shit floating around in my gray matter that at the very least, I could have made it easier for Megs.

"Yeah, unfortunately I was in a session." Megs focused on me, her mind probably getting a reboot courtesy of the memory. "I tried to get him out of there as soon as I could. I should really book him into a relief counselor."

"Megs, listen." I had no idea if talking to the kid had made shit worse or better but it still didn't change the fact I'd done it. Last thing I wanted is for her to be blindsided when she went back or worse, think I was hiding shit. "I know we probably shouldn't have, but we talked."

"You talked to my patient?" She didn't seem mad; more surprised and super curious. Her eyes on me as she waited for me to join the dots on how I came to be have a D and M with one of her patients.

"Yeah, he was feeling guilty and I was trying to tell him that shit wasn't his fault. He overheard what happened. We didn't go deep or anything, but he came clean about probably not being the easiest kid to get along with. He thought that had something to do with it."

"Oh my God, no." She shook her head and sunk into an armchair. "I can't have him taking that on. He already has enough."

I dropped to my knees beside her, there was more to the conversation than what needed to be said. Not that I was a shrink and hell, who knows if I'd made things better or worse, but I'd opened my mouth and I was fessing up.

"Which is what I told him. I don't know, Megs— I don't know this kid and maybe I saw something I wanted to see. But he seemed to understand that you were only trying to help him. He even told me that he was looking forward to next time when you guys had a session."

Her eyes got wide, almost like she hadn't bought my version of events. "He said that? He actually said he was looking forward to our next session? He hates our sessions."

"Well not those exact words but we agreed my version was probably what he meant. He even apologized to his mom for making her worry." The paraphrase was a definite improvement, no way was I ever going to say the kid was a shit.

"You got him to say sorry? Troy, that's huge. I know you don't understand but trust me... it's massive." She scooted forward in her seat, her excitement earning me some lip action as she pressed her mouth against mine.

"So you're not mad? I know there is all kinds of gray area there about talking to kids and shit." Yeah as in, don't fucking do it.

"Troy, you weren't impersonating a psychologist, and from what you said he approached you. As long as you weren't talking about our therapy sessions or giving him prescribed treatment there's nothing unethical with you having a consensual conversation. Besides, it sounds like talking to you was exactly what he needed. Sometimes, all it takes is one thing to set off a chain reaction of change."

"Well, I just didn't want to fuck anything up." Not for the kid and not for Megs.

"You didn't fuck anything up." She gave me one of my favorite smiles. The ones where the corners of her mouth pull up so much it lights up her entire face. The kind of smile you couldn't fake.

"Awesome." I leaned in and gave her a kiss on the forehead. "Why don't you return your call and I'll hit the shower. I can't do anything about a change of clothes but at least I won't smell."

Maybe I had a clean T-shirt lying around somewhere? In any case, our living arrangement needed to be sorted at some point in the very near future, and one of us going to be relocating. Best we could save that dilemma for after we fed our faces.

"Yes and then fooooooooood," Megs added, seeming to read my mind.

I shot her a wink before strolling off into the bathroom, not forgetting the promise I'd made to her. "And coffee."

28

Megan

Troy had been right about one thing—his parents had been ecstatic when he broke the news to them about our impromptu I-do's. He had called them after his shower and even put the phone on speaker so I could hear. There weren't any shocked gasps or tearful accusations— so basically the opposite of my parents— and they were both just so lovingly supportive that it made me teary all over again.

My work emergency had turned out to be just Carrie checking in on me. All my appointments had been postponed with all my high risk patients being re-allocated for care in the interim. It made things a little easier that there was one less thing for me to worry about.

Breakfast for lunch, as Troy had called it, had been sublime. While the pancakes had been delicious, it had been my extra large, extra hot with an extra shot of coffee that had ricocheted me straight off the planet and into outer space. It was like welcoming back an old friend and went a long way in making me feel less zombiefied. I pledged my renewed fealty to the caffeine master and tried not to sound like I was having an orgasm when taking the first sip. Not going to lie— it hadn't been easy.

"They know about the baby, right?" My palms were sweaty as we loitered outside Dan and Ash's door. I hadn't seen or spoken to either of them since it happened and really wasn't up for detailed run through.

I shouldn't have had that second coffee; I was so jittery my teeth were rattling.

"Yeah, I had been with Dan when you called me so he knew something was up. I gave him a call and filled him in while I was in the waiting room." Troy gave me a sideways glance, like he was unsure of what my reaction was going to be. My lack of an emotional explosion prompted him to go on.

"I didn't know if it was going to leak out or not, and figured it was better they heard it from me. I told the rest of the band too, and Lexi— she made sure that nothing showed up in the press."

I hadn't even thought about the press and how much worse it could have been with a camera in my face asking us about our loss.

"I'm glad you told them, they should know. It's not like we can pretend it didn't happen." That would have been so much worse.

"You ready to go in? We can go hang at my place for a while." Troy jangled his keys temptingly.

It would be easy to run away, but it was only a matter of time before our Vegas jaunt made news. I was surprised *TMZ* hadn't been at the airport, no doubt *MTV* would have the story by the evening. Ironically, Ashlyn's prediction about me never being featured would be a bust, however it wouldn't be my recorder prowess that would earn me headlines, but the sparkly new finger wear I was sporting. In truth— I sucked at the recorder.

So my new philosophy was to *own* being Mrs. Troy Harris, consequences be damned. Besides, I really liked saying his last name.

"No, I'm good." My head bobbled a little too enthusiastically, the full effect of the caffeine running havoc on my nervous system.

Troy didn't look convinced as he knocked on the door. His concern evident as he wrapped his arms around me and pulled me closer to him.

It was either that or he was expecting me to drop to the floor and have a cardiac arrest— not out of the realm of possibility given how much I'd been buzzing.

"Megs!" Ash screamed, pulling me out of Troy's arms and into her own as she opened the door. "Oh, crap. I didn't hurt you, did I?" She eased her hold on me as she led me through the doorway, Troy walking in casually behind us.

"I'm fine, I'm fine." Well, as fine as I was going to be. Certainly not about to fall apart, which was a plus.

"Troy." Ash gave him a slightly less emotional hug than the one she'd given me.

"Hey, Ash." Troy returned her hug before lifting his head to address Dan. "Hey, douchebag."

"Hey." Dan tipped his chin hello. It wasn't just his subdued greeting weirding me out a little, it was the absence of the trailing "numbnuts" which was also odd. He was almost like an anti-Dan, respectfully standing back and observing without insults or innuendo. I hadn't been the only one who had noticed, his scaled down behavior earning him a raised eyebrow from Troy.

"Soooooooo." Did I launch into our big announcement or did I let things be awkward a little while longer? I wasn't sure what the protocol was. "Troy and I got married." My mouth made the decision for me, with my left hand flying out in front of me. The big rock on my ring finger to serve as exhibit A for submitted evidence.

"You got married?" Ashlyn's eyes widened as she snatched my hand and examined my ring. "When did you have time to get married?" She continued to talk to my *Van Cleef and Arpels* diamond rather than address me directly. Not that I blamed her, I had a hard time not breaking into a *Gollum* impersonation and stroking *my precious, my precious* myself.

"When did they have time? They've been dating like ninjas since God knows when, I'm surprised we're only celebrating their wedding and not their freaking first year anniversary." Thankfully the Dan I remembered came back with a vengeance, leaving behind whatever the previous reincarnation had been. Better the devil you know I say.

"Dan, you promised you wouldn't be an ass." Ash gave him a gentle shove in the shoulder. The mystery of anti-Dan solved.

"I didn't even call Troy an asshole, even though he called me a douchebag. Can't I get credit for that?" He rubbed his shoulder with his hand indignantly, no doubt annoyed his sacrifice hadn't been acknowledged.

"Ash, thanks for the sentiment but it feels weirder if he tries to act normal. Just be yourself, Dan."

"Thank you, Megs." He shot his wife-to-be a smug grin. "See, I'm a regular freaking delight, babe. Don't know why you were worried."

"Anyway," Ash rolled her eyes ignoring Dan's now inflated ego. "When did this all happen?"

Troy took over and explained our snap decision to go rogue and elope.

"I'm so fucking disappointed, dude." Dan paced, his agitation showing as Troy recounted the story.

"I'm sorry, man. No one was there. We didn't even tell our families." Troy's apology attempted to ease Dan's disappointment. Both of us genuinely touched that Dan had been bummed about missing out on the wedding.

"No, not about not being there. I totally get that. You wanted to get married, you got married. I can respect that." Dan waved off Troy's apology.

"So what's the problem then?" Troy asked, neither of us closer to working out why if it hadn't been his lack of attendance that had upset him, what he'd got worked up over.

"That fact that you two idiots weren't married by a fat Elvis wearing a satin jumpsuit. You were in Vegas, dude. That's like going to the Coliseum and not seeing the Pope. The King is rolling around in his grave right now. I hope you two fuckers are satisfied." He passionately informed us of our squandered opportunity as he pointing his finger at us accusingly.

"The Pope lives in the Vatican, you moron, not the Coliseum and The King didn't need our business. It's fine." Troy laughed off Dan's concerns of us ruffling the deceased rock star's blue suede shoes.

"I'm just sayin' next time you're in Memphis you should probably head to Graceland and apologize to the Velvet Elvis just to be sure."

Velvet Elvis would probably be waiting a while, but I didn't bother informing Dan.

"Yeah, we'll get right on that." Troy rolled his eyes, pretending to humor him.

We stayed and chatted for a while, Ash giving me concerned looks but I remembered to nod enough and give her the I'm-okay smile. It wasn't a lie; deep down I knew I would be. The laughter certainly helped, but our adventure-filled night had left me tired, so Troy and I wrapped it up and said our goodbyes, talking the walk across the hallway. Our destination—his apartment.

"You want to lie down?" Troy tossed the keys on his kitchen bench; it had been awhile since we'd been in his apartment. The venue for our late night rendezvous had been usually my place.

"Yeah." I smiled as I pulled him toward me. "I think we should live here." It was sudden— my snap decision on where we should call home—but it seemed to fit. Everything about our relationship had either been out of sequence or fly-by-the-seat-your-pants, why change it now?

"Megs, we can live anywhere you want. I can move to yours or we can buy something new. It's just space, it's what's in it that counts." Troy kissed the top of my head.

"I know but it feels right that we move here. Beside, this is where we spent our first night together and our second. It's where the craziness began."

Troy shot me a sideways glance. "That a good thing or a bad thing?"

"It's an *us* thing."

It had been two weeks and I was back at work, my routine slipping into something resembling normal. Normal if you took into account I was married to Troy Harris— I still wasn't used to it, the Zsa Zsa diamond on my hand a constant reminder.

My parents had also come around, which was another win. Once the shock of my changed marital status wore off, they not only accepted both the marriage and Troy, but also actively welcomed him into the family. My dad and husband had even scheduled a man-date on the green. Troy had been quoting *Caddyshack* all week and I had bought a pair of suitable hideous pants I had planned on making him wear, the laugh alone worth every penny I'd spent on them.

"Dr. Harris, your three o'clock is here." Carrie buzzed through my intercom.

"Thanks, Carrie, send him in."

Oh and another thing, I totally did the name change. The freedom from the legacy of my father's last name, liberating. No more having to endure *Harry Potter* stares when people met me for the first time, or whispers about who my parents were behind my back. Their wonder in me— moving forward —would be on my merit alone. Unless they were Power Station fans and then I was shit out of luck.

I stood as I waited for my patient to arrive, the door opening to reveal my three o'clock appointment.

"Hi, Brad, take a seat."

He quietly slumped into the chair opposite my desk as I retook mine.

"Look, before we start I just wanted to talk to you about our last session. I know you followed up with Dr. Meyer and spoke about what happened, but I just wanted you to know that I'm okay now."

It was a fine line in talking about something personal with a. a patient and b. a minor, but as long as I kept the details out of it, ethically I could reassure him that I was okay without crossing any lines. It's not like we could ignore the elephant in the room either— he knew about Troy and the baby.

"I'm really glad, Dr. Winters...I mean, Dr. Harris." Brad fidgeted nervously with the drawstring of his hoodie.

"You can call me Dr. Winters if it makes you feel more comfortable. I don't mind." Change could sometimes be a trigger, and the last thing I wanted to do was have his progress pushed back on something as trivial as my name change.

He shrugged. "Your name is Dr. Harris now, so if it's cool with you, that's what I'd like to call you."

"Of course. I'd like that. So I read over your notes from the last two weeks. Seems like you and your parents came to an agreement about school?"

"Yeah, it's no big deal. I promised my mom I would graduate high school even though it's fucking lame." He shifted uncomfortably in his seat, his hair flicking into his eyes.

"That's fantastic. I'm so proud of you." The fact he'd made the commitment, massive progress in itself.

"Like I said, no big deal." Another shrug.

"Would you like to talk about something else?" I shifted gears, not wanting to push too hard on our first session back.

"I started playing drums." His eyes met mine.

Drums? It was too strange to be a coincidence and I had to wonder if a particular drummer hadn't influenced the decision to pick up the sticks.

"Interesting choice of instrument. Was there any particular reason you chose drums?"

"Yeah, a set showed up at my house one day, with a note."

Drums just showed up on his doorstep? That was even stranger. My gut told me the responsibility of this random act of kindness fell at the feet of someone whose name began with *Troy* and ended with *Harris*. Of course it was all purely speculation, but if I'd been hedging a wager, I'd be going all in.

"You wouldn't happen to have the note would you?"

"Yeah, it's here." Brad pulled the folded piece of paper from his pocket and placed it on the desk in front of me. The deep lines and wear on the paper indicating it had been read and refolded numerous times.

Dear Brad,

When I was younger I'd sometimes get mad too, but instead of beating myself up, I'd take it out on the skins. Maybe it's worth a shot? It doesn't have to be musical, just make some noise. And don't be scared to hit them hard — trust me, they can take it.

The note was incredibly sweet and had all the hallmarkings of Troy. I could almost hear him reading it to me himself. It seemed that Brad and I then embarked on a game of let-me-say-one-thing-but-I-actually-mean-another. I was actually really good at this game, and short of have telepathy; I could read the subtext pretty damn well. This is how the conversation went and what was my interpretation.

"It's not signed?" Translation— Do you know who sent it?

"Nope, no return address either." Translation— someone obviously hiding their identity.

"Well it's a really nice gesture, who ever sent them." Translation— let's dance around the fact that it was probably Troy who did it.

"Yeah, he must be pretty cool." Translation —I know it was your husband.

"Yeah, he must be." Translation — yeah okay, so we both know it was my husband.

See. It's a great game and anyone can play. Now let's get back to therapy so I can find out whether this grand gesture was just a social experiment or if it actually helped the kid.

"Has it helped?" I leaned forward in my seat, already knowing the answer to what I was asking. "Playing the drums?"

"Yeah, I feel less angry." The evidence of that in his less explosive responses and the massive drop in expletives used when talking. "I'm even taking lessons."

"That's really great, Brad."

We spent the rest of the time we had discussing strategies, but I could tell by the change in him already that he would make it. It wasn't going to be a cakewalk, and he had a long road ahead, but for the first time since that angry boy had stepped inside my office, he seemed to want the change.

We said our goodbyes and I instructed Brad to make another appointment and he'd barely shut my office door when I reached for my phone.

"Megs." He answered on the second ring.

"Troy Harris, do you have something you need to tell me?"

He had to have known I'd eventually find out. I mean, Brad's my patient, talking is what we do.

"Okay, Megs, I'll come clean. All the people on *Lost's* Oceania flight 815 were dead the whole time." He barked out a laugh.

"Ha, ha. Very funny. No something else."

"Is this about the lingerie in the back of the closet?"

"What? No. You bought me lingerie?"

"No it's for me actually, but sure I guess you can wear it."

He was having way too much fun with this. There was something about the two of us on a phone. I don't think he had the capacity to have a serious conversation with me.

"It's not about underwear." My fingertips massaged my temples as I calculated how much longer to let this play out.

"Can I buy a vowel?"

"Troy." Okay so obviously not very long. "Did you buy a drum kit?"

"As in ever?" He laughed, my question clearly ridiculous.

"Okay, you're going to make me ask, aren't you?"

"I say we keep playing this game. It's fun and kind of like charades with audibles. Sounds like…"

This conversation was going nowhere fast. "Troy did you send Brad Hemsworth a drum kit?"

"That's odd, did he say I did?" He didn't sound half as surprised as he was trying to.

"No, the note was *anonymous*." The emphasis on the last word for his benefit, not mine.

"Oh see, I'm *Harris* not *anonymous*, both end in *s* so I can see how you got confused." He annunciated the words— both his last name and anonymous— slowly for effect.

"Troy!" I actually huffed into the phone.

"Megs!" He mimicked, but with less huff and more chuckle.

"Tell me," I demanded. Did we establish eons ago, I have an acute need to know?

"Assuming I did and I'm not saying I did but purely for this exercise let's work on the hypothetical." There was finesse in Troy's voice that was smooth and un-frazzled. Clearly I hadn't been the only one who'd watch CSI.

"Fine," I humored him. "Say it *might 've* been you."

"Okay, so based on that assumption if I had sent a drum kit wouldn't it stand to reason that you best not know anything about it, where it could cause a conflict of interest in your treatment of him?"

Of course he was right. His silence was protecting me from a wading through an ethical minefield. I mean technically it wasn't breaking any rules but Troy contacting one of patients? Even if his intentions were pure… Yeah, let's file that under *it would probably have given me a nervous breakdown had I known at the time.*

"Troy, I know it was you. How did you get his address?"

There was no way he would have been able to access my patient information. Not unless he was moonlighting as a computer hacker.

"Well, *hypothetically* you're not the only person who knows how to use *Google*."

"Even though I can't sanction what you did, it was a really good thing and I love you." My heart swelled for this amazing man who never ceased to amaze me.

"I love you too." His voice oozed sweetness. "Oh, but while we're doing confessionals." He paused and I had no idea where he was going with it. "You want to tell me how a pair of my autographed sticks found their way into one of your storage boxes?"

Ooooooooohhhhhhhh. Yeah. Those. Totally forgot about the sticks I swindled from Dan when he'd pumped me for information for Ash's birthday. Probably should have hidden those.

"Is that kind of creepy?"

Did I really need to ask?

"Nah, the photoshopped picture of us at the *AMAs* is waaay creepier."

Huh? What photo? I cast my mind back to try and recall if I'd ever done that. Let's face it. It did sound like me.

"I did not photoshop myself into a photo with you at the AMAs."

Or at the very least I was ninety-nine percent sure I hadn't.

"No, I did. It looks great too." Troy chuckled. "Thinking of making it our Christmas card."

The smile spread across my face. Yeah, we were made for each other.

"Bye Troy, love you."

"Bye Megs, love you more."

29

Troy

"DUDE, WE ARE SO LAME. CAN YOU BELIEVE WE WENT TO *SCORES* and spent more time talking to each other than checking out tits? I got bored half way through the lap dance and actually paid the chick fifty bucks to stop." Dan and I stepped out of the elevator and into our shared hallway. Times were definitely a-changin'.

"It's where you said you wanted to go, douchebag. Did you not specifically ask for a strip joint for your Stag party?" If I'd had my way, we'd have gone and shot some pool at *Donavan's*, maybe smoked some cigars. Watching chicks bump and grind the pole was not my idea of a good time, and it hadn't been in a long while.

"Yeah but it's no fun any more. I mean—if anyone is going to be rubbing my junk, I want it to be Ash." Dan swung his keys around his fingers, ready for us to do the catch-ya-laters.

"You are such a romantic, dude. Brings a tear to my eye."

"Hate all you want to hate. Going inside to my girl."

"Later."

The key went in and the lock turned, the door creaking slightly as it opened. I cursed under my breath, it was late and I didn't want to wake Megs.

We'd been out to celebrate Dan's last few weeks of freedom but I'd been lucky if I'd had three beers. It wasn't the ring on my finger that was stopping me from having a good time; it was the zero desire I had to look at any other woman that wasn't my wife.

My wife. Best fucking thing that ever happened to me was that blonde powerhouse that was tucked up in my bed, and not a day didn't go by that I couldn't believe my luck that she was mine.

Trying to keep the noise to a minimum, I did my usual strip on the way through routine, dumping my clothes in the hamper before heading to bed. The smell of stripper's perfume and cigarettes left behind as I made the familiar walk to my bedroom.

Megs was naked, sprawled out on our king size bed, her hair all over her face with her head on my pillow. The big-ass grin spread across my face as I watched her sleeping, her legs kicked out taking up most of the room, her hands lying on the space I'd usually be occupying.

I quickly hit the shower, rinsing off the stench of my ordinary night out. I toweled off and headed back into our bedroom, hoping the water hitting the tiles hadn't been enough to disturb her.

Still sleeping.

My eyes focused on Megs's body, which had inched over slightly while I'd been getting clean, giving me just enough room to crawl onto the mattress. The smell of her got me instantly hard the minute I'd slid in between the sheets.

"Holy Fuck." My voice echoed louder than I'd meant. Megs wrapped her hand around my cock as soon as my ass hit the bed, barely giving me enough time to turn and see her huge smile.

"Hello, Troy Harris." Her voice purred, clueing me in that maybe she hadn't been sleeping the whole time.

"Did I wake you, sweetheart?" I tried not to focus on her hand slowly moving up and down my shaft.

"Tell me, Troy Harris." She ignored my question, instead shuffling up the bed, giving me more wrist action as she continued to talk. "This hard-on, is it for me? Or did you see something else you liked tonight?"

"Only you, Megs." My eyes nailed her as she tightened her grip around my cock.

"I've missed you." Something in her tone had me guessing that she hadn't meant just tonight. The last time I'd been inside her had been over three weeks ago.

"I've missed you too." My hand itched to touch her skin as it moved over her tits. "You sure about this?" I asked, needing to know this was exactly what she had in mind.

She didn't answer, instead dipped her head into my lap and swirled her tongue around the head of my dick, her teeth gently pulling on the ring on the tip. So I'm assuming that would be a yes.

"Fuck, Megs." I cursed out a breath, the feeling of her mouth on me better than I'd remembered.

"That's what I'm trying to facilitate here." She mumbled as she pulled my cock out her mouth. The words familiar, kicking us back to our first time.

"Yeah? Well who am I to deny my wife what she wants."

My interest in the blowjob was superseded by the need to get my mouth on her, my body moving quickly as I splayed her out on the bed. The green light had gotten me so juiced up I wasn't sure which part of her would be getting my attention.

She yelped as her ass hit the mattress, my mouth making the decision as it licked her nipple, my hand palming her other tit.

"Troy." She moaned as my tongue got reacquainted with her pink peaks, moving from one and then other. It wasn't like me to play favorites, making sure each of them got enough of the loving feeling.

Being the dedicated guy that I am, I continued the mouth action down her body; the echoing of my name acting as my soundtrack as I gently parted her thighs. She was so fucking wet.

She arched her back, giving me better access as my tongue invaded her pussy. The "Holy Shit" while she bunched the sheets beside me all the encouragement I needed as I sucked and licked her clit.

"Don't stop." Her hands locked around my head holding me in place as she twisted her fingers through my mohawk.

If I could have told her that telepathically and not by actually stopping what I was doing, I would have let her know that there was zero danger of that.

She thrashed as I slid two fingers inside her, my tongue keeping busy as it circled her clit.

"Troy," she moaned as her hands moved from my head to her body, her fingertips kneading her tits as her legs started to shake.

She was close, and with one last flick of my tongue, she was pushed over. Her beautiful tits heaving up and down as I teased out the rest of her orgasm with my fingers.

"Mmm. I love watching you come." The fingers that had been buried in her pussy found their way to my mouth, my lips closing around them, as I tasted her one last time. "You want to go to sleep now?" I teased, with no intention of putting the brakes on. Nope. Not until I'd sunk my cock deep into her and felt her come at least one more time.

"I want you in me," she panted, her hands fixing on my shoulders and pulling me down onto her. Her mouth clamped over mine as I tried not to crush her.

My arms wrapped around her body and I rolled her on top of mine, adjusting her so my cock hit her in all the right places.

"What part?" I palmed my hard-on, circling the opening of her wet pussy.

"That, I want that." She moaned as she rubbed herself against my hard-on

"What's that? You need to be clear with me. I'm having a hard time understanding," I hissed out not sure who was I was torturing by holding back— her or me.

"Your cock. I want your cock," she all but screamed.

Well then, you heard the lady. My dick got into position, demanding I put us both out of our misery as it slid in an inch.

It was quick—way quicker than I had meant to —but I sunk into her in one fluid thrust, her pussy fisting me as I entered her. The skin on skin contact drove me insane as I moved slowly out, and then pushed in again. It was like I was on autopilot as my cock slid inside of her.

"Megs." I pulled back, my drive to sink into her giving me temporary amnesia, and the fact we hadn't done this in a while not getting the attention it deserved. "Did I hurt you?" I couldn't see her face, her head buried in my neck as she breathed heavily.

"I said." She kissed my neck as she shuffled up my body, her knees hitting the mattress as she straddled me. "I want your cock."

"I love your fucking dirty mouth," I hissed through clenched teeth as I pulled her back down onto me.

She didn't give me a chance for another thrust, linking her hands into mine, using them for leverage as she pushed down to bury my cock deep inside her.

She writhed on top of me, my mouth no longer capable of talking as she met every one of my thrusts with one of her own.

"Troy." She begged me, her body not quite there as she rode me.

"Right here, sweetheart. Feel me?" I pushed deeper inside her as my hand reached down and thumbed her clit.

"Yes," she screamed, the extra attention my hand was giving her enough to tip her over. "Oh. My. God." Her pussy milked my cock as she exploded on top of me. Her body collapsed onto mine as she rode out the rest of her orgasm.

"Megs, I need to come." I couldn't hold out any longer, the pulsing that was travelling up the length of my shaft driving me fucking insane. One more thrust was all it took and I shot my load into her, kissing her hard as I emptied into her.

Movement was obsolete, my arms the only part of me still operational as I snaked them around her body and held her, both of us still shaking.

CRASH RIDE

"Are you okay?" My hand brushed her hair off her shoulder, slightly pissed at myself I hadn't been able to rein it in and give her more *making love* and less *fucking*.

"I'm fine now." Her giggles vibrated against my chest, her face still pressed against my body.

Her fingers traced the lines of my new tattoo, the one that I'd gotten just an hour after saying "I do."

"I love this." Her lips kissed the gray-scale tiny feather that sat just above my heart, a smaller replica of the ones that decorated her skin. A tribute not only to Megs but also to the little life we'd lost.

"Yeah, me too." It made it a little easier knowing that they would both always be with me.

"Megs." Thinking about the baby gave me a different kind of wake up call. "I wasn't wearing any protection and you're not on the pill anymore."

Sure we were both sporting matching rings and the same last name, but I assumed we'd need to have a sit down and discuss whether we were going to try for another baby or not. Have the second time around happen with a little less of an OMG moment. Probably a conversation we should have had thirty minutes before we'd started fucking.

"I kind of realized that once I felt the ring inside me, but there was no way I could ask you to stop." She rested her head on my shoulder, those blue-green eyes owning me as she smiled.

"So how would you feel if we just made a baby?" I didn't know what the chances were— but sex without any barriers—it was a definite roll of the dice.

Her wide eyes blinked as if the realization had finally hit her, the possibility higher than average.

She didn't give any words, instead pushing her lips down on mine, my mouth getting on the same page as I kissed her.

"Megs, do you want to make a baby?" I rephrased the question, thinking that the new improved way of asking had a nicer ring to it. My cock that was still buried inside her, stirred with renewed interest.

"Yes, Troy Harris. I want to make a baby." Her eyes started to glass, rapid blinks chasing down her tears.

"Well then, Megs Harris, let's get you knocked up."

EPILOGUE

Megan

"DAN, STOP TOUCHING MY ASS. MY DAD IS RIGHT OVER THERE." Ashlyn very unconvincingly smacked away Dan's hand. Her lips curved into a smile as her other hand brought the glass of champagne to her mouth. Despite being manhandled, there was no hiding how happy she was.

"Oh come on, babe, I'm dying here. Can't we sneak off for a quickie?" Dan almost pleaded. His eyes filled with lust as they raked over his new wife. I would have thought Ash should be more worried about the come-sit-on-my-face vibes he was throwing off rather than hands on her ass, but who was I to judge.

"No, we have a few more hours of the reception and then I'm all yours." She giggled as she lowered her champagne glass back to the table.

"Hate to break it you, babe, but you're all mine now. I'm just being respectful by not having sex with you right here and now," Dan not so quietly whispered into her ear. His hands disappeared under the white table linen of the bridal table. The grin getting wider hinted that they weren't sitting idle in his lap. My role as maid of honor earned me a front row seat to the shenanigans, catching an eyeful as I sat to their left.

The wedding had been beautiful. My dress had even been a stunning slate grey chiffon full-length gown. Not a pink tutu in sight. The whole vibe was traditional and simple, with the bride and groom exchanging vows in a catholic church in Manhattan before a stunning reception in the Manhattan Ballroom of the Grand Hyatt hotel. The ornate tables all but deserted as guests danced to a live five-piece band. They weren't anyone famous, but knew just about every chart topping song from the last thirty years.

It was all very low key considering whom the groom was. Although given that the night wasn't over, there was still time for a bunch of bikini-clad babes to jump out of a cake or something.

"You should probably do the flower toss and call it a day. Save us and everyone else from an indecent display." Troy popped open a button on his tailored tuxedo jacket to reveal a fitted charcoal vest as he sat down beside me. The contradiction of the mohwak he was rocking, making the suit look even more delicious.

"Did I tell you how sexy you look, Troy Harris?" My arms snaked around his broad chest. God, he looked good. Maybe Dan had the right idea? Holy hell. I'd just agreed with Dan. Maybe it was best we called it a night.

"Yeah? You got a thing for the monkey suit?" Troy gave me a suggestive look, his grin widening as he leaned back in his chair. The power of his smile making me tingle all over.

"I have a *thing* for you." I tiptoed my fingers along the seam of his vest.

"Yeah we know." Dan laughed, apparently done with fondling his wife in time to eavesdrop on our conversation.

In fairness, I hadn't been quiet about it. I had a couple of rings on my finger than told me I didn't have to be. Oh, and I didn't have to worry about stalking charges now either. I was able to ogle Troy Harris all I wanted, and it was total legal. It was winning all the way around.

"Wow." Jase nodded, taking a swig from his beer as he pulled up a chair beside us. "I feel like I should be busting out a rendition of "Can you feel the love tonight?" That, or cry into these expensive napkins at the beauty of all of it. The struggle is real." His voice dripped with sarcasm as he joined us at the bridal table.

"Yeah, whatever, asswipe. You're next." Dan tipped his chin, giving him a pointed glare. Jase being the only member of Power Station not with a significant other.

"Nah, someone has to keep us on the most eligible bachelor lists." Jase's smile widened as he brought the bottle back to his lips and took another drink. With his dark suit fitting snuggly against his toned body, he could have easily been a model for GQ.

"Five large says he ends up in knots over a girl within the next three months." Troy smirked, his hand resting on the back of my chair.

"I say let's make it ten, but Jase likes putting in the ground work. The guy isn't even dating anyone, so I think it would be closer to six," Dan piped in, Ashlyn giggling by his side.

"You know I'm right here, assholes." Jase rolled his brown eyes. "And I can't believe you are gambling on my relationship status. I feel so fucking cheap."

"Done." Troy agreed, his wager with Dan apparently decided as they both ignored Jason.

"I'll drink to that." Dan raised his glass of champagne before pausing. "Hey, why aren't you drinking?" His eyes floated over to the lack of alcoholic beverage in front of me. I'd been sipping water all night.

"Wait. What?" Ashlyn's attention now also directed on my apparently offensive glass. Obviously her being busy getting married had distracted her enough to not notice. "Why are you not drinking?" She pointed a finger at my glass accusingly, her eyes peeled wide as she looked down at the glass of water and then at me. "Megs!"

"Wow, Ash. No need to yell at her, babe. It's only a drink." Dan rubbed his wife's arm oblivious as to why she was getting excited.

"Megs. Don't you hold out on me." Ash showed no signs of letting it go.

Let's face it. When it came to keeping secrets, I sucked. Also in the list of things I didn't do well was lie. So combine the two, and I was pretty much a goner when it came to hiding that just two days ago, peeing on a stick had given me two very clear lines.

"Okay." I admitted as I slowly rose to my feet, Troy's arms circling me as I continued. "It's early and we just found out. We're being cautious." Not to mention petrified, but elated and crazy happy. Oh and I'd had cried about fifteen times in the last forty-eight hours. I was sure that wasn't normal either.

Ash squealed, leapt out of her chair and gave me a hug, her display of affection drawing curious stares from people close by. Lucky for us they didn't give us much more interest. A bride squealing on her wedding day wasn't exactly a surprising occurrence.

"Nothing bad is going to happen this time." Troy gave my hand a subtle squeeze being that Ash was still dominating my personal space. They were same words he had been reciting to me since I'd held the EPT test in front of his face. My vocabulary had been limited to "Oh my God" as the significance of those two lines sunk in.

It's what we both wanted, had hoped for but it didn't mean that I didn't freak the hell out. It seemed to be my natural reaction so this time around I didn't fight it. Troy was his usual calm self and even though I suspected he was just as scared as I was, he was wearing an ironclad poker face.

"Congrats, man." Jase clapped Troy over the shoulder. "So happy for you guys." He turned his attention to me and pulled me into a warm one-armed hug. "Awesome news, Megs. Oh and thanks for the heat off my love life. I owe you one."

"Thanks." My eyes started to leak again. I swear, by the end of this pregnancy I was going to be hospitalized for dehydration via tear ducts. Could that even happen? Crap. I needed to drink more water.

"You're knocked up?" Dan shot us a sideways glance, clearly needing the clarification.

"Yep." Troy grinned not even trying to hide his excitement. "We sure are."

Dan gave us his excited congratulations like everyone else had and I gave up trying to stop from crying again. Ash joined me, proving what a team player she was, not leaving me to ruin my mascara all by myself. So much for my initial concern about bringing drama to her wedding—yeah that ship had sailed. I know there was a saying about even the best intentions going down the tube, but I couldn't remember it, and in the end it didn't matter.

Troy and I, we didn't know how to do ordinary, and that was okay, because like he'd told me months ago, where's the fun in an easy ride? I was buckled up and ready to go.

No one needed to give me a guarantee this was going to work out, I already knew. Why? Because I had Troy Harris.

See **MORE** of Dan, Ash, Megs and Troy in **JASE'S** story **BACK STAGE** coming later in 2015.

ACKNOWLEDGEMENTS

THE BIGGEST THANKS WILL ALWAYS GO TO MY FAMILY. They put up with a lot so these books can be written with this one being no exception. **Gep, Jenna, Liam** and **Woodley**, I'll never write enough words to express my gratitude so I won't try. Instead I'll write just three—I love you.

Thank you to my girls who have been there from the start and will be there until the end. **Mini, Sam, Nat, Cayte, Shell, Juzzie, Jo, Grace, Bec** and **Kirsty** each one of you has seen me at my worst and at my best, and none of those times have you left. You've got me and I've got you.

To an **amazing beta team** who between the three of them make sure I don't drop the ball and churn out something subpar. **Amy, Terri** and **Maz**, thank you for your honesty, your time and all your effort. I know this book is what is because of your notes and suggestions even if they weren't always easy to hear.

Thank you the authors who either haven't ejected me from the club just yet or have at least been discreet when they obtained retraining orders. **Lili Saint Germain, JB Hartnett, Skyla Mardi, CJ Duggan, Lilliana Andersen, Rachael Brookes, JD Nixon, KM Golland, TJ Hamilton, Jill Patten, Chantal Fernando, Kim Karr, SC Stephens, Joanna Wylde** and **Kylie Scott**. Thanks for the support, the laughs and the outstanding reads. Honored to call you my peers and humbled to call you my friends.

Thank you to **Hang Le** for the back cover, teasers and other super sexy graphic stuff. It is an absolute pleasure working with you; you get my vision each and every time. It's no lie I adore you.

Thank you **Dr. Gian** for another kick-ass cover. This one could well be my favorite. You never fail to slam-dunk in the design department and I'm going to miss your work on my covers—I suppose your students and faculty do need you more so I won't fight it. Be awesome.

Thank you to psychologist **Jo-Anne P** for technical and medical information and support. I write books, you save lives. Thanks for the amazing work you do in your field as well.

Thanks to **Angelique Ehlers** for front cover photography.

Thank you to the bloggers and blogs who have supported me. **Helen S-** Kinky Book Klub, **Kelly O-** Kelly's Kindle Konfessions, **Marie M-** Surrender to Books, **Jodie O-** Fab Fun and Tantalizing Reads, **Rebecca** and **Nicole** – Author Groupies, **Tammy M-** A Slice of Fiction, The Book Nuts and The SubClub, **Francessca W** – Francessca's Romance Reviews, **Sam** -Forever Me Romance, **Mel L**– Sassy Mum book Blog, **Debbie O-** Hard Rock Romance, **Tash D-** Book Lit Love, **Stephanie G** – The Lemon Review, **Kristine B-** Glass Paper Ink Bookblog, **Karen H-** A Thousand Lives Book Blog, **Belinda** and **Lily-** Hopelessly Devoted 2 Books, **Amy J** – The SubClub, **Paige** and **Kylie** –Give me Books, **Tash D-** Book Lit Love, **Sian D** - Rauchy, Rude and Readers blog, **Laurie F** – Book Fancy, **Jo W-** Four Brits and a Book, **Erin-** Read and Ramble, **Sarez-** Talk Supe, **Bianca** – Martini Times Romance blog, **Rosarita-** iScream Books, and sorry to anyone I have forgotten. I love you all.

Thanks to the **T Gephart Entourage**, it's not a street team, it's a support crew. Love you ladies.

Thank you to **Jemina Venter** at BookNerdFanGirl Designs to breathing life into my boys. Love your designs.

Thanks to my Fictionally Yours, Melbourne team- **Penny** and **Simone**. #WordWizard #ShutUpAndWrite #FanGirl

Thank you to my editor **Nichole Strauss** from Perfectly Publishable. I'm not the easiest person to edit, having very strong ideas on my work, but you worked tirelessly to give me a beautiful clean manuscript. I appreciate your time and your patience even if you disapprove of my shouty caps. Sometime huge needs to be written as HUGE, it's all in the telling.

Thank you to **Max Henry** from Max Effect for my stunning formatting. My pages never looked so beautiful.

And a HUGE (yes shouty caps are necessary) **thank you to the readers**. Yeah, I mean you. All of you. Now, hustle in for a big group hug! Thanks so much for spending your time with my characters and me.

ABOUT THE AUTHOR

T GEPHART is an indie author from Melbourne, Australia.

T's approach to life has been somewhat unconventional. Rather than going to University, she jumped on a plane to Los Angeles, USA in search of adventure. While this first trip left her somewhat underwhelmed and largely depleted of funds it fueled her appetite for travel and life experience.

With a rather eclectic resume, which reads more like the fiction she writes than an actual employment history, T struggled to find her niche in the world.

While on a subsequent trip the United States in 1999, T met and married her husband. Their whirlwind courtship and interesting impromptu convenience store wedding set the tone for their life together, which is anything but ordinary. They have lived in Louisiana, Guam and Australia and have traveled extensively throughout the US. T has two beautiful young children and one four legged child, Woodley, the wonder dog.

An avid reader, T became increasingly frustrated by the lack of strong female characters in the books she was reading. She wanted to read about a woman she could identify with, someone strong, independent and confident and who didn't lack femininity. Out of this need, she decided to pen her first book, A Twist of Fate. T set herself the challenge to write something that was interesting, compelling and yet easy enough to read that was still enjoyable. Pulling from her own past "colorful" experiences and the amazing personalities she has surrounded herself with, she had no shortage of inspiration. With a strong slant on erotic fiction, her core characters are empowered women who don't have to sacrifice their femininity. She enjoyed the process so much that when it was over she couldn't let it go.

T loves to travel, laugh and surround herself with colorful characters. This inevitably spills into her writing and makes for an interesting journey - she is well and truly enjoying the ride!

Based on her life experiences, T has plenty of material for her books and has a wealth of ideas to keep you all enthralled.

CONNECT WITH T

Webpage
http://tgephart.com/bio/4579459512

Facebook
https://www.facebook.com/pages/T-Gephart/412456528830732

Goodreads
https://www.goodreads.com/author/show/7243737.T_Gephart

Twitter
@tinagephart

BOOKS BY THIS AUTHOR

THE LEXI SERIES
Lexi
A Twist of Fate
Twisted Views: Fate's Companion
A Leap of Faith
A Time for Hope

THE POWER STATION SERIES
High Strung
Crash Ride
Back Stage (2015)

Made in the USA
Charleston, SC
31 May 2016